SPECIAL MESSAGE TO READERS

This book is published under the auspices of

THE ULVERSCROFT FOUNDATION

(registered charity No. 264873 UK)

Established in 1972 to provide funds for research, diagnosis and treatment of eye diseases. Examples of contributions made are: —

A Children's Assessment Unit at Moorfield's Hospital, London.

•

Twin operating theatres at the Western Ophthalmic Hospital, London.

•

A Chair of Ophthalmology at the Royal Australian College of Ophthalmologists.

•

The Ulverscroft Children's Eye Unit at the Great Ormond Street Hospital For Sick Children, London.

You can help further the work of the Foundation by making a donation or leaving a legacy. Every contribution, no matter how small, is received with gratitude. Please write for details to:

THE ULVERSCROFT FOUNDATION,
The Green, Bradgate Road, Anstey,
Leicester LE7 7FU, England.
Telephone: (0116) 236 4325

In Australia write to:
THE ULVERSCROFT FOUNDATION,
c/o The Royal Australian and New Zealand College of Ophthalmologists,
94-98 Chalmers Street, Surry Hills,
N.S.W. 2010, Australia

Barbara Cleverly lives in the middle of Cambridge, surrounded by ancient buildings and bookshops. She was born and educated in the north of England at a Yorkshire grammar school and then at Durham University.

Folly du Jour is the seventh in the Joe Sandilands series. The previous books have been warmly received. The first, *The Last Kashmiri Rose*, was a *New York Times* 'Notable Book of 2001', and the third, *The Damascened Blade*, won the prestigious Crime Writers' Association Award for Historical Fiction.

FOLLY DU JOUR

Paris, 1927. It's springtime in Paris and Joe Sandilands, a Scotland Yard detective, has flown in to attend an Interpol conference. However, he is promptly diverted to the Quai des Orfèvres where his old friend, Sir George Jardine, has been arrested for murder. George is confined to a cell at police headquarters, his evening dress stained with the blood of the man he is alleged to have knifed to death at the Folies Bergère. Beaten by his interrogators, George is in a sorry state. Why, then, is he so reluctant to confide in Joe? The detective's enquiries reveal a dark current of vice and murder lurking underneath the gaiety, champagne and dancing — and Joe comes within a whisker of death before finding the killer.

Books by Barbara Cleverly
Published by The House of Ulverscroft:

THE LAST KASHMIRI ROSE
RAGTIME IN SIMLA
THE DAMASCENED BLADE
THE PALACE TIGER
THE BEE'S KISS
TUG OF WAR

BARBARA CLEVERLY

FOLLY DU JOUR

Complete and Unabridged

CHARNWOOD
Leicester

First published in Great Britain in 2007 by
Constable
an imprint of Constable & Robinson Ltd.
London

First Charnwood Edition
published 2008
by arrangement with Constable & Robinson Ltd.
London

British Library CIP Data

Cleverly, Barbara
Folly du jour.—Large print ed.—
Charnwood library series
1. Sandilands, Joe (Fictitious character)—Fiction
2. Police—France—Paris—Fiction 3. Paris (France)
—Fiction 4. Detective and mystery stories
5. Large type books
I. Title
823.9′2 [F]

ISBN 978–1–84782–344–1

Published by
F. A. Thorpe (Publishing)
Anstey, Leicestershire

Set by Words & Graphics Ltd.
Anstey, Leicestershire
Printed and bound in Great Britain by
T. J. International Ltd., Padstow, Cornwall

This book is printed on acid-free paper

For my son Steve
with many thanks for his help,

and for Gary
whose enthusiasm for the
Paris Music Hall was inspiring.

Prologue

Paris, 1923

Harland C. White of Pittsburgh, Pennsylvania shuffled resentfully after his wife, May, through the Egyptian rooms in the Louvre museum. One vaulted stone room after another. You could lose yourself in here. Or lose your mind. He wondered whether this was a good moment to suggest they go for tea on the new roof terrace over the Samaritaine store.

'Say! May!' he called after her. 'This is the fourth roomful of sarcophaguses — okay, then, sarcophageeee — we've done. How many more?'

They'd had lunch at Ciro's. The food and wine had made him sleepy, the size of the check had made him grouchy. $1.00 for a slice of melon? $2.25 for a Baby Lobster? Still, lunch at Ciro's was on his schedule. You couldn't go home and not say you'd lunched at Ciro's. Had to be done. Same thing, apparently, with the Louvre.

Maybelle (May, since she'd discovered all the girls over here had short names . . . though it didn't have quite the kick of Zizi or Lulu or Kiki) had come to a halt in front of a huge, dark-painted coffin box and was doing that thing with her hands . . . Tracing the shapes in the air — hieroglyphs, she called them — and silently mouthing the sounds that went with them.

Clever girl, May! She'd been to classes. She'd grown chummy with the arty folks at the State Museum. She'd gotten hold of a book called *The Mummy* by some feller called Wallis Budge and had learned — or so she told him . . . what would *he* know? — to read the sounds out loud. She'd tried to teach Harland to do it but his attention had faded after he'd mastered '*Tut — ankh — amen*.'

'Come look, Harland! This one's kind of special and I can work out the name of the occupant.'

His friends at the Country Club — swell blokes every last one of 'em — had been full of good advice: 'So, you're going to Paris? Peppy Paree! Ah! It's the top of the beanstalk — you'll just love it. Give my regards to Harry . . . and Henry . . . and Bud at the Dead Rat . . . and Joe Zelli — now he's a real live wire!'

Two days down and all he'd met were three-thousand-year-old guys who lived in boxes. And here was another introduction coming up.

'*Kham — nut — see*,' said May.

'I'm looking, I'm looking!' he said, trying to lighten the gloom.

'Chump! That's his name. *Kham — nut — see*,' she intoned again. 'High Priest of Ptah.'

'Do you *have* to spit your baccy on my brogue, May?' he said, never knowing when to give up.

May ignored him. 'At Memphis.'

'Memphis?'

'That would be Memphis, Lower Egypt, not Memphis, Tennessee.' May could be very squashing.

'Well . . . whoever . . . your buddy's just sprung a leak,' he said crabbily. He didn't like the look of adoration on Maybelle's face — the way she opened shining wide eyes and moistened her lips. Never looked at him that way. He pointed to the foot of the upright coffin. 'There. He's sprung a leak — or taken one.'

The ticking off for loose language he was expecting didn't come. May was staring at the marble floor at the base of the mummy box. He looked again. A dark red-brown glutinous fluid was ponding there.

'Ah! I'll tell you what that is . . . it's embalming fluid,' said Harland, decisively. 'Come away, May. Time to move on, I think.' He tugged at her arm.

'No, it's not embalming fluid,' said May. 'It's blood. You ought to know that. I'll stay here. You go get help. Somebody's climbed in there and died.'

'But not four thousand years ago . . . No, you're right, Maybelle — that's blood. And it's still flowing!'

⋆ ⋆ ⋆

Oddly, the room guardian wasn't at his post. Nor was the one in the preceding room. What was this — the tea break? He saw not another soul until he came to a grand staircase he remembered. A party of four men, all carrying briefcases and paper files of notes, were coming down, laughing together and chatting in several languages.

‘Hey there!’ shouted Harland. ‘Anyone here speak English?’

One of them, a smart-looking Anglo-Saxon type, all floating fair hair and ice-blue eyes, detached himself from the group, responding to the urgency in the American’s voice. ‘I do. Can I help you, sir? Jack Pollock, British Embassy.’

‘Thank God for that! I need someone to come and inspect a mummy. There’s a High Priest of Memphis, Egypt, down there and he’s bleeding to death!’

* * *

Jack Pollock should have his name added to the list of live wires about Paris, Harland reckoned. In minutes he’d managed to send for the chief curator, the specialist in Egyptology, the police and a doctor, and was relaying what was going on to his party. And all in a babble of English, French, Italian and German.

A crowd had gathered — now where in tarnation had *they* all sprung from? — clustering around the case, gesticulating. They jostled each other in their eagerness to get close to the coffin and Pollock, using his height and a headmaster’s voice, had set them at a distance, firmly requiring Mr and Mrs White, as discoverers, to stand by and hold themselves in readiness for a police interview should it prove necessary. He wasn’t a man to argue with. In any case, wild horses wouldn’t have dragged them away from the scene of discovery. *Their* discovery. This was going to go down a treat at the Club when they got home.

A lively Frenchman was doing a lot of shoulder-shrugging and pooh-poohing and Harland made out that he was telling Pollock this was all a load of nonsense and he should mind his own business. Just some fluid, polish probably, spilled by the cleaning detail.

'My dear Marcel,' said Pollock, in a kindly voice, pointing to the floor, '*flies* are not, I believe, attracted by polish. I have never seen a fly in the Louvre before. It would take something frightfully delicious to lure them in here. But here, as you see, they most certainly are.'

* * *

A smart navy-suited *agent de ville*, with képi and baton, swept in and gave orders to clear the room immediately. He waved his arms about. He tooted his whistle. He made threatening gestures with his baton. He tried to arrest Pollock. Not one of this crowd took any notice and he had to content himself with making them all take a step back and sending for reinforcements.

Harland was uneasy. Ghouls! Worse than the flies. One whiff of blood and there they were, mouths open, eyes staring. A doctor bustled in. Was Harland the only one to find the speed of his arrival surprising? No, to give him due credit, the feller himself seemed to be a bit astonished . . . 'I got a message telling me to . . . Dr Moulin, from the Institut Médico-Légal, Quai des Orfèvres . . . Oh, my goodness! Yes, that's blood. And relatively fresh blood. Good Lord, there may be someone still alive in that box. The top must come off at once!'

That was what they wanted to hear. At last — they were to be treated to the bit of theatre they'd all been waiting for.

Six strong men, the policeman and Pollock included, heaved and strained, taking their instructions from the senior Egyptologist who'd hurried down from his office. The box, far taller than the tallest of the men, was lowered flat to the ground on its back and at a word from Pollock, three on each side, they flexed their muscles, ready to lift up the bulky lid.

Before the final revelation, Pollock called a halt and addressed Harland. 'I wonder if perhaps the lady might like to be excused this next bit?'

'Naw!' Harland replied. 'Maybelle's as tough as my old army boots!' and knew it could have been better expressed.

He and May were the only tourists present. All the rest were — he'd have sworn — academics. Staffers perhaps. Harland was a salesman and a damned good one. And you didn't make the money he'd made by not being able to read faces. Individuals or in groups. Harland didn't read much but he read people all right. And this collection puzzled him. It was downright weird! He'd seen a scene like this in one of May's books. It was entitled *The Opening of the Mummy Case*. Earnest professor types gathered round a table, all eyes on the box laid out ready in front of them.

Harland glanced around the faces of this crowd. They'd known just how far they could push the cop. They'd retreated exactly when they had to, conceded no more than was necessary to keep him on board. Thinking as one. Like a good platoon. Struck by his insight, Harland tried but failed to spot the senior officer present. Well, whoever these people were, they knew when to keep quiet.

No one spoke. Harland didn't even hear a gasp when the lid finally went up. He tried to cover May's eyes but she bit him and he took his hand away. And then, a voice broke the stunned silence.

'Ah. A double occupancy. It's a bit crowded in there, wouldn't you say?' said Pollock, lazily confident. 'I think we can safely identify the passenger on the lower deck — and looking a teeny bit ruffled — as the High Priest of Lower Egypt. But — I say — anyone recognize the passenger in first class accommodation on the *upper* deck?'

'It's Lebreton! Professeur Joachim Lebreton!'

'Ha!'

'Well! Well!'

' 'Struth!'

A communal breath was exhaled by the gathering. Wondering looks were exchanged. Most made the sign of the cross. But, strangely, Harland saw not one look of distress or sorrow. One or two even gave — he was certain — a bitter smile.

The doctor took over, sweeping the helpers aside. He summoned the policeman to his side and spoke tersely into his ear. Harland could follow his gestures, and all present could see for themselves what had happened to the professor.

He was dead. A wound to the heart. A knife wound, Harland judged. Two years of soldiering in the infantry during the war had taught him all anyone would ever want to know about bullet wounds. This was no bullet wound. The poor guy looked like he'd been bayoneted. Slit down the middle. The body had clearly been propped on its feet at the moment of death because the flow of blood down the front of his beige jacket and trousers had been copious and had ponded in his shoes to overflow into the bottom of the box. Harland thought it must have gathered there in quantities, waited for him and Maybelle to stroll by, and started to seep its way through on to the floor.

Oddly, there was something white sticking out of the dead man's mouth. It looked grotesque and Harland wanted to rush forward and pull it away. The doctor seemed to have the same urge. He chose a pair of pincers from the bag he had laid out open at his feet and tugged at the — cotton, was it? A thin roll of white fabric about two and a half inches wide emerged from the mouth. Moulin pulled again. A further length came out.

'Linen. Mummy bandage,' said someone in the crowd.

Another voice specified: '*Ancient* mummy bandage.'

'Well — it's outdated rubbish,' drawled the Englishman standing in front of Harland, to his neighbour, 'what else would we expect the dear professor to spew forth? Let's just hope they won't feel obliged to check the other orifices. I, for one, should have to leave.'

A waft of some sweet, spicy scent began to wind its way through the crowd. The inside of his grandpa's old cigar box? Cloves? Cinnamon? Myrrh? What did myrrh smell like? Just like this, Harland imagined. His memory, triggered, went off with a bang. His mother's apple pie! Suddenly uncomfortable, he reached into his pocket for his handkerchief.

A small gold object fell from the now bloodstained bandage and landed with a tinkle on the marble at the foot of the Chief Egyptologist. He didn't hesitate. He picked it up and held it aloft between thumb and forefinger. 'Gentlemen. I think we all recognize the ugly, dog-headed god of Egypt?' he announced. His arched eyebrows, quizzical, superior, assumed a special knowledge in his audience. He could have been taking class.

Harland itched to put up his hand. 'It's Anubis,' he whispered to May. He knew two Egyptian gods. Ra was the other one.

Maybelle didn't even hear his mistake. She was staring at the gold trinket. She had turned very pale. '*Set*! It's Set!' she hissed in Harland's ear. 'I don't like it here. I don't like these people. It's crowded, it's creepy and it's making me nauseous. Get me out, Harland, or your wing-tips really will suffer!'

Serious efforts were made to bar their way. The policeman's hand went to his holster. Orders were yelled in several languages. But Sergeant Harland C. White, survivor of Belleau Wood, supporting his wife with one arm, extended the other, stuck out his jaw and charged for the door.

Out in the main corridor and sounds of pursuit fading, they encountered two newsmen carrying cameras armed with those new-fangled exploding light bulb devices. They were looking about them eagerly.

'Show's back there,' said Harland, nodding over his shoulder. 'Better hurry, you guys. You've missed the first act.'

1

Paris, 21st May 1927

'I know monsieur will have a most enjoyable evening.'

The young woman who'd shown him to his seat offered him a smile at once shy and knowing. She held out her hand for his tip and slipped it swiftly away with a murmured word of thanks. The solitary Englishman hesitated, eyeing the pair of gilt chairs snuggling cosily together in the empty box with sudden misgiving.

'Mademoiselle!'

He detained her with his call as she turned to dart away and offered his ticket stub again for her inspection. 'Some mistake, I think?'

The girl took the ticket and looked with exaggerated care at the number. She was an *ouvreuse* — yes, that's what they called them over here, he remembered. Though what they actually 'opened' was a mystery to the Englishman . . . unless you counted the opening of those little bags into which their conjurer's fingers made the notes and coins disappear.

'No, there is no mistake, monsieur. This is indeed your box number.' She tilted her head and the smile appeared again, this time without the softening element of shyness. 'You have the best seat in the house.' Her eye ran over the handsome features, the imposing figure, taking in the evening dress, correct and well-cut. She remembered his generosity and paused in her scurrying to cast a glance, amused and complicitous at the second chair. 'A little patience!' she teased. 'I'm sure it will not be long before monsieur has company.' She took the time to add: 'There are ten minutes to go before the curtain rises. And it is no longer fashionable to be late. Certainly not for this show.'

She whisked away in a flutter of black silk and a tantalizing trace of rather good perfume, leaving Sir George Jardine standing about in something of a quandary.

He had an increasing feeling of unease. He was displaced. He ought not to be here. But the momentary touch of vertigo was chased away by a stab of impatience with himself. With the man he had become over the years. Would he ever be free to lay aside the burden of his training? Years of forethought, political skirmishing, and — yes — out-and-out skulduggery had imbued him with a watchfulness that was not lightly laid aside, even when he was thousands of miles away from the arena of his intrigues. Here he was, in the pleasure capital of Europe; it was time to let go the reins and leave the bloody Empire to look after itself.

For at least the next six months in fact. George had gone on working after many would have retired, the guiding force, the continuity behind the last two Viceroys of India. He'd been looking forward to getting away from Delhi, leaving behind the heat, the scandals, the undercover chicanery. It had been a good idea to break his journey at Marseille and take the Pullman up to Paris. Yes, no doubt about that. A week or two of relaxation and stimulation before he did his duty by his ageing family back home had been hard earned.

A summer in Surrey. He needed to fortify himself. Experience the latest sensations . . . work up a few stories . . . bank a few topics of conversation. At home in England one couldn't go on for long talking about India. It pained him to see eyes glaze over when anything other than a passing reference to the subcontinent was made. At the mention of Delhi, people started to twitch and to look anxiously over your shoulder for rescue, but just let drop that you'd been in Paris and they clustered round for news. George determined to have fascinating things to report.

Before taking his seat, he patted his pockets with a familiar sensation of expectation. His opera glasses, cigarlighter, wallet, spare handkerchief and a roll of currency were present and correct. Along with a folded envelope.

Bit of a puzzle, this.

It had been handed to him the morning after his arrival in Paris — an envelope addressed to him in a careful English hand, care of the Ambassador Hotel. There was nothing in it but a scribbled note and a theatre ticket. For the Théâtre des Champs-Élysées. The clerk at reception had no knowledge of its delivery. No one, George could have sworn, knew that he was to be in Paris this evening. And who the hell was 'John'? Which 'John' of his acquaintance

— and there were many — had, in black ink, written:

George, old man — welcome to Paris! Thought you wouldn't be able to resist this. Tickets are like gold dust so make sure you enjoy yourself. But — there you are — I owe you one! Yrs, John.

A mystery? George had no time for mysteries. His first reaction was of irritation rather than puzzlement. Why on earth couldn't the wretched fellow have appended his surname? Unless he was so well known to him that it would be considered unnecessarily stiff? A moment's further reflection and he had it. With a passing embarrassment (was he getting old? losing his grip?) he remembered he had a cousin called John — though he'd always called him Jack — and that cousin was, indeed, in Paris, engaged in some clandestine way in the diplomatic service. And, yes, George did recall that the younger man owed him a favour. Quite a favour, in fact. A ticket to the theatre — though the star was the most talked-of, most scandalous woman in the world — was a pretty frivolous offering as a counterbalance. Bad form. George didn't at all object to being sent the ticket but he felt it was . . . ah . . . undignified to mention the moral debt at all. What are influential relatives for, if not to ease your path through the career jungle? You accept the leg-up, are duly grateful and the matter is never referred to again. Well — all would, doubtless, be revealed. Jack would pop up, late as usual, and they'd have a laugh together, slightly uneasy to catch each other enjoying such a spectacle as was promised. George was glad he'd had the sense to order a tray of whisky and soda for the interval. They'd enjoy a glass and his cousin would know that he was expected.

And here he was, the sole occupant of what in London would have been called the Royal Box, the target of lazily curious glances from the audience gathering below. A public figure and constantly on parade, George was unperturbed. He automatically made a gesture to adjust his already perfectly tied black tie, he smoothed his luxuriant grey moustache and eased his large frame into the spindle-legged gilt chair further from the entrance, thinking to allow easy access for his cousin when he appeared.

He settled to stare back boldly at the audience, conveying amused approval. This gathering risked outshining the performers, he thought, so brightly glittered the diamonds in the front stalls and the paste gems in the upper gallery. The gowns glowed — silks and satins, red and mulberry and peach apparently the favoured colours this season, standing out against the stark black and white of the gentlemen's evening dress. His nose twitched, identifying elements of the intoxicating blend of tobaccos curling up from the auditorium: suave Havana cigars, silky Passing Clouds favoured by the ladies, and, distantly, an acrid note of rough French Caporals.

And every seat taken, it seemed. Definitely *le tout Paris* on parade this evening. George checked his programme again, wondering if he'd misunderstood the style of entertainment on offer. A turnout like this was exactly what you'd expect for the first night of a ballet — he'd been part of just such an audience, tense with anticipation, in this theatre before the war. He'd seen Nijinsky leap with superhuman agility in *The Rite of Spring*, delighting some, scandalizing others. George had counted himself delighted to be scandalized. On this stage, Anna Pavlova had thrilled the world with her performance of *The Dying Swan*. And tonight's crowd was seething with expectation of an equally significant display. All was movement: faces turned this way and that, hands fluttered as friends were greeted across the breadth of the hall, places were hurriedly swapped and the unmistakable musical rise and fall of a chirruping French crowd on pleasure bent swirled up to him.

The sounds of such conviviality made him for a moment conscious of his solitary state. Unused to being alone, and certainly never unaccompanied at an evening's entertainment, George swallowed the joking aside he would have murmured to his aide-de-camp. He felt in his pocket and took out a pair of ivory opera glasses. The audience were freely scanning *him*, he'd return the attention and search out a familiar face among them. The odds were that he knew someone down there. Might note them, wave and see them in the bar after the show perhaps?

A poor haul. His glasses passed swiftly over the barely remembered features of someone he'd been at school with and didn't care to see again. He was probably mistaken . . . a passing resemblance. And that was it.

He was on the point of giving up when a stirring in the box opposite caught his attention. An usherette had entered to show the occupants to their seats. An inquisitive application of the glasses confirmed that the girl was *his* pretty *ouvreuse*. Obviously i/c boxes for the nobs. A favoured position, most likely. He scanned the scene, watching as a young lady followed her in, clutching her blue and gold programme. The newcomer smiled back at her escort, trailing behind. She waited for him, turning her head in a regal gesture as he tipped and dismissed the attendant, and went to stand by a chair, pausing until he came forward to hold it ready for her. As he sat down by her side, she threaded a white arm through his in a familiar way. Ignoring the man, George trained his glasses on her. What a corker! Blonde and flamboyantly pretty. And what quantities of make-up young girls wore these days, he reflected. The tiny pair of glasses was almost concealed in his great hand and he discreetly trained them lower to take in her figure. He smiled. What should he report back to the ladies of Simla regarding the latest fashions? They were certain to ask. He would say that necklines appeared to be retreating southwards while hems were advancing rapidly northwards. Disastrous collision inevitable.

An attractive colour, though, the scrap of silk the goddess opposite was wearing. Colour of a peacock's throat. It glinted in an exotic way, flashing two colours over the void at him. George sighed. Lucky bastard — whoever he was — to have this girl on his arm! He eased his glasses sideways to take in her companion.

Christ Almighty! George lowered them hurriedly. He dropped his programme deliberately and bent to retrieve it, head lowered, using the seconds floundering about on the carpet to decide what he should do next. This could prove to be, socially, a jolly awkward moment. What bad luck that the only other person he recognized for certain in the whole theatre should be seated exactly opposite him. In clear view. Lieutenant Colonel Somerton, now a knight of the realm if George had it right, and one-time soldier. Their last meeting had been decidedly unpleasant.

But surely the scoundrel would, even after all these years, be lying low, not flaunting himself in a box in full view of the cream of European society? George was assailed by sudden doubt. He risked an eye over the edge and looked again, taking his time. The black hair was as thick as ever, with not a trace of grey as far as George could make out, and the moustache, always the man's affectation, still in place and looking, he thought, rather outdated. The hawk-like features which had struck such terror in the ranks were less sharp and he watched in surprise as the face he had always perceived as humourless softened into a smile when his lady-friend whispered in his ear. Well, well! Steamroller Somerton! George had thought never to encounter him again. And now what? Greet him at once or spend the rest of the evening avoiding his gaze?

He made up his mind. Straightening again and glancing around, he made a show of catching sight of his old acquaintance for the first time and tilted his head slightly in surprise. With a short, stiff nod, unaccompanied by a smile, he acknowledged him and held his eye until the man responded similarly. George made no attempt to extend his courtesy to the female companion. The absent Lady Somerton, he felt, wherever she was (and it most certainly wasn't Paris), would not have considered it appropriate.

This was one of the dangers you ran in a European capital. Away from the hothouse world of India where you couldn't smile at a girl without running the risk of rumour, you suddenly felt free to turn your long-held fantasies into reality. How appalling for the chap opposite to see that he'd been recognized — caught out — and by a man he had no reason to call his friend. Deeply embarrassing. But it occurred to George that any sympathy he was prepared to expend on the situation would be wasted on a rogue like Somerton. No, it was the girl on his arm who deserved his concern.

He glanced at her again, suddenly shrewd and objective. All appearances were that she was a professional lady-friend, hired by the night. French, he would have guessed, judging by the liveliness of her hand gestures and her confident chatter. Well able to take care of herself — or summon up some protective chap from her murky organization to do it for her. George was not familiar with the arrangements in Paris. In

Simla or Delhi, had such a situation arisen, an aide would have been dispatched and the problem would have dissolved before his eyes.

But he was troubled. He found he could not dismiss the little miss opposite as a world-weary and experienced . . . what did they call a tart of this quality in France? *Poule de luxe*, that was it! Below all her surface glamour he sensed that she was young — barely twenty, he would have guessed. And, whether dubiously employed or a free agent, she was someone's daughter, for God's sake! Had the silly little thing *any* idea of what she was getting herself into? It would take more than a tap on the cheek with a fan to control Somerton if he turned nasty. George shuddered. The man, he recalled with a rush of foreboding, was rotten to the centre of his being. He couldn't say 'soul' — there was no evidence that he had one. George chewed his lip in irritation.

He should have had the man shot when he'd had the chance.

He stirred in his seat, checked his watch and considered his options. Did he have time to negotiate the lengths of corridor chock-a-block with latecomers on a dash over to the box opposite? And what would he say when he arrived there with the performance about to start? He pictured himself crashing into the box, breathless, perspiring, and in the grip of a Quixotic urge. A ridiculous figure. He had no authority, civilian or military, over Somerton . . . he would have to appeal to the girl directly. But how would he find the words to warn her?

There'd be accusations followed by argument, protests, denials. *Your remarks are slanderous! I'll see you in court, Jardine!* And — heaven forbid! — suppose the girl turned out to be something entirely innocent such as . . . his niece? George watched surreptitiously as Somerton leaned close and whispered something in her ear, lifting his head slowly and trailing his pomaded moustache lingeringly over her cheek. Almost retching with disgust, George concluded this was no niece.

He pressed down on his arm rests and the chair wobbled under him as he prepared to take action. A moment later he sank back in frustration. He never embarked on any course unless his strategy was clear, his tactics well worked out, the outcome predictable and in his favour; the reason he'd survived for so many years when others had not. And he was not about to abandon the careful habits of a professional lifetime on account of a stab of juvenile sympathy. George could foresee the result of any irruption of his into the box opposite. At the best, he'd be ejected by a hurriedly summoned bouncer; at the worst, he'd be trapped over there with the pair of them until the interval.

His conflict was cut short by an arresting fanfare of notes on a trumpet followed at once by a blaring blue jazz riff from the orchestra pit. He was aware of a simultaneous dimming of the electric house lights. The blonde girl across the way opened her mouth in anticipation and wriggled forward in her seat with the eagerness of a six-year-old at a pantomime. George sighed and came to a decision. In the seconds before the light faded, he did what he could. Oblivious of the hush descending on the crowd, he rose to his feet and slipped on his white gloves. He sought out and held the eye of his opposite number.

Imperious, imperial and impressive, over the width of the auditorium, Sir George Jardine delivered a command.

2

Abandon target! Withdraw at once!

The soldier's silent hand language flashed, eerily blue in the dimming house lights, across to the opposite box. Unmistakable to a man who had been a fellow officer. On the Frontier, grappling often in hand-to-hand combat with lethally savage tribesmen, officers had learned from their enemy that in close proximity you communicated in silence as they did or you got your head shot off. Would Somerton remember and respond? Or would the man summon up what vestiges of self-respect he still had, to affect ignorance or rejection of the old code? George calculated that he could not depend on touching any finer feeling, on awakening any sense of regimental pride across the void. No — ugly threat was the only weapon left in his armoury. To emphasize his point, he added a universally recognized gesture. He drew the forefinger of his left hand slowly across his throat. *Do as I say or else . . .*

At that, Somerton threw back his head and laughed. Shaking with amusement and hardly able to keep his hands steady, in the moment before the last light went out, he returned the signal: *Message received and understood*.

* * *

Bloody French audiences! George remembered they always took their time settling. But the musicians seemed to be well aware of this and mastering the situation. The trumpet solo had silenced most and there now followed, as the last mutterings faded, the last shuffling subsided, a clarinet performance which stunned George with its fluency. Not his style of music at all. Jazz. But he could see the point of it and had been made to listen to the quantities of recordings that had filtered through to Simla and Delhi along with the ubiquitous gramophone. It was one of his party tricks to discuss in an avuncular way the latest crazes with his young entourage. And this was an experience he would want to share with them on his return. What he was hearing, all his musical senses were telling him, was exceptional. He rummaged in his pocket and took out his cigar-lighter. A discreet flick of the flame over his programme gave him the name: Sidney Bechet. English? French? Could be either. Even American perhaps? He'd file the name away. The chap was an artist. Could take his place in the wind section of the Royal Philharmonic any day. Given the right material to play.

He was so absorbed by the music, leaning forward over the edge in an attempt to get a clearer view of the almost invisible soloist, he didn't hear her enter. The presence of a stranger in his box was betrayed by a rush of remembered scent carried towards him on a sudden air current as the door opened quietly and closed again. The effect on George was instant.

Memories had ambushed him before he could even turn his head.

The scent of an Indian garden at twilight . . . L'Heure Bleue he'd been informed when he'd dispatched some gauche young subaltern to make discreet enquiries. The aide had returned oozing information, parroting on about vanilla, iris and spices. George had been gratified and amused that the young man had been received with such voluble courtesy by the wearer. Amused but not surprised; she had always been able to charm . . . enslave wouldn't be too strong a word . . . his impressionable young men.

The name said it all. The Twilight Hour. He didn't need to listen to accounts of top-notes and bases. It spoke, for him, in a voice soft as velvet, of the swift, magical dark blue moment between sunset and starlight. But, intriguingly, it brought with it an undertow of something sinister . . . bitter almonds . . . the scent of death. George shivered. The scent of a woman long dead. A woman he had mourned for five years. Silently in his heart, never in his speech.

And here, in this gaudy box, in frenetic Paris, the scent seemed as out of place as he was himself. He whirled angrily to confront whoever had invaded his privacy and — idiotically — with a thought to challenge the invader for daring to wear a perfume which for him would forever be the essence of one woman: Alice.

'Alice?'

George's voice was an indistinct croak expressing his disbelief, his raised hand not a greeting but an exorcism, an instinctive gesture of self-protection, as he peered through the gloom, focusing on the dark-clad figure standing by the door. An elegant gloved hand released the hood of the opera cloak allowing it to slide down on to her shoulders. He could just make out, with the aid of the remaining dim light from the orchestra pit, the sleek shape of a blonde head but the face was indistinguishable. Her finger went to her lips and he heard a whispered: '*Chut!*'

In a second, the woman had slid into the chair at his side and had grasped his hand in greeting. She leaned and whispered into his ear: 'George! How wonderful to see you again! And how touching to find you still recognize me — and in the dark too! Alice? Am I then still Alice for you?'

'Always were. Always will be. Alice,' he mumbled, struggling for a measure of control. He hunted for and caught her hands in his, pressing them together, moving his grasp to encircle both her slim wrists in one of his great hands, his gnarled fingers closing in an iron and inescapable grip.

'And, Alice Conyers, you're under arrest.'

3

She laughed and winced but made no attempt to struggle. 'Let's enjoy the performance first, shall we? And . . . who knows? . . . perhaps I'll surrender to you later, George?'

Her purring voice had always, for him, spoken with a teasing double entendre in every sentence. He had dismissed it as a delusion, the product of his own susceptibility, a fantasy sprung from overheated and hopeless senile lust. No one else had ever remarked on it. But the voice he was hearing again, the style, the breathed assumed intimacy — all this was telling him that it was indeed Alice he held in his grasp.

'I do hope you're prepared, George? This can be rather stimulating! The show, I mean! Elderly gents carted off, blue in the face and frothing at the mouth, every evening, I hear. Got your pills to hand, have you? Last will and testament in order? Perhaps you should tell me whom to ring just in case . . .' She broke off at the first twitch of the pearl-grey curtains. The lightly insolent tone was unmistakable and he remembered how he'd missed it. George swallowed painfully, unable to reply.

With a thousand questions to ask the woman at his side, a thousand things to tell her, he was reduced to silence by the swish of the curtains as they swung back revealing a brilliantly lit scene. George stared at the kaleidoscope of vivid colours filling the stage, a controlled explosion of fabrics and patterns. The set conjured up the interior of a sumptuous Parisian department store — or was it meant to be a boutique on the rue de la Paix? Silks, velvets, chiffons and furs hung draped about the stage, arranged with an artist's eye for effect. After the minutes of darkness, the assault on the sense of sight was calculatedly overwhelming. Another surprise followed swiftly. Set here and there against the background colours, a number of dressmakers' dummies — mannequins, they called them over here — gleamed pale, their pure, sculpted nakedness accentuated by the profusion of clothes behind them. At a teasing spiral of sound from the orchestra the figures came to life and began to parade about the stage.

They were actually moving about! Dancing! George could hardly believe his eyes. He released Alice's wrists at once and cleared his throat in embarrassment. A scene of this nature could never have been staged in London. He tensed, wondering whether he should at once set an example and make noisily for the exit, tearing up his programme and tossing it into the audience like confetti in the time-honoured tradition, snorting his disapproval. Writing off the remainder of what promised to be a disastrous evening. Apparently catching and understanding his sudden uncertainty, his companion put a hand on his arm, gently restraining.

George watched on. Was it his imagination . . . or . . . ? No. He had it right. The girls, without exception, were tall and lovely and

— yes — one would expect that of chorus girls. Rumour had it that they were all shipped in from England. But this bunch were all blonde or titian-haired with alabaster-white skin. After the years of exposure to Indian-brown limbs, this degree of paleness struck him as exaggeratedly lewd. While he was pondering the reasons for this blatant piece of artistic stage management, the girls started on their routine.

To his bemusement the chorus-girl-mannequins were beginning to act out a scene of shopping. They were selecting garments held out for their inspection by a group of *vendeuses* whose sketchy notion of uniform appeared to be a pair of black satin gloves and a black bow tie. Their clients inspected the garments on offer and saucily began to put them on, layer by layer, tantalizingly and wittily not always in the expected order. It was a while before George realized what was going on and when he did he began to shake with suppressed guffaws.

Alice leaned close and whispered: 'A striptease in reverse. They start naked and end up in fur coats. Different, you'd have to admit! You're to think of this as an aperitif,' she murmured.

The girls, fully clothed at last, eventually took a bow to laughter and applause and swayed off, flirtily trailing feather boas, silk trains and mink stoles, leaving the stage empty.

The lights went out at once and a backdrop descended. A single spotlight was switched on, illuminating in a narrow cone of blue light marbled with tobacco smoke, an area of stage front right. It picked out what appeared to be the contorted limbs and trunk of a tree. The drums took up a strong rhythm and a tenor saxophone began to weave in and out, offering a flirtatious challenge to the beat, tearing free to soar urgently upwards.

The shape on stage began to move.

George could have sworn that a boa constrictor was beginning to ripple its way down the trunk then he gasped as the tree straightened. A second light came on from a different angle, compelling his eye to refocus. He now saw a massive black male figure carrying on his back, not a boa, but a slim, lithe and shining black girl. George forgave himself for his failure to make sense out of the contorted figures: the girl was being carried upside-down and doing the splits. Her limbs were distinguishable from the man's by their difference in colour — hers, by the alchemy of the blue-tinted spotlight, were the colour of Everton toffee, his gleamed, the darkest ebony. She twined about lasciviously, her body moving in rhythm with the pounding drumbeat, naked but for a pink flamingo feather placed between her legs.

The athletic undulations continued as the spotlight followed the black giant to centre stage. Once he'd mastered his astonishment, George decided that what he was seeing was a pas de deux of the highest artistic quality. Yes, that was how he would express it. But he wondered how on earth he could ever convey the shattering erotic charge of the performance and decided never to attempt it. The relentless sound of the drums, the stimulation of the dance and the overriding pressure of the enigmatic presence by his side were beginning to have an effect on George. He ran a finger around his starched collar, harrumphed into his handkerchief and breathed deeply, longing for a lungful of fresh air — anything to dispel this overheated soup of tobacco, perspiration and siren scents.

On stage, the dancing pair were writhing to a climax. The giant, at the last, determined to rid himself of his unbearable tormentor, plucked the girl from his back, holding her by the waist in one great hand, and spun her to the floor. He, in turn, collapsed, twitching rhythmically.

'Thank God for that! Know how you're feeling, mate!' George thought and knew that every man in the audience was experiencing the same sensation. He watched, with a smile, for any sign of Alice's predicted rush for medical attention for the elderly but saw none. To enthusiastic applause and shouts the lights went out, allowing the pair to go offstage, and the curtains swished closed again.

'Would you like me to loosen your stays, Sir George?' Alice asked demurely. 'No? Well, tell me — what do you make of her, the toast of Paris? The Black Venus? La belle Josephine?'

'Miss Baker lives up to her reputation,' he said, ever the diplomat. 'A remarkable performance. I'm glad to have seen it.'

'And you're lucky to have seen it. This was the first act she impressed the Parisian public with when she arrived here two years ago. Her admirers have pressed her to repeat it for some time and at last they've persuaded her partner

— that was a dancer called Joe Alex — to perform with her again. The order of performance, for various reasons, has been changed this evening, you'll find. Word got out, which is why the theatre is packed tonight.'

'Is she to reappear?' he asked, trying for a casual tone. 'Or have we seen all of Miss Baker that is to be seen?'

'She'll be back. Once more in this half — doing her banana dance — and then again in the second. We're to hear her singing. She has a pleasant voice and an entertaining French accent. Now, George, why don't you sit back and enjoy the rest of the acts?'

George could well have directed the same question at her, he thought. He felt he could have better entered into the spirit of the entertainment had his disturbing companion herself been at ease. But she was not. He hadn't been so distracted by the spectacle that he'd failed to notice the tremble of her hand, the bitten lower lip, the anxious glances around the auditorium. Troubling signs in a woman he had always observed to be fearless and totally confident. And if Alice Conyers had no fear of the influential Sir George Jardine with his powers to effect her arrest for deception, embezzlement and murder, culminating in repatriation and an ignominious death on an English gallows, then whom *did* she fear? He concluded that there must be, lurking somewhere in this luxuriously decadent space — in her perception at least — someone of an utterly terrifying character.

He followed her gaze. Her eyes, under lowered lashes, were quartering the theatre like a hunter. George sighed with frustration. This refurbished and enlarged theatre now housed, on a good night, up to two thousand souls. And of those, all but two were strangers to him. He wondered how many were known to Alice. And in what dubious capacity? Everything he knew of the woman's past suggested that her associations were likely to be of a criminal nature, after all. And he'd never been aware of a leopard that could change its spots. Good Lord! Could it be that the woman might actually be thinking herself safer in *his* custody than running loose in Paris? That the grip of his improvised handcuffs about her wrists was not threatening but welcome?

4

London, 21st May 1927

Croydon Aerodrome. Gateway to the Empire, the hoarding announced.

'Arsehole of the Universe, more like,' Joe Sandilands corrected.

It was fear that, eight years after the war, still reduced him to the swearing and mechanically filthy reactions and utterances of the common soldiery. He looked about him, distracting himself from his terror by examining the other lunatics queuing up to experience three hours of danger and discomfort.

Rich, expensively dressed and unrestrainedly loud, they smiled when they showed their passports and plane tickets, keen to be off. They waved goodbye to their Vuitton luggage, their hat boxes, golf clubs and tennis racquets, as a uniformed employee of Imperial Airways wheeled it all away on a trolley to be stowed in the hold. Joe clutched his Gladstone bag and briefcase firmly when his turn came to face the booking clerk, his steely expression discouraging any attempt to wrest them from him.

'My luggage has gone ahead. I'll be keeping these with me,' he said firmly, flashing his warrant card. 'Work to do during the flight, you understand.'

'As long as the light lasts, sir,' the clerk agreed

reluctantly. 'Will you be requiring supper during the flight, may I ask? I believe we have Whitstable oysters and breast of duck on the menu this evening, sir.'

Joe tried to disguise an automatic shudder. 'Thank you but I shall have to decline.' He smiled. 'Late dinner plans in Paris.' The reciprocal smile showed complete understanding.

'Full complement of passengers tonight?' Joe enquired politely as his tickets were checked and chalk scrawls made on his bags by a second employee.

'No, sir. By no means. Thirteen passengers. You're the thirteenth. We can take twenty at a push but the season isn't in full swing yet. You'll find it pleasantly uncrowded. Fine clear skies reported over the Channel,' he concluded encouragingly.

'This lot must be first-time flyers,' Joe decided as he shuffled along in file with the chattering group ahead of him to take a temporary seat in a room equipped as a lounge. 'They won't be grinning and giggling for much longer.' One of his friends, like-minded, had summed up the short flight: 'They put you in a tin coffin and shut the lid. You're sprayed with oil and stunned with noise. You're sick into a bag . . . twice . . . and then you land in Paris.'

The passengers, who all seemed to know each other, swirled around the quiet, dark man absorbed by his documents, offering no pleasantries, attempting no contact. Something about the stern face, handsome if you were sitting to the east of him, rather a disaster if you found yourself to the west . . . war wound, obviously . . . kept them at arm's length. The men sensed an implacable authority, the women glanced repeatedly, sensing a romantic challenge. Everything about him, from the set of his shoulders to the shine on his shoes, suggested a military background though the absence of uniform, medals, regimental tie or any other identifying signs made this uncertain. His dark tweed suit was of fashionably rugged cut and would not have looked out of place on the grouse moor or strolling round the British Museum. The leather briefcase at his feet was a good one though well-worn, and spoke of the businessman hurrying to Paris. But there were disconcerting contradictions about the man. The black felt fedora whose wide brim he'd pulled low over his eyes gave him a bohemian air and the gaily coloured silk Charvet scarf knotted casually about his neck was an odd note and, frankly . . . well . . . a little outré. An artist perhaps? No — too well dressed. Architect? One of those art deco chappies? Bound no doubt for the exhibitions that came and went along the Seine.

A pretty redhead wearing a sporty-looking woollen two-piece and a green cloche hat changed places with one of her friends to sit beside the stranger. She leaned slightly to catch a glimpse of the papers which were so absorbing him. Joe wondered what on earth she would make of the learned treatise he was scanning: *Identification of Corpses* by G. A. Fanshawe, D.Sc. (Oxon) with its subheadings of *Charred*

Bodies, Drowned Bodies, Battered Bodies . . .

Aware of her sustained curiosity, Joe mischievously shuffled to the top a printed sheet of writing paper. Under the bold insignia of Interpol, and laid out in letters so large she would have no difficulty in reading them, was an invitation to The Commissioner of the Metropolitan Police, Scotland Yard, London, to attend the second conference of Heads of Interpol in Paris. A detailed programme of lectures and events followed. Joe took out a pencil and began to make notes in the margin.

She addressed him with the open confidence of a fellow passenger aboard a boat, all companions for the duration of the voyage. 'I see you're not on pleasure bent in the capital of frivolity? Er . . . Commissioner? Should I address you as Commissioner? Is that who you are?'

He grinned and passed her a card. 'Not Commissioner, I'm sorry to say. He's the villain who's deputized me to come along in his stead. This is me. I'm Joseph Sandilands. How do you do, Miss . . . ?'

'Watkins. Heather Watkins.' And she read: '*Commander* Sandilands. DSO. Légion d'honneur. Ah, I was right! I took you for a military or naval man of some sort. But Commander sounds very impressive!' And she added in a tone playfully inquisitive: 'May we look to see 'Commissioner' on your card one day?'

'I do hope not! Annoying my boss is one of my chief recreations. I should hate to find myself at the top of the pyramid keeping order. Who would there be to keep *me* in order? I should have to do it myself!' Good Lord! That was the first time he'd given words to any such feeling. And he'd expressed it in unbelievably artless words to a complete stranger. It must be the fear of the next few hours that was sweeping away his defences, making him reckless.

The arrival of a steward in Imperial Airways livery made unnecessary any further revelations and they were called for boarding. The group, jostling and joking with each other, surged forward. But, at the point of putting her foot on the ramp, the lively and confident Miss Watkins, who had trailed behind finishing a conversation with Joe, balked. She shook her head like a horse refusing a fence, turned pale and began to breathe raggedly. Joe, close behind, recognized the symptoms and put a comforting arm under hers. 'Don't worry,' he said. 'And, above all, don't be concerned if the wings appear to wobble alarmingly. They're supposed to do that. Watch them carefully and, should they stop wobbling, then you may start to worry. These big planes are perfectly safe, you know, and the company has an unblemished record. Look — do you see — it's an Argosy. That means it's got four wings, three engines and two pilots. That should be enough to get us through.' He wished he could believe all this rot himself. 'And, look, Miss Watkins . . . Heather . . . take this. I find it really helps.' He passed her a lump of barley sugar.

A second steward in spanking white mess jacket and white peaked cap welcomed them aboard what he proudly called 'the Silver Wing service' and, taking them for a couple, ushered them towards a pair of seats alongside at the rear of the plane.

'Every passenger has a window seat, you see,' said Joe, helping her to settle. 'Though you can always draw the curtain across, should you have vertigo.'

They braced themselves for take-off. It came with the usual terrifying snarls of the engine and bumps along the runway and then there was the stomach-clenching moment of realization that the machine had torn itself free of the earth and was soaring at an impossible angle upwards. A glance through the oil-spattered glass showed the grey blur of London disappearing below them. Higher up, the sunlight brightened and they caught the full glow of the westering sun gilding the meadows and woods of southern England.

'It will be dark before we arrive, won't it?' Heather Watkins asked, suffering a further pang of apprehension.

'Yes,' Joe admitted. 'This is technically the night flight, after all. We should touch down just before ten o'clock.'

'But how will the pilot . . . ?' Hearing the naïveté of her question, Heather fell silent.

'Beacons all the way along the flight route,' said Joe confidently. 'But while the light lasts, he'll just follow the railway lines. Look — over there!' He pointed out a group of buildings below. 'You can see exactly where we are. Do you see — it's Ashford. That was the railway station. They paint the names of the main stations on the roof in big white letters all the way to Paris. They have emergency landing strips every few miles. And even in the dark the pilot can't mistake the Eiffel Tower. It's lit like a Christmas tree!'

Miss Watkins checked every few seconds to see that the wings were wobbling satisfactorily, the railway lines still beneath them, and finally began to relax.

'Doing anything interesting in Paris?' Joe asked when he judged she was capable of a sensible reply.

'Oh, the usual things,' she said. 'Shopping and shows for a few days then we're all off to the south of France. For the tennis tournament.' She fell silent.

'Do you observe or compete?' he asked.

'Oh, I play. Not very well. I mean I'm not in the Suzanne Lenglen or Helen Wills league yet but I'm improving. The boys,' she indicated the four young men sitting ahead of them, 'are all players. My brother Jim — that's him with the red hair — is the team captain and general organizer. The other two girls are team wives. I'm the odd one out.'

'Very odd,' Joe agreed. 'Most unusual. I've never met a lady tennis player before. One who plays seriously.'

'There aren't many of us in England. In France it's thought rather dashing and quite the okay thing to be! We're even allowed to wear skirts up to our knees over there.'

She rummaged in her handbag. 'Look — here's where we're staying . . . well, you never know. It's a little hotel on the Left Bank. In the rue Jacob. Handy for the bookshops. And a stone's throw from the police headquarters, funnily enough . . . ' she added with a gurgle of laughter. 'It's right opposite the Quai des Orfèvres!'

'I'm booked in at the Ambassador on the Right Bank, handy for the Opéra,' he said lightly. 'And a few steps away from the department stores. Au Printemps . . . Galeries Lafayette, funnily enough . . . One way or another, I think it's very likely in the way of business or pleasure our paths will literally cross again. And if my mental map of Paris serves me well, that'll be just about at Fauchon's, Place de la Madeleine. In time for what they call 'the five o'clock tea'.'

So that was the way to conquer a fear of flying — sit yourself next to a beautiful, athletic redhead and flirt your way there — Joe thought as they began to circle Paris, preparing to land at Le Bourget airfield just to the north-east. He wished he'd suggested something a little less staid than a *salon de thé*. The Deux Magots in St Germain would have struck a more adventurous note. Well, it was just a few stops on the electric tram and taxis were everywhere.

'How are you getting in to the city?' Joe asked. 'It's quite a few kilometres distant . . . '

'Oh, Jim's ordered a couple of taxis. You?'

'A colleague from the Quai des Orfèvres is coming to collect me. In a police car, I expect,' said Joe. 'All screeching sirens and flashing lights — that would be his style!'

He smiled at the mention of his colleague and relished the thought of the warm greetings they would exchange. Inspector Bonnefoye. Late of

Reims. Now, thanks to his undeniable talent and his great charm, promoted to the Police Judiciaire squad in Paris. A useful contact. Relations between the English and the French police departments were not often easy. Joe had made known his plans for attending the conference and Bonnefoye, with Gallic insouciance, had set about pulling strings and calling in favours, making promises — who knew what? — to get himself appointed to the French contingent at the Interpol jamboree. Not that Bonnefoye seemed prepared to take it seriously. His telephone conversations had been full of plans of an entertaining nature which had little to do with international crime fighting.

The Argosy circled the Eiffel Tower, Joe judged for the satisfaction of the passengers rather than in response to any navigational imperative, then headed off to the northeast and lined itself up, head into the wind facing an illuminated landing strip, and made a delicate touchdown. Everyone breathed a sigh of relief.

It was the stewards' odd behaviour that warned Joe. Suddenly unconfident, they advised the passengers to remain seated: ' . . . until we have taxied up to the hangar. There appears to be an impediment on the runway,' one of them improvised. The other climbed the stairs communicating with the cockpit to confer with the crew and he returned looking no less puzzled. The doors remained closed. No staff came forward to open the door and release them. And something was going on outside the plane.

Peering through the gloom, Joe saw, to his astonishment, shadows moving on the tarmacked runway, lights from torches and flares skittering everywhere. The passengers sat on, docile and puzzled.

Joe got to his feet and, with a calming gesture to the two stewards, made his way down the gangway to the front of the plane. With a bland smile he murmured: 'I speak a little French.' They nodded dubiously and made no attempt to remonstrate with him. No one ever challenged a man confident enough to make such an assertion on foreign soil, he found. He nipped up the steps and located the two pilots seated in the open cockpit.

'Captain! Commander Sandilands here. Scotland Yard. What's the problem?'

'Problem? I'll say!' came the shouted reply. 'People! It's worse than a football crowd. Look at them! They're standing ten deep up there on the viewing gallery. And they're milling around everywhere, all over the runways. Damned dangerous, if you ask me! And where are the airport staff? Can't move until they've cleared this mob away. What the hell's going on? Some strange French Saturday night entertainment?'

'Oh, no!' Joe groaned. 'I think I can guess what's going on. It's Charles Lindbergh! Attempting the transatlantic crossing. It was on the wireless — he was sighted over Ireland this afternoon. Made much better time than anyone expected and I'd guess this mob's gathered to watch him land. We must have beaten him to it by a few minutes. Dashed inconvenient! And we're a huge disappointment to all these idiots on the runway. It's not us they've come out from Paris to see. Ah, look! At last — they've twigged. They're pushing off, I think. They'll leave us alone now.'

'Lucky Lindy!' said the captain. 'Well, well! Never thought he'd do it! I can see a space now. Sir — would you mind returning to your seat? I think I can get through to the hangar.'

Joe made his way back to his place, passing on the news to the passengers as he moved down the aisle. Heather Watkins was thrilled to hear it and at once called forward to her brother: 'Jim! I want to stay to see Charles Lindbergh! Take care of my luggage, will you? If we get separated I'll meet you back at the hotel!'

Joe was amused to hear the decisive and energetic girl emerge from the heap of anxiety he had sat next to for three hours but felt he ought to offer advice: 'Do hang on to someone's arm, Miss Watkins. It's a menacing scene out there. Stay close to your group!'

The plane taxied on to an apron by the Imperial Airways hangar and, with no exterior staff in evidence, the stewards opened the door themselves and released the passengers on to the tarmac. They stood, paralysed, unable to negotiate the crowds, wondering which way to turn. Joe's eyes were searching for the familiar form of a police car when he felt his arm seized by a strong hand.

'Joe! I had no idea you were so popular!' said Inspector Bonnefoye. 'Welcome to Paris! The car's over there. Let me take your bags.' He gestured to a police car parked, lights on, engine running and pointing in the direction of the city with the driver at the wheel. They pushed their way over to it and threw the bags into the back seat.

'Bonnefoye! Never more pleased to see you, old man!'

'But you didn't tell me you were to be accompanied?' Bonnefoye was eyeing Miss Watkins with interest.

'A fellow passenger separated from her group. Miss Watkins,' said Joe, surprised to find that she'd followed him but relieved to see she'd abandoned her notion of staying to see Lindbergh touch down. 'I say, would you have room for her? She's bound for the city centre also. Her taxi doesn't seem to have made it through.'

'I'm sure I can squeeze Miss Watkins in the back,' said Bonnefoye easily, and Joe was amused to hear the automatic gallantry in his voice.

Before they could get in they were startled by the whining and coughing sound of an engine low over their heads, making for the runway. The crowd screamed and pushed its way to the sides as the monoplane, gleaming briefly silver as it passed between the searchlights, throttled back noisily and set down on the runway, continuing onwards towards a dark part of the airfield. In evident confusion, the pilot stopped and turned the plane around, nose pointing back to the hangars. But before he had gone far in this direction, he cut the engine abruptly, no doubt in regard for the crowd as people surged back again, risking loss of limbs, unaware of the danger of the scything propeller blades. For a moment the Spirit of St Louis stood in the middle of the track way, small, battered, oil- and salt-caked and unimpressive once out of its element of air. And then, as the engine spluttered its last, souvenir-hunters moved in and began to pull strips of canvas from the wings, tugging anything that yielded from the framework of the plane. Press camera bulbs flashed and popped, trained on the door.

'For God's sake!' Joe shouted, horrified. 'Do something, Bonnefoye! Those maniacs will tear the poor bugger apart! He's been flying solo in an open cockpit for a day and a half over the Atlantic — he won't be in any fit state to face up to a reception like this!'

As he spoke, the pair of them were already shouldering their way back through the crowd, using their height and aggressive energy to forge their way through to the door. Flourishing their warrant cards in a valiant attempt to keep the masses at bay, they stood together, arms extended, holding an uncomfortably small space free in front of the plane. After a moment, a window slid open and a voice called uncertainly: 'Does anyone here speak English?'

'We do!' Joe shouted back. 'Captain Lindbergh! Welcome and congratulations! I think it might be a good idea if you were to get out, sir, and we'll escort you to the hangar.'

The door opened and the tall figure of Charles Lindbergh appeared, blinking in the spotlights and the flash of the cameras. With a cry of concern, Bonnefoye put an arm under his shoulders and helped him to the ground, murmuring words of welcome. The pilot was pale and weary and looked much less than his twenty-five years. He stared in dismay at the jostling mass between him and safety and Joe remembered that, by all accounts, the young man was terrified of crowds. Taking his other arm, Joe felt his panic and the stiffness of his limbs and came to a decision.

'Captain, this is an impossible situation you've flown into. Idiotic, unplanned and damned dangerous! If only we could get you over to the hangar . . . Look — why don't you give me your flying helmet and take my hat instead?'

Lindbergh's eyes brightened with instant understanding. 'A decoy? That what you have it in mind to be, sir?'

'Might work. I'm tall. I can keep my hair covered, shout cheerful platitudes in English. That's all they want. In any case, I don't suppose they've any idea what you look like. Anyone in a flying helmet and talking English is going to get the attention of this crowd. Let's give them a run for their money, shall we?'

The American grinned and nodded. 'Well, I'd call that a very sporting offer . . . and good luck to you, sir . . . '

They ducked down and, crouching under cover of the wing, swapped headgear.

'They'll never think of chasing after a couple,' said a confident English voice and Heather Watkins pushed forward. She stood on tiptoe and adjusted the black fedora firmly over the aviator's golden hair. Companionably, she tucked an arm through his. 'Right, er, Charles, the hangar's that way. And just by it there's a police car with its engine running and a driver who knows where he's going. How about it?'

They strolled off, unimpeded, and Joe heard with amusement her cheerful voice: 'Now — tell me — how was your flight?'

And the laconic response: 'Why, just fine — and yours?'

Joe had no time to hear more. He straightened and moved to arrange himself with a tentative wave in the searchlight now trained on the cockpit door, helmet strap dangling provocatively. 'Well, hi there, folks! I guess this must be Paris . . . '

He got no further. In a second he was swept up with a howl of triumph on to the shoulders of two men in the crowd and carried off in parade down the runway towards the terminal building. The throng on the viewing gallery cheered. Joe turned this way and that, nodding and waving to his admirers, shouting the occasional greeting or navigational direction in English. Worse than riding an elephant. His back was slapped repeatedly, his hands wrung, he was lowered and hoisted on to fresh shoulders several times. A painful experience and not one to be endured for long.

Eventually, after spending what he considered an overgenerous amount of his time on this performance, he bent and informed his bearers that after more than thirty hours in the air he needed to have a pee. Urgently. He reckoned they had ten seconds to set him down. It seemed to work. Once his feet were on the ground, he made off at speed towards the hangar, tearing off the helmet as he ran. The front door of Bonnefoye's car opened at his approach and he flung himself inside. Bonnefoye and Miss Watkins were sitting together on the back seat.

'What have you done with our hero?' panted Joe.

'Dropped him off at Reception in the hangar. He'll be all right. The American Ambassador's taken cover in there with him, offering medical aid, engineering assistance and a bed and breakfast at the Embassy when they can make a break for it. And now, Sandilands, if you've quite finished horsing around and showing off, perhaps we can extricate ourselves from this mêlée and get ahead of the crowd before they all block the road back into Paris.' Bonnefoye looked anxiously at his watch. 'If you'd taken many more curtain calls we'd have missed the best of the entertainment at Zelli's, which is where I'm planning we'll make a start.'

5

Act followed act and George settled to enjoy himself. Music Hall. This was something he could respond to. And the quality of the turns was high — the best the world had to offer, he would have thought, and lavishly staged. He admired especially a slender woman in a tight black sheath, and was moved to wiping a sentimental tear from his eye as she sang of the fickleness of men. He wasn't quite sure about the androgynous creature who swung out over the audience on a Watteau-like, flower-bedecked swing and, at the end of the act, peeled off a blonde wig to reveal a man's hairless scalp. Not entertaining. But he enjoyed the lines of chorus girls, performing complex manoeuvres to the split second. Some backstage drill sergeant deserved a commendation, George reckoned.

To huge enthusiasm, Josephine Baker made a second appearance just before the interval but this time she sang. Coming forward and involving the audience with a touching directness she warbled in a thin, little-girl's voice, strange but, once heard, unforgettable, of her two loves: *J'ai deux amours, Mon pays et Paris . . .*

Everyone including George was enchanted. Except, apparently, for Alice. She leaned over and whispered: '*Two* loves? Is that all she's declaring? Ha! And the other thousand!' Miss Baker bowed and laughed and made her way offstage, the curtain was lowered and the lights began to come on again in the auditorium. Alice started to fidget. Under the pretence of stretching her legs, she moved her chair stealthily back a foot or so and lifted the hood of her cape to cover her head again. Odd behaviour. George wondered whether he should remark on it and decided to give no indication he'd noticed anything strange. If she wanted to tell him, she would tell him in her own good time of whom she was so afraid. But he rather thought it was not her intention to confide in him at all. Do you whisper your terrors to the trunk of a sheltering oak tree when the lightning is flashing all around? No, you stay under its branches looking out, with just the anxious eyes Alice was trying to hide from him, until the storm was over. But perhaps there was some revealing reaction he could provoke?

'Ah, the interval already,' he exclaimed jovially. 'I say, Alice, I was rather expecting my cousin Jack would be with me tonight. I've ordered up a tray of whisky . . . not at all suitable for a lady. I'll just speed off and change that to champagne, shall I? Or is there something else you'd prefer? Now what was that pink drink you used to like?' He started to get up. 'Though — we could go and show our faces in the bar?'

Her reaction was instant. She seized him by the arm, trying to hold him in his place. 'No! You're quite wrong, George. I'll drink whisky with great pleasure. Don't go off into those crowds, you'll never find your way back and we'll lose minutes of precious time. It's been five years

— you must have such lots to tell me. Let's just stay quietly here, shall we? And talk about old times.' And then, with relief: 'Ah — here are our drinks.'

So — he hadn't imagined her nervousness, her undeclared need to stay close to him. She decidedly didn't want to be left alone up here, ogled by the crowd.

Even the waiter came in for a searching look from Alice and she fell silent, watching his every move until he left with his tip. George poured out two glasses, offering her one of them.

'Let's drink to absent friends,' he said, still probing.

She smiled. 'So many of them! But I'm thinking of one in particular. Of Joe. Joe Sandilands. My handsome Nemesis. Do you remember? Do you know what became of him?'

'Indeed. A dear friend. Joe's doing well. I follow his career with interest. We've arranged to see each other in London when I move on there. I understand he's gone on dodging bullets and breaking hearts — you know the sort of thing.'

Alice gurgled with laughter. 'I rather think he broke my bullet and dodged my heart,' she said. 'But I'm glad to hear he's being a success.'

George noticed that she sipped delicately at her whisky, controlling her features to hide her dislike. He decided to torment her. 'Not too fond of the hooch, I see? I'd have expected you to down it in one with a resounding belch — seasoned gun-slinger that you are.'

He settled back into his seat, pleased to have evoked — and, he was sure, accurately interpreted — an instinctive reaction. The slightest twitch of her right hand towards her right side told him all he wanted to know.

'Don't worry — it doesn't show,' he confided. 'The bulge, I mean. That cape covers a multitude of sins.'

In India, for many good reasons, she'd always gone about armed. He'd met her just after the war when she'd first come out from England. The unexpected inheritor of an old-fashioned family trading company of international importance, young Alice had set about reorganizing the business with dash and inspiration. Her hands on the reins had been firm and capable and she found many to applaud her performance. For her admirers — and George counted himself one of the foremost of these — Alice was beautiful, talented and enchanting. But the ruthlessness she had inevitably needed to exercise had made her enemies. Enemies who would not shrink from removing her permanently from her post at the head of the company. Her own husband, George remembered, had led this faction.

And, it seemed that for Alice Conyers, though thousands of miles separated her from the scenes of her alleged crimes, there were still people she needed to defend herself against, even here in civilized Paris. She smiled and raised an eyebrow in affected incomprehension at his remark and launched into a bright inconsequential chatter which she maintained with some skill throughout the interval. A surprisingly easy conversation. She gave every sign of enjoying the gossip he had to lay out and added a few insights and reflections of her own which took him by surprise. 'But I had no idea, Alice!' he heard himself exclaiming. 'I say — can you be certain of that? Well, I never! Deceitful old baggage! And her daughter was . . . ? You don't say!'

Any third party joining them would have heard a friendly couple talking with enthusiasm and good humour of mutual acquaintances, of experiences they had shared. They were professionals in their own separate ways, the pair of them, George reflected. They could play this game till the cows came home. And often had. But they both greeted the removal of the tray announcing the start of the second half with relief.

At least he would now be able with some confidence to hand her over to the authorities with a warning: 'Disarm her and don't listen to a word she says.' Something on those lines. He doubted that the flics would know what he was on about if he talked of Circe and her spells, the ensnaring silver sounds of the Sirens. No, better just to say the woman's got a pistol under her cloak and she's wanted on two continents.

* * *

A considerable feat of engineering, he judged, was what they were witnessing. To more preparatory blasts of jazz music, a huge egg of highly decorated Fabergé fantasy, its shell trimmed all about with golden flowers, began to descend slowly from the great height of the theatre roof and slowed to hover low over the orchestra pit. After a moment, the device burst open like a flower, the petals thrust apart by the person crouching inside. The floor of the golden oval gleamed and shimmered in the carefully placed spotlights, a mirror reflecting the figure of the occupant. Josephine Baker stood, slender, motionless, arms slightly extended towards her audience with all the naked dignity, George thought, of the wondrous Tanagra figurines he'd seen in the Alexandria museum. The same rich earthenware colour, the same grave attitude and finely modelled features. A goddess.

But then the deity grinned — a very ungodlike smile — wide and flashing with good humour. Her elbows went out to her side, akimbo, her legs, apparently disjointed, echoed the movement, and, twitching frenetically in rhythm with the band which now belted out a Charleston, she danced. Shocking, mad but compelling, her movements caused the only piece of costume she wore — a string of silvery bananas around her waist — to jiggle and bounce, catching and reflecting the light.

The dance was soon over. The petals of the flower closed over her and she was hoisted slowly back up into the shadows of the roof, to deafening applause.

More acts followed, thick and fast and with little continuity, but all were first rate of their kind. The audience remained appreciative, knowing they were to see one more appearance by the star who always, according to Alice, returned to join the dancing troupe and the other performers for a huge and lavishly dressed finale — the 'Golden Fountain'.

But this evening they were treated to an extra, unscheduled appearance by Miss Baker. In the hour or so between her acts when she might have been expected to be relaxing in her dressing room, she suddenly, between two turns, dashed on to the stage and came forward to speak into the microphone. The spotlight operator had just followed offstage a handsome young crooner and was taken aback, as was everyone, but recovered to track back and highlight the star. Her stagecraft overcame her excitement and she waited until she was illuminated to claim the full attention of the audience. She looked around the auditorium, her hands extended in the peremptory gesture artistes use to indicate that applause would not be welcome at this moment. Her head flicked from side to side, involving the occupants of both boxes, and she was ready. George listened, breathless with anticipation. He had the impression she was speaking directly to him.

'*Bonnes nouvelles!* Ladies and gentlemen,' she said in her warm American voice, 'Charles Lindbergh has arrived! The Spirit of St Louis has landed in France!'

The outburst that greeted this simple statement was extraordinary. George put his hands over his ears then took them down again to join in the clapping. Shouts, whistles and cheers rang out. Most of the male members of the audience, and some of the women, climbed on to their seats, the better to express their enthusiasm. The din went on in many languages as people translated for each other. Americans in the auditorium were singled out for especially warm congratulations.

George's trained observer's eye delighted in identifying the different nationalities' reactions amongst the audience. The unrestrained whooping of the American contingent was unmistakable, the clapping and murmuring of the English a counterpoint and, underpinning all, the squealing, fluttering expressiveness of the French. He wouldn't have expected such warmth from them, he thought, saddened as the nation was by the news that its own French entrant in the race to make the crossing had been lost at sea only a week ago. He wondered cynically whether they rightly understood that the St Louis whose spirit was now amongst them was a southern American town — and, coincidentally, the home town of Miss Baker — and not, as they might be forgiven for understanding, a reference to their own saintly king of France.

He leaned to share this thought with Alice, to find that he was once again alone in his box.

Wretched girl! His first feeling of self-recrimination for his careless lapse in attention was followed very quickly by one of intense relief. There was absolutely nothing he could do about it. He luxuriated in the feeling for a moment. She was no problem of his. He pictured her scuttling away to hide herself in a city she'd made her own. He could never find her now. Useless even to think of pursuit. He struggled with a reckless and bubbling joy, acknowledging for the first time the nature of his concern for the woman. Against all his fears, she was alive and had taken the time to show herself to him. The irrepressible thought that came to mind was: 'Good luck, Alice, wherever you're going. I hope you get away with it at the last! Whatever you're up to . . . '

He acknowledged that the glamour had faded from his evening but sat on and admired the last flourish — the ensemble gathering staged amidst miles of golden satin, tulle, sequins and bobbing ostrich feathers — and clapped heartily as the curtains swung closed for the last time. As the house lights came on, he glanced across to the opposite box to check on the rogue Somerton.

'Ah! So your girl's cut loose too!' he muttered to himself, surprised to see that his acquaintance was alone. Surprised also to find that Somerton was sitting slumped over the rim of the box, fast asleep. 'Through all that din?' George was instantly alert. The man's posture was unnatural. No man, however elderly, could have snoozed his way through that performance. Alice's warning words concerning heart attacks among the susceptible flashed into his mind. Good Lord! The poor old bugger had had a seizure! No more than he deserved but — all the same — what bad luck. And the girl must have gone off to seek assistance.

George gathered himself together, preparing to battle his way to the exit through the still over-excited crowds. He fought against his sense of duty but it won. Suppose the girl didn't speak English? That she didn't know the identity of her escort? That she had just abandoned him to be swept up with the discarded chocolate boxes?

His diplomat's antennae for international scandal were sending him signals he could not ignore. The villain was, after all, a baronet, now possibly a dead baronet, and if the gutter press were to get hold of the circumstances, he could imagine the headlines. But the other news of the evening, luckily, George argued with himself, would squeeze the plight of an English aristocrat off the front pages. Nevertheless, and cursing his compulsion always to take charge of any delicate or dangerous situation, George hesitated and then, mind made up, turned resolutely to shoulder his way against the tide flowing towards the bar and the exits and headed for Somerton's box.

He gave a perfunctory tap and walked straight in. Somerton was indeed by himself and, to all appearances, fast asleep, head comfortably cushioned on the padded upholstery. George cleared his throat noisily and followed this with a sharp exclamation: 'Somerton! Come on, wake up! Show's over!'

The absolute stillness and lack of response confirmed all George's fears. He moved over to the man and knelt by his chair placing a finger behind his right ear where he might expect the absence of a pulse to tell him all. He snatched his finger away at once. He looked at his hand in horror. Black and sticky in the discreetly dim light of the box, there was no mistaking it. With a surge of revulsion, George seized hold of the chair-back to hoist himself to his feet. He had not thought to calculate the effect of his considerable weight being applied in a desperate manoeuvre to the elegant but insubstantial modern chair. It tilted and the body of Somerton heeled over, threatening to land in his lap. The expressionless face was inches from his own, eyes staring open but focused on a presence beyond George. George's hand shot out in an instinctive attempt to support the back of the lolling head which seemed about to roll away. A wide slash across the throat had almost severed the head from the rest of the body and quantities of blood had gushed all the way down his shirt and evening dress.

Ignoring the protests of his arthritic old knees and gargling with disgust, George staggered upright, taking the weight of both the chair and the lolling body against his chest, struggling to right them.

A gasp and a squeal made him turn his head in the middle of this black, Keystone Cops moment and he saw 'his' *ouvreuse* standing huge-eyed and speechless in the doorway.

6

The hammering on the door of his room at the Ambassador Hotel had been going on for a while before Joe Sandilands swam up to consciousness. He looked at his watch. Seven o'clock. The last thing he'd done before his eyes closed was put out the 'Do Not Disturb' sign on his doorknob. He'd planned to sleep until midday at least. And now, only three hours after he'd slumped into his bed, here was some lunatic going against all the well-oiled discreet tradition of a French hotel.

Joe cleared his throat and reached for his voice. 'Bugger off! Go away!' he shouted. 'Don't you know it's Sunday morning?'

A silence was followed by another fusillade. More peremptory this time, sharper. An authoritative voice called out to him: 'Monsieur Sandilands. This is the manager here. You are requested to come down at once to the lobby. We have England on the telephone. Long distance and they are holding. Scotland Yard insists on speaking to you.'

Joe was alarmed. Always cost-cutting, the department didn't waste money on trunk calls unless they had something serious to impart. He shouted back his thanks and said he'd come straight down to the reception desk.

Minutes later he was enclosed in the guests' phone booth in the lobby taking a call from the Assistant Commissioner himself. Major-General

Sir Wyndham Childs, i/c CID. His dry soldier's voice leapt straight to the point with no preamble.

'Having a spot of bother with the French police . . . thought you might be able to help out . . . and how fortunate we are that you're right there on hand. Look — we know you're scheduled to attend the Interpol conference — starting when? — tomorrow. Just put that on hold, will you? We'll send out someone to cover for you and you can rejoin your party as soon as you can see your way through. There's been a rather nasty occurrence. Over there in Paris. One of our countrymen murdered in his box at the Théâtre des Champs-Élysées last night. Knifed to death, I am informed. The French police have made an arrest and a suspect has been detained in a cell at the Quai des Orfèvres where he's currently giving a statement.'

Joe marshalled his thoughts, regretting last night's excesses. 'That is sad news indeed, sir. But there's not a great deal I can do. The victim may be English and I'm sorry to hear it, but if, as you say, the murder was committed on French soil it must be the province of the Police Judiciaire. We couldn't possibly interfere . . . ' Joe hesitated. He wasn't thinking clearly. Sir Wyndham knew all this perfectly well.

A stifled exclamation of irritation which might have been 'Tut!' or 'Pshaw!' or even a click on the line startled him into adding hurriedly: ' . . . unless there's something I could do towards identification of the body. Do we know who the unfortunate gentleman is?'

An awkward silence was followed by: 'They

have a strong suspicion that the deceased is an English aristocrat and ex-soldier. Sir Stanley Somerton.'

Joe used the pause following this pronouncement to search his mental records. 'Sorry, sir. Unfortunately, I have no knowledge of the man.'

'No. I don't wonder.' There was no warmth in the reply. 'He did spend most of his time travelling abroad after all. And kept well out of our sphere of activities.'

'Have you been asked to send out any members of the family to confirm identity, sir? I'd gladly be on hand to receive them and guide them through the process — it's all rather different over here. The Paris morgue is not a particularly . . . well . . . you shouldn't think of sending in someone of a nervous disposition. Perhaps someone at the Embassy could — '

'Stop rattling on, Sandilands! We're sending over his wife. Lady Catherine has been informed and is packing as we speak. She'll be on the noon flight arriving at teatime — you know the score — and I want you to arrange to see her when she fetches up at police HQ. No need to go to Le Bourget to meet her — the Embassy are taking care of all that. *You* can do the hand-holding business in the morgue.'

Joe was encouraged by a lightening in the tone to reply: 'Right-o, sir. I'll parade with smelling salts and handkerchief at a time to be arrested. Um . . . have they told us whom they have arrested for this crime?'

'They have indeed.' The Assistant Commissioner was once again deadly serious. 'And this is where you come in, Joe. You will want to be involved in whatever capacity you can contrive for yourself when I tell you that the suspect they've arrested is George. George Jardine. Friend of yours, I understand? When we heard, someone said straight away, 'Get Sandilands out there.''

Joe mastered his astonishment and disbelief to reply firmly: 'Terrible news. But not the disaster you suggest, surely, sir? It must be a misunderstanding . . . a mix-up with the language . . . failure to communicate one way or another at any rate — Sir George is a diplomat. And a top one at that! He has immunity. He might have shot dead the whole front row of the chorus and he could be lounging at ease with a reviving cup of tea in the shelter of the British Embassy out of reach of the Law. Why is he in a police cell? This is outrageous!'

'Ah, you don't know . . . you hadn't heard?' A gusty sigh down the telephone and then: 'George no longer has diplomatic status, I'm afraid. He resigned his post a couple of months ago. He's retired. Hasn't quite severed his links — talks of returning — but, officially (and that's all that counts with the French), he's a free agent, no longer employed by HM Government and no longer under the umbrella of diplomatic immunity. Unlisted. A huge loss. One might have expected them to show some respect for his past position and let the matter drop. But the chap I spoke to who seems to be handling the case is one of those heel-clicking martinets you trip across sometimes over the Channel. Brittle.

Self-important. You know the type. We're not short of a few over here . . . Anyway, I see from your file, Sandilands, which I have before me, that you have experience in dealing with this style of Gallic intractability . . . interpreter during the war, weren't you? We must have a drink when you've sorted all this out — I'd like to hear your slant on old Joffre. Anyway. Mustn't keep you. Get on down there, will you? Let me see . . . their HQ is at . . . now where did I . . . ?'

'36, Quai des Orfèvres, sir,' said Joe. 'Staircase A. I've visited before. Makes our HQ look like Aladdin's palace. I'll do what I can and report back, er, this evening.'

'Very well. Oh, and, Sandilands — feel free to reverse the charges, will you? No expense to be spared on this one. Better take down my home number. Got a pen?'

Joe replaced the hand-set and stayed on in the booth for a moment or two, deep in thought. He went to the reception desk where the manager was still hovering nervously with a solicitous eye to the English gentleman now revealed to be an agent of the British police force. Joe spoke in a reassuring undertone requesting more telephone time. He needed to put a call through to this number. He handed him a card, carefully avoiding using the word 'police'. Guests were beginning to trickle through on their way to breakfast in the dining room and Joe recollected that hotel management the world over had a horror of any suggestion of police activity, even benign activity. Luckily Jean-Philippe Bonnefoye's card simply gave his name and telephone number.

Joe went back into the booth and waited through several clicks and bangs for the ringing tone that told him the manager had successfully made contact with the number. Disconcertingly, it was a young woman's voice that answered sleepily. He asked to be allowed to speak to his colleague Jean-Philippe.

'Colleague? If you're a colleague you should know better than to ring him at such an unearthly hour! He's only just gone to bed. Push off!'

He shouted something urgently down the telephone to prevent her hanging up on him and unleashed a torrent of words in which 'distress . . . emergency . . . international incident . . . ' played a part.

At the words '*entente cordiale*' she finally hooted with derision and gave in. A few moments later Bonnefoye grunted down the phone. He recovered his wits rapidly as Joe concisely and twice over conveyed the information he'd just had from the Yard.

'Martinet?' he said. 'Know who you mean. He's a bastard. But most of the blokes in the Crim' are good guys. Look — why don't you give me time to get myself organized and I'll see you down there. I'm not involved . . . yet . . . but I can at least perform a few introductions and blather on about international co-operation. Ease your path a bit. In one hour? I'll see you at the coppers' entrance. You know it? Good! I'll just go and soak my head and drink a gallon of coffee. Suggest you do the same.'

* * *

The doorman whistled up a taxicab when he emerged from the Ambassador, showered and shaved, and dressed, calculatedly, in conservative English fashion. Thanks to his sister's careful packing, his dark three-piece suit had survived the journey in perfectly wearable condition. He had put on a stiff-collared shirt and regimental tie. Sadly no bowler hat which would have impressed them; Joe did not possess such a ridiculous item of headgear. No headgear at all, since his fedora was lost somewhere at Le Bourget.

The morning traffic was thick and the taxi, weaving its way through the press of horse-drawn cabs and delivery lorries, was making slow progress. Once or twice in his anxiety for Sir George, Joe contemplated getting out and racing along on foot. The exercise would clear his muddled head, the sharp air would purify his lungs and the sight of Paris, magnificent and mysterious in the dissolving river fog, would delight his eye, but he decided it might make better sense to conserve the physical resources left to him after last night's experiences. He didn't want to ride to George's rescue sweating, foaming and breathless. Calm, confident and helpful — that was what was required. In any case, they were bound to be stunned by his timely appearance on their doorstep and his title was impressive. Deliberately so. A 'Commander' with its naval flavour got attention, largely because no one seemed to have the slightest idea what it entailed or dared to ask and some even confused it with 'Commissioner' and took him to be the face of Scotland Yard.

With so little information at his disposal Joe could not do much to prepare himself for the interview — even assuming he would be granted an interview with the chap in charge. He planned to speak in French from the outset. Occasionally it was an advantage to fake ignorance. Not many English could converse in foreign languages anyway and the French didn't expect it. Talking unguardedly amongst themselves, they would often reveal useful bits of information but Joe intended to play no such deceitful tricks on this occasion. Too much at stake. He wanted to raise no hackles. And he wanted no reluctant English-speaking officer with a sketchy knowledge of the case to be pushed forward to handle the communications. Direct access to facts and theories was what he wanted. A face-to-face talk with the martinet. But mostly what he wanted was a chance to see Sir George.

His taxi driver, impatient with his progress on the boulevards, took a chance and nipped down the rue de Richelieu, emerging on the rue de Rivoli at the Comédie Française. They skirted the busy area of the market place, unimpeded. The thick traffic from the supply barges on the Seine to the Halles Centrales had been over with some hours before. A right turn at the crossroads of Le Châtelet took them over the bridge and on to the Île de la Cité. And into the ancient heart of the city.

Joe checked his watch with the ornate clock on the side of the Conciergerie as they turned off the quai. The old prison of Paris had the power to make him shudder even on a spring morning. The arrogant grandeur of its exterior, its pepper-pot turrets flaunting a military past, hid an interior of dismal rooms and thick walls soaked in sorrow. Prison, law courts, police headquarters, medieval hospital, the most magnificent Gothic cathedral in the world — all crowded on to this small, boat-shaped island in the Seine, its prow pointing downstream to the sea. Joe constantly expected it to sink under the enormous weight of its cargo of stone architecture.

Five minutes to eight and they were on the island. He'd do it.

What time did the shows end at the Champs-Élysées? About ten? So poor old George had been banged up in the cells for ten hours. Probably had a worse night than he'd had himself. Joe was surprised that he was still in custody. Such was the man's presence, strength of character and charm, Joe would have expected the flics to have bowed him out with an apology and an offer of a lift back to his hotel in a police car. A passing unease tugged at him. At any rate, with his talent for putting everyone at ease and getting precisely what he wanted, George would probably be discovered holding court in his cell and ordering up breakfast.

His taxi passed the imposing Law Court building and dropped him outside the police headquarters. He made his way through to the small courtyard where he counted ten police cars and two *paniers à salade*, empty of prisoners, lined up on the cobbles. Joe wondered briefly as he walked by whether George had been brought here in one of these Black Marias with their metal grilles. They trawled the streets bringing in a nightly haul of vagabonds, thieves, knife-wielding Apaches and other villains. George would not have much enjoyed their company.

Bonnefoye was waiting by the policemen's entrance. The two men greeted each other ruefully. A painted sign announced: *Direction de la Police Judiciaire. Escalier A* it added over an unimpressive door. Ancient, narrow and battered, it would not have looked out of place in any Paris back street. The stone slab under the door was worn to a hollow in the centre, witness to the thousands of nailed boots that had clumped their way over the threshold during the centuries. Nostalgically, Joe placed his Lobb's black half-Oxford right in the centre. Putting down a marker for Scotland Yard. Marking out new territory.

Bonnefoye looked at him through bleary eyes. 'What a night, eh? I've seen you look sharper!'

'Do I look as bad as you do, I wonder?'

'Twenty years worse!'

Bonnefoye pushed open the door and hesitated. 'Are you ready for this?' he asked. 'It's a hundred and forty-eight steps up to the fifth floor. And no lift! But I think we may find out what we want to know by the third floor.'

The building smelled rather unpleasantly of new paint, old linoleum and stale air, with, far in the background, a waft of coffee. Apart from the swish of brooms, the flick of dusters and the mumbled conversation of the cleaning ladies, it was very quiet. Joe could hear the peremptory toot of a barge on the river and the distant ringing behind a closed office door of a telephone that went unanswered. He silently compared his surroundings to the marble-tiled magnificence of the vestibule of Scotland Yard with its mahogany reception desk manned by helpful, uniformed constables and the ceaseless movement of policemen in and out whatever the time of day or night.

'Where is everyone?' Joe asked as they began to climb the staircase.

'It's early.' Bonnefoye shrugged. 'Night shift's left and the morning crowd won't get here for another hour.'

They stopped off at the third floor and Joe followed his escort into a green-painted waiting room which seemed to have been furnished by the local junk shop. They settled on two mismatched chairs and Bonnefoye asked for a further report on Joe's telephone conversation. He listened to Joe's brief background details on Sir George and smiled.

'As you say, Sandilands — quite obviously a misunderstanding. I'm sure you'll be able to clear it up in no time. I don't expect that I'll be of much help. I'm very recently arrived here, remember. They don't know my face yet. But I'll do whatever I can. And I'll start by marking your card over the Chief Inspector. If it's who I think it is, his name is Casimir Fourier and he's an unpleasant bastard. Sour, forties, unmarried, fought in the war, very ambitious. Said to have clawed his way up from lowly origins. What else can I tell you? No known virtues. Except that he's reputed to be very efficient. He has an exceptional record for extracting confessions.'

'Confessions?'

'You know our system! You can be discovered by a dozen independent witnesses — and half of them nuns — with your hands about a victim's throat and the state will still demand a confession. The magistrates expect it. It absolves them of any guilt should any contradictory evidence arise after the event. And by 'event' I mean execution. Monsieur Guillotin's daughter still does her duty in the courtyard at La Santé prison. There's no arguing with *her*. I imagine your friend is busy providing Fourier or his deputy with a *procès-verbal* of the events.'

'But, taking down a written statement . . . I can't imagine that would last ten hours, can you?'

Bonnefoye looked uncomfortable. 'Depends on whether he's saying what Fourier wants him to say. Perhaps he's not such a co-operative type, your friend?'

'Oh, he is. Very much the diplomat. Experienced. Worldly. Knows when to compromise.' Joe grinned. 'And he always comes out on top. But he doesn't suffer fools — or villains — gladly and your Casimir Fourier may find he's bitten off more than he can chew if he confronts George. And — let's not forget — he's not guilty! Hang on to that, Bonnefoye!'

'Wait here, I'll go and tap on the Chief Inspector's door and let him know we've arrived.' He headed off down the corridor towards the inspectors' offices.

Bonnefoye returned a minute later. Not at ease. 'Fourier's got your friend in there. As I thought, they're working on his statement. And not pleased to be interrupted, I'm afraid.' He looked at his watch. 'Told me to go away and not to bring you back before ten o'clock. He'll see you then.'

Joe could not keep the annoyance out of his voice. 'Spreading his tail feathers! Showing who's boss! He doesn't endear himself!'

'Tell you what . . . pointless kicking our heels here . . . why don't we nip out and get some breakfast? The Halles are a short walk away. The blokes normally go there at the end of a night shift. There's a good little café where you can get onion soup, wonderful strong coffee, croissants, fresh bread . . . '

Joe was already heading for the door.

* * *

He reckoned it was not so much the onion soup that fortified him as the dash of brandy that the waiter stirred into it. But whatever it was, he returned with Bonnefoye, fully awake and having got his second wind. They repeated their ascent to the waiting room and stood by the open door. Distantly the bell of Notre Dame sounded ten and, taking a deep breath, Bonnefoye invited him with a gesture to accompany him to the Chief Inspector's room.

The Frenchman tapped on the door and

listened. A peremptory bark was interpreted as a signal to enter. As the door swung open, Joe was taken aback by a wave of used air, over-warm and sooty, thick with rough tobacco and rancid with perspiration. At a desk too large for the room lounged the Chief Inspector in his shirtsleeves, tie pulled loosely aside. His stare was narrow and truculent, dark eyes hooded in a sallow face. Joe was gratified to note the dark stubble on the broad jaw. Fourier looked rather less appetizing than himself or Bonnefoye and was clearly still finishing off his night's work. Not yet into the new day. He made no effort to greet them, merely watching as they came in to stand in front of him, raising his eyebrows as though to enquire what could possibly be the reason for this interruption to his day.

'A moment, please,' he said before they could speak and rang a bell.

A young sergeant entered from the room next door and looked at him enquiringly. 'Do you want me to take over, sir?'

'Not just yet. I'm still going strong. Good for a few more hours yet,' Fourier said, ignoring his guests. 'Just check the stove, would you? Oh, and get me another cup of coffee.'

The sergeant went smoothly about his duties, pouring out a cup of badly stewed coffee from an enamel pot simmering on the stove and finding a space for it on a tray alongside a green bottle of Perrier water and an empty glass by the Chief Inspector's hand. No offer of refreshment was made to the men standing in front of him. And as there was no chair in the room but the one on which Fourier sat, stand was all they could do.

All Joe's attention had been for the silent prisoner in the middle of the room but he forced himself not to react to what he saw and turned back to the Chief Inspector as Bonnefoye performed the introductions. He handed over his warrant card and waited patiently while Fourier read it with exaggerated care, turning it this way and that. 'If he holds it up to the light, I shall certainly smack him one,' Joe thought, relieving his tensions with a pleasing fantasy.

'I see. And you claim to be . . . what am I supposed to assume? . . . a Commander of Scotland Yard?' The voice was dry and roughened by years of cigarette smoke. Joe glanced at the ashtray stuffed full of yellow butts and wondered if he should advise the use of Craven A. Kind to the throat, apparently.

'Your deduction is correct,' Joe replied mildly. 'I *am* a Commander. You may not be familiar with the hierarchy in the Metropolitan Police? I direct a department of the CID — the equivalent of your Brigade Criminelle — specializing in military, diplomatic and political crime of a nature sensitive to His Majesty's Government. I report to the Chief Commissioner himself.' As well as clarity and exactness the statement also carried the underlying message that Commander Sandilands outranked Chief Inspector Fourier by a mile.

Fourier dropped the card carelessly on to his desk amongst the disordered piles of papers cluttering the surface. 'But a commander who has no crew, no ship and has entered foreign waters. Seems to me you're up the creek without a paddle, Commander.' Fourier's hacking, gurgling cough, Joe realized, was laughter and a sign that he was enjoying his own overworked image. 'You seem to have a turn of speed at least though, I'll grant you that! How in hell did you manage to get here so fast? Crime wasn't committed until late last evening.'

Joe decided to ignore the slight and respond to the human element of curiosity. 'Wings,' he said with a smile. 'Wings across the Channel. The night flight from Croydon. We landed a second or two before Lindbergh. I was coming to Paris anyway. I'm to represent Britain at the Interpol conference at the Tuileries.' Joe's smile widened. 'I'm due to give a paper on Day 3 . . . You might be interested to come along and hear . . . It's on international co-operation, illustrated by specific examples of Franco-British liaison.'

A further bark expressed disbelief and scorn. Joe held out his hand. 'My card? Would you? I'm sure I saw you drop it into this rats' nest.' He kept his hand outstretched and steady — an implied challenge — until his card was safely back in his grasp.

'And now, to business,' he said briskly. 'Perhaps you'd like to introduce me to your prisoner and outline the grievance you have with him.'

At last he felt he could turn and look at George with a measure of composure. Had he reacted at once according to his gut instinct, he would have hauled Fourier over his desk by his greasy braces and smashed a fist into his face.

George was almost unrecognizable. Old and weary, he had been put to stand in the centre of the room, back to the window, in bloodstained undervest and drooping evening trousers. Braces and belt had been taken away, his shoes gaped open where the laces had been removed. A familiar procedure. But used here, Joe guessed, not so much to prevent the prisoner from hanging himself as to humiliate him. One eye was blackened and a bruise was spreading over his unshaven jaw. He seemed uncertain as to how to greet Joe and embarrassed by his own appearance. His slumped shoulders straightened when Joe and Bonnefoye turned to him and he shifted slightly on his feet, planted, Joe noticed, in the soldier's 'at ease' position. But there was nothing easy about George's circumstances.

Joe decided to play it unemotionally and by the book. 'Sir! How very good to see you again after all this time. My sympathy and apologies for the plight in which you find yourself. I'm at your service.'

George licked his lips and finally managed, in a ghost of his remembered voice, to drawl: 'Jolly good! Well, in that case, perhaps you could rustle up a glass of water, eh? Perhaps even some breakfast? Hospitality around here not wonderful . . . I've eaten and drunk nothing since a light pre-theatre snack yesterday. Though I discern . . . ' he said, waving a hand under his nose, 'that you two boulevardiers have been at it already. Onion soup, would that be?'

Bonnefoye looked down at his feet, unable to meet Joe's eye.

If he gave way to the explosion of rage that was boiling within him, Joe realized he would be thrown off the premises at best, perhaps even arrested and lined up alongside. At all events, he might expect a damning report on his conduct to be winging its way to Scotland Yard in a mail bag aboard the next Argosy with all the predictable consequences for his future career with Interpol. A passing expression of cunning on the Chief Inspector's face, the proximity of his finger to the bell on his desk, told him that this was precisely what he was anticipating.

For George's sake, he calmed himself. His old friend, he calculated from the evidence of his senses, had been kept standing here in this ghastly room for twelve hours with no water or food while his interrogator lounged, coffee in hand, taking time off from his questioning through the night, relieved by his sergeant at intervals. Joe imagined Fourier had a camp bed somewhere about the place to which he could retire when the proceedings began to bore him.

Joe glanced with concern at George's legs. Long, strong old legs, a polo player's legs, but he was aware of an involuntary twitching in the region of the knees. There were shadows of exhaustion under his eyes. One of those eyes was almost closed now by the spreading purple bruise. The other bravely essayed a wink. With a stab of pity, Joe determined to make a clandestine but close inspection of the knuckles of both Chief Inspector and sergeant. Whichever had done the damage to George's face would pay.

Fourier gave him sufficient time to absorb the prisoner's condition and to spring an attack and, as it did not materialize, he added further fuel to Joe's anger. 'Breakfast? Not quite sure where *milord* thinks he is . . . the Crillon, perhaps? As he seems to be prepared to react to *you* perhaps you could convey my regrets. No information, no refreshment. I can keep him here for a further twelve hours, though I would not like to mar my reputation with the magistrate for speed and efficiency.'

The scornful '*milord*' had given Joe an insight into Fourier's character. He had already noted the countryman's accent. He was not experienced enough to identify it but it quite definitely was not a Parisian voice and it was not the voice of a man who prided himself on his culture as did most of the Frenchmen Joe had met. This implacable, humourless man could, in a past century, have taken his place on the Committee of Public Safety alongside Danton, Marat, Robespierre and the other bloodthirsty monsters who had spawned the Revolution. Only three generations separated him from his sans-culotte ancestor, Joe supposed. And here was the descendant, still flaunting his traditional twin hatreds: the aristocracy and the English. George was doubly his target.

Joe's fists clenched at his sides but it was Bonnefoye who cracked first.

7

Joe had been aware for some time that shame had been doing battle with disciplined deference in his friend. But the young Inspector was a Burgundian by birth and possessing the Burgundian traits almost to the point of caricature. Merry, deep-drinking, wily and — above all — proud.

Bonnefoye stalked to the desk, seized the Perrier bottle by its elegant neck and proceeded to fill the water glass with the deft movements of a waiter. 'The Crillon it clearly is not,' he said affably, 'nor yet is it the Black Hole of Calcutta.'

He presented the glass to George and watched him empty it with one draught, bubbles and all. George handed it back with an appreciative belch.

'Eternally grateful, young man.'

'George, this is my colleague Jean-Philippe Bonnefoye. Inspector Bonnefoye,' said Joe. 'Though not for much longer,' he added to himself with an eye on Fourier. Expressionless, the Chief Inspector had unscrewed the cap of his fountain pen and was making a note on a pad at his elbow.

Was recklessness a Burgundian characteristic? Or was it Gascon? Joe wondered. Whichever it might be, Bonnefoye was demonstrating it with relish. His next act of defiance was to reach over and ring the bell. The sergeant came in at once.

'We need some chairs in here. Fetch three,' said Bonnefoye.

'Yes, sir,' muttered the sergeant. He looked sideways for a countermanding order, but, receiving none, bustled out.

Another note was scratched on the pad. Fourier's mouth twisted into an unpleasant grimace which Joe was alarmed to interpret as a smile.

A moment later three stacked chairs made their appearance and Joe and Bonnefoye took delivery, lowering Sir George with creaks and groans down on to one of them. They seated themselves one on each side of him, protective angels. Joe sighed. He feared Fourier's pad was going to be overflowing with damning comments before the hour was up. He exchanged a grin with Bonnefoye. Ah well . . . in for a penny . . .

'And now, Fourier, if you wouldn't mind — your *procès verbal*. How's it coming along? The sooner his statement's in, the sooner we can get it to the clerk's office . . . *le greffe*? Is that what you'd say? And then we can all get out of your hair and you can get back to the business of arresting someone for the killing in the theatre.'

'I have him. The killer sits between you,' said Fourier in a chilling tone. 'Here's what Jardine has confided. Here — why don't you take it. Read it. Come to your own conclusions.'

Joe was alarmed to hear the certainty verging on gloating in his voice. He took the meagre account, amounting to no more than two sheets of paper, and began to read. He was quick to pass the report to Bonnefoye who ran through it and looked up, disturbed.

'Sir George,' Joe began, 'I'd like you to go through this with me, confirming, if you would, that the Chief Inspector has not misinterpreted anything you had to say. Adding anything you feel has been overlooked. Bonnefoye and I between us ought to be able to hack together something solid. Now . . . you detail your reason for attending this particular performance . . . The gift of a ticket, you say?'

'Not actually a ticket,' corrected George, opening in the voice of the meticulous witness, 'one of those annoying tokens they issue. A sort of ticket for a ticket — you cash the first one in for the real thing when you get to the theatre. It's a ridiculous system for extracting more francs from — '

'Sent to you by a cousin, you say?' Joe set him back on course.

'No, I don't say. Not for certain. I kept the note that came with the token. Fourier has it,' he said.

Fourier passed over a torn envelope and a short note.

'John? Just 'John'? Could be anyone, surely? Does this help?' Joe asked.

'No help at all. I must know about two dozen Johns and most of them likely to be passing through Paris sometime during the year. I took it to be my young cousin John who's posted to the Embassy here though I didn't at first catch on — always call him Jack, you see. These people,' George waved a gracious hand in the direction of the Chief Inspector, 'allowed me a phone call at least though they insisted on doing it for me. They got hold of him at the Embassy and I'd guess it's due to his efforts on my behalf that you're here, Commander.'

'You may also wish to see this,' smiled Fourier. He passed over a scrawled report on a sheet of Police Judiciaire writing paper. 'I sent out an officer to interview the gentleman, of course.'

Joe summarized the statement, reading aloud: ' 'Confirm Sir George Jardine my cousin . . . no knowledge of any gift of theatre tickets. Didn't even know he was in Paris.' Ah. Some mystery there, then. Well, moving on: you arrived at the theatre — '

'Where he was ambushed by a second mystery,' Fourier interrupted. 'Are you now, in this welcome rush of revelation, going to disclose the identity of the lady who joined you in your box, monsieur?'

Enjoying Joe's surprise, he added, 'The *ouvreuse* in attendance on the boxes yesterday evening is a lively young woman and very alert. She it was who discovered your friend in the act of slitting his compatriot's throat. She identified him as the gentleman from Box A across the theatre. She was able to tell us that, moments before the performance started, monsieur was joined by a woman. A Frenchwoman, she thought, from their brief conversation, and wearing an opera cape. The hood was up and she would be unable to identify her or indeed, remember her face. From the closeness of the chairs in that box, when I examined it, the two knew each other well, I'd say. Or at least were friendly. The bar reveals that both occupants drank a glass of whisky in the interval. And — I would ask you to note — the drinks order was placed before the lady arrived. She was clearly expected. By Sir George.'

'George? This is nothing but good news! If we can find this lady, she will provide your alibi, surely? Who on earth was she?'

'No idea! She just turned up moments before the performance started.' George's mystification was evident. 'A lady of the night, I assumed. Well — wouldn't *you*? Most probably a gesture from the magnanimous John. Whoever he is. Can't say I approve much of such goings-on! I say — is this sort of behaviour becoming acceptable in Paris these days? The done thing, would you say?'

His words ran into the sand of their silent speculation. Joe paused to allow him to expand on his statement but George appeared unwilling.

He pressed on. 'You were not able to furnish the Chief Inspector with a description of the lady?'

'Sadly no. She was wearing one of those fashionable cape things . . . Kept it on over her head. She came in after the lights went out . . . '

'The lights went on during the interval?' Joe objected quietly. He was beginning to understand some of Fourier's frustration.

'Jolly awkward! I mean — what *is* one to say in the circumstances? Any out and out dismissal or rejection is bound to give offence, don't you know! I chatted about this and that — put her at her ease. She didn't have much to say for herself

. . . comments on the performance . . . the new look of the theatre, that sort of thing. I gave her a glass of the whisky I'd ordered in expectation of a visit from my cousin Jack who's very partial to a single malt — '

'The lady,' said Joe. 'What do you have to report?'

'Um . . . didn't like the scotch but too polite to refuse. She'd probably have preferred a Campari-soda . . . I think you know the type . . . ' He paused. His mild blue eye skittered over Joe's and then he drawled on: 'French. Yes, I'm sure she was French. Spoke the language like a native, I'd say. Though I'm not the best judge of accents. Not perhaps a Parisian,' he added thoughtfully. 'Cape all-enveloping, as I've said, no clear idea of her features. But — average height for a woman. Five foot something . . . ' He caught Joe's narrowed look and amplified: 'Five foot five. Slim. Well-educated. Obviously from a top-flight establishment. Suggest you start looking there. I expect the Chief Inspector is well acquainted with these places? In the line of professional enquiry, of course.'

Joe hurried on. 'Moving to the finale . . . You say there was a commotion when Miss Baker announced the arrival of the Spirit of St Louis . . . '

'Commotion? It was a standing ovation! Went on for at least ten minutes. Stamping, shouting and yelling! Quite unnecessary and embarrassing display! And that's when she disappeared, I think. My unknown and unwanted companion.'

'And at the true finale — Golden Fountain,

you call it? — you observed your acquaintance Somerton to be slumped in his box opposite.'

'I feared the worst. Well, not the *worst* I could have feared, not by a long chalk, as it turned out . . . Thought he'd had a heart attack. Anno domini, don't you know . . . Stimulating show and he'd been twining about a blonde of his own . . . ' George bit his lip at his faux pas, hearing it picked up in the energetic scratching of Fourier's pen, but he ploughed on: 'A spectacular girl — I've given the description.'

'Yes, I see it. Remarkably detailed, Sir George. She obviously made quite an impression?'

'The girl thirty metres away was clearly more vivid to Jardine than the one who was practically sitting in his lap,' offered the Chief Inspector acidly.

'Opera glasses, George? . . . Yes, of course.'

'And she disappeared from her box . . . oh, no idea, really,' said Sir George vaguely. 'Sometime before the finale, that's as near as I can say.'

'And you decided to go over there in a public-spirited way to see if you could render assistance?'

'Old habits die hard, you know. Taking charge of potentially awkward situations . . . always done it . . . always will, I expect. Interfering old nuisance, some might say.'

'Sir George has run India for the last decade,' Joe confided grandly, probably annoying the hell out of Fourier, he thought, but he pressed on: 'Riots, insurgencies, massacres . . . all kinds of mayhem have been averted by his timely intervention. A disturbance in a theatre box is something that *would* elicit energetic action.'

'As would intent to murder,' replied the Chief Inspector, unimpressed.

'Tell us what happened next, will you? I see that this is as far as you got in twelve hours, despite vigorous encouragement from the Chief Inspector. No wonder he's looking a bit green around the gills.'

George described with accompanying gestures the scene of discovery. The Chief Inspector scribbled.

At last when George fell silent, Fourier put down his pen, a look of triumph rippling across his features. 'And this story meshes splendidly with the eyewitness account we are given by the helpful *ouvreuse*, but only up to a point.'

With a generous gesture, he peeled off another police witness sheet and allowed Joe and Bonnefoye to read it.

'The lady says . . . I say, shall we call her by her name since she seems to be playing rather more than a walk-on role in this performance? Mademoiselle Francine Raissac states that she came upon the two Englishmen in Box B in the course of her nightly clearing-up duties. The man she refers to as 'the ten franc tip' — the large good-looking one (Sir George) — was in close contact with the smaller weaselly one ('the five franc tip') and she took the former to be in the act of cutting the throat of the latter since the blood was flowing freely between the two and Sir George, who turned and looked up on hearing her scream, was covered in his compatriot's blood.

'The men were alone in the box, the partner of the five franc tip being no longer present. Mademoiselle Raissac declares she is unable to furnish us with a full description of the lady. She had never seen her before. She remembers she was young — less than twenty-five years old — and had fair hair. Mademoiselle Raissac further declares the girl must have been speaking French since she (Mademoiselle Raissac) was not conscious of any accent. Mmm . . . '

'A second elusive fair beauty. How they cluster around you Englishmen! I do wonder what the attraction is,' scoffed Fourier.

As George seemed to be about to tell him, Joe changed the subject with a warning scowl. 'I should very much like to see the corpse,' he said, 'and hear the opinion of your pathologist . . . '

'But certainly,' agreed the Chief Inspector. 'And perhaps you would also like to examine the murder weapon? Oh, yes, it was discovered. At the feet of the corpse on the floor of the box where Sir George dropped it. A finely crafted Afghani dagger.' He turned and looked for the first time at George. 'I understand, Jardine, that you were, at one time, a soldier in Afghanistan?'

'A long time ago,' said George. 'As was Somerton. We both served for a spell on the North-West Frontier. The blade was most probably his own. He had a fondness for knives. And a certain skill with them. It definitely wasn't mine. I have an abiding aversion for them. I favour a Luger these days for self-protection. Though I make a point of never going armed to the theatre. Too tempting to express an over-critical view of the performance. And these closely tailored evening suits — anything more substantial than a hatpin completely ruins the line, you know.'

Joe was reassured to hear a flash of the old Sir George but was becoming more anxious for his safety as the sorry tale evolved. His old friend, the man he admired and trusted above all others, was in serious trouble.

Fourier clearly didn't believe a word he said and was looking out for a quick arrest. Possibly within the twenty-four-hour limit he prided himself on achieving. If George had killed this man, Joe was quite certain Somerton had deserved it. But he determined to know the truth. His compulsion was always to go after the truth using any means at his disposal; he had no other way of functioning. And having found out the truth? And supposing it didn't appeal to him? He smiled, recalling the wise words of an old member of the Anglo-Indian establishment . . . what had been her name? . . . Kitty, that was it. Mrs Kitson-Masters.

'What could be more important than the truth?' he'd asked her one day some years ago in Panikhat, at a moment when he was being, he remembered, particularly officious, annoyingly self-righteous. And, gently, she'd replied: 'I'll tell you what: the living. They're more important than the dead and more important than the truth.' And, as long as George was among the living, Joe would lay out all his energy and skill to keep him there.

But there was bargaining to be done. Agreement to be reached. Feathers to be smoothed and arms to be twisted. Joe grinned. He was going to have to discount the pathetic and confused old person sitting next to him and call on all the skills he'd learned from the man he'd first met as Sir George Jardine, Governor of Bengal, Adviser to Viceroys and discreet Spymaster of India.

And the first of these skills had been: never to lose your temper, and the second: to deploy what Joe had always thought of as a type of mental ju-jitsu. Identify and assess your opponent's strength and, under the guise of accommodation and reason, use its energy against him to propel him arse over tip on to the nearest dung-heap.

He turned a tentative smile of relief on Fourier when he looked up from the notes which were now flowing fast from his pen.

'I'd say this is going rather well, wouldn't you, Fourier? But if you're thinking the magistrate is not going to be happy to accept so much conflicting and inconclusive evidence without the underpinning surety of a confession — well, then, I'd be the first to agree with you.'

Fourier scowled at him suspiciously.

Joe leaned forward in his chair, hands on his knees, fixing his opposite number with a keen stare. He spoke to him with quiet force. They could have been the only two people in the room. 'I'm an ambitious man, Chief Inspector,' he confided. 'You've seen my card. You are aware of how I am currently . . . placed — '

'*Poised*, I'd have said,' interrupted Fourier.

Joe smiled. 'As you say — 'poised' will do very well . . . poised for advancement. I make no secret of the fact that I have my eye on the directorship of one of the more interesting divisions at the Yard. 'Assistant Commissioner' would not be out of the question. There is much competition, many excellent candidates. Not a few are military men who know how to plan an effective campaign. I expect it's the same over here? And it's the man who can forge a reputation for himself who will win out. The one who can make himself stand out from the rest. 'Ah, yes — Sandilands. Isn't he the bloke who cleared up that killing in Paris?' I believe I have a nose for an interesting, attention-grabbing case. And we have one here!' He paused for a moment to allow his excitement to be caught on the other side of the desk.

Fourier yawned.

'A front-page, sell-every-copy story that could rival the Whitechapel murders. On both sides of the Channel. It has everything one could ask for! Pretty girls, daggers, gallons of blood spilt in the most spectacular of settings . . . And — cherry on the cake — the victim is a *rosbif* — an Englishman for whom we need feel no sympathy. Probably got no more than he deserved . . . I challenge you to invent three possible headlines for this case. Go on, man!'

Joe took out his notebook and pencil and began to scribble. Before Fourier had a chance to call a halt to his games, he rushed on. 'Got it! I've got one for the English press. Not sure that it will do much for you. You'll have to invent your own. *Death du Jour*,' said Joe. 'What do you say?'

'Not bad. I'd use something a bit longer and more dramatic — that's the style of our papers. They like to involve a famous person: *Did the Black Venus witness the Angel of Death?* They're bound to pick up the fact that the star of the show could well have been onstage at the very moment when Jardine struck the blow — only a few feet away as it happens,' Fourier speculated.

George tensed, preparing to object, but stayed silent, aware of Joe's tactics.

'They might use *Throat-slashing at the Folies . . .* ' Fourier went on with ready invention and it occurred to Joe that his mind had already been running in just such a direction. He wondered if George, his mentor, had seen it? Joe had rightly guessed the Chief Inspector's imperative, his motivation. He'd judged Fourier's craving for advancement to be at the same time his strength and his weakness and, by ascribing the same ruthless ambition to himself, Joe had made it appear acceptable in his eyes. More than acceptable — commendable. He had bracketed them together, two like-minded cynics ready to exploit a situation for their mutual benefit. Somerton, Sir George, even Bonnefoye were marionettes, their strings in the hands of two hard-eyed professionals.

Joe wasn't quite there yet but he was on his way to using the power of Fourier's forward rush to kick him into space.

'Two Englishmen fight to the death for the

favours of a mysterious *fille de joie*. Plea for the blonde beauty to come forward.' The Chief Inspector was enjoying himself. He shrugged. 'Well, these news editors — they'll say whatever they like. Of course, sometimes they respond to a confidential suggestion in their ear.'

He looked at the clock and glared at Sir George. The obstacle between him and his story. 'Pour the man another glass of water, Bonnefoye,' he said. 'It seems to loosen his tongue.'

'Fourier, may I have a word in private?' Joe asked.

He left the room with the Chief Inspector, a companionable hand on his shoulder. They returned a minute or two later and Joe went to stand almost to attention by Fourier's desk, alongside him and facing the other two men.

Fourier cleared his throat and gathered up his documents. 'Gentlemen,' he said, 'the Commander and I have come to a decision. In order to pursue the case further, I will be releasing the prisoner from police custody into police custody. Jardine is to be handed over to Sandilands with the assurance that he will not attempt to leave the city. I retain his passport and his documents. I require him to attend for a further interview as and when I deem it necessary.'

He rang the bell. 'Sergeant — the prisoner's clothes are to be kept as evidence. Can you find an old mackintosh or something to cover the mess? And you may bring his shoelaces and braces back. Gentlemen — go with the sergeant. He will walk you through the process of signing out the prisoner. Oh, and Commander — your request to examine the corpse — I grant this and will leave instructions at the morgue accordingly. Now — Bonnefoye! I'm not au fait with your schedule . . . Remind me, will you?'

'Mixed bag, sir. The suspected poisoning in Neuilly — toxicology report still awaited. The body under the Métro train — no ID as yet. And there's last night's floating *bonne bouche* dragged from the St Martin . . . And the conference, of course.' He smiled blandly back at the Chief Inspector.

'Then I recommend that you get yourself back on track at once.' Fourier added with menacing politeness: 'Your contribution to the proceedings has been noted.'

Joe thanked him and, taking advantage of the spirit of burgeoning co-operation, asked if he might fix a time to escort Lady Somerton to the morgue for purposes of identification. Fourier was beginning to see the advantages of having an Englishman on hand, Joe thought, as his response was quick and positive. His own response would have been the same. The dreadful scene of the widow wailing over the remains was always the one to be avoided, particularly when the grieving was being done in a foreign language. It added an element of awkwardness to a situation requiring sympathy and explanation. Fourier seemed to have no objection to passing on this delicate duty. They eyed each other with a gathering understanding and a mutual satisfaction.

* * *

The unanimous verdict burst from the three men as they reached the safety of the courtyard below:

'Arsehole!'

'Qu'il est con!'

'Fuckpot!'

Without further exchange or consultation, they quickly made their way out on to the breezy quayside where George came to a standstill, content to stare at the river traffic, enjoying its bustling ordinariness. He listened to the shouts, the hoots, the throbbing of the engines; he narrowed watering eyes against the brilliance of the spring sunshine dancing on the water. He waved and shouted something teasing at a small terrier standing guard on a passing barge. It barked its defiance. George wuffed back and laughed like a boy in delight. An escaper from one of the circles of hell, Joe judged. A night in clink with Fourier for company would make anyone light-headed.

With something like good humour restored, Joe began to lay out a programme for the rest of the morning. He was interrupted by Sir George. 'The hotel can wait,' he declared. 'Now we're free of this dreadful place, I want some breakfast! Some of that soup wouldn't come amiss. Where did you get it?'

Joe eyed his dishevelled state and was doubtful; George was looking even less appetizing in the bright light of morning. He could have strolled over to join the dozen or so tramps just waking under the bridge a few yards away and they'd have shuffled over to make room for a brother. But at least, the worst of the bloodstains were hidden under a dirty old wartime trench coat two sizes too small.

Bonnefoye was more confident. 'Excellent idea! Looking as you do, we won't take you to a respectable café. Au Père Tranquille — that's where we'll go. Back to the Halles, Joe. It's a workmen's café — they'll just assume Sir George is a tourist who's fallen foul of some local ruffians. Or an American artist slumming. Wait here by the gate — I'll flag down a taxi.'

⋆ ⋆ ⋆

After his second bowl of soup with a glass of cognac on the side, a whole baguette and a pot or two of coffee, George's colour was returning and his one good eye had acquired a sparkle.

'I'm curious! Are you going to tell us, Joe,' Bonnefoye asked, 'what precisely you said to the Chief Inspector that made him change his mind? Rather a volte-face, wasn't it? I could have sworn he was all set to have another go at harrying Sir George. Perhaps closing his other eye?'

'No, no! You're mistaken, young man,' said George. 'I tripped and banged my head against a corner of the desk. But — you're right — I have a feeling I was about to execute the same tricky manoeuvre on the other side. What *did* you say, Joe, to turn him through a hundred and eighty degrees?'

Joe stared into his coffee cup. 'I merely suggested that if Fourier had it in mind to apply the thumbscrews, he might like to know that Sir

George had been for years a soldier in the British forces, battling the bloodthirsty Afridi to say nothing of Waziri tribesmen in the wilderness west of Peshawar. I enquired whether he was aware that George had at one time been captured by the enemy and subjected to torture of an inventive viciousness of which only the Wazirs are capable. Rescued in the nick of time, more dead than alive after three days in their hands, but having divulged no information to his captors. Not a word. Name, rank and number and that's it. Surely Fourier, during his physical inspection of his prisoner, had remarked the scars on his back, the dislocation of the left shoulder, the badly repaired break to the ulna . . . ? I think he decided at that point that any action he was planning against such a leathery old campaigner was a bit limp in comparison.'

'Good Lord!' said Bonnefoye faintly, inspecting Sir George with fresh and wondering eyes.

'Joe! Come now!' George reprimanded. 'Ulna? Wasn't aware I had one . . . Are you quite certain that's not one of Napoleon's victories?' He turned confidingly to Bonnefoye. 'It wouldn't do to believe everything this man tells you,' he advised with a kindly smile for the young Inspector. 'He enjoys a good story! Keen reader of the *Boy's Own Paper*, don't you know!'

'Oh, I see!' Bonnefoye was embarrassed to have been caught out so easily. 'Well, for a moment, Commander, you had me fooled too! But then, I was always a sucker for tales of derring-do.' Bonnefoye looked from one to the other, suddenly wary and mistrustful of these two Englishmen who seemed to share the same lazily arrogant style, the same ability to look you in the eye and lie.

He flicked a speculative glance at Joe. Surely he was aware? Could he possibly have been taken in by that performance in the interview room?

'And now — back to your hotel, George,' said Joe. 'Where are you staying?'

'Hotel Bristol. Rue du Faubourg St Honoré. D'you know it?'

'Ah, yes. Handy for the British Embassy. Well, a bath and a change of clothes and about twelve hours' sleep are all on the menu. And when you wake up, there'll be a policeman by your bedside waiting to take down your statement. Leaving out the invention and prevarication, this time. No more lying! Nothing less than your *uncensored* revelations will do. And the policeman will be me.'

8

As they approached the hotel, George became increasingly agitated. In his hatless, beaten-up state he had been receiving some questioning looks from the smartly turned-out inhabitants. One lady had even crossed the road to avoid encountering him.

'I say, you chaps,' he said fifty yards short of the Bristol, 'better for everyone if I don't cross the foyer looking like this. I'd be an embarrassment to the management as well as to myself. There's a side alleyway they use for deliveries to the kitchens. I'll use that. I know my way about. I'll nip up in the service lift. See you in my room. That's 205.'

He would listen to no argument and slipped away without a further word.

Joe and Bonnefoye pressed on to the Bristol and requested the key. Bonnefoye produced his badge and asked the maître d'hôtel to summon a doctor and send him up with the utmost discretion.

Once over the threshold of his own room, George rallied and tried again to dismiss his attendants. 'No need to wait on me, you chaps. No need at all. I can manage. I'll see the medic if he appears, for form's sake, but — really — no need of him. Let's keep the fuss to a minimum, shall we?'

'No khitmutgars here,' said Joe cheerfully,

pushing past him into the room. 'Not even a valet. You'll have to make do with us. Jean-Philippe — run a bath, will you, while I hunt out his pyjamas and dressing gown. Is this what you're using, George? This extravagantly oriental number? Good Lord! Now, just sit down will you, old chap . . . you're teetering again . . . and you can start peeling off that disgusting vest.'

Bonnefoye returned from the bathroom lightly scented with lavender to catch sight of Sir George in his underpants, slipping a purple silk dressing gown around his shoulders. He stood still and exchanged a startled look with Joe. When George had disappeared into the bathroom he hissed: 'Sandilands! That mess on his back! Scars? Weals? What in hell was it?'

Joe was recovering from his own astonishment at the brief glimpse he had caught. 'Good Lord! It seems I wasn't exaggerating. I was just retelling an old story that does the rounds in India. I had no idea it was accurate.'

'Tough old bird,' murmured Bonnefoye. 'Fourier had no idea what he'd run into.' And then: 'He never would have signed a confession, would he?'

'No,' said Joe. 'But that doesn't mean he has nothing to confess. There's something wrong with all this. He's hardly begun to explain what he's involved in. I think he's been lying to the Chief Inspector but, if he has, there'll be a damned good reason for it. Fourier couldn't beat the truth out of him and we, my friend, must use other methods. As soon as we've got him settled

I'm going back to the morgue to take a look at the man at the bottom of all this — our mystery man, Somerton. No — no need to come with me — I'll report back. You should go back to your duties, Jean-Philippe — I've taken up too much of your time already.'

'No one will notice. I was given a couple of days to prepare for the conference. Unfortunately, I can't get out of that and I'll have to turn up and show my boss my grinning face, I'm afraid. You can telephone me at the number you have at any time — if I'm not there someone will take a message. It's pretty central . . . Left Bank . . . nothing very special but my mother's happy there. The rue Mouffetard — do you know it?'

Joe knew it. A winding medieval street of old houses, market stalls, cafés and student lodgings, one of the few to escape the modernizing hand of the Baron Haussman.

'Just south-east of the Sorbonne? Near the place de la Contrescarpe?'

'Exactly. You need the place Monge Métro exit. Let me write the address on the back of the card I gave you.'

Joe was amused. 'You don't give out your address to all and sundry?'

'Matter of security,' said Bonnefoye. 'Mine!'

'You have an apartment?' Joe asked.

'No. It's my mother's apartment. On my salary it will be some time before I can afford to rent one of my own. You have to pay fifteen thousand francs a year for a decent place in Paris. It's the foreign invasion that's put up prices.'

‘Invasion? You’d call the tourist influx an invasion, would you?’

‘Hardly tourists! Ten thousand semi-permanent residents have flooded in, mostly American, some British, all keen to take advantage of what they consider the low prices in France and all able to pay more than an ordinary copper for a decent place. Do you know how I’ve spent my time, this last month? Sorting out cases of grievous bodily harm and damage to property on the Left Bank. The *indigènes* of Montparnasse have started to show their resentment of the way the Yanks have taken over whole quartiers. They don’t like the way they buy up cafés and turn them into cock-tail bars, they don’t like the food they consume or the way they consume it . . . they don’t like their loud voices . . . they don’t like the way they look at their girls . . . You know the sort of thing. It’ll only take a spark to blow the lid off. Might try raising that with Interpol.’

The hastily summoned doctor examined Sir George and passed him as perfectly well — suffering from shock, naturally, as one would, being the victim of a street robbery — and from the obvious contusions but otherwise nothing to be concerned about . . . Nothing broken. No — a very fit specimen for a man of his age, was the reassuring verdict. All the same, the doctor grumbled, attacks like this were growing more frequent. And on the Grands Boulevards now? Tourists to blame, of course. A honey pot. Too easy and tempting a target for the local villains. It was quite disgraceful that a respectable gent like the patient couldn’t return from the theatre to his hotel along the most civilized street in the world without being beaten up. Where was the police presence in all this, the good doctor wanted to know.

A complete rest with plenty of sleep was his prescription. Of course, there was always the danger at any age of a delayed reaction to a head wound. Was there someone they could summon to sit with him . . . just in case . . . a compatriot perhaps would be most suitable in the circumstances. He left his card and took his leave.

'A nurse?' Joe, eager to dash off to the morgue was impatient at the doctor's request. 'Is that what he's suggesting? Where on earth do we dig up a nurse at a moment's notice?'

Bonnefoye grinned. 'This you can leave to me, Joe. I think I can work my way around the problem.' He took out a small black notebook and began to flip through the pages. 'You go off and interrogate the corpse. You'll find all well when you get back.'

* * *

On the ground floor a lean-faced man in his mid-thirties, unremarkable in sober city clothes, was waiting for a friend. He watched Joe step out of the lift, cross the lobby and greet the doorman. He looked at his watch, shrugged and decided to abandon his assignation. Following Joe outside, he stood patiently by, next in line. He heard Joe speak to the driver of the cab: 'Île de la Cité. Institut Médico-Légal.' The man smiled and walked back into the lobby.

* * *

Joe was admitted with courtesy into the Institut. Sombre, forbidding and dank, the building was everything Joe expected of a morgue and forensic pathology department combined. He was going to have to return in the evening escorting Somerton's widow and he wanted to be certain that he could find his way about, to be prepared to answer any questions she might have. The usual run of grieving relatives tended not, on first confrontation with the corpse, to be particularly searching with their queries. A combination of feelings of loss and the oppressive atmosphere of the viewing room was enough to reduce them to an inarticulate silence, a nod or a shake of the head or, at best, a few muttered words, most frequently: 'Did he (or she) suffer?'

Somerton certainly suffered. But not for long, Joe estimated, staring down at his corpse. The pathologist in charge of the case who had officiated at midnight the night before had returned, he now told Joe, straight after breakfast to continue his examination. Le docteur Moulin was wearing the white overall, cap and gloves of a surgeon and was as cheerful as the depressing circumstances allowed. His intelligent brown eyes were the only source of warmth in the whole building, Joe thought. He was expecting Joe and looked only briefly at his identification before leading him past three other livid corpses laid out in a row to a marble-topped, channelled table where the body of the Englishman was laid out.

'Were you gentlemen acquainted?' asked the doctor, extending a hand to Somerton.

'Not in the slightest. I'm here to investigate, not identify. He has been named by the man who discovered the body and his papers confirm his identity. The widow, Lady Somerton, is on her way and will attend this evening to sign any documents you may present. Before she turns up, I'd like to familiarize myself with the details, so that I can guide her through it, if you have enough to go on . . . '

'Oh, yes. More to do, of course, but peripheral to the police enquiry, I'd say. I shall be obtaining a toxicology report, checking stomach contents — the usual — but the cause of death I think you'd agree is pretty obvious.'

Joe stared with pursed lips at the body laid out on the slab. He was struck by the way in which the hair and moustache, retaining their luxuriance and dark colour, were at odds with the waxen flesh from which the humanity seemed to have drained away. What was the dead man telling him? What could he possibly learn from the already decaying features of a man he'd never seen alive, had never heard speaking? Joe recalled a phrase the usherette had used in her statement: '*Visage de fouine*.' Weasel-faced. Yes, he could see why she might say that. The sharp nose and chin in a narrow face offered a contrast with George's broad and handsome features. The expression and animation of the living man would also most probably have coloured the girl's impression of him and on this Joe would never be able to form an opinion. The eyes were closed, the thin, well-shaped lips set in a tight line.

The five franc tip, Joe remembered. What a frightful epitaph!

The knife slash that had killed him went from ear to ear. Cleaned and closed, it was still a fearsome sight. Joe could only imagine the shattering effect on George of discovering his friend — dead? dying? — with blood pumping by the pint from the gaping wound.

'Have you any views on how the wound was administered?' Joe asked.

'I have. Dealt from behind, I'd say. I understand the victim was watching a performance at the Folies? In a box either by himself or accompanied by a young lady? A question for the police to clear up. Obviously, if she were sitting or standing next to him the lady would be drenched in blood. When she went to the *vestiaire* to retrieve her coat, someone would have noticed her state.'

'He's quite a tall man, the victim?'

'About five feet ten inches and, though he must be in his mid-fifties, his musculature is in good condition.'

'Difficult to subdue a man of that height unless you are yourself taller and more powerful, you're thinking?'

'As are you, Commander. He's hardly likely to oblige by standing there, sticking out his chin and closing his eyes! A man like this would have fought back against a *perceived* assailant.' The pathologist pointed to the hands and forearms. 'No signs of wounds received during self-defence, you see. No attempt to repel a knifeman. It's my theory that his attacker came up behind him while he was still seated, seized him — possibly left hand over his mouth — and slashed and sawed his throat from ear to ear. Standing behind your victim, you would not be showered by his blood which would be projected out and down. You then allow the body to flop forward on to the padded edge of the booth where the obliging upholstery absorbs most of the litres of blood. Velvet, quilted over cotton wadding, I understand.'

'And if you're a careful killer,' added Joe, 'and I'm sure our man was just that, you'd have taken off your opera cloak and put it on the peg by the door, murdered your victim and then put your concealing cloak on again before leaving. If you've timed it just right, your exit will coincide with the moment everyone was streaming out of the theatre.' He knew that moment. Everyone preoccupied with his or her own immediate plans . . . taxis, supper, romance. No one wanted to catch the eye of a stranger in the crowd.

Joe went to fetch a chair, placed it at the foot of the marble slab and sat down on it. 'Doctor, would you mime the action of the killer as you judge it to have been carried out? I'll be the victim.'

'Of course. And, in the pursuit of authenticity — a moment — I'll just fetch the weapon.'

Moulin bustled away into his office, returning with a cardboard box filled with material conserved from the corpse. 'We're holding all this until the police and the magistrate are satisfied. You know the routine?' He waited for Joe's nod and went on: 'The personal effects will be returned to the next of kin. Not sure they'll want to keep this as a souvenir though,' he said, producing from a paper bag a dagger with an eight-inch blade and a carved ivory hilt.

'I'd like the lady to take a look, if she can bear it,' Joe said. 'Just in case she can identify it as her husband's own property.'

'You can take hold of it,' said Moulin, offering it by the point of the blade. 'It's been tested for fingerprints and cleaned up. No prints, by the way. It had been wiped clean — just some unusable smears left.'

Joe took the object with distaste. 'Afghan.' He turned the blade flat and slid it over the back of his hand, slicing through a few hairs. 'Sharp as a razor.'

'It would need to be to go quickly through such an amount of muscle and gristle. The throat is not an easy option. But it is quick and sure. Think of pig-killing. In my village they always go for the throat. And a pig's flesh has more or less the same density and resilience as a man's. This knife went upstairs to the laboratory for inspection. Under the microscope you can see the signs of the use of a sharpening implement on the blade. Very recent sharpening was done. Perhaps with the killing in mind?'

'Ah? A workmanlike tool. Not a cheap blade but not lavishly produced for display, I'd say. It's not as ornate as many I've seen. An inch or so shorter than most. Discreet. An efficient killing blade.'

'Indeed. Now this is what I think happened. For the record — I'm five foot eight inches tall, so we're possibly looking for someone two to four inches taller. And almost certainly more powerfully built.' The doctor took the knife in his right hand. He mimed taking off his cloak and hanging it up then he moved silently behind Joe who leaned slightly forward in the attitude of someone engrossed in the performance on the stage below.

'Ah! In the dark and with your head tilted forward like that it's not so easy to get a hand around your mouth. I'm going to change my plan slightly,' said Moulin.

He grasped Joe by the hair and pulled his head back, applying the dagger blade to his exposed throat. Joe could not repress a shudder as the cold steel gently touched the skin behind his left ear.

'Yes, that's how it would have been done!'

'What about the noise, doctor? Would he have had time to let out a scream?'

'Oh yes. Think of any pig you've ever heard being slaughtered. They manage a few seconds of hideous squealing before their voice box is cut. It must have been done at a moment of intense surrounding noise.'

'I agree. The finale?'

'Yes. Clapping and cheering and, these days, with such a large foreign element in the audience, you tend to hear whistles and squeals of a very un-French nature. And that theatre is the largest in Paris. There must have been close on two thousand people creating a din. Now, if his companion for the evening had been there *during* the murder she would have been an accomplice or — if a witness — would have been, I presume, made off with — eliminated? — by the guilty party. In some other place, at some other time, as there were no signs of further violence in the box, I understand. I would fear for the young lady's safety, wouldn't you?'

'Accomplice? Witness? Not necessarily,' said Joe. 'She might have been the killer. What would you say?'

'A woman?' The doctor was taken aback. 'Physically it's certainly possible, I suppose . . . if she approached him from behind as I've demonstrated. You'd need a considerable rush of energy — determination, hatred . . . ' His voice tailed off doubtfully.

'You don't like the theory?'

Moulin smiled. 'No more than I observe you do, Commander! We both know this is not a woman's method.'

'True. In my experience, when women plan a murder — and from whatever rank of society they come — they choose more subtle methods. Poison and the like. Anything from rat poison to laudanum. When the killing is done on the spot and the result of an overriding urge, or a desperate attempt at self-protection, they use the nearest weapon to hand — usually a domestic tool which, depending on their circumstances, may be a frying pan . . . a silver sconce . . . '

'Contents of a theatre box not much use, I'd have thought. Could you throttle someone with all that gold braid?'

'I wouldn't want to try it. No. Someone chose to take this dagger into the box and use it. And leave it behind for all to see. This particular dagger. It's distinctive. Meaningful. Personal, I'd say. The victim had fought in Afghanistan, his fellow soldier tells me. There's a possibility that it may be from his own collection. Carried there by the victim himself and turned against him in an unpremeditated attack?' Joe sighed. 'Much work to be done yet, I'm afraid.'

Rising from his chair, Joe was struck by a sudden thought. He walked over to the corpse and lowered his head to sniff the improbably dark hair. He looked up and said: 'Pomade?'

Moulin joined him and repeated the process. 'Certainly,' he agreed. He sniffed again. 'Unpleasant. Not French. Much too heavy. I'd say something like Bay Rum, wouldn't you? And it's sticky.' He took off a glove and tested a strand of hair between thumb and forefinger.

Joe did the same. He peered at the crown of the man's head. 'Well-barbered hair though a little long for most tastes, I'd have thought. Plentiful and would give a very good grip to anyone choosing to sink his fingers into it. As you demonstrated. Left parting and — look — it's disordered on top. Could have happened involuntarily at any moment after the death of course, during the manhandling of the body by the authorities. But if your theory's right, doctor, the killer must have had a disgustingly sticky left hand — and not sticky with blood. It's not much but . . . '

He accepted Moulin's offer of soap and water and towel in a side room and they washed their hands in a companionable silence together, each deep in thought. 'I thank you for working through all this with me, doctor,' Joe said, walking back to pick up his briefcase. He hesitated and then made up his mind to ask: 'Shall I hope to see you later on today when I bring the widow Somerton? Or will you have handed over to a colleague by then?'

Moulin smiled. 'I shall arrange to be here, Commander. More dead than alive myself by that hour but . . . ' He shrugged. 'You'll find me here. I'm very bad about delegating. Particularly when a case has caught my attention as this one has.'

* * *

Emerging from the depths of the stone Palais de Justice building, Joe experienced again a rush of relief and pleasure. He took a minute or two to raise his face to the sun, to breathe in the not-unpleasant river smell, to be thankful that he wasn't laid out on a slab or filed away in one of the steel drawers that lined the walls. He'd taken a liking to Moulin — an admirable man, professional but not stuffy. A brother. But he did wonder how he managed to stay sane working in that chill, haunted place. Above all he asked himself how bearable would be the claustrophobic effect of those thick walls on a recently widowed Home Counties lady. He looked at his watch and calculated that she was in mid-air over the Channel, delicately refusing the oysters most probably.

Lunch! Suddenly hungry, Joe decided to make for a café and find something he could eat within half an hour. The place St Michel was just over the river. Food over there on the Left Bank was cheap and quickly prepared. The were mostly students and Joe enjoyed the informality, the laughter and the sharp comments he heard all around him. He settled at a pavement table on the square and decided to order a croque-monsieur. Always delicious and quick to produce. He wondered what to drink with it and thought his usual beer might finally send him to sleep. A bottle of Badoit or a plain soda water might be more —

Soda! Campari-soda! The shock of realization was so intense he looked furtively around him to see if anyone was conscious of his reaction to the sudden thought. Ridiculous! These chattering strangers, even if they'd been looking in his direction, wouldn't have given a damn for an Englishman whose startled expression was that of a man who'd just remembered — too late — his wife's birthday.

'Campari-soda'! George had been trying to pass on a message and he'd missed it. Pink and decadent, light but lethal. And always, for him, to be associated with that woman.

George had been attempting to let him know he'd spent the evening trapped in a box with a viper.

Joe, all appetite vanished, chewed his way through his sandwich and planned his next move. Looking around him, he remembered that he was just a few steps away from the rue Jacob and he frowned.

Good Lord! It seemed a week ago he'd met that redhead on the plane. What was her name? Heather, that was it. And she was staying at a small hotel down there. Raking his memory, he had a clear impression he'd promised to meet her again, though he'd left it all a little vague. He doubted she was the kind of girl to sit in her room waiting for him to contact her but, all the same, it would be too rude to do nothing. He could at least explain that he'd run head-first into the most frightful bit of trouble and wouldn't be at liberty to enjoy Paris with her as he'd hoped. Paying his bill, Joe strode off down the rue St André des Arts and crossed over into the rue Jacob. He wandered along until he found a pretty, flower-bedecked hotel whose name rang a bell.

The receptionist at the Hotel Lutèce admitted he had a guest of that name but Mademoiselle Watkins had gone out over an hour ago and — no — she had not said at what time she expected to return. With some relief, Joe scribbled a note and left it in her pigeon-hole.

And now, he was free to concentrate on a second lady who'd caught his attention. He took out his notebook and checked the address he'd hurriedly memorized from the Chief Inspector's interview sheets and copied down later. An address in Montmartre. He looked up and north, seeking but not finding, for the press of rooftops, the gleaming white dome of the Sacré Coeur, presiding over the huddle of cottages, mills and cabarets that made up the old village on the hilltop. Too far to walk in the time he had. Joe went back to the place St Michel and picked up a taxi.

'*Montmartre. La rue St Rustique*,' he said. '*Le numéro 78*.'

'Another liar!' he thought and began to plan how best he could lay a trap for her.

9

Joe decided to tell the driver to drop him in the place du Tertre in the heart of Montmartre. The cab moved off easily northwards, threading its way according to Joe's directions, along the Right Bank, taking a westerly route through Paris's most spectacular streets and on up the rue d'Amsterdam. They turned on to the boulevard de Clichy which wound like a necklace along the wrinkled throat of the ancient village on the hill.

As they crossed the place de Clichy, he glanced at the billboards of the Gaumont Palace cinema with its imposing Beaux Arts façade. *Le plus grand cinéma du monde*, it announced. Today they were offering a matinée programme, a repeat showing of a pre-war thriller: *Fantômas III. Le mort qui tue*.

Fantômas, Part Three. The Murderous Corpse. One of a series of horror stories that had swept France. Joe was not a fan. He'd stopped reading them after the second book when he'd worked out that the Emperor of Evil whose sadistic exploits were recounted always escaped the law. At the end of every story one implausible bound set him free from the clutches of the tenacious policeman who'd vowed to bring him to justice. Joe lost patience with the good Inspector Juve. But he was a human like Joe, overworked, mortal and fallible and fighting a hydra-headed, super-human essence of wickedness. A completely implausible villain, for Joe. He much preferred Professor Moriarty. Though *he* had shown a tendency to survive unsurvivable plunges into waterfalls.

They attacked the hill by way of the rue Lepic, lined with market stalls. Progress up the cobbled streets was slow. They were impeded every few yards by two-man push-and-pull handcarts whose pushers and pullers stared in disdain at any motor vehicle attempting the steep incline, taking their time, demonstrating defiance. The worst blockage was caused by a two-wheeled cart being pulled along by an ambling old horse. His sole interest was in the contents of the nosebag he wore and he eventually ground to a halt outside a grocer's shop. La Bordelaise looked prosperous, its windows bright with bottles of wine and oil, baskets of olives and dangling saucissons. Sticking his head out to assess the delay, Joe was caught by the scent of roasting coffee beans. On impulse he called to the driver to wait and dashed into the shop. A moment later he climbed back into the taxi with a fragrant bag of beans in his hand.

He paid off his taxi in the place du Tertre and looked about him, getting his bearings. He strolled off along the north side of the square, getting a feeling for his surroundings. More strident than it had been in its heyday half a century ago when Pissaro, Cézanne and Renoir had sat at their easels on exactly this spot, painting the crossroads scene. More self-consciously colourful, tricked out, alluring, completely aware that it had something valuable to sell. Itself. Montmartre was a tart. But people fell for her charms every time. And he was gladly allowing himself to be seduced.

The gaudy square was surrounded by poor streets. He turned left into one of them. Here, the children playing in the street were ragamuffins like the ones in the East End of London. Barefoot some of them, all scrawny but cheeky enough to shout rude comments at a stranger. He brushed aside offers to shine his shoes, take him to a jazz bar and other more dubious propositions. He skirted around ball games and dodged urchins swinging out across the pavements on ropes suspended from gas lamps — a dangerous game of bar skittles in which the passer-by risked losing his hat or, at the least, his dignity. Joe, in a moment of playfulness, could have wished he was wearing a top hat for them to aim for and quickly took himself in hand. Such a spurt of frivolity was not appropriate. He blamed it on the freshness of the air up here on the hilltop, the blossom, the new leaves, the wad of bills in his pocket and a feeling that all was possible. He gave the lads his police stare, put on a show of knowing exactly where he was going and they left him alone.

Every narrow street he looked down called to mind a scene already captured in paint or waiting to be captured. He turned a corner into the rue St-Vincent and found himself following a few paces behind a figure from the last century. In baggy black suit and wide-brimmed gypsy hat, guitar slung across his back, a *chansonnier* strolled on his way to perform perhaps at the Lapin Agile. Conscious that he was wasting time, Joe tracked him until he disappeared into the dilapidated little cottage, his entrance marked by raucous cries of welcome and a burst of song. For a moment Joe paused, tempted to go into the smoky depths. He remembered that in an earlier age it had been known as the Cabaret des Assassins.

Who would he see in there if he slid inside and took a table? He narrowed his eyes and pictured the scene. Letting his fancy off the leash, he saw: Picasso . . . Apollinaire . . . Utrillo . . . Jean Cocteau . . . and he grinned. He probably wouldn't understand a word of the conversation! Avant-garde, fast-living, arty . . . But he knew who would understand and almost turned to share his thoughts with young Dorcas. He felt a stab of regret that his adopted niece who'd trailed through France with him last summer was not by his side. She'd have felt at home here. She'd have greeted the gypsy guitarist and talked to him in his own language. Her raffish father, Orlando, must have spent hours drinking and yarning with his fellow painters in this picturesque hovel, judging by the quantities of canvases it had inspired. And his daughter was probably on first-name terms with half the clientele!

He looked at his watch. Better left for another day. Yes, he'd come back some other time. With Dorcas. Why not? He reminded himself to find a suitable postcard to send to her in Surrey. But a different girl was higher on his agenda today.

He had work to do. A self-imposed task but tricky and not one to be attempted light-heartedly. Not heavy-handedly either though. He looked around and caught sight of a flower seller's stall on a corner of the square. Five minutes later, armed with half a dozen of the best red roses the seller could provide, done up in a silver ribbon, he locked on to his target.

Everyone who could be outside on that May afternoon was out on the pavement. The concierges of the lodging houses had settled in chattering groups, shelling peas, their chairs obstructing the pavements. From open doors behind them drifted the fragrant smell of dishes cooking slowly in some back room. Mothers fed babies or crooned them to sleep.

Around a corner to the north of the square he came upon the faded blue sign he was looking for: rue St Rustique. The oldest street in the village and quite probably the narrowest. The three- and four-storey houses had known better days. Shabby grey façades retained interesting architectural features: elegantly moulded architraves graced doorways, Second Empire wrought-iron grilles added dignity to windows whose shutters stood wide open on to the street. Bourgeois net curtains gave seclusion and an air of mystery to the interiors.

Joe located number 78. The patch of pavement in front of the house and the cobbled road as far as the central gutter were freshly cleaned. A broom was propped against the wall to the right of the open door, two large pots of daisies stood to attention and an eye-watering waft of *eau de javel* leapt from the interior and repelled him. Joe read the sign painted in art nouveau letters above the door's architrave: *Concierge*.

He froze. There she was, filling the doorway, barring his entrance. Redoubtable. Cerberus? The Cyclops? He reckoned he had about as much chance of getting past her and into the building as he would have had facing up to one of those monstrous guardians. She stood, four-square, bulldog face peering at him over gold half-moon spectacles. She was holding a pile of letters to the light and shuffling through them. Sorting out the residents' afternoon post, he guessed, and she was not counting on being disturbed. She was dressed like a badly done-up parcel; her clothes were all in shades of brown, shapeless and hanging in layers to her mid-calf. Here the tale of sartorial disaster was taken up by a pair of drooping socks and bulging slippers.

Joe did not often find himself at a loss for words and was angry with himself for hesitating to address her. He regretted now the bunch of roses in his hand. What a twerp he must look.

'Yes? Who are you?' Her voice would not have disgraced a sergeant major.

The challenge provoked a military response. He stood at ease in front of her with what he hoped was an air of languid confidence and managed a tight smile. 'An English gentleman to see Mademoiselle Raissac. I understand she lives here.' He began to reach into his pocket for his warrant card.

She stopped him with a gesture. 'She's not seeing callers today. She's not well. Come back tomorrow.' The concierge turned and, as an afterthought, seized her broom as though she thought he might run off with it. She made to go back inside.

'Police! Wait!'

That claimed her attention. She came towards him. 'Shh! Keep your voice down! This is a respectable street,' she hissed at him. 'Police? *Again?* She's given a statement. Can't you leave her alone?'

'I will see her here, discreetly, in her own room, for half an hour or I will haul her off to the Quai des Orfèvres for a rather lengthier interview. I'm quite certain neither you nor the young lady would relish the appearance of a *panier à salade* outside your front door, madame.' Joe was not at all certain that one of these sinister motorized cells would be deployed at his request for the conveyance of one suspect but the old dragon appeared impressed by the threat.

'You'd better come in then . . . sir. And you can show me your proof of identity.' Her voice would never be capable of expressing deference but at least it was now verging on the polite. 'You can wait in my parlour while I go up and see if she's prepared to see you. Through here.'

She took him to her two-roomed *loge* on the ground floor off the hallway and offered him a hard-backed chair. The small room which served as both kitchen and living room was sparsely furnished but neat and well polished. A few ornaments twinkled on the mantelpiece above an open fire on which a blackened pot had been left to simmer. Monsieur's supper no doubt.

She wiped her hands on her pinny and reached for the warrant card he held out to her. Every aspect of it came under her searching eye and finally: 'Well, it's good that the flics are taking a serious interest in this tragedy. Bit unusual, isn't it? Not something we're used to round here — courtesy visits from the Law with roses in its hand. Have a glass of water while you're waiting, young man. You look overheated,' she said, surprising him, and poured a glass from the tap. 'Don't pull that face! No need to be fussy! Paris water is good water.'

Joe drank gratefully, puzzled but relieved by her change of attitude. On a whim, he reached into his pocket and took out the bag of coffee beans. 'For you, madame. I hope you can drink coffee?'

The tight lips twitched slightly and she took the bag from him, squinting at the label. 'From La Bordelaise! I can certainly drink that! Thank you very much.' She set it down on a dresser beside the polished copper funnel of a coffee-grinder and went to summon her lodger. In the doorway, she turned and spoke to him over her shoulder in her clipped, machine-gun phrases. 'Francine is a good girl. Never been in trouble with the law. She works every hour God sends. As good as a daughter to me. And she's still reeling from the shock. You're to treat her with respect.'

Joe's saluting arm twitched in automatic response to the tone.

As her slippered feet thudded up the staircase,

he eyed the coffee. A sop to Cerberus? It still seemed to work.

* * *

A sleepy face peered round the door at him, focused blearily on his card and, after a delay calculatedly long enough to register her protest, she opened the door with a grudging: 'You'd better come in, I suppose.'

Her room was untidy and, Joe thought at first glimpse, perfectly charming though he would not have relished the task of carrying out a detailed search of the premises. The afternoon sun streamed in through the window illuminating, on the opposite wall, an open armoire densely packed with dresses of all colours and fabrics. They spilled out to hang in bunches on hangers along the picture rail. A treadle sewing machine with a piece of work still clamped across the needle plate stood under the window to catch the light. Against one wall of the single-roomed apartment was a bed, made up and covered with a gold brocade eiderdown. A low table held a row of unwashed coffee cups and one or two baker's shop wrappers covered in crumbs and patched with grease.

Once he was inside, she rounded on him. '*Two* interviews in as many hours? What's going on? I'm a witness not a suspect! Couldn't you leave me alone to get over it? And why are they sending me the handsome inspectors? Is this a new tactic? Are there any more of you lurking round the corner? I'm not in the chorus line, you know! Though you seem to think so — are those for me?' She seized the roses and went to put them in a jam jar that she filled with water from the wash basin in a corner of the room. 'Doesn't it cross your mind that you might be ruining my good name? Arriving here with flowers? Wish I'd got dressed . . . '

Francine Raissac was wearing a creased white silk dressing gown embroidered — and rather richly embroidered — with black and red dragons. Her eyes were puffy and last night's mascara smudgily outlined her dark eyes, giving her the comical air of a cross panda. Joe said as much and she looked at him first in astonishment, then with a flash of amusement. He rushed on while he had this slight advantage. '*Handsome* inspectors, did you say? I thought I was the only stunner they could field . . . ?'

'The previous one was better,' she said, looking closely at him, giving the question her serious attention. Her response told him the light approach was probably the effective one. 'You're very nearly handsome. But you're older and you don't have a Ronald Coleman moustache.'

'Ah! I think I recognize my colleague, Inspector Bonnefoye?' said Joe, trying to keep a tetchy note out of his voice.

'Jean-Philippe.' She managed a tease and a confirmation in one word. 'You mean you didn't know he was coming here?' she asked. 'Doesn't the right hand know what the left's getting up to at the Sûreté? Or aren't you speaking the same language?'

'We have different roles,' Joe said, recovering

from his surprise. 'My questions will not be the same as his. He has other fish to fry.'

'Ah, yes, of course. I understand that.'

'I am, as you've noticed, English. I'm representing the interests of the gentleman who was taken in as a suspect.'

'Not the interests of the *murdered* Englishman, then?' she asked sharply.

'His interests also,' Joe hurried to add. 'Indeed, I am shortly to meet his widow and conduct her to an identification of the body. An inconvenience to the French authorities and an embarrassment to us that what may prove to be a quarrel between two of my countrymen should be played out on French soil. I am doing what I can to assist the Police Judiciaire and working under the auspices of the British Embassy, of course. Interpol also, of which — '

'All right . . . all right! You're a big shot! Got it! Will Your Eminence deign to take a seat?' She heaved an armful of fabrics off a sofa and Joe lowered himself on to it. 'Oh . . . carry on then! I'm listening. I suppose I should be grateful they've not sent old sourpuss . . . the Chief Inspector . . . um . . . '

'Fourier?'

'That's the one!' She rolled her eyes. 'He interviewed me at the theatre. Looks and talks as though he's sucking an acid drop.'

'You take, I detect,' he said with a grin, pulling a straight pin from under him, 'more than an amateur interest in couture?'

'I'm sure you're not here to count my dresses and check their provenance.' She sounded slightly on her guard. 'I'll tell you straight, Mr Detective, that every last frock you can see has been acquired legally. Working in a theatre, they're easy to pick up, if you know the right people. Did you know there's a whole workshop underneath in the basement, sewing away day and night? I go down there sometimes and chat to the girls. They're always pleased enough to hear news from the world above! The show clothes aren't much use to me, of course — all ostrich feathers, tulle and lamé — but the girls pass on the occasional remnant that I can use.

'The stars are my best source. Now — Josephine! She's incredibly generous and if you know just when to show your face — as I do — she'll shower you with stuff she doesn't want or gowns she's only worn once. We're much the same size and sometimes she asks me to model a gown for her to help her make up her mind.'

So that accounted for the head-hugging hairdo with the over-sized curl slicked on to her forehead. Francine had a dark complexion for a Frenchwoman, Josephine had a light skin for a black American. The two girls met somewhere in the middle. But the conscious attempt to mirror the looks of the star was more than just flattery. Josephine must have found it useful to see herself from a distance in this bright young woman. And the thought came to him: 'Probably enjoys her company, too.'

'You get on well with the star?'

'Yes, I like her. We French *do* like and admire her. It's the Americans — her own countrymen — and the English who give her a rough time.

Her dancing is too scandalous for some and she's black. There are those — and some are influential people — who'd like to see her closed down and put on the next liner home. Not the French. We don't care at all about her colour. And her morals . . . ' Francine shrugged. 'Well, that's up to her, isn't it? She's entertaining and stylish and we love her for it.'

'I expect she suffers professional jealousy — one so successful at such a young age? What's the name of the Queen of Paris Music Hall? She must be feeling a bit miffed!'

'Mistinguett? Yes, she's a rival but she's big-hearted, you know. Reaching the end of her career . . . she must be in her fifties, though she still has the best legs in Paris. She can afford to rise above it. But there are two younger stars, French, both, at the Casino de Paris and the Moulin Rouge, who hate Josephine's guts. She's rather stolen their thunder. Either one might have hoped to inherit Mistinguett's ostrich feather crown as *meneuse de revue*. And one of them has a very wealthy protector. A banker. You'd know his name. He sends his Rolls Royce to the stage door for his little mouse every night.'

'Does Josephine mind? All this antipathy?'

'Too busy enjoying herself. I'd say she doesn't give a damn! In fact,' she added dubiously, a sly, slanting question in her eyes, 'those close to her think she doesn't care *enough*. For public opinion or her own safety.'

Joe seized on the word: 'Safety?' he murmured.

'Everyone thought when she had her accident last year — '

‘Accident?’

‘Not actually. It could have been nasty . . . In one of her acts, she’s lowered in a flowery globe down over the orchestra pit. A breathtaking bit of theatre! Luckily she’d decided to rehearse in the damn contraption before the actual performance.’ Francine shuddered. ‘She was on her way down from the roof in this thing when one of the cables jammed. That’s what they said. A mechanic was sacked afterwards and everyone heaved a sigh of relief. The globe suddenly tilted over and swung wide open. She *ought* to have been thrown out into the pit. But she’s a strong girl with fast reactions. She jumped for one of the metal struts and hung on like a trapeze artist until someone could get up into the roof and haul her up again.’

‘Good Lord! What would have happened if she’d fallen?’

‘She’d have been dead. Or so badly injured she’d never have walked again.’

‘Dangerous place, the theatre.’

And a breeding ground for all kinds of overheated nonsense, he reckoned. Scandal, exaggeration, petty jealousies. He was allowing his own tolerance of gossip to put him off track and guided Francine Raissac back on to the subject he wanted to pursue. ‘These clothes the generous Miss Baker gives you — where do they come from?’

‘Gifts. They arrive at the theatre in boxes for her to try. If she doesn’t like something, she’ll tell me to take it away. I found her knee deep in Paul Poiret samples the other day. Wonderful things! She'd just had an almighty quarrel with him and was throwing the whole lot away. Before she'd even tried them on!' The girl was filling the space between them with irrelevant chatter, taking her time to get his measure, he guessed. And, unconsciously, going in exactly the direction he'd planned to lead her.

'Does she have a preferred designer?'

'Hard to say. I doubt if she can tell one style from another. She hates turning up for fittings so they take a chance on what she'll like and send her lots of their designs, hoping she'll be seen about town wearing them . . . *I* think Madame Vionnet suits her best and Schiaparelli . . . her bias cut is very flattering . . . Lanvin . . . of course . . .'

'And your outlet for these dazzling couture items?' he asked. 'I'm assuming you don't acquire them simply to decorate your room.'

'I send them on to my mother. She has a little business in Lyon. We started it together when my father died. *Location de costumes* — but not your usual rag and bone enterprise. We're building up a well-heeled client list — plenty of money about down there. Industry's booming and it's a very long way from Paris. Everyone wants a Paris model for her soirée!' She indicated her sewing machine. 'I can undertake adjustments here at source if I have a client's measurements. Then the lady's box is delivered and she tells her friends it's straight from Paris — just a little confection she's had specially run up for the Mayor's Ball or whatever the event . . . And the label — should her friend happen to catch a glimpse of it — has a good deal to say about the success of her husband's enterprise. And *her* taste, of course. We rent out things by the day, the week. A surprising number we sell.'

'I'm talking to someone with a keen eye for fashion then? Someone acquainted with the work of the top designers of Paris?' he said, raising an admiring eyebrow.

'I'm sure you didn't come here to talk fashion,' she said doubtfully, 'but — yes — you could say that. I could have been a mannequin if I'd been three inches taller. If I'd been five inches taller I could have been a dancer. But I'm not really interested in 'could have been'. I'm a going-to-be,' she said with emphasis. 'Successful. Rich. I haven't found my niche quite yet. But I will.' And, angrily: 'It won't, of course, be in the professions or politics or any of the areas men reserve for themselves. We can't vote . . . we can't even buy contraceptives,' she added, deliberately to embarrass him.

'But some girls have the knack of attracting money and don't hesitate to flaunt it . . . Does it annoy you — in the course of your work — to be seen in rusty black uniform dresses when the clientele are peacocking about in haute couture?'

'No. Why would it? The black makes me faceless, invisible. The work is badly paid — no more than a starvation wage — but the tips are good. Men are so used to being greeted by old harridans with scarlet claws whining for their *petit bénéfice*, they are rather more generous to me than they ought to be. Sometimes, I flirt with the older ones,' she said with a challenge in her look. 'And, before you ask — no, I don't take it any further. But they toy with the illusion that it might develop into an extra item on the programme and tip accordingly. No man wants to be perceived as a tight-wad.'

'A five franc tip?' he reminded her.

The eyes rolled again. 'I pitied that girl!'

'Ah yes. Now tell me . . . the dress she was wearing . . . '

She put her hand over her mouth and stared at him over it. 'Ah! So you really *did* come here to talk fashion! Well, I talked myself into that, didn't I?'

'You did rather,' he agreed. 'So, come on! Expert that you are — I think we've established that much — tell me all. You divulged almost nothing to the Chief Inspector. What was it now . . . ? Under twenty-five and fair? Oh, yes? Bit sketchy, I thought. Huh! Your poor old ten franc tip with his rheumy old eyes gave a fuller description of the disappearing blonde from thirty yards away! A seam by seam account of her gown! And he wouldn't know his Poiret from his Poincaré . . . I want to know everything about her appearance and — perhaps more importantly — why you chose to pull the wool over Inspector Acid Drop's eyes.'

She went to sit at the bottom of her bed, demurely adjusting the belt of her Chinese gown, tucking up her bare feet under her. Joe swallowed. 'Man Ray, where are you? You should be here with your camera, fixing this moment,' he was thinking, seized and dazzled by the theatricality of the scene. This girl with her high cheekbones, sleek black hair, snub nose and huge, intelligent eyes made Kiki of Montparnasse look ordinary. He reined in his thoughts. She was also deliberately distracting him, making time to weigh his question, possibly to plan a deceitful answer. After a further diverting shrug of the shoulder, she began her account.

'Well, for a start, it was expensive — eight hundred francs at least, probably more. That shot silk fabric — there's not a great deal of it about yet and the designer who's been using it this season is Lanvin. Her shoes were Chanel T-straps. Blue satin. Her opera cloak was silk. Midnight blue. She shopped about a bit, this girl, but it was all well put together. She was carrying it under her arm — the cloak. When she came up the stairs. Her escort hung it up at the back of the booth. They often do that. Sometimes it's to avoid tipping at the *vestiaire* but with the box clientele it's usually to avoid the queue to pick it up at the end.' She gave a twisted smile. 'The gentlemen don't like to be kept waiting at this stage of their evening. Now I did manage to catch a glimpse of the label on her cape. It was a Cresson. Rue de la Paix.'

'Are you able to give me a description of this garment — an idea of the fabric?' he asked unemphatically, pencil poised.

She thought for a moment, and deciding apparently that the information was routine and could not harm her in any way, chose to co-operate. He noted the details. In a show of helpfulness which told him he was almost certainly heading down a cul-de-sac, she even got up and walked to a basket overflowing with fabric remnants. Stirring them about, she finally produced, with an exclamation of triumph, a piece of heavy silk. Dark blue silk.

'Not this exact fabric but — very nearly. Her cloak was made of some stuff like this.'

He thanked her and put it away in his pocket.

'And — Cresson . . . Lanvin . . . Chanel . . . you say. These are all impressive names you mention, I think?'

'The very best.'

'With a distinguished client list?'

'Of course.'

'And if I were to traipse along the rue de la Paix to the boutiques of those you've mentioned and apply a little pressure or charm or cunning I might find the same name coming up?'

'If you choose to waste your time like that . . . I wouldn't bother. Some of these houses are hysterical about piracy. And they're always wary of having their clients snatched by a rival. The *vendeuses* are well trained and they have a nose for wealth.' She looked at him critically then smiled. 'You're an impressive man but you don't look like the kind who'd spend a fortune indulging his girl!'

Joe regretted his meagre half-dozen roses.

'Far too clever. I think you'd have considerable trouble extracting the information.'

'So — you're going to point out a short-cut?'

'Why should I? The girl had nothing to do with the murder. And this answers your second question. It wasn't *her* I found covered in blood. She was working for a living. If she'd been willing to give evidence she'd have hung about, wouldn't she? But she had the sense to leg it. I'm not going to make her life difficult for her by involving her with the flics. They're shits! And they have a hard way with *filles de joie*. There but for the grace of God and all that . . . If things don't go so well for me — well, that might be the next step. Who knows? Cosying up to old farts like the five franc tip isn't my idea of a career but I'm not stupid. I see lots of girls making a lot of money that way. I've had my propositions! And I see it sometimes as an easy option. A good deal of unpleasantness for a short time but the rewards are good.'

'Francine, don't think of it!' Too late to snatch back the instinctive exclamation.

While he looked at his feet in confusion and she smiled in — was it triumph or understanding? — the attention of both was caught by plodding footsteps on the stairs. The concierge's peremptory voice called out: '*La porte!*' and Francine went to open it. Joe got to his feet, fearing that his interview was about to be cut short, ready to repel the intrusion, but instead he hurried forward to take the tray she was carrying from the old woman's hands. He carefully balanced the weight of the silver coffee pot, two china mugs, a jug of milk and a plate of Breton biscuits, adding his own thanks to those of Francine: 'Oh, Tante Geneviève, you shouldn't have!'

The dragon looked around and, apparently happy with what she saw or didn't see, cleared the top of the table to make way for the tray, gathering up the dirty cups and wrappers, grunted, and went out.

'I don't have much experience of concierges,' said Joe, 'but I'd have thought room service of this kind is a bit out of the ordinary? Did I hear you claim that lady as a relative?'

'I call her 'Aunty' and I've known her forever, but she's my godmother. Her husband was wounded in the war. Has never worked since. They scrape a living. My mother would only agree to my continuing to live alone in the wicked city if I was under someone's wing.' She smiled and added thoughtfully: 'And she was quite right. It's not always convenient to have a mother hen clucking after you, but the advantages are considerable. My rent is fair, not extortionate as it can be for most young girls trying to live by themselves. No spirit stoves allowed in the rooms, of course.' She looked around at the quantities of fabrics festooning the room. 'And this would be a fire hazard if I attempted to use one. So — occasionally, she brings me coffee. Inspector Bonnefoye rated one too.' Francine sniffed the coffee as she poured it out. 'But not as good as this! Mmm! Moka? And no chicory!' She looked at him with fresh speculation. 'The old thing's brought out her best for the English policeman. Now what on earth did you do to provoke this attention?'

They sipped the coffee appreciatively for a moment or two and then Joe said mildly: 'So — your attempt to pervert the course of justice by withholding vital information (six months in La Santé if Acid Drop were to find out) was occasioned by a feeling of solidarity for a fellow working girl? No more than that? Am I expected to believe this?' He left a space in which she was meant to reflect on her predicament and assess his power to carry out his threats, veiled, as they were, by a charming smile and delivered in a pleasantly husky voice. 'But loyalty is something I can understand. It is my motivation also in pursuing this case,' he confided. 'The suspect, Sir George Jardine, is an old friend of mine, a distinguished public servant, a much-decorated soldier and a man of impeccable honour. He is not a man to sink a dagger into the throat of a fellow officer, to hear his death rattle, to soak up his blood.'

Fearing he was raising George's virtue to an unbelievable height, he paused.

'Are you telling me such a man never killed before?' she said, cynically. 'Come on! A politician and a soldier? To me that combination shrieks power and violence. I saw him — you forget. He is a man capable of killing.' She surprised him further by looking him in the eye and adding: 'Like *you*.'

Joe was alarmed by the accuracy of the girl's insight. 'He's a competent man. Such a messy killing is not his *style* at all. Completely implausible. If circumstances ever forced a man like Jardine to contrive the death of a fellow man — and I can't imagine what they might conceivably be — ' he lied, 'he would do it from afar . . . He would not do it before an audience of two thousand. And — I can tell you — he would not be discovered floundering about with blood on his own hands.'

'Exactly! You're getting there! From afar — you've said it! Perhaps the victim was no pushover? A soldier might be expected to fight back? Your elderly friend not too keen to get close enough to sink a blade in him? I wonder how much your Sir George laid out for the distancing? Money can take you anywhere in this city, Inspector. If you know where to go. The right address. A thousand francs will buy you a night of passion you never dreamed of . . . If your desires are of a more sinister nature, the same sum will buy you a death.'

10

'And if all I hear is correct, both may be obtained at the same establishment,' she whispered.

'*Établissement?*' he queried, apparently not understanding the word, and waited for her explanation. A trick he must use sparingly, he thought. She was clever and would soon realize that, in offering a simplified and expanded version of her comments, she was giving away more than she had intended. He listened carefully to her reply and nodded his understanding.

She made an effort not to look about her and Joe was aware of a lowering of her voice even though they were unobserved. Was this done for effect? He thought he'd better be prepared to reserve judgement on Mademoiselle Raissac.

'If this is an agreement you're offering, Inspector,' she went on, 'I have to accept, but I want your assurance that it will not be known that this information comes from me. Nor will I involve others. They don't like loose ends. They cover their tracks and they don't leave witnesses.'

'They?' he questioned lightly. 'Did you mention a name? Did I miss it?'

'They have no name but they have a reputation, amongst those who need to know these things, for efficiency and even — ' she shuddered — 'a certain style.'

‘What are you suggesting?’ He glanced around at the couturier’s silk and satin confections. ‘An element of *design* in their deaths? Bespoke killing? Made-to-measure murder?’

‘Don’t scoff! You have no idea!’

The words burst from her, raw and vehement. What emotion inspired them, he wondered — fear, despair or fury at his wilfully obtuse comments? He had a knack of making people fizz with rage when he chose to use it. Anger frequently knocked down carefully erected defences and left his suspect exposed. But this girl had not yet reached that pitch. Her emotion — whatever it might be — was still surging and gathering. In an anxious effort to impress on him the gravity of her situation, the gestures accompanying her words became intense and urgent.

‘If they found out I’d spoken of this . . . I’d be discovered dead, my mouth sewn up with scarlet thread and a pair of scissors through my heart. Do you understand?’

He affected dismay. ‘Am I to suppose, then, that the — shall we now call it ‘assassination’? — of Somerton was a *commercial* undertaking? That someone approached the nameless organization you have in mind and ordered up his death?’

‘Yes. The dead man was probably lured there by this blonde girl who at an agreed moment abandoned him to his fate. At the finale, I’d guess, the killer entered and cut his throat, leaving the knife behind. They usually take the weapon away with them. This knife must have been significant, wouldn’t you say? I caught a glimpse of it. They picked it up with a handkerchief from the floor at the man's feet. It looked foreign to me. And it wasn't a zarin, which is the most popular knife in use in Paris.'

'Zarin?'

'It's like a stiletto. The street gangs use it. For ripping and stabbing. Like this.' She held an imaginary weapon in her hand using a backwards grip and demonstrated. Her face was impassive but her breathing was increasingly fast and shallow.

'I've seen just that action somewhere,' he said vaguely.

'Well, this weapon was no zarin. It was short . . . fancy carved hilt.'

'Ivory. Very distinctive. The dagger in this case was from Afghanistan,' he said calmly. 'A country in which Somerton had served some years ago, before the war.' He calculated he was giving nothing away. It would be all over the newspapers tomorrow. And her response would tell him what he needed to know about Mademoiselle Raissac. Would she fall for the stimulus of the exotic blade he was offering and be inspired to spin out her story?

Yes, she would. Her eyes gleamed, her hands fluttered in expressive embroidery of her tale: 'Well — there you have it, then! You should be looking for someone with a grudge going back to that time. A clear case of vengeance, wouldn't you say? Someone with enough money and enough hatred, after all these years, to have the man very publicly killed. Payback for something murky in the past? That's what the scene would have shown if your poor old friend hadn't stumbled into the box prematurely. And now he's got himself arrested and it all looks like an exhibition of jealous rage between two old codgers who ought to know better. A fit of rage that got out of hand.'

She considered for a moment and added: 'They might not like that. An expensively staged act of retribution reduced to a sordid squabble. The customer who paid for his bit of theatre might not be entirely satisfied at the outcome.'

'Not sure where you're going with all this. *He* — whoever *he* is . . . Client of *them* perhaps? — can hardly say: 'Excuse me — may we see that bit again, from the top?' can he? It's not a dress rehearsal we've been treated to! More of a live — or rather *death* — performance.'

She scowled. 'Nothing I can say will make you take this seriously. I've said enough. I've said too much. Who knows what he's deciding at this moment? What they are planning? You'd better leave now. But before you go — I'll remind you of our bargain. What was it? Six months in La Santé or spill my guts? Now, the question is, do I trust a policeman? (Am I naïve?) An English one? (Am I barmy?)' She put her head on one side and considered. 'No. I'm not stupid. And I'm not taken in by an affected lack of understanding that comes and goes, or by a handsome face and a pair of grey eyes that, with a little guidance, could find my soul. I'm going to take you for an honourable man. I couldn't serve time in prison. Not even a day. I know what it's like. The river . . . or the canal

. . . would be my way out of that. So, unless you want my death on your conscience, you'll keep your word.'

It was not the moment to tell her that so far she'd revealed nothing he could use. *He . . . They . . .* Nonsense. But sensing that she was still working her way through to offering something he stayed silent.

'Look, can I ask you to do something for me before I give you the one bit of information I have that may help you? By coming here you've put me in danger. You must do what you can to put things right. No effort on your part involved! Agreed? Good.'

* * *

Ten minutes later Joe emerged into the sunshine. He looked around him, a man in an unfamiliar street, getting his bearings. He appeared oblivious of the passers-by though he was noting them through eyes narrowed against the sun: the two men strolling down the middle of the road, the tramp scavenging for cigarette butts in the gutter, the fashionably dressed young hostess on her way to her shift at one of the jazz clubs. Any one of them could be disguising an interest in a man leaving Mademoiselle Raissac's apartment. Joe loitered on the doorstep as he'd promised Francine he would. She leaned briefly from the window, hitching up the shoulder of her silk gown, and called down to him: 'Darling — I should have asked — can you make it two hours later next week?'

As a bonus, Joe made a show of adjusting his trousers with a louche smirk. Francine ducked back inside the room, unable to hold back a burst of throaty laughter. He looked at his watch, sighed with satisfaction and made off back to the square, whistling.

Better to compromise her good name rather than her neck, she'd judged. He'd been impressed by Mademoiselle Raissac. Mannequin? Dancer? No. Her modest stature might have deprived the boutiques or the Folies of her talents — but it was the stage of the Comédie Française that was the true loser. She would have graced any one of Molière's plays. Dorine in *Tartuffe*? Perfect! What a performance the girl had put on for him! Emotion threatening to overflow at every verse end.

Charming girl, but she'd clearly been watching too many overblown dramas — onstage and backstage. Probably spent her spare time at the matinées in the Gaumont cinema, terrifying herself watching the adventures of Fantômas, Emperor of Evil. Joe shuddered as he recalled the image on the posters, known all over the world, but very particularly French in flavour: a mysterious gentleman, elegant in evening dress, inhuman green eyes glowing through his black mask, stalked a city-scape of Paris with giant strides. His left hand, kid-gloved, cupped his chin thoughtfully, as he selected his next victim. His right hand, slightly behind him, held in a backwards grip a blood-smeared dagger. And the grip was the very one Francine had demonstrated with such vigour. He wondered whether

her storytelling was a part of her character, her way of enlivening an otherwise hard-working but humdrum life, or whether she was making a special effort to mislead the police.

The young nightclub hostess he'd marked down earlier must have doubled back. He was disconcerted to find her suddenly in front of him, coming towards him. How had she slipped by? He was getting careless. A few more strides and she was face to face with him on the narrow pavement. With an exclamation of apology Joe stepped to the side. But he chose to hop to the unexpected side, away from the road. Put out by his clumsiness, she dodged. They got in each other's way, setting to the side and back again, partners in a country dance, disguising their impatience with embarrassed smiles. She began to speak to him. 'I wonder if monsieur is looking for an encounter of a more intimate nature?' she murmured, and then the familiar, shyly delivered, '*Tu viens?*'

Joe relaxed. A street walker after all. All was well. Training made him keep up his pretence of Englishman eminently satisfied by his experiences in Montmartre and he said politely: 'Awfully sorry, my dear. Couldn't possibly! I'm afraid you've picked just the wrong moment . . . if you understand me? Ha! Ha! Some other time?' He rolled his eyes in an expression meant to convey both satiety and anticipation of a pleasure deferred and walked on.

Francine's nervousness must be affecting him. 'They don't leave witnesses,' she'd said, wide-eyed. Once round the corner, Joe's pace increased. Belatedly catching her anxiety, he broke into a trot. Witness? He was thinking of another witness who'd had a clear view of the murder box. The chief witness, you might say, and one who had yet to make his full testimony. One he'd personally removed from the protection of police custody and left behind asleep in a hotel room. He began to run. Had he abandoned, unguarded, a loose end to be tidied up?

11

With a crowded lift just taking off upwards from the lobby, Joe ground his teeth and dashed for the stairs. He arrived panting and took a moment outside the door of George's room to ease and check the Browning revolver in his pocket and to put his ear to the woodwork.

'Liar!' George's voice boomed. 'You're not getting away with that! Lying cheat!' he added.

Joe burst in, revolver in hand.

'Oh, I say! Great heavens! Don't shoot! I was just about to come clean anyway!' Heather Watkins put her hands in the air and shook with laughter. The playing cards she was holding began to slide from her hands and flutter on to the counterpane between herself and Sir George.

George was sitting up in bed, rubicund with rage or good humour or bruising, it was hard to tell. He was crisply dressed in nightshirt and dressing gown. 'Ah! Commander!' he said. 'There you are. What an entrance, my dear fellow! As you're positively bristling with authority, you may as well arrest this young lady. Cheating at cards is the charge.'

'What . . . what in hell's going on here?' Joe blustered, slipping the Browning away in confusion.

'Good afternoon, Joe. I see you are well,' said Miss Watkins, primly ignoring his loose language.

'But . . . Heather . . . You weren't at your hotel when I called . . . '

'I imagine not. I was summoned this morning by Jean-Philippe to come to the assistance of a fellow countryman. He's very persuasive, your French friend, Joe.' She smiled and Joe saw for the first time that she had a very pretty dimple in her left cheek. 'Well, in less time than it takes to tell, I was here receiving instructions in the nursing care of a distressed old gentleman.' She waved a hand at George who put on a pathetic face. 'Not so old, not very distressed and I'm not so sure about the gentleman bit of the billing either. He's ruthless when it comes to cards! We were playing Cheat. Do you know it?'

Joe could only nod in reply.

'I was told to bring a book and to expect to sit by his bedside while he slept and be there, all cool hands, reassuring smile and soothing words when he woke. Which I was led to believe might be in eight hours or so. Hmm! It was difficult to get him to agree to go to bed at all and he only slept for three hours and then snapped awake. It's taken a lot of ingenuity and force of character to keep him where he's supposed to be — in bed,' she huffed in a nannyish way.

The warm smile she exchanged with her patient told Joe all he needed to know about the developing relationship.

'An inspired idea! And what luck Jean-Philippe had your telephone number, Heather,' he said innocently. 'Thank you indeed for giving up your day to ride herd on my old friend. Did the Inspector tell you — we had to wrest him from the hands of the Police Judiciaire who were determined to wring something — anything — from him by means of the third degree?'

'He did!' Heather reached over and squeezed George's hand. 'Monsters! If I ever get hold of that dreadful Fourier, I'll give him what for! If only I could be trapped in a lift with him with a tennis racquet in my hand! How *could* he? And Sir George already distressed by the death of his friend . . . So unfeeling!'

George grimaced, trying and failing by a mile to look pitiable. 'Well, Joe, with all this female sympathy deployed, how could I not have perked up and made a full recovery? Miss Watkins has been wonderful! A breath of crisp English air in all this overheated foreign nonsense.' He looked sideways at Joe and added: 'And — as it seems you're counting, Joe — she's been good enough to give *me* her address too. Her address in England. Look forward very much to continuing our acquaintance, my dear,' he said, turning to Heather, 'when you get back from your tennis tournament. You must tell me all about it . . . show me your medals, swap gossip from the Riviera. I shall want to know the truth behind that liaison we were speaking of . . . '

'The gigolo and the English countess?'

'Shh! Discretion, my dear Miss Watkins!'

'Of course!' Heather Watkins stood up and began to collect her things together into the small travelling bag she'd brought with her. 'Well, it would seem my work is done here, for the time being at any rate. Look, Joe, Sir George, I consider myself on hand if required, for the rest of my stay in Paris. Don't hesitate and all that . . . '

'Heather, you don't have to rush off?' Joe began.

Her eyes twinkled as she looked from one to the other. 'I'm quite certain you have things to discuss. Serious things. Crime things. I'm very happy to go about my business which — you won't be surprised to hear — involves a quick trip to the Galeries Lafayette. I saw a darling little day dress in their window on my way here in the taxi.'

After an affectionate goodbye to George she tucked him up again under his covers, ran a hand over his brow and spoke gently to him: 'Why don't you try to take another forty winks now that Joe's back? You're quite safe, you know.'

She paused, bag in hand, by the door and Joe went to open it for her and show her out. 'Hang on a minute! Gosh, I wouldn't make a good agent, would I — I nearly forgot! Jean-Philippe told me to tell you he'd be back by French teatime.'

'Five o'clock, then.' Joe grinned.

'Oh . . . and you might like to tell him that he was quite right to warn me about attempted incursions by strangers.'

Suddenly chilled and alert, Joe asked quietly: 'What was that, Heather? Are you saying someone tried to force his way in here?'

'Not force, no,' she said thoughtfully. 'Much more subtle. And I'm probably being over-suspicious in the light of Jean-Philippe's warning . . . Well, you can judge, Joe. About a quarter of an hour after he'd left, there was a tap on the door. I looked around. George hadn't gone to bed — he was in the bathroom with the door shut. Avoiding me, I think. Hoping I'd go away. The bed was made up, the room neat. I chucked that mucky old trench coat away behind the chair, picked up my bag, looking for all the world as though I'd just that minute arrived, and opened the door a crack. There was a stranger there. A man. Thirties? Forties? French, I'd say. Dressed in black jacket and trousers. Room service, you'd have said. Except that no one had called for room service.'

'Go on!' Joe could hardly bear the pause as she marshalled her impressions.

'Well, I took the initiative. 'Yes? Who are you and what do you want?' I said in English.

''Reception, mademoiselle, I have a message for the gentleman,' he said. He was trying to speak English. And doing it well, I thought.

''What gentleman?' I asked. And without looking up at the number on the door I said: 'This is Room 205. You must have got the wrong number.' At this point I opened the door properly . . . didn't want to appear to be hiding anything . . . or anybody. His eyes darted . . . yes, they darted . . . inside. I thought for a moment he might try to get in so I squared up to him, barring his way.

''Sir George Jardine,' he said. 'It's very urgent. I must deliver the message directly and into his hand.' He was holding something in his right hand which was stuffed into his trouser pocket, I remember.

‘‘Well, I’m sorry about that,’ I said. ‘But, hard luck — you’ll have to enquire elsewhere. I’ve just been shown to this room which of course has been vacated. There’s no one under the bed — I always check. Silly, I know! And now if you wouldn’t mind — I’m just about to take a bath. Look — obvious question, but you *did* check with Reception before you came up, didn’t you? Perhaps,’ I suggested helpfully, ‘your Sir John was here last night? But he’s not here now. Perhaps they gave you the wrong floor? Yes, I’d go back to Reception and ask them what on earth they think they’re doing. They’ll set you straight.’ ’

Joe must have been looking shocked. With a wary eye on him, Heather asked anxiously if she’d done the right thing.

‘Exactly the right thing. Wonderful presence of mind, Heather!’

She was encouraged to ask quietly: ‘Who was he, Joe?’

‘I’ve no idea,’ he said and, displeased by his answer which, though true, was unsatisfying and unworthy for a girl who had, by her quick thought and courage, most probably saved George’s life, he added: ‘Someone sent to tidy up a loose end, I fear. Thank God you were here, Heather, holding the gate!’

* * *

When Heather had left, Joe turned from the door to survey the loose end. Sir George had fallen fast asleep again and a gentle, rhythmic rumbling suggested it might go on for a few hours.

Thoughtfully, Joe picked up the deck of cards and put them away, then settled to write up some notes in his book. He had depressingly little. He drew arrows from one word to another, isolated some in balloons, began again. Times might prove vital, he felt, and he reconstructed the day as accurately as he could from several perspectives. He looked again at his material, searching for links, threads, coincidences even and finding none. The only words that compelled his attention were the words Francine had used: 'He . . . They . . .'

And an address in Montparnasse.

* * *

At precisely five o'clock, Joe was waiting by the door and heard Bonnefoye's quick rap and his voice identifying himself. He entered, seemed reassured by the peaceful scene and said as much.

'Yes, old mate, and it's by the grace of God and Miss Watkins that George there is sleeping the sleep of the just and not the just dead. Why didn't you tell me you knew his life might be at risk? I'd not have left him!'

'What! You mean to say . . . ? But tell me, man!' Bonnefoye's dismay was acute.

Joe repeated Heather's account of her sinister visitor and Jean-Philippe groaned and exclaimed. 'And, coming after my interview with Francine Raissac who raised not a few suspicions in my mind, I've been sitting here, imagining horrors.'

'But I didn't seriously expect anyone to try to get in,' said Bonnefoye. 'You know me — careful, exact, always taking precautions . . . ' Joe wondered whether he really did know Bonnefoye. 'I thought . . . just in case those buggers at headquarters decided to change their minds — not unknown! — and rearrest Sir George, we'd give them the runaround for a bit. Good girl, though! I say — I would think twice about playing tennis against her, wouldn't you . . . or any other sport, come to that. I told her to repel boarders, yes. And I took the precaution of asking them at Reception to cancel George's booking. Said he was shaken up and going to stay down the road at the Embassy and all enquiries should be sent there. Meantime my friend Miss Watkins would be pleased to take the room for the next two days. I gave them her details. It ought to have looked right in the books. The management know who I am,' he said thoughtfully. 'They wouldn't annoy the PJ. And I can't see them divulging details of an English guest to anyone. Large part of their clientele are British diplomats. They wouldn't want to upset one.

'But, Joe, what's all this about Mademoiselle Raissac? What were you doing over there in Montmartre? And what's the connection?'

'Like you, I saw from Fourier's notes that the girl was only telling a part of the story. In her job, she would be able to give a far more detailed description of the disappearing witness. She was hiding something. I thought I'd get over there and find out what it was before she disappeared herself.'

Joe recounted his interview, down to the last detail of his confrontation with the streetwalker. 'Well, that's me. And now — do tell — what did *you* and your moustache manage to charm out of her?'

Bonnefoye looked aside shiftily, Joe thought.

'Not charm. No time for charm. Living up to the rough-tough image of the PJ, I'm afraid. And I had some bad news to impart.'

'What have you got on her? She seemed to me, if not innocent exactly, at least uninvolved in shady goings-on?'

'She's a law-abiding woman — your impression was right. Agreeable and hard-working. And very protective of her younger brother who is none of those things. We have nothing against Mademoiselle Raissac but young Alfred has a sheet as long as your arm.'

'Good Lord! She didn't mention him. A Parisian?'

'Lives in the thirteenth arrondissement. On the fringes of the student quarter. Bad area. Full of thugs and villains. Thirty years ago, he'd have been running with a gang of Apaches.'

'Apaches? Why do you French always speak of those villains in a hushed tone? Dead and gone, aren't they? Nothing but a musical-comedy memory?'

'I looked up the word one day,' said Bonnefoye. 'Couldn't think why French gangsters should be named after a tribe of North American Indians . . . you know — Geronimo's mob. And, after a while, you realize you've left it too long and it becomes impossible to actually *ask* anyone without being laughed at. It's from a native word, *àpachu*, meaning 'enemy'. And the tribe in question was notorious for the savagery and boldness of its attacks. They had a certain style.'

There it was again, that word. Francine Raissac had used it, hadn't she? Or had he used it himself?

'And a dashing image was what the Parisian Apaches aimed for! They wore hats with visors pulled low over their faces, red scarves, polished boots, waistcoat, black trousers and a stiletto. A uniform. Liked to see themselves and their exploits all over the front pages of the press. They swore undying loyalty to each other and, though gangs fought each other all over Paris, they'd always join forces to take on the police. There were those who found that sort of skulduggery attractive. Smart. Some romantic fool wrote a poem about them. It's suspected that they actually hired themselves out to stage knife fights on the pavements in front of particular cafés to attract customers. Nothing like a little frisson with your absinthe!

'And they had a very short way with informers. They didn't take bribes and they didn't squeal. Vermin! But stylish vermin. They disappeared in the war. Swept up for cannon fodder. And now it seems they've been reborn.'

'The Sons of the Apaches?' Joe's voice was laced with irony.

'Just so. They're alive and kicking on the

fringes of the boulevards. And this lot are tougher and smarter and less conspicuous. They don't advertise themselves and they avoid being written up in the press but the crime figures speak for them. Never stray south of the boulevard St Michel after dark, Joe!'

'And poor little Francine has a brother mixed up with this crew?'

'Francine doesn't acknowledge her brother. Claims to have cast him off. Never mentions him. Did she mention him to you? No! She pretends he doesn't exist. But I've seen the records. She's always there in court pleading for him with the magistrate, bailing him out, when things go wrong for him. I think he's used up a lot of her money. Drug user when he can get his hands on the stuff. Do anything for the price of the next shot . . . you know the sort of thing. But if he's not in the centre exactly of the criminal underworld, he hears things that ripple out. Might have passed them on to his sister. That's probably the stuff she was spinning into a tale for you. The framework of a few authentic details and a lot of embroidery on top — she's good at that. Send the impressionable copper away thinking he's heard something useful from a helpful citizen when all he's got is a headful of nonsense.'

'Not a very flattering picture but I do hope you're right,' said Joe soberly. 'Because the alternative might be to suppose that Heather and George were standing a whisker away from the stilettos of the Sons of the Apaches.'

Bonnefoye laughed silently.

'But before you write off my fishing expedition as a trip down the garden path, answer me this — is there any reason why Francine Raissac might decide to confide in a bloke like me? I didn't invoke my charm particularly, nor did I resort to strong-arm tactics . . . A little light coercion, perhaps, but nothing she couldn't have seen through and side-stepped if she'd wanted to. I'd say she was playing my game. Why would she choose to pass on to a man she's never met before, and a foreign policeman at that, a piece of information that might be vital to the solution of last night's murder?'

Bonnefoye was silent, tugging at his moustache, unable to meet his eye.

'What reason?' Joe insisted.

Finally, 'Listen,' he said quietly. 'I told you I had three urgent cases on my books?'

Joe nodded.

'I was supposed to shelve them or delegate them until the end of the week for this conference. But, you know how it is . . . '

Again Joe nodded. 'Can't be done. Especially when you see threads running through them which fresh eyes might not be able to connect.'

'Right. Well, one of them involves this hooligan brother, this Alfred. It's thought he was in a fight with three or four other men down by the Canal St Martin. Some bargees reported a scuffle and screams. Nightly occurrence! No one took much notice. Alfred disappeared on that night and hasn't been seen again since. His sister reported him missing. She was supposed to be having coffee with him as she always does on a Sunday afternoon — passing on some of her wages no doubt. She gets paid on a Saturday. He didn't turn up. She made an incursion — brave girl — into his territory and caught hold of one of his pals. He told her nothing but the terror in his reaction, she reports, was enough to make her fear the worst. And then, late last night, before I came out to meet you at the airport, on my desk, a note from the morgue.

'A body of a young man fished from the canal. No identification but the description fits Alfred.'

'Have you had time to go and see it?' said Joe.

He had a memory of walking past three dripping bodies on slabs on his way to view Somerton. 'The night's catch,' the pathologist had commented. 'A poor haul.'

'No. Been too caught up with your business, Joe.'

'Cause of death? Is it known?'

'Oh, yes. It was very clear. And it wasn't drowning.' Bonnefoye's sentences were growing shorter and shorter as his tension increased. 'The ultimate cause of death was a stiletto to the heart.'

'Ultimate?' Joe picked up the word.

'Yes. That's what killed him. Finished him off. But before he died, his lips had been sewn together. With a length of black cobbler's thread.'

12

Joe groaned and put his head in his hands.

Not histrionics, he thought, but hysterics or verging on it. Francine Raissac had been mourning her brother, still raw from the Inspector's description of his death, bruised, no doubt, by what Bonnefoye called 'his rough-tough image', when the English policeman had come bumbling in on his two left feet, making, with insouciance, silly remarks about her panda's eyes. Eyes swollen not, as he'd unthinkingly assumed, by interrupted sleep but by grief. Mascara smudged by tears.

Joe tormented himself and Bonnefoye by insisting on going over some of his worst remarks. ''Bespoke killing . . . made-to-measure murder,' I said! Can you believe that? How crass! How hurtful!'

'How were you to know? You weren't, Joe. And with all that sewing equipment about the place — I have to say — rather an apt if unfortunate image. Now stop this!'

'She hinted at it, you know . . . said she might herself be discovered with her mouth sewn up with — I think she said scarlet — thread. And scissors in her heart. She was using the facts of the death you'd just dropped into her lap to illustrate something — something she was frightened to disclose but . . . '

'I think her grief pushed her to tell you too

much. She didn't tell me, she was still stunned. Gave me nothing. I've seen this before. Shock makes them clam up. Then the anger begins to build up. By the time you got to her and flashed your understanding eyes at her, the desire for revenge had taken over and she was ready to pop. You were treated to her explosion and didn't have the facts to help you to make sense of it. But her insinuations — that there's a clandestine assassination agency with a flair for the dramatic out and about and doing business in Paris — what do we make of *that*? Ludicrous, surely? And it has no name. What in hell *would* you call it?' He grinned. 'Shakespeare & Co.? No, that's been used. Bookshop, I think. How about Death by Design?'

'Bonnefoye, there are two corpses laid out side by side in the Institut Médico-Légal. Alfred Raissac and Sir Stanley Somerton, unlikely morgue-mates. Knifed to death, the pair of them, and they're not laughing with us.'

'Sorry, Joe.' He sighed. 'Sometimes it's the only way through the nastiness. But it's not like you to be such an old misery guts? La belle Francine seems to have had quite an effect on you. Always a danger with these girls.'

'No, Jean-Philippe! That's the problem. She isn't just one of 'these girls'. I thought she was a very fine young woman. And I'm deeply sorry that I must have — albeit unconsciously — offended and upset her at a distressing moment in her life.'

'Hard to avoid that in this job,' commented Bonnefoye. 'Always offending someone. But

— look — put her out of your mind and concentrate on the most important character in all this. We've hardly given *him* a thought since it started.'

'Yes, of course. Somerton. The victim. The moment George wakes up I'm going to want to know exactly how the two are connected. There's something he's not told us. George is an accomplished liar. It's not like him to do it *badly*. That's what concerns me. But, if he hasn't told us, can you blame him? — we haven't got around to asking him yet. Though I'm sure old Fourier must have made the attempt.'

They both turned to the bed where, from his pillows, George gave a fluttering and extended snore. They waited for him to turn and settle again before they continued their hushed conversation.

'While you're filling in background on Somerton, I'll go off and take a look at this address in Montparnasse,' said Bonnefoye. 'The one Francine confided. I'm getting to know that area quite well. I'll be able to make more sense of it than you would, I imagine. Oh — and don't forget you're due to escort the Lady Somerton to the morgue.'

He took out a notebook and checked a page. 'A message came to headquarters. I ring in every hour and there's usually something for me. Six o'clock at the British Embassy. Can you pick the lady up there? The Embassy's just down the road from here. Very convenient. Oh, they stipulated number 39, rue du Faubourg St-Honoré. That's the residence of the Ambassador — not the offices next door. That gives you forty minutes to smarten yourself up. No time to go back to your hotel . . . Why not borrow one of Sir George's shirts? You're about the same size. He's got a drawer full of them over there. And a hat? Never did get your louche fedora back but you'll find something suitable if you look in the wardrobe.

'And look, Joe . . . ' Bonnefoye weighed his next announcement, suddenly unsure of himself. 'You'll probably think I'm overreacting to circumstances . . . put it down to Gallic hysteria if you like . . . but I think we should move Sir George out of here. To a safer place.'

'I agree. Sensible proposal,' said Joe. 'What do you have in mind?'

'The rue Mouffetard,' he said. 'My mother's apartment. She's used to soldiers. My father and uncles were in the army. She'll take good care of him. I'll take him out the back way through the kitchens. When you've finished at the morgue why don't you come along and check his accommodation? He's technically in your custody, after all! It's above the baker's shop halfway down. Got a map? Here let me show you . . . '

'Before you start dressing to impress the widow, Joe, why don't you get acquainted with my razor?' George's jovial voice was brisk. Not in the least sleepy. 'No newfangled patent safety razor on offer, I'm afraid. I always use an old-fashioned cut-throat. You must pardon the expression in the circumstances.'

Bonnefoye shrugged and grinned and went with the smooth efficiency of a valet to select a shirt.

'Let me mark your card, Joe.' This was the old Sir George, good-humouredly in charge, presiding. 'Now, the present Ambassador is the Marquess of Crewe. Can't help you there. Never met the chap. Though I was well acquainted with his predecessor. Hardinge. Viceroy of India for many years. And a good one. Anyway, play it by ear and if it seems appropriate to do so, convey my respects and good wishes to whoever seems to be expecting them . . . you know the routine, Joe.'

'I don't suppose the top brass will be parading for a mere Scotland Yard detective and a widow on a lugubrious mission, sir.'

George pursed his lips for a moment, assessing the social niceties of the situation. 'You're probably right, my boy. Six o'clock. Dashed inconvenient time for them to be landed with handing a distraught old lady over to the bluebottles. They'll be preparing to welcome guests for whatever shindig they've got planned for tonight. Sociable lot at the Embassy! Always some sort of soirée on. You'll probably find they've tethered the old girl to a gatepost outside, awaiting collection.

'No, Bonnefoye! Not that one! Wherever did you get your training? He's not bound for the golf course! Find a boiled shirt, my dear chap! Yes, that'll do. Collars top left. Grey felt hat in the cupboard. Nothing grander. Don't want to look as though you've turned up for the canapés.'

* * *

At five minutes to six Joe stood, getting his breath back, in front of the Embassy, transfixed by the perfection of the Louis XV façade. Balanced and harmonious and, in this most grandiose quarter of Paris, managing to avoid pomposity, it smiled a welcome. He almost looked for George's gatepost but of course there was none. An elegant pillared portico announced the entrance; doors wide open gave glimpses of figures dimly perceived and moving swiftly about in the interior. As he watched, electric lights flicked on in all the windows of the first two floors. The reception rooms. Obviously a soirée about to take place.

He collected his thoughts and strode to the door.

The liveried doorman barely glanced at the card in his extended hand. 'You are expected, Commander. Will you follow me?'

He passed Joe on, into the care of an aide in evening dress who came hurrying into the vestibule to shake his hand. 'Sandilands? How do you do? So glad you could come. Harry Quantock. Deputy assistant to the Ambassador. You'll have to make do with me, I'm afraid, sir. His Excellency sends his greetings — he's at the moment rather tied up with the string band.' At the upwards flick of an elegant hand, Joe caught the sounds of a small orchestra essaying a piece of Elgar somewhere above their heads. The deputy assistant grimaced. 'French band, English tunes . . . not a good mix. I sometimes think they do it on purpose.'

'Still seeking revenge for Waterloo?' suggested

Joe. 'Ouch! I'd surrender at once.'

'We won't hear them in the red salon, come with me.' Quantock led him across the impressive space in front of them. Airy, well proportioned and sparely decorated. '*Le hall d'entrée*,' announced his guide with a perfect accent.

Joe had an impression of cool grey and white marble tiles leading the eye to the graceful curve of a great staircase. The delicate wrought-iron handrail outlining it sparkled with gold and bronze, promising further wonders as it wound upwards.

Quantock leaned to him and confided: 'Most of the refurbishment was done with impeccable taste by Napoleon's favourite sister. And there she is — Pauline Borghese.'

Joe nodded in acknowledgement as they passed her portrait. The young princess, slim and lovely in her high-bosomed gown, was as handsome as her house.

'Pity about the curtains, don't you think? Red velvet!' Quantock was shuddering. 'Too Edwardian for words! And the theme continues through here in *le salon rouge*.' He paused by a closed door. 'Your charge, Lady Somerton, is in here, taking sherry and flirting with the Duke of Wellington. They *will* do it! His Grace still exerts a certain power over the ladies.'

Joe entered a room richly decorated, in contrast with the restrained hall. In the centre, a gleaming round mahogany table stood precisely in the rosette of a deep red turkey carpet and was overhung by a stunning chandelier. Gilded mirrors applied to each of the red walls reflected the flickering lights of candles in sconces, and in the middle of all this magnificence Joe had to hunt for the figure of Lady Somerton. She was standing at the end of the room, empty sherry glass in hand, still, black-clad, almost a shadow. She was looking up at a portrait. Transfixed, she did not hear them enter.

As they drew near she began to speak: 'Arthur Wellesley. The Iron Duke. Now there was a man one can admire! So handsome! So competent! I'm just surprised, after what he did to the French, that they allow us to display him, Mr Quantock.'

'His Grace was himself Ambassador for a year here in 1814, immediately before his victory at Waterloo, your ladyship,' Quantock reminded her. 'And therefore takes his rightful place on these walls.' He performed the introductions. 'May I refill your glass? And how about you, sir? Would you like some sherry?' He went to pour the drinks himself from a sideboard, tactfully leaving Joe to continue the conversation.

'His quality leaps from the canvas, don't you agree?' she continued, determined apparently to hear his views.

'It's all in the nose, I believe,' said Joe, annoyed that the widow appeared far more interested in Wellington than in himself.

'I beg your pardon? The nose, did you say?'

'Yes. Look at it. An ice-breaker! A promontory! Your hero could have fought a duel with Cyrano and they would have needed no other weapons.'

At last she smiled. 'Noses. In the Bois. At dawn. I'd have put my money on the Duke.'

Her attention caught, Joe moved easily into the routine of expressing sorrow for the death of the lady's husband. His smooth sentiments were graciously received, helped along with sighs and sips of sherry. Quantock politely sought the most recent information on the tragedy and Joe gave him an acceptable and highly edited account. The task before him was to point this uncertain dark horse at a rather taxing fence and he wanted to avoid scaring her off. Without appearing to do so, he studied the widow, assessing her strengths and qualities. Exactly what he was expecting. Apart from her age. She was middle-aged, possibly as much as forty, but at any rate, more than a decade younger than her late husband. Quite a normal age gap in military families. He could imagine that, with promotion in mind — possibly Colonel the next step — Somerton had been taken on one side by a superior officer and advised to marry. And, one summer, on home leave, he'd met and courted this woman. What had she said her name was? She'd rather particularly during the introductions corrected young Quantock. 'Lady Somerton no longer,' she'd informed them. 'With Sir Stanley dead and the title gone to his son, my daughter-in-law is the present Lady Somerton. I am now to be addressed as *Catherine*, Lady Somerton.' The voice was educated, Home Counties.

Her face was pale, enlivened by a gallant touch of rouge along the cheekbones. Quenched but pretty. Her hair was light brown, not greying yet, her eyes hazel. She'd chosen her dress well. Black, of course, but silk and well cut. The drama was relieved by a double strand of pearls around her throat and matching pearl earrings that peeped out just below her bobbed hair.

Joe enquired amiably and sympathetically about her flight over the Channel. She declared she'd enjoyed it but he set her brave comment against the betraying rise and fall of her pearls as she failed to restrain a gulp. The conversation, which was never going to be an easy one, felt as discordant as the strains of the Gallic version of 'Nimrod' filtering along the corridor and all three were relieved to draw it to a close.

Harry Quantock escorted his guests back to the front door where, to Joe's surprise, an Embassy car was waiting for them. A manservant hurried forward with madame's cape and monsieur's hat. After routine farewells, Quantock handed Catherine Somerton into the back seat, closed the door and turned to speak softly to Joe: 'His Excellency will be keen to hear the outcome of this business, you understand, Sandilands?' A light smile softened the command. 'As will Jack Pollock. Sir George's cousin. He sends his respects and good wishes. He'll be in touch.'

* * *

The morgue, illuminated as it now was by electric bulbs, was all the more sinister. The light had the effect of deepening the many dark corners, emphasizing the roughness of the walls and highlighting things better left in the shadows. Like shining a torch in the face of an old whore, Joe thought. Disturbing and unkind. But at least they were not faced, on entry, with a line-up of freshly delivered corpses to pass in review as had been the custom from the Middle Ages to the recent past. All the bodies apart from one had been filed away in the sliding steel cases along the back wall, Joe was relieved to see.

Dr Moulin was still at his post and waiting for them. He greeted Joe warmly and the two men went into their routine. Dignified and considerate, he checked that the lady was prepared for the sight of her husband's corpse. Catherine Somerton hugged her cape about her, clutched her pearls, shivered and nodded.

'Do you think we might take a look at Exhibit A before we begin?' Joe asked and Moulin nodded his agreement. The dagger was produced for her inspection.

She made no attempt to handle it but looked at it carefully and turned a co-operative face to Joe. 'I'm sorry, Commander. I've never seen it before.'

'Did Sir Stanley keep a collection of knives at home?'

'Ah. Where *was* his home? We had no such objects in the house in Kent. But you should be aware, Commander, that my husband lived for many years in India. He had a passion for the country that I could not share. I joined him there for the first year of our marriage but the climate did not agree with me and I returned. He could have amassed a collection of such artefacts and I would be unaware of their existence. This is, I take it, the very blade that did the deed?'

Joe and Moulin murmured in unison.

She peered at it more closely, then shook her head. On the whole, a good witness, Joe thought. When the doctor moved to the head of the sheeted figure she moved with him and stood waiting on the other side. Joe watched her carefully as the cover rolled downwards to the waist. There was at first no reaction. Finally, she drew in a deep breath and whispered: 'That's Somerton. My late husband.' And, as Joe had predicted, there came at last the inevitable question: 'Tell me, doctor, did he suffer?'

The doctor also was prepared for this. But he was a scientist, not a diplomat, and he gave an honest reply. 'His death must have come very quickly, madame. He did not linger in pain. But the wound — you may see for yourself — is a savage one, almost severing the head. The initial assault would have caused a degree of pain, yes.'

'Good!' said the widow, suddenly bright. 'But however painful it was, it could never have been painful enough!'

In the stunned silence, she rounded on the corpse and for a moment Joe felt his muscles tense. Fearing what? That she was about to inflict a truly painful blow of her own? Incredibly — yes. The doctor had put out a restraining hand. She gestured it away impatiently and went to stand close by the head. She bent and spoke directly to the corpse, her lips inches from his ear: 'I hope you're in hell, you rotter! I hope that

Lucifer in person is turning your spit. Look at you! Oozing your stinking essence on to a slab in a foreign dungeon. Dyed hair! Pomaded moustache! You lived — a disgrace; you died — a disgrace.'

She took a step back and gave her last, formal farewell: '*Down, down to hell; and say I sent thee thither.*'

Joe was uneasy. The vehemence was spontaneous but the quotation from *Henry VI* had been, he calculated, prepared with some forethought. The whole outpouring appeared the distillation of years of resentment. He looked again at the dead face, softening in decay, and speculated on the qualities that could provoke such hatred.

The widow collected herself and struggled for a more level tone, addressing the two men: 'You may have his remains burned or whatever you do. I don't want to take them away with me or have them posted on. Send the bill to the Embassy. And now, if you're ready, Commander . . . ? We must be on our way.'

She threaded her arm through Joe's and turned for the last time to her husband, unwilling even now to let him go in peace, her parting words meant for him: 'I have an engagement on the Champs-Élysées. At Fouquet's.'

She began to drag Joe towards the door, calling out still over her shoulder her taunts: 'Champagne . . . foie gras . . . asparagus . . . the first of the wild strawberries . . . '

Joe paused in the doorway and looked back at the startled doctor, mouthing silently: 'Not with me, she hasn't!'

13

She swept out ahead of him and stood by the car door until he opened it. When they were settled inside she gave him his instructions. 'Tell the driver I'll drop you off before he goes on to Fouquet's. Where would you like to be set down, Commander?'

Without waiting for his answer, she took a velvet bag from the deep pocket of her cape and fished about until she found a small flacon of perfume. 'Do you mind if I apply something a little fresh? I'm quite sure I must smell of — what was that fluid? Ugh! Formaldehyde, would it be? That stink?'

'Death and bleach, Lady Somerton,' said Joe tersely.

He addressed the driver, who was sitting patiently waiting for instructions. 'Driver — would you take me across the river on to the Left Bank, please? I'm bound for the place de la Contrescarpe. Do you know it? And then, the lady requires to be set down in the Champs-Élysées. She will direct you.'

The big car moved off and Joe reeled at an over-enthusiastic application of perfume. Rose and sandalwood? Chanel's Number 5 was easily recognized. And what had Mademoiselle Chanel saucily said about her creation? 'Perfume should be applied in the places where a woman expects to be kissed.' Joe watched in fascination as

Catherine Somerton dabbed the contents of her tiny flacon behind her ears, at the base of her throat — and, when she thought he'd turned to look out of the window, he saw, in the reflection in the glass, her forefinger steal down into the hollow between her breasts to lay a seductive trail.

For whose nose? For whose lips? Joe smiled to himself. He hoped Fouquet's had got the champagne on ice.

The car rolled to a halt, held up by the press of early evening traffic fighting its way across the Pont Neuf on to the island. On an impulse, Joe spoke to the driver again. 'Look — I'll get out here. With the traffic as it is, Lady Somerton will find herself late for her assignation in the Champs-Élysées if she makes a detour to drop me off. I'm happy to take a taxi.'

She made no demur, not even noticing his slight reproof, even thanking him for his consideration. Mind elsewhere. Impatient to be off. In the advancing headlights her eyes flashed, her pearls gleamed, and although nothing about her appearance had substantially changed, Joe suddenly saw, where had been the downcast widow in her weeds, a sophisticated woman, elegantly dressed and eagerly looking forward to an adventure.

'Give my regards to the Duke,' he called to her before he slammed the door shut. 'I trust his olfactory powers will be in fine fettle this evening.' He enjoyed her puzzled expression.

Joe watched the car crawl away again and turned on his heel, trotting back across the bridge to the morgue. Hoping he wasn't too late.

* * *

The lights were still switched on. Moulin was there, putting away instruments and equipment, when Joe burst in. He seemed pleased to see him.

His cheerful voice echoed the length of the room, dispelling the shadows. 'Oh, hello there! You managed to escape? I'm glad of that! Wouldn't want to find *you* on one of my slabs with a mysterious mark on your throat. It can be pretty poisonous, the bite of *Latrodectus mactans*, I've heard. The black widow spider. Its venom is thought to be sixteen times more virulent than the rattlesnake's.'

'I leapt out of the car! If I weren't so exhausted, I'd have been tempted to go along to Fouquet's, bribe someone to give me a table in a corner, and lurk to see who she's got caught up in her web.'

Moulin eyed Joe with concern. 'You *do* look all in, Commander. Come and have a mug of coffee in my lair. I've just put a pot on. Take the weight off your feet. Get your breath back and ask me the question you've passed up an evening at Fouquet's to come back and ask.'

* * *

They sat clutching mugs of strong coffee in the small and calculatedly bright study across the corridor from the morgue building. Not so much a study as a retreat, an affirmation of his humanity, Joe thought, looking around with pleasure. And wouldn't you need one! He'd sunk gratefully into the depths of one of a pair of old-fashioned armchairs piled with cushions and topped off with lace antimacassars. Thoughtfully, Moulin kicked up a footstool for him. The room had probably, in its first use, been some sort of torture chamber, Joe calculated, but no signs of a lugubrious past lingered after the determined application of rich lengths of drapery to the walls, Tiffany shades to the lamps, rows of books, and a gently puttering gas fire warming the room. On a desk and smiling out into the room, the silver-framed photograph of a very pretty dark-haired woman. The ticking of a deep-throated clock soothed Joe to a point where he had to shake himself awake and take a sip or two of his coffee.

Under the influence of the strong brew, the good company and fatigue, Joe recounted his day to a pair of willing ears. But the warm smile, the understanding comments and the ready humour dried up at the mention of Francine Raissac's flight of fancy. Joe caught the sudden stillness.

'Yes, that's what I've come to ask. I try not to leave any accusation unchecked however ridiculous it sounds on first hearing. The girl's theories began to sound less crazy when I heard — from another source — that her brother is a customer of yours. Filed away in a steel drawer, I should think? Fished out of the Canal St Martin.'

'Alfred? Drawer number 32,' said Moulin. 'She hasn't been in to identify him yet. Poor girl! It's all deeply unpleasant, I'm afraid. I've taken the waxed cobbler's twine out of the lips so it doesn't look quite so frightful but I can't obliterate the wound altogether. The lad was very young. But physically in rather bad shape. Emaciated. Taking drugs, I shouldn't wonder. And are you saying you see a connection between this poor specimen of humanity and an organization run by some sort of super criminal? A Fantômas reborn?' Dr Moulin laughed and pointed to a shelf of lurid novels over the desk. 'I have the whole collection, you see! You're very welcome to help yourself if you like.'

Joe shivered. 'I gave up after the second book. Too utterly terrifying for a law enforcer like myself. Fantômas, if I remember rightly, never died,' he explained. 'He's immortal — a god of Evil. Nightmare! But yes, I wouldn't mind taking a look at the third one in your line-up. *Le mort qui tue*, I think it's called.'

Moulin gave him a startled look and counted along the shelf, extracting the book he'd mentioned. 'Here you are. I shall leave the gap there! I'm going to insist on having it back, then I can be sure you'll come again and entertain me with a further episode in your horror story. Will you have a little brandy in your coffee? It can strike chill in here in spite of my efforts to dispel the gloom.' He reached behind a row of leather-backed novels and found a bottle of cognac.

'I think you can guess what I'm going to ask,' said Joe seriously. 'Inspectors each have their own case loads. Three corpses is what Bonne-foye's got on his books at the moment. They may not have the time to exchange theories with each other, or see anything but their own narrow picture of crime in the city . . . *You* would see it. You examine all — very well, most — of the bodies. They pass through your morgue and under your scalpel for an hour or two — a day possibly — and you move on. But you see the wider landscape of murder . . . '

'I know where you're going with this. And I know you don't want to wait while I dig out screeds of notes, sheets of records — all of which are available, by the way — so I'll ask — will memory be a good enough guide? It will? Let me think then . . . ' He got up and wandered to his stove, pouring out more of the liquid inspiration.

'Over the last four or five years? Is that enough? That's as far back as my current appointment goes.'

Joe nodded, thankful that his notion hadn't been dismissed out of hand with a pitying shake of the head.

And then he waited, unwilling to press Moulin, understanding that this was the doctor's first and alarming overview of the crime pattern.

'Like your Jack the Ripper — a killer in series — but yet quite unlike him. The victims in his case were all of the same profession, sex and situation. They — and the killer most probably — were living within a few doors of each other. The Paris corpses I have in mind are male and from varied backgrounds, they're of different nationalities, killed over a period of years and in vastly different scenarios. No one would dream of linking them together as a group because apart from their being male — which the victims of violent death predominantly are — they have only one thing in common — a totally fanciful notion. In Francine Raissac's head, in yours and now — in mine! Curse you! No, it won't do, Sandilands.' He shook his head in an attempt to dismiss ideas too shocking to entertain.

'And there's the question of motive,' he persisted into Joe's silence. 'Motive could be guessed at in most of the cases. Or should I say motives? They were varied but run-of-the-mill.'

'Financial gain, provocation, revenge, hatred . . . ' Joe started to list them.

'Yes, yes . . . a bit of everything. And I'm not sure it tells us much in these cases.'

'Would you like to bring some of them into the daylight again — just as a matter of speculation, of course,' Joe encouraged.

'No, I try rather to forget them.' Moulin stirred uneasily and turned up the fire a notch. 'Working here, you'd think I'd become — if I wasn't already — some sort of automaton. I haven't. I don't think I could do the job adequately if I had. I feel something for each 'customer', as you call them. And bury a little bit of myself with each one.' He smiled to see Joe's eyes flare with concern. 'Don't worry! I shall know when to stop.'

Moulin pointed to the row of thrillers. 'You're not to think, on the cold winter evenings between post-mortems, I allow my imagination to be fired by these things! Lots of people you might admire enjoy them. Jean Cocteau, René

Magritte, Guillaume Apollinaire, Salvador Dali . . . Blaise Cendrars called them 'the Aeneid of Modern Times'!'

'And you can add to your list of playwrights, poets and artists: Sandilands of the Yard,' said Joe comfortably, sensing that the learned doctor was slightly embarrassed to be caught out in his enthusiasm.

'Very well — you're prepared, then? To explore a really outlandish idea?'

Joe nodded.

'Before we start, I must insist — no notes! This is just a chat between two weary men whose brains are ticking over faster perhaps than they should. Agreed?'

'Agreed,' said Joe.

'In 1924, the body of a priest was found. I remember it was the night before All Saints' Day. Your Hallowe'en, I believe?'

Joe nodded again, saying nothing. He sensed that it would not take much of an interruption to put him off a track he was plainly uncomfortable to be following. The man was a scientist, after all. Rational. Logical. Not given to fervid speculation. Intolerant of ridicule.

'I wondered later if that was significant. The man was dangling by a noose to the neck on a bell-rope. The rope was the one that hung from the bell tower of the curé's own church. The tolling started in the early hours of the morning, as the body swayed — in the breeze? It was a windy night . . . Or from a push? We don't know. The sound went unregarded for an hour or so as the good citizens of the well-to-do faubourg huddled deeper into their goose-feather eiderdowns. They might have decided he'd committed suicide — not unknown in the priesthood — had it not been for his other wounds. His robe had been slashed from neck to hem and was heavily bloodstained down the front. His male member had been cut off. Before death.'

'Revenge for some kind of abuse committed by the priest?'

Moulin shrugged. 'I would expect so. No one ever came forward with accusations, let alone evidence. Case closed. Unsolved. The Church, in any case, was glad enough to hush it up.

'And then, later that same year, a rich industrialist whose name I'm certain would be familiar to you died in bed. Not his own bed, but that of a common prostitute in a picturesquely low quarter of the city. The lady was absent and never surfaced again. The corpse of our louche old money-bags was discovered naked, tied up with scarlet velvet ribbons to the bedpost — hands and feet. He'd died from an overdose of hashish. The gentlemen of the press had been alerted before the police and were instantly on the scene with their flash bulbs. Everyone was horrified. Except for the man's five sons. They were now to inherit his fortune, clear of any fear of premature depletion by the extravagant young actress whose charms had led him, a month or so previously, to propose marriage.'

Joe gave a wry smile. 'Next?'

'Last year. Picture the Eiffel Tower. A favourite jumping-off point for the suicidally minded. The body of a young man falls from a crowded viewing platform to splatter itself all over the concourse below. It happens every month. No one sees anything. No one is aware of any suspicious circumstances. The man's fiancée, the spoiled daughter of one of our prominent politicians, is aghast. 'But why the Eiffel Tower?' she sobs. 'The very place where he declared his love and asked me to marry him!' She is distraught. She is inconsolable. But her best friend reveals — spitefully perhaps? — that the boy in question had, in fact, changed his mind since the tryst on the Tower and decided to marry *her*. The first fiancée was, luckily, far away in Nice on holiday with her family at the time of the death and could not possibly be involved in any dirty work.'

'This is a mixed bunch of motives, I'm hearing,' said Joe.

'And here's one for the connoisseur! I've saved the best for last. But, for me, it was the *first* in the sequence, I suppose. Though it wasn't for some weeks that I realized I'd had a pretty strange experience. In 1923. Newly appointed to the Institut and rather overawed by the big city, I wasn't quite sure what to expect — except that everything would be faster, more exciting than I was used to in Normandy. I got a phone call from upstairs telling me to grab my bag, jump into a police car and get over to the Louvre. To the Egyptian rooms on the ground floor. Pandemonium when I got there! And something very odd going on. An American couple alone in one of the galleries had come across a pool of blood at the foot of one of the mummy cases.

You know — those great big ornate coffin things . . . weigh a ton . . . '

'I know them.'

'When I got there — ten minutes after receiving the call — the body hadn't even been discovered. It didn't strike me as strange until later, mesmerized as I was by the quality of the communications in the city: phone, telegraph, police cars standing at the ready outside . . . 'So this is the modern pace!' I thought. 'Must keep up!' And there was a lot of activity to distract me at the museum. A whole chorus of academics — curators, Egyptologists, students — had assembled to see what was going on. Newsmen weren't far behind!

'Luckily, a British official of some sort who happened to be leaving a meeting was collared by the distraught American who'd just avoided putting his foot in something very nasty and this Briton, using the several languages he spoke, backed up by — shall we say — a certain natural authority . . . ' Moulin paused and grinned apologetically at Joe.

'Arrogance, you can say if you wish,' suggested Joe easily. 'We learn it on school playing fields — or charging enemy machine-gun nests armed with a swagger-stick and shouting: 'Follow me, lads!' But I can imagine what you're going to say and — I'd have done the same, I'm afraid.'

'Well, the Englishman took charge. Jack Pollock, his name was, and thank goodness he was there.'

Joe had reached automatically for his notebook but, remembering his promise, he relaxed.

'He calmed everyone down and sent for all the right people. A policeman was on the spot to see fair play, I remember.'

'And you found a body in the case? Dripping blood on to the floor? Not very well hidden?'

'No. I think it was meant to be found. And the finding was timed . . . orchestrated, you might say.'

'Who was in the box?'

'Two bodies. Below: the rightful occupant, a High Priest of some sort, and on top: an alien presence. A professor of Egyptology. Stabbed. Messily. The killer knew enough about knife work to ensure that the body drained itself of blood. Weapon? A type of butcher's knife, I wrote in my report. Something capable of stabbing and ripping open. A pig farmer could advise perhaps? It was never found. But we did find, in the throat, and sucked right down into the breathing passages of the deceased, wads of linen bindings. Ancient linen. Taken from the body of some other mummy. He'd been forced to swallow the stuff.'

'Deeply unpleasant!' Joe could not contain his revulsion.

'That wasn't the worst. I say, you won't arrest me if I make a confession, will you, Sandilands?'

'Good Lord! Depends what you're confessing. If you want to tell me you're the Mastermind behind all this, I'll have you in cuffs at once!'

Moulin smiled, got to his feet and went to take a small box from a shelf. 'I'm going to show you something I stole. From an evidence file. It comes from the scene of the crime.'

He handed the box to Joe who raised his brows in alarm on catching sight of the contents.

'You can handle it. It's been sterilized.'

'Why would you need to do that?' asked Joe, cautiously.

'I removed it from the bloodied bandage lodged in the throat of the corpse of Professor Joachim Lebreton. It was sticky with various body fluids and an oil that had been used to ease the descent of the fabric down the tubes.'

'Charming!' Joe took the golden object gingerly and held it to the light between finger and thumb. 'An amulet?'

'No. Not my job, of course, to establish the provenance of exhibits but no one else seemed interested enough to do it. In the police report it's listed as 'imitation gold medallion, value 5 francs'. It would have been chucked out after a year but I was curious enough to preserve it. Oh, it's not valuable. It's not even ancient. A modern copy — gilded. Crudely done. Anyone with a bit of tin, a chisel and a pot of gold paint could produce the equivalent. Any *mouleur-plaquiste* could churn them out by the hundred. But you'd need to know your Egyptology. This is a bona fide, head and shoulders portrait, you might say.'

'It's a disgusting image! Whoever *is* this fellow? Or is it an animal?' Joe peered more closely. 'It seems to be half god, half bad-tempered greyhound. I know just enough to recognize that it's *not* the rather stylish *jackal*-headed god, Anubis.'

'You're right. But he is a god all the same. And at one time widely venerated in Egypt. It's the son of Ra and brother of Osiris.'

Joe shook his head. 'We're not acquainted. Don't particularly wish to be.'

'You show good taste! His name's Set. Set murdered his brother and scattered his body parts all over Egypt. He debauched his own nephew Horus. In his capacity as Lord of the Desert, he had the power to stir up terrible storms. For the Ancient Egyptians, Set was utterly terrifying — the embodiment of Evil. The God of Evil.'

Joe put the gilded trinket back into its box. 'I'm bringing no charge, Moulin. Let's just keep the lid on him, shall we?'

Moulin, smiling, agreed. 'And why don't you take him away with you? I think I was just hanging on to him until someone who knew what he was about took an interest. You know, Sandilands, I think the purpose of that thing was to drop a hint as to motive for the crime. Out of the victim's mouth came evil? Something on those lines? Again — no suspect was ever arrested. But, bearing in mind the closed circumstances, you'd have to say — an inside job. The man had many enemies. Archaeologist himself, he'd been ruthless in his acquisition of artefacts and had plundered his students' and his fellows' learned works for his own glory. He'd wrecked promising careers by his vitriolic criticism, his sly innuendoes. At least fifty academics must have raised a glass on hearing about the circumstances of his death. Now, they couldn't *all* have been present at the discovery of the body but, Sandilands, a good many *were*. It never occurred to anyone pursuing the case to ask why so many experts, all known to the deceased, were right there on the spot.'

The doctor fell silent. Then: 'There was a moment . . . When the amulet emerged, it dropped to the floor. Someone fainted at the sight of it and had to be taken out and I had the strangest sensation . . . I was acting in a drama. Onstage. Pushed on into the middle of a scene and left to improvise my part. The crowd — who should never have been allowed to remain — weren't a crowd. They were . . . *an audience*. An *invited* audience.'

Moulin took a deep breath, relieved to have unburdened himself. 'I say, Sandilands, does any of this make sense?'

'Certainly does. My friend Sir George was himself pushed in, almost literally onstage, last night to perform the same function. And he *was* actually sent a ticket to the event! But, being an Englishman of a type you recognize, he bustled in rather too actively and got himself arrested for the murder. But, Moulin — four cases, in as many years? Is that all?' Joe asked. And, tentatively: 'If this were some sort of syndicate — shall we say? — taking commissions to carry out crimes spectacular to the general public or crimes deeply satisfying to the one who orders them up, well — we are rather assuming a business, I suppose. And businesses exist to make money. Not sure I'd take the enormous risks involved for the return. Are you? What must they charge? One killing per year? Overheads, knifemen, underlings to pay? Hush money! It wouldn't work.'

Moulin's expression was grim. 'There are many more than four possibilities. I didn't want to over-face you with detail but, if you can give me a week, I'm sure I can make out an expanded list for you. And there might be as many as twenty cases on it. Some less uncertain than others. And that's just Paris. What do we know of other towns? But I agree with your unstated thought — it's not just the financial returns, is it? There's an underlying sense of . . . enjoyment?'

'A sadistic indulgence?' Joe said. 'And with an added element of self-forgiveness — a twisted feeling of justification for the crimes. Someone else has paid for this. Someone else supplied the ingenious requirements of the death — the means, the scenario. So — someone else is to blame. The brain which devised the murders, the executive producer if you like, holds himself no more to blame than the dagger that came bloodstained from the heart of the victim. The guilt can be as easily washed away as the blood. Am I being fanciful?'

'I've no training in psychology!' said Moulin. 'So you must put your theory to others. But I have to say I've travelled that same path, Sandilands.'

'And the latest victim, congealing in one of your drawers? I wonder who dialled up *his* death?' Suddenly decisive, Joe said: 'I'm going to find out who's behind the mask, Moulin. Whose hand held the Afghani dagger *and* whose voice asked for it to be done. I'm going to have 'em both. I can't go back four years in a foreign country, crusading for belated justice, but I can get to the bottom of this one that's landed in my lap. And I'll only get close to the truth by digging up the nastier bits of Somerton's past. Not much chance the widow will confide but I know a man who I can persuade to cough up some details.'

Sensing that his guest was ready to leave and on the point of exhaustion, Moulin got to his feet. 'Wait here, Sandilands, while I nip out and whistle up a taxi for you. Oh, and thinking of the rogue Somerton . . . ' He tapped the cover of the book Joe was still clutching. '*Le mort qui tue*. Read the title again. That's *le mort*, not *la mort*. Dead man — not Death itself. The corpse that kills. Be warned! Have a care for your friend. We don't want an innocent man, blundering in on a sorry episode, to pay for his well-meaning interference on the guillotine. I suspect this man, Somerton, has caused enough havoc in his life, I don't want to think that, from the depths of the morgue, he has the power to kill again.'

14

He chose a dark side street behind the place de la Contrescarpe to pay off his taxi. Feeling mildly foolish but in no way allowing this to make him lower his guard, he waited in a doorway until he was sure he hadn't been followed. When he was fully confident, Joe wandered into the small square lined with cafés and restaurants. The aperitif hour was swinging to a close and the tables were rapidly filling with diners. He browsed the menus displayed on boards outside or scrawled on the windows and made his choice. The Café des Arts, being the biggest and noisiest, had claimed his attention and he went inside to the bar, ordered a Pernod and paid for a telephone connection.

He'd committed Bonnefoye's number to memory and destroyed the card and, in his state of fatigue, hoped he'd got it right.

The same lively female answered his tentative: '*Umm . . . allô?*'

'There you are! Just in time for supper. You know how to get here? Good. See you in two minutes! Bye!'

No names, no details, he noticed. And none asked for. Whoever she was, Bonnefoye's female was well trained. And hospitable.

Joe was conscious of the unusual honour the Inspector was doing him and Sir George by extending this invitation to take shelter in his own home. The French rarely asked friends to dinner at their flat or house. Friendships were pursued in the café or restaurant or at shooting weekends in the country. If the Englishman's home was his castle, the Frenchman's was a keep with the drawbridge permanently up to repel invaders or visitors.

Bonnefoye had been surprised and enchanted with his first taste of British hospitality the previous winter. Welcoming the Frenchman on an official visit to London, Joe had taken responsibility for the young officer and invited him to spend a long weekend with him at his sister's house in Surrey. An instant love-affair had flowered. The English family had fallen for Bonnefoye at first sight and Jean-Philippe had been equally smitten. He probably considered he was in Joe's debt in the hospitality stakes but Joe was, nevertheless, surprised and charmed by the gesture.

And concerned. The man kept his address a close secret and doubtless for excellent reasons. Joe had no intention of bringing danger within his orbit. He was keeping up his guard. He ambled around the square again, marking his exit, and when he was sure he was unobserved, he slipped off into the rue Mouffetard. A lamp-lighter was moving down the street creating romantic pools of light and Joe hurried to get ahead of him, hugging the shadows. He was looking for a baker's shop. In the alleyway to the side of it he found a door which opened at his tap.

He was greeted by Bonnefoye who closed and

bolted the door behind him. 'We've got him settled in,' he told Joe as he led the way up a flight of stairs. 'All's well! Through here — it's a bit crowded and you'll have to share a room with me if you want to give the Ambassador a miss tonight. I gave Sir George our only guest room.'

Sir George was sitting at a kitchen table shelling peas. He was under instruction from a middle-aged woman who, with her striking dark looks, could be no other than Bonnefoye's mother, and he appeared to be doing well at his task. His manicured thumbnail was slicing along with skill, making short work of the pods. When his mentor turned to greet Joe, he stuffed a podful of peas into his mouth and was sharply rapped on the knuckles.

'Now add the spring onions and the butter . . . more lettuce leaves on top . . . tiny drop of stock . . . don't drown it . . . and there you are! Put it on the stove. Back burner . . . So glad to meet you at last, Commander!' The voice from the telephone. Youthful, bossy and eager. 'I'm running a little late this evening and I've had to call up reinforcements.' She flashed a devastating smile at George. He grinned and mumbled a greeting across the table, content to take a back seat in the proceedings.

Madame Bonnefoye was much younger than George — perhaps fifty years old but, in the way of Frenchwomen, still attractive. She whisked off her grey pinafore to reveal a black widow's dress enlivened by a pink scarf draped at the neck. Bonnefoye's father, he had told Joe, had fallen at Verdun.

'Jean-Philippe! A glass of wine for the Commander! It's one from our home village in Burgundy. We bring it back in quantities. You boys have ten minutes to exchange information before you present yourselves at table. It will be a very simple supper: I made some soup to start with, then the butcher had some excellent veal which will be good with George's *petits pois à l'étuvé*, followed by cheese and, since Jean-Philippe tells me you Englishmen are fond of sweet things, I've got some chocolate éclairs from the pâtissier.'

Joe decided he'd died and gone to heaven and, as he'd always thought it might, heaven smelled of herb soup and rang with a woman's laughter.

He went to sit in the small salon of the apartment with Jean-Philippe, listening to the chatter from the kitchen. George's stately but adventurous French sentences rolled out, to be punctuated by sharp bursts of amusement and exclamation from Madame Bonnefoye.

'First things first,' said Joe. 'Security. I'm as sure as I can be I wasn't followed here. You?'

'Sure. But we mustn't reduce the level of precaution. A message came by telephone late this afternoon. From Miss Watkins, I'm afraid. One of my staff took it down and I've translated it but I think it's very clear. All too clear!' He passed Joe a scrap of paper.

My new boyfriend very keen! He even came shopping with me. Was compelled to go on the offensive. He has a two-inch red scar on his left jaw.

Joe was aghast. He picked out the word which most alarmed him. '"Offensive', she says?'

Bonnefoye cleared his throat. 'This ties in with a report we had from the Galeries Lafayette,' he said. 'To be precise — from the ladies' underwear department. A customer lodged a complaint against a man she alleged was following and threatening her. Two assistants, who remarked the young lady grappling with a tall man in a dark overcoat, went to her aid and attempted to detain him. Unfortunately he was able to effect an escape.'

'And the scar? I hardly dare ask!'

'. . . was already a feature of his physiognomy before he encountered Miss Watkins.'

'Thank goodness for that! But we should never have involved her.'

'I agree. And it's too late now to *uninvolve* her.' Bonnefoye sighed. 'But look — if these people are as good as we think they are, they'll make enquiries and discover that she has absolutely no connection with Sir George and leave her to get on with her hearty tennis life. They'll assume that she was just spooked by an over-zealous piece of shadowing. He'll probably get a ticking off from his boss — should have had more sense than to follow her into the lingerie section. And Miss Watkins has certainly got closer — physically at any rate — to the tool they're using than we have.'

'That scar? Any use to us?'

'Yes, could be. I've reported it to the division that keeps our Bertillon records. All marks of that kind are listed, classified and kept on card. If the chap has committed a crime before, his features will be on file and indexed. They ought to be able to come up with a few suggestions.

'The thing that's worrying me, Joe, is their apparent preoccupation with Sir G. They seem to have him in their sights. But why? Did he see something he's not told anyone yet? Does he know something he ought not to know? You'll have to grill him. I can't seem to get near him. Any attempt on my part at putting a few questions gets batted aside — with the greatest good humour of course. Genial, avuncular, smelling of roses — and he's as slippery as a bar of soap. But tell me — how did you get on with the widow?'

After a draught or two of the Chablis he was handed, Joe launched into an account of his evening.

'She was off to Fouquet's, eh?' Bonnefoye was entertained by the thought. 'I'll make enquiries. We'll know tomorrow who she met, what they ate, what time they left and where they went afterwards! Are you thinking — there's one lady who is delighted that old Somerton was done to death?'

'She told me she had no idea her husband was in Paris — they hadn't communicated for years. And, of course, she was hundreds of miles away from the scene of the crime . . . ' Joe began dubiously.

'Well, if your mad theory about the crime-order-catalogue business is correct, she *would* be. That's the whole point of it. They have the telephone in England and the wires run as far as Paris, remember.'

'Not sure she fits the frame,' said Joe. 'Glad enough, yes, to be rid of the old boy. As, indeed, might be the *son* I discover she has. The one who succeeds to the title. And who knows what else! We might check on *him* and the size and nature of his inheritance. But why would she or he or they bother with all the palaver? I mean the showmanship element? The theatre . . . the dagger. I watched her examine the knife. I'll swear it meant nothing to her. She was curious, fascinated even in a ghoulish way, but there was no flicker of recognition. Just an element of his past life she'd rather not think about. Why didn't they simply have him pushed under a bus or off a bridge? And why wait all these years?'

Bonnefoye shrugged and poured out more wine. 'Still — glad enough to have them as suspects two and three. I like to collect a good hand.'

Joe raised a questioning eyebrow. 'Your first suspect?'

Jean-Philippe was suddenly grave. 'Sir George, of course. I don't like it any more than you do but the man's up to his neck in whatever's going on. You'd have to be blind not to see that.'

Joe produced the doctor's copy of *Le mort qui tue* from his pocket and slapped it down on to the table between them. 'Look at the title, Jean-Philippe. If we work with your suppositions, Sir George will die. An innocent man guillotined for a corpse we haven't the wits to account for. Somerton will be the death of him, and with our co-operation. I can't shake off the feeling that someone's pulling our strings, playing the tune we're dancing to. And that puts my back up! The pathologist, Dr Moulin, had some interesting observations to pass on. He's formed theories which support Francine Raissac's strange ideas.'

He took the small box from his pocket and revealed the contents. 'Exhibit B. He passed this on too. And listen, will you, to the story the doctor had to tell.'

Bonnefoye listened, wholly involved in the story, turning the gold amulet between his fingers, his face showing fascination and revulsion at the ugliness of the features of the god. Finally: 'The God of Evil, you say? Brother of the good God, Osiris? And his murderer?'

'Yes. Set was worshipped throughout Egypt for many centuries. But as a god of goodness. He and Osiris were peas in a pod. But then, apparently, he turned to wickedness and was struck off everyone's calling list. His subsequent career plumbed the depths of iniquity, you might say. A recognizable myth — in many cultures you find a reference to the evil obverse of a coin. Cain and Abel . . . And take Lucifer — after all, the name means 'Bringer of Light'. He started off on the side of the angels. *Was* one of the angels.'

Bonnefoye picked up the crime novel and began to riffle through its pages. 'Have you seen it yet? The link between your book and your amulet?'

Joe shook his head.

'Good stories, these! The theme still fires the imagination, you see? Down the centuries and right through into the twentieth.'

Joe didn't quite see.

'The evil Fantômas is pursued in each story by a police inspector from my own outfit, the Brigade Criminelle, no less. Inspector Juve, the good guy! And no prizes for guessing Juve's secret identity. He's the long-lost twin brother of Fantômas.'

'Juve and Fantômas, Osiris and Set?'

'Two minutes, boys! Heavens! Is this how you waste your time? The Série Noire? Don't you have enough real life crime to occupy your time? And who's your ugly friend? Not sure I want *him* in my drawing room.'

'He's the man we're looking for, Maman, and who's looking for us! Let me introduce you — he's the God of Evil. And our nameless killer I think now has — according to Joe — an identity. Let's call him Set, shall we?'

Madame Bonnefoye considered for a moment and then said soberly: 'Well, if Set comes calling, he'll run into some fire-power! Your Lebel, Jean-Philippe, the pistol I see the Commander has on his right hip, the Luger Sir George has tucked in his upper left-hand inside pocket and my soup ladle. Come to table now!'

⋆ ⋆ ⋆

After a long and delicious meal, Jean-Philippe's mother herded the men back into the salon with coffee and brandy, closed the door on them and began to clatter her way through the clearing up.

Sir George put on an instant show of affability and frank co-operation. 'Now — I'm sure you chaps must have a question or two of your own to . . . ' He was expansive, he was slightly wondering why they had held off for so long from questioning him. He knew he was cornered.

'Indeed, we do, George, and this time you're not ducking them,' said Joe firmly. 'People's lives — including, I do believe, your own — depend on your answers. So you must stop all this bluffing and circumlocution and come clean. I will know if you're lying. Now, I have a list of questions to put to you.'

Sir George nodded.

Joe decided to catch him off balance by launching an easy throw but from an unexpected quarter. Start them on the easy questions; establish a rhythm of truthful responses and the slight hesitation before a lie is told will be picked up by a keen ear.

'John Pollock?' he said. 'Or Jack Pollock — whichever you prefer. Tell us about him.'

'Cousin Jack? Oh, very well. Son of my father's very much younger sister, my Aunt Jane, who married a man called Pollock. Only son: John Eugene. He was never a friend, you understand. Twenty-year age gap. Looks on me more as an uncle. Little Jackie! A delightful child! Clever boy and with the Jardine good looks! He must be in his mid-thirties by now. He's working in Paris, as you remember from Fourier's notes. He was keen on a diplomatic career when he came out of the army and I was able to put his name in front of someone who was, in turn, able to give him a leg up. Find him a niche, you might say. And they haven't regretted it. Doing well, by all accounts. Haven't seen him since a year or two after the war ended. 1921? Possibly. I remember he wasn't looking too sharp then — recuperating in London. But he had a good war. Quite the hero, in his way.'

'Your cousin sends his regards and promises he'll be in touch.'

'Good. Good. I look forward to that.'

'I'm afraid we'll have to tell him any meeting between the two of you will have to be put on hold. Officially you're in the custody of the Police Judiciaire in a lock-up somewhere on the island. No one but the three of us knows you're here and that's how it must remain until we've cleared you.'

'Very well. Sensible precaution. He'll be the first to understand and approve. Very security-minded, naturally. Next?'

'Now, sir.' Joe gathered his thoughts. The next bit was not so straightforward. 'I'm hoping you feel able to supply us with the name of someone who witnessed your appearance at the theatre and can vouch for the fact that you were in your place across the width of the hall when the murder occurred — assuming it to have happened during the finale?'

'Yes, I do. Been thinking about it. Racking the old brain, you know. And the name's come back to me: Wilberforce Jennings.'

'Who?' Joe was startled. This was not what he was expecting. He'd been leading George to expand on the information he had slid into — or allowed to escape into — the conversation in

Fourier's office. Joe's mind was running on a beautiful and unscrupulous woman with a penchant for Campari-soda. And murder and blackmail and extortion and deceit. But here was Wilberforce Jennings stealing the spotlight.

'Old school chum. 'Willie', we called him. I was surprised to see him. You know how you gaze around the audience to see if there's anyone you know — well, there was. Jennings. The most frightful little creep, I remember, and I may have completely misidentified him, but he was in the sixth row of the stalls at the end of the row. No idea whether he recognized me. You could always ask, I suppose. If you can find him. He may have allowed his gaze to rest on me in the concluding moments.'

'When he could be looking at la belle Josephine and a hundred chorus girls wearing not so much as a bangle between them? Worth a try, I suppose. You never know your luck,' said Joe doubtfully. 'Can you oblige, Bonnefoye?'

'Easy. We have access to records of every foreigner using accommodation in the city. There are about six hotels the English prefer to use. We'll try them first.'

'And now, George, we've got you in your box . . . The chairs — pulled into a companionable huddle . . . the tray of convivial drinks served and consumed. Tell us about your mystery guest. Who was she? Why are you twisting about in an effort to keep her identity from Fourier?'

Irritated by George's dogged silence, he tried a full assault. 'Alice Conyers paid you a visit, did she? Yes, I knew she'd survived. Though I had no idea she was in France.'

'It's hard to imagine, eh, Joe? You're expecting your cousin and there bobs up at your elbow a girl you thought had died in terrible circumstances five years ago. I was never more surprised! She seemed well and happy and sent you her fond regards.'

'She has good reason to remember me with fondness,' said Joe bitterly. 'But why did she show herself to *you*? I always thought the two of you were pretty thick but . . . all the same . . . ' Too late he heard the tetchiness amounting to jealousy in his voice. 'A risky manoeuvre on her part, I'd have thought,' he said more firmly. 'You could have arrested her!'

'I did. She escaped.' George was breezily defiant.

Joe snorted in exasperation. 'Sir, are you saying you had the woman in your grasp and you let her loose?'

'That's about it. Yes. And, Joe, that's exactly where I want her — on the loose. At liberty, to go where she pleases.'

Into the astonished silence he set about his explanation. With rather less than his usual confidence he spoke: 'I've resigned my position, you know. I'm free for the first time in my life of duty, protocol, intrigue, politicking of any kind. I'm not so old I can't enjoy the rest of my life. Got all my faculties and bags of energy. Knees not wonderful but I hear they can do amazing things in Switzerland with knees. Funnily enough, at the very moment when *you* might say my life was hanging by a thread, I've realized the value of it. It came to me on the bank of the Seine this morning. I'm going to make good use of whatever years are left to me and I'm not starting on them by taking the life or liberty of another. Especially not a woman like Alice whom you rightly surmise I have always held in esteem and affection.'

The expression in the blue eyes he turned on Joe was, for once, not distorted by guile, amusement or cynicism. The eyes were direct and piercing and Joe found it hard to meet them. How could he accuse George of negligence in letting Alice Conyers go free when he'd done exactly the same thing himself five years before?

'And lastly, before you fall asleep, my boy, you'll be wanting to hear about the rascal Somerton. Do try to concentrate. You really ought to know what it was he did to make a mighty number of people want to stick a dagger in him. Including yours truly!'

15

George took a fortifying swig of his brandy and lapsed into thought.

'Look here, chaps,' he said finally, 'I know you're both men of the world and violence is your stock in trade, so to speak, but what I have to tell you is shocking and offensive. In the extreme. You must be prepared. It may be that, when you understand the kind of man he was, you'll be less eager to pursue his killer. A plague-infested rat . . . a striking cobra . . . Somerton . . . the world would always be well rid of them.

'He was commanding officer of a military station in the north of India. Before the war. Known to me — we'd met briefly during a tour on the Frontier and I'd formed a dislike for the fellow then. The affair I'm about to mention was hushed up to avoid bringing disgrace on the British Army at the time so — if you'll excuse me — I'll respect that and give you no names, no pack drill.

'You'll know, Joe, that when outfits turn rotten, you always find the cause of it is the commanding officer. And Somerton's was a rotten outfit. Oh, outwardly crisp — their drill and appearance could never be faulted. Indeed, in the way of such men, he was a stickler for detail, regimentation. So, the fact that he was running a brutish, bullying crew, moulded by him in his own image, was likely to be overlooked. They were never seriously tested militarily — I'm speaking of the period before the war when there was always the danger of units turning soft through inactivity and boredom — so I can't speak for their fighting qualities. After the event, the whole corps was broken up and dispersed. I presume they went to France and many must have perished on the battlefields, along with the rest of the army of the day. I'm probably the only man left alive who would be willing to tell the tale but there must be many more who remember and will always stay silent.

'There was a native village on the outskirts of the station . . . usual arrangement. Many of the local men undertook work for the army. One day the rubbish collectors, going about their business, found a body on the rubbish tip. It was the corpse of a young girl from their village. They all recognized her. She was the daughter of the dhobi — the laundryman.' Sir George was uneasy with his story, his delivery flat and deliberately uninvolving. 'They thought at first she'd been torn apart by jackals. The station doctor was summoned. Fast turnover of doctors in that unit. They never stayed long before asking for a transfer and this one was newly arrived. He involved himself before consulting the commanding officer. Had the body brought in for examination.

'The girl had been the victim of multiple assaults. Of a sexual nature. She'd been raped. Many times. Also beaten and cut with a dagger and, finally, strangled. She was twelve years old.' George's head drooped and he seemed unable to carry on.

Joe and Bonnefoye could find no words to encourage him.

'Somerton tried to cover it all up. No need of a report for such a matter. Who was lodging a complaint? The father? Pay him off! A few rupees would close his mouth. But the medical officer was made of stern enough stuff to stand up to him. He sent in a full report to Somerton's superior officer and he sent a copy to me.'

'Was a proper investigation conducted?' asked Joe.

'I insisted on it. I put my best men in to get to the bottom of it and when I heard what they'd discovered I took steps. They found that the girl had been sent — against her will and against custom — into the camp to deliver items of laundry urgently needed by the CO. Women never ventured near the place as a rule — the men had a reputation for savagery of one sort or another. The poor child must have been terrified to be given the errand but girls in that country obey their fathers. She'd delivered it to Somerton's quarters. She'd been seen going inside and coming out again. This was the story my men picked up from every witness. A word-perfect performance, they judged. Too perfect. Rehearsed. They went to work and after some days finally found sitting before them at interview a young chap fresh out from England and as yet untrained in the ways of that regiment. He spilled the beans.

'Put his own life in danger, of course, by his assertions and we had to take him away directly to a place of safety and hold him in reserve for the trial. He stated that the girl had indeed come out of the CO's quarters but thrown out screaming and bleeding and in great distress — by Somerton himself. Some of his men had gathered round on hearing the din and our recruit had been horrified to hear his instructions: 'She's all yours, lads, if you can be bothered!'

'Our chap ran away and hid and no one was aware that he'd seen anything, but he was able to give a full list of those involved. We had the names and rolled it up from there. The men had bragged about it to each other openly afterwards. They never knew exactly who had shopped them. It wasn't difficult to get a confession from most of them.'

'And you left him alive, George?' said Joe quietly.

'A court martial was held and he was found guilty. Kicked out of the army with every ounce of parade and scorn they could muster. A pariah for the rest of his days. I thought that was punishment enough. At the time. I wish now I'd had the bugger shot. I could have arranged it.'

'Why did you hold off?' Bonnefoye wanted to know.

'The fellow had a wife and young son back home. And, on the whole, a cashiering makes less of a splash than an execution.' He sighed. 'Discretion, always discretion.'

Suddenly angry, he burst out: 'And now see

where discretion and pity have landed me! In danger of losing my head because the silly bugger's got his comeuppance! And *I* didn't even have the satisfaction of plunging a dagger into his snake's heart! It's a thankless task you two fellows have got on your hands. If you find out who ordered up this assassination I shall have to ask you to congratulate him before you slip the cuffs on.'

⋆ ⋆ ⋆

'He *didn't* kill Somerton, did he?' Bonnefoye commented when Sir George, finally exhausted, had excused himself and gone off to his room.

'What makes you change your mind?'

'At the end, when he lost his temper and spoke without restraint . . . I believed him when he said he would have plunged the dagger into the man's heart. He would have done just that. Quick and soldierly. He'd quite forgotten for the moment that Somerton had died from a gash from ear to ear. I can't see Sir George sawing away like a pork butcher to bleed a man to death, can you?'

'No, I can't. But I'll tell you what, Bonnefoye — the wretched man's gone off to bed leaving us with a mass of things to do tomorrow. I say, will you . . . ?'

'Yes. I've arranged for a deputy to take my place and bring me notes of the conference afterwards. I'll be of far better use to international crime-fighting if I pursue this case actively. We'll allocate tasks in the morning

. . . Though I leave the Embassy to you — I think you have the entrée!'

'And, speaking of entrées — your evening, Bonnefoye. How did you get on in the boulevard du Montparnasse?'

'Ah, yes! Mount Parnassus, home of Apollo and the Muses! Well, there was music and verse, certainly, but it wasn't at all classical. The address Francine Raissac gave you turned out to be a jazz café. And, you know, Joe, I'd have gone in there anyway! The music I heard as I was passing was irresistible. The performers were a mixture of black and white. There was a guitar but a guitar played very fast, a violin and a clarinet and something else I can't remember . . . a saxophone? Odd assortment of instruments — you'd swear they only just met and put it together. But brilliant! And the crowd was loving it.'

'Did it have a name, your café?' asked Joe, intrigued.

'Oh Lord! Some animal . . . they're all called after birds or animals, have you noticed? Le Perroquet . . . Le Boeuf sur le Toit . . . L'Hirondelle . . . Le Lapin Agile . . . And here's another one — Le Lapin Blanc — that was it. It's a bit further out than the Dôme and not as far as the Closerie des Lilas.'

'What sort of people were in the crowd? Did you know any of them?'

'No one on our books, if that's what you mean. Upright citizens, I'd say. Large number of Americans — you'd expect it in that part of Paris. Poets, painters, photographers and their models and muses all packing the place out. Sixth arrondissement bohemian, to use an old-fashioned word! But living up to it — you know, a bit self-conscious and not the real thing. Every client looking over his shoulder spotting the latest outrageous artist. And every outrageous artist looking over *his* shoulder spotting the *mouchards* from the police anti-national department. Who's likely to be snitching on *them*? The local commissariat is still on the alert for extreme views of one sort or another. Marxism, Fascism, intellectualism. Dadaism. Is that a word? They especially don't like that! We're supposed to be on the watch for it. Not sure what we're expected to do with it if we find it . . . '

'Anyone spot *you*?'

'No, indeed! I thought I blended in rather well. And no one was making inflammatory statements. The clientele weren't annoying anyone when I was there. Usual mixture of thrill-seekers and thrill-providers. Well-heeled but quirky. Silk scarves rather than ties, two-tone shoes, little black dresses and cocktail hats — you'd have felt very much at home, Joe.'

'I'd never wear a cocktail hat to a café,' muttered Joe.

'Unless you were going on somewhere. No . . . the seediest customers were a couple of gigolos . . . nothing too flamboyant . . . and a pair of politicians. The rest were businessmen, rich tourists and poseurs, I'd say. It's obviously the place to be seen this month.'

'Nothing unusual? No dope? No under-the-counter absinthe?'

'None that I noticed and I notice more than most. The only odd thing, and it didn't occur to me until I was on the point of leaving, was that two of the men had gone off into the back quarters, separately, and neither had come out again. I followed the second of them after a discreet interval. Cloakrooms, as you'd expect. The gentlemen's accommodation was impressive — as good as a top hotel — and I'd assume the ladies' was of equal comfort. Nothing untoward going on. The man I was pursuing was not in the room. He'd disappeared. Alongside the cloakrooms was a carpeted staircase.'

'You didn't resist?'

'Whistling casually, I followed on up to a landing. A table with a lavish display of flowers and three closed doors. No numbers. They each had a — fanlight? — a pane of glass over the top. Well, I judge the management have some sort of mirror system in place because the middle door opened at once, before I'd even knocked, and a maître d'hôtel type appeared. Large, ugly, unwelcoming but exquisitely polite. Well trained. He sent me straight back downstairs. I was trespassing on private property, apparently.'

'Some sort of house of ill repute, are you thinking? A house of assignation?'

'Yes. Something in the nature of the Sphinx which is close by — just off the boulevard by the cemetery. There's a call for it. Tourists seeking thrills and well able to pay over the odds for their indulgence. And citizens come over from the affluent Right Bank into the Latin Quarter in search of a slight frisson of danger, a whiff of spice, but not the out and out dissolution on offer round every corner in Montmartre. Another attraction is that the *maisons d'illusion* of this type guarantee anonymity. From a perfectly innocent meeting place, thronged with people — like the jazz club — clients present themselves, are checked and gain entrance through an antechamber. They leave through a different door. All very discreet. You could run into your brother-in-law who's an archdeacon and you needn't blush for your presence there. You'd be just another fan of that wonderful saxophonist.'

'This Sphinx you mentioned . . . ?'

' . . . is generally reckoned the top of the tree. It's reputed for the calibre of its girls. They started with fifteen and now have about fifty. Beautiful of course but also well-educated and charming — good conversationalists. Many of them — or so it's said — have aristocratic pretensions: Russian princesses, Roumanian countesses, English nannies.'

'Top drawer stuff!'

'And it's fresh and modern. Forget the red plush decadence of the Chabanais and the One-Two-Two! The Sphinx is avant-garde, art deco . . . Good Lord! It's even air-conditioned! It's the sort of place where responsible fathers take their sons for their first serious experience with the fair sex.'

'And our nameless establishment over the White Rabbit jazz club may have set up as a rival?'

'Perfectly possible. There's an increasing

demand. Every luxury liner disgorges thousands of eager sensation-seekers. Restaurants, theatre, night spots — they've never been so busy. And of course the brothels are going to cash in too. The Corsicans who used to run this side of life have suddenly lost authority and the market's ripe for the taking. The North Africans are moving in but there's a strong challenge from the lads of the thirteenth arrondissement. They're flexing their muscles, getting Grandpa's zarin down from the attic, and are ready for the fight.' Bonnefoye became suddenly serious as he added: 'But more than knives. Some of them have guns they didn't turn in after the war ended. And the men themselves . . . they're not untried lads. They survived the war. They're trained killers. Killers who perhaps got used to the excitement of war and miss it?'

'But if the guard dog was told not to admit a clean-cut and clearly solvent chap like yourself — well, that's a bit strange, isn't it? I'd have expected them to have dragged you in the moment you stuck your head over the parapet.'

'Yes. I was quite miffed! I went back down into the bar and got myself a drink. Found myself next to the two I'd marked down as politicians — I vaguely recognized one and, since they were talking about government grants on animal fodder in Normandy, I think I got that right. I'd parked myself next to the two most boring men in the room! I knocked back my vermouth and was on the point of leaving when the conversation next to me started to break up. It's always worthwhile listening when good-byes are being said. People say things with their guard down that perhaps they ought not to — and more loudly.'

'Like — 'Remember me to your brother and tell him to count on my help. The Revolution's next Tuesday, is it? I'll be there!' '

Bonnefoye grinned. 'In fact, my man said, 'Remember me to your wife. Her soirée's next Saturday, isn't it? I'll be there!' It was the bit he added that was worth hearing. At least I *think* it was worth hearing. You must be the judge. He leaned over and in a hearty, all-chaps-together voice said: 'I'm just off to the land of wonders . . . interested? No?' And he walked out through the back door.'

'Say it again — that last bit,' said Joe uneasily. 'The bit about wonders. Where did he say he was going?'

Bonnefoye repeated his words in French: ' . . . *au pays des merveilles* . . . '

'*Au pays des merveilles*,' murmured Joe. He was remembering a book he'd bought for Dorcas the previous summer to help her with her French reading. It hadn't been well received. 'Gracious, Joe! This is for infants or for grown-ups who haven't managed to. It's sillier than Peter Pan. I can't be doing with it!' His mind was racing down a trail. He was seeing, illuminated by a beam of hot Indian sunshine, a book, fallen over sideways on a shelf in an office in Simla, the cover beginning to curl, a peacock's feather marking the place. The same edition. *Alice au pays des merveilles*. *Alice's Adventures in Wonderland*. Alice.

Surely not. He knew what Dorcas's judgement would have been if he'd confided his mad notion: 'Sandilands in Fairyland.'

The idea would not go away. Alice Conyers, fleeing India, Gladstone bag stuffed with ill-gotten gains of one sort or another, stopping over in Paris — might she have used her formidable resources to set herself up in a business of which she had first-hand knowledge? She might well. Bonnefoye waited in silence, sensing that Joe was struggling to rein in and order his thoughts.

'Tell you a story, Bonnefoye! At least Part One of a story. I think you may be about to make a bumbling entrance with me into Part Two. As the Knave of Hearts and the Executioner, perhaps?'

Bonnefoye was intrigued but scornful. 'That's all very fascinating but it's as substantial as a spider's web, Joe!'

'But we'll only find out the strength by putting some weight on it, I suppose. Your face is known there now. My turn to shoot down the rabbit hole. It's my ugly mug that they'll see leering in their mirrors next time! And, if madame's there, I think I know just the formula to persuade her to let me in. There's something I shall need . . . Two items. Didn't I see a ladies' hat shop down there in the Mouffe? Two doors north of the boulangerie? Good. What time do they open, do you suppose?'

16

Harry Quantock was again performing front-of-house duties at the Embassy. He recognized Joe at once and greeted him breezily.

'Good morning, Commander! Good morning! We got your message and it's all laid on. Come along to the back quarters, will you? You don't merit a *salon rouge* reception today,' he teased. 'Much more workaday surroundings, I'm afraid. Jack Pollock's expecting you in his office. Being on the Ambassador's staff, an attaché, if you like, at least he's housed in relative comfort.'

Joe was shown into a ground-floor office at the rear of the building, looking out on to a courtyard garden. It was high-ceilinged, wood-panelled and stately. The walls were studded at intervals with sepia photographs of pre-war cricket teams. Joe noted the progression from public schoolboys to the undergraduates of an Oxford college whose first eleven was outstanding for its striped blazers, striped caps and ugly expressions. These were followed in the line-up by examples of the University side. The only touch of modernity was a black and gold telephone sitting on a mahogany desk next to a silver vase of spring flowers. A tall window was open, letting in the scent of lilac blossom and the sound of traffic rumbling along the Champs-Élysées.

The attaché was seated behind his desk

thumbing through a file, one eye on the door.

Joe was prepared for a family resemblance but, even so, he was taken aback by the young version of Sir George who leapt from his seat and bounded across the room to greet him with a cheerful bellow. Pollock's handshake was dry and vigorous, his welcome the equal of — and reminiscent of — that of any large yellow dog that Joe had ever met.

'You'll have a cup of coffee, or do you prefer tea, Commander? Tea? Harry — could you . . . ? Let's sit down, shall we? I won't waste your time — busy man — I'll just say how sorry I am that you've been dragged into this mess, Sandilands. Lucky for us you were here on the spot, or in mid-flight to be precise, when all this burst over our heads. But — first things first — how are the Varsity doing?'

'Varsity? Doing?' For a moment, Joe was perplexed.

'The Surrey match,' Pollock prompted. 'First fixture of the season.'

'Ah, yes. Last I heard, I rather think they were losing 3–1 at half-time.'

The stunned silence lasted only a second. Pollock threw back his head and laughed. 'Of course — Edinburgh man, aren't you? Like my old relative, George. And how you must be cursing him! He might have expected to get into some trouble or other by taking a box at the Folies — might even have been relishing the thought — but surely not trouble of this magnitude. Never heard the like! He has told you that the ticket didn't come from *me*, has he?

Good! I wouldn't like it assumed that I was remotely responsible. Not my style! But, I say, Sandilands — if *I* didn't send the fatal billet — are we wondering who did? It must be someone, apart from myself, who knew he was going to be in Paris and is aware of our relationship. It could only be known through an ambassadorial contact — here in Paris, in London or in Delhi, I suppose.'

'You've just narrowed it down to a thousand people,' said Joe. 'Thank you!'

Jack Pollock grinned, leaned over the desk and added: 'I can narrow it more usefully to someone who knows that there's no way in this world my cousin would have recognized my handwriting. I'd swear the last sample he had was the gracious note I wrote in appreciation of the mechanical tiger he sent me when I was at school.'

Pollock's eyes twinkled at the memory. He looked at Joe, friendly but calculating. 'Wonderful contraption! With a bit of devilish skill, a dab or two of honey and lashings of schoolboy callousness I contrived to get my tiger to snap up flies!'

'The Tipu Sultan of the Lower Third?'

'Exactly! I was allowed to demonstrate it on Sundays after tea. George had taken me to see the original life-sized tiger at the Victoria and Albert — you know — the one Tipu had made . . . *His* tiger was in the act of eating a British soldier. I'll never forget the roars and screams it emitted when someone wound it up! And the way the victim's arm twitched as the tiger held him in his jaws!'

Joe laughed. 'George would know how to please. He has a certain magic with children. I've watched it working.'

'Pity the old feller has none of his own,' said Pollock, suddenly serious again. 'What a waste of many things.' He snapped back into the conversation he had himself interrupted. 'But the note — I have no reason to suppose he'd recognize my scrawl. We were never frequent — or even regular — correspondents. Distance and the exigencies of the war rather put paid to intimacy of that kind. And the transition from uncle-nephew to equal adult cousins has never had a chance to take place. Not sure how it will all pan out . . . we'll just have to wait and see.'

Joe listened to the outpouring of eager speculation and confidences, smiling and agreeing.

'Now tell me — what have you done with him? I'm assuming you've put the boot in imperially and sprung him from whatever hell-hole they'd banged him up in?' The question was put abstractedly, Pollock's attention on the tray of tea a manservant carried in. 'Just set it down over there, will you, Foxton? Milk or lemon, Sandilands?'

'Milk, please.'

Returning to the first question he'd been asked: 'I'm afraid not,' said Joe carefully. 'Still incarcerated, I'm sorry to say. Reasonably comfortable, I insisted on that, but still in a lock-up on the island. The authorities appear to be unimpressed by Sir George's standing. I shall have another try later today. It may come down

— or rather up — to a personal representation from the Ambassador himself.'

Pollock was angry. Whoever said that blue eyes could only be cool should have seen Pollock's at this moment, Joe thought. They blazed. 'What impertinence! Poor old George! He must be let out before the end of the day. Ring in and reassure me he is comfortably settled back in his hotel — where's he staying? The Bristol? Of course. Well, the moment he gets there I'll go and see him. And you, Sandilands — where are you staying?'

'I'm at the Hotel Ambassador on the boulevard Haussman.'

Pollock made a note.

'And all went well with the widow yesterday? Thank you for undertaking that unpleasant task!'

'Unpleasant perhaps but not the harrowing experience it most often is. The lady seemed not particularly grieved to find her husband dead.' Joe wondered how far he could pursue this line but the slight nod of agreement he received from Pollock encouraged him. 'In fact she emerged from the identification scene a changed woman, I'd say. Reassured. Confident. Feeling a certain amount of release, no doubt? She was looking forward to an evening's assignation at Fouquet's with a companion whose identity is as yet unknown to us.' He caught the echo of deadly police phrasing and added: 'Give a lot to know who the lucky chap was!'

'Oh, I think I can help you with that!' said Pollock, enjoying the intrigue. 'Doubtless the gentleman she sat next to on the plane — her travelling companion. Her constant companion for the past year, I understand. A Major Slingsby-Thwaite.' Pollock lowered his voice though there was no risk of his being overheard. 'Between you and me — bit of an adventurer! But then . . . perhaps that's exactly what the lady's after — a bit of an adventurer — after all those bleak years of being married to a murderous swine. I take it my cousin has filled you in on the activities of the unlamented Somerton?'

'I've had a pungent account of the case. And agree with Sir George — the man got no less than he deserved. But you seem to be very well informed as to his movements, Pollock? Why does His Britannic Majesty's Government take such an interest in an ex-this, a disgraced-that? A wandering has-been?'

'Current nuisance! For many a year. We've always kept tabs on him, watched his movements around Europe. Passed him on to the next chap with a sigh of relief. The man made many enemies — he was always likely to be a target for revenge or embarrassing mayhem of one sort or another. And a thorough cashiering, though well-deserved, doesn't, in my experience, turn a villain into a saint overnight. 'Off with his buttons!' is in no way as effective as 'Off with his head!' '

Pollock frowned for a moment and looked at Joe with speculation. 'You may not approve, of course. But I see you are a military man. You must agree with Richard III when he was having his problems with . . . now who was it . . . ?'

'Lord Hastings, it was, who provoked that famous order for execution, I believe,' said Joe, coming to his rescue. 'In Shakespeare's play.'

'Quite right! Someone ought to have advised Sir George similarly at the time — 'Off with his head!' Overtly or covertly if necessary. Either method easily available in that locale, you understand. No questions asked. Death closes all. George slipped up there. When they're given the sack, some of these villains take the honourable way out of their situation — the revolver and the brandy on the terrace after a good dinner, a friend's steady hand on the elbow — but the ones who go on fighting the judgement — you need to keep an eye on *them*. Trained soldiers, used to command, wily and unscrupulous — can cause havoc if they take it badly! Even in death, the wretch Somerton's causing problems. And it all happened on my watch! I'd have thought he was harmless enough boxed up at the Folies. Glad he's gone!'

'As perhaps may be his son? I understand that Somerton was a baronet? So, the title is a hereditary one and will pass — has already passed — down to his only son.'

'Yes. The world now has Sir Frederick Somerton to reckon with. An effortless way of acquiring a degree of nobility. Though a tarnished title. And one some might not be eager to parade. I'll look into all this. The contents of the will, if the man left one, are not yet known. I'll inform you if anything interesting comes up. Are you thinking that the young man got fed up with waiting for his absent reprobate father to drop off the twig? Young Frederick can't have been easy, aware that the old man was roving about Europe, spending the family fortune. I understand this to have been quite sizeable at one time. Perhaps he decided to hurry things along a bit? Makes sense to me. He'll have an uphill task, trying to burnish up the family name again, though. Old Somerton left quite a stink behind him!'

Intrigued by the nuances of speech and the unusual ideas they hinted at, Joe felt himself steered into asking with more familiarity than he would normally have assumed: 'How are you placed, Pollock — dynastically speaking?'

He seemed ready enough to reply. 'I'm not impressed by dynasties, successions, and all that family rubbish. I suppose I take that attitude from my father. My mother — oh, it's well known — married beneath her, as they say, and my father brought me up to be very dismissive of all that inheritance nonsense. I went to a Good School where the other boys merely confirmed me in my prejudices. On the whole, the grander the nastier, I concluded. But — the system seduces us all, I suppose you'd say. Did I refuse my cousin's offer of a recommendation to the right person? No. And I have to confess, Sandilands, that . . . ' Again he lowered his voice, taking Joe into his confidence, slightly embarrassed at what he was about to reveal. ' . . . there's a chance . . . a good chance . . . that there'll be an honour in the offing for me before very long. Knee on the velvet cushion, sword on the shoulder, 'Arise, Sir John' stuff! And, do you know — I shan't feel inclined to turn it down. I'll have earned it. It will be my own achievement and will owe nothing to a scheming old ancestor having pleased some capricious monarch in the dim and distant.'

'So, if we were making a book on the runners and riders in the Somerton slaying, we'd be giving short odds on the new baronet?'

'I'd certainly leave him on the list until we have more information. And his mother. At slightly longer odds, of course. Any more suspicions?'

'Vague ones. Tell me, Pollock — there's been a suggestion that the whole thing was staged deliberately to be witnessed by Sir George . . . or for the delectation of someone else in the audience. What's your opinion on that?'

Pollock frowned. 'A bit far-fetched but not out of the question, I suppose,' he replied cagily.

'I wonder if it had occurred to you that there might be a similarity with another crime scene you were dragged into some four years ago? I only mention this because the officiating pathologist at both crimes turns out to be one and the same — efficient fellow called Moulin.'

Pollock's face livened at the name. 'I remember. Yes, indeed. Good man! Effective and businesslike. And the scene was in the Louvre of all places! Good God, is it really four years? To me it's as clear as if it happened yesterday. Did he fill you in . . . ?'

'Yes, he gave me the details of the discovery of the body, the means of killing, the identity of the corpse and so on. But the most interesting thing he had to say was that, in common with that of Somerton, the murder was undertaken as a form of display to an invited audience of Egyptologists and academics, who all had reason to hate the man. Did you have the same feeling, I wonder?'

'Certainly did! The whole event was — well, just that! — an event. Apart from the representatives of law and order, there were three of us non-combatants, so to speak, caught up in the sorry scene. A very nice couple of Americans who raised the alarm when they caught sight of the blood pool under the coffin box — and me.'

'What on earth were you doing in the Louvre? Did anyone orchestrate *your* movements on that day?'

'Do you know — that thought never occurred to me! No . . . I'd say it was impossible. I was newly at the Embassy. Relatively low-ranking, of no significance in this context. Has George told you how I spent the war years? No? Well, knowing something of Egypt, and speaking a few languages, I was posted into Intelligence there. I picked up first-hand experience of the tricky political situation in the country. Powder keg! Wanting its independence from Britain, France, Italy, Turkey and every other piratical nation that thought it had a claim on its archaeological resources, to say nothing of its strategic and geographical advantages. After demob which came at very long last — always one more dispute to preside over — it was thought I could use the skills I'd acquired on the ground, here in Paris.

'I owe my present position to George — were

you aware of this? When I got here I found that the war was still being fought out amongst the archaeological cliques! And that's what I was doing at the museum that day. On neutral territory, away from embassies, we were having a meeting, trying to reach an agreement between four nations growling like dogs over a bone. Well, several thousand bones, as it happened. A whole newly discovered burial chamber. And the digging rights were in dispute. Not as straightforward as you might expect — many borders were still being negotiated in those days after the war.

'We'd come to something approaching a position all could accept and were gratefully on our way home when we were accosted by a frightfully concerned American who thought he'd discovered someone bleeding to death in a coffin case. Well, I assume the doctor who arrived shortly after that has filled you in?'

He paused, marshalling his thoughts. 'Moulin did not mislead you. I agree with him. There was something very strange going on. I was so occupied with keeping the peace I was perhaps a bit slow to catch on. It wasn't until later at police headquarters . . . The Americans — the Whites — fled. The wife was feeling ill. Got clean away. But their consciences overcame them afterwards and they duly reported to the police, who set up the interview and took their statement. Mr White asked particularly if I could be present to help with the language. A sensible arrangement and a task I was pleased to carry out. Very nice people, as I said. He was an army sergeant who'd been decorated for bravery on the Marne, I believe.

I've never understood why they call those Yanks 'doughboys', have you? Most unfortunate. Conjures up images of puffy-faced, spotty youths, soft to the touch. This man was as hard as a well-seasoned oak beam. And smart. We talked later, off the record, so to speak, and he put his ideas to me. I had to agree with him. He'd seen more than I had and made better sense of it. And his wife's insights were even more acute!

'Sandilands, the audience were there by invitation, I'd swear it. Someone had arranged the whole thing. A ringmaster of sorts. Set the scene, knowing it would go down well. A much-hated man had got his just deserts.'

'Would it be too fanciful, do you think, to assume that this, um, ringmaster had gone on cracking his whip? Organizing spectacles of this kind? Perhaps this wasn't the first? Perhaps it wasn't the last?' Joe suggested tentatively as though the idea had just occurred to him. He spoke with the diffidence of one putting such a ridiculous suspicion into words.

Pollock was astonished. Then he smiled. 'You didn't know? Well, how could you be expected to know? Just nipped over the Channel for a few days . . . no access to records . . . Oh, I do beg your pardon! How rude of me! It's just that . . . you've shown such insight . . . delved so deep in no time at all — the temptation is to assume Scotland Yard is omniscient. It takes a diplomat with fingers in many pies, a nosy bugger like me, someone with months to reflect on it, to get the full picture.'

Joe's easy smile showed that he was not at all put out by Pollock's frankness.

'The murderer was indeed in the room. Enjoying his little show. When I thought about it, I was only surprised he didn't take a bow or lead the applause.'

Pollock became suddenly serious and Joe caught sight of the tenacity and moral muscle that lay beneath the insouciant surface. 'There were several nationalities involved, you understand, Sandilands. At least three Englishmen present and participating. There were men I had had dealings with in the past and with whom I could expect to deal in the future, men whose hospitality I would be accepting, men on whose good will I would have to count. But I hadn't been so long in the business that I no longer cared whether the hand I was shaking had blood on it. I made a few enquiries, put two and two together and came up, I believe, with the right answer.'

'You have his identity?' Joe tried to keep his voice level.

'Certainly have! And the excellent Maybelle White confirmed my suspicions!'

17

Joe waited, allowing him to savour his moment of intrigue.

'The murderer wasn't concealing himself or his motive with very great care. What a show-off! I expect *you*, sharp fellow that you are, would have been waiting by the door to finger his collar.'

The ball had been patted back into his court and Joe wondered whether he was being tested in some mildly playful way. Readying himself to provide an entertaining belly-flop, he slipped a hand into his trouser pocket and checked that what he was seeking was there. He remembered the details of Dr Moulin's story and plunged in. 'It was, of course, the jocular prestidigitator who pulled the gold amulet of the god Set out of his victim's mouth! Rather in this manner . . . '

Joe flourished the trinket he'd palmed, holding it between finger and thumb, enjoying Pollock's astonishment. This was followed swiftly by a burst of laughter.

'You've got him! Good Lord! I never would have expected to see that piece of nonsense again! Wherever did you come by it? And the murderer produced it that day in front of that learned crowd, just as you've demonstrated! Probably with a wink for his admirers, but I'll never know — he had his back to me at the time. And, like everyone in the room with the exception of Harland C. White, I was able to interpret the symbolism of the gesture: here was a man who was opening his mouth one last time to Spew Out Evil. Mrs White had a good deal of interesting remarks to make about the Egyptian burial rite of 'The Opening of the Mouth' but we decided that line of thought might be a little over-adventurous.'

'And what's become of your ringmaster?' Joe asked. 'Your entrepreneur of crime? Is he still flourishing? I should very much like to talk to him. Is he still here in Paris?'

'In a manner of speaking, yes, he is! He's in Père Lachaise. The cemetery. Committed suicide last year. Down in the south somewhere . . . Cannes, that's it. Left a full confession. More tea, Sandilands?'

Joe accepted a fresh cup using the mechanical gestures to disguise his surprise and disappointment.

'The murder in the Louvre wasn't the only thing he had on his conscience.' Pollock shook his head, in distaste. 'A really terrible man! Almost the equal of the man he'd had done away with. Two of a kind! But then, the profession, which it now claims to be, has always attracted unscrupulous rogues of all nationalities. And all ranks of society. From Napoleon to the ten-year-old native tomb-robber.'

After a carefully calculated interval, Joe put down his teacup and began to draw the interview to a close, thanking Jack Pollock for his help and interest: formulaic phrases cut short by Pollock's bluff response: 'Think nothing of it, old chap!'

His warm hand reached again for Joe's and gripped it firmly. 'If there's anything — the slightest thing — I can do, I'm your man. Keep me informed, won't you?'

At the door he paused. 'French views of Law and Order not the same as ours, you know. Stay alert, Sandilands!

'And where have you decided to have luncheon today? May I recommend somewhere?' he asked as they crossed the hall on the way to the front door. 'At your hotel? The Ambassador, I think you said? Excellent reputation for its cuisine. Good choice!'

* * *

So. Moulin and Francine Raissac — and he swiftly added himself to the list — had fallen victim to an over-coloured story, a lurid, crime-novel notion of villainy. Relief and disappointment were flooding through Joe, fighting for control. Of course Pollock's theory was correct and it was supported by a confession. The scene at the museum had to have been staged by a man with influence enough to clear rooms, to lure in the victim, to have him dispatched with all that chilling ceremony, to arrange for an independent witness to stumble on the body, and to have the insider's knowledge to invite just the right people to participate in the finding. No one but the Americans and Pollock was there by chance.

The whole presentation had been a work of art. A labour not of love but of hatred. And, with a final directorial twist, the case had been solved and brought to a conclusion by the perpetrator himself. Very proper. Inevitable. The death had occurred down south in Cannes and Moulin had not been aware or involved. 'I've saved the best till last,' the doctor had told him. And the best — the most astonishing — case in the series of unexplained crimes now proved to have been no such thing. A one-off. Solved. Case closed with Père Lachaise finality. And, with that key element dislodged, the whole house of cards tumbled down.

Joe surrendered to relief. And yet he was left feeling foolish. He was still saddled with the problem of assigning responsibility for Somerton's killing and had wasted a precious day. But at least now he could concentrate on the motive he had originally thought most likely: vengeance. And he could probably discount the unlikely phone calls from the Somerton residence in England to an undisclosed agency in Paris: 'The name's Somerton. You'll find him at the Crillon . . . Dagger would be most suitable . . . How much? You *are* joking, of course? Ah well . . . I suppose it will be worth it . . . '

He could forget about Sir George's presence being an element in the planning. It was most likely that there had been no planning at all. Perhaps some Anglo-Indian, retired from the army, someone with a grudge against the man, had seen him lording it in a box at the Folies accompanied by an attractive young girl and this had been the trigger for a vengeful act of fury. It was the unconsidered flaunting of power and position that could incite lesser men to rage. Many men had come back from India with daggers in their possession. They might, with all the alarming stories of the revived Apache gangs, have chosen to carry a knife from their collection instead of the more usual swordstick as a means of self-defence in this dangerous capital.

Joe wondered wearily if he could ask Bonnefoye to release names from the information he knew the French police kept on foreigners residing in the city, permanently or temporarily. Hours of patient checking would be called for and he was very far from certain that such a request would be taken seriously by the police authority. In any case, Fourier would have lost patience long before results were available and rearrested George.

But, looking on the bright side, Sir George was no longer to be considered the target of some mysterious Set or Fantômas figure, stalked through the streets of Paris by a scar-faced acolyte. And Joe could now return safely to his hotel without slinking along like a polecat. He badly needed to change his clothes. Toothbrushes and other essential items had been provided by the industrious and early-rising Madame Bonnefoye and he had spent a comfortable night in a pair of Jean-Philippe's pyjamas, but he wanted to touch base.

But what of Heather Watkins? Her encounter had been with a flesh and blood menace. Twice. Could the shadowing of Miss Watkins be explained by the girl's obvious attractions? Her vivid hair and fresh Celtic looks would always attract masculine attention, he thought. They had attracted *his*. He knew that many men on the lookout for just such loveliness haunted the foyers of even the best hotels. Perhaps she was being pursued by some theatrical impresario? To be recruited into the ranks of high-kicking chorus girls? She had exactly the right height and athletic appearance. And he didn't doubt that, like every other English girl he knew (always excepting Dorcas Joliffe of course), she'd been to ballet classes. Bonnefoye had confessed that certain nameless limbs of the government actually kept lists of spectacular girls — attractive and good conversationalists — who might be summoned to escort visiting royalty or the like about the city. Joe wasn't quite sure he believed him. At the worst, she might be the target of the gangs of confidence tricksters who ran the 'badger games' from hotel lobbies. Beautifully dressed, well-spoken and plausible, the female bandits they employed would lure men freshly arrived and looking forward to adventures with a sob-story or an involving smile and in no time they'd have the gold out of their pockets — and their teeth.

He reined in his thoughts. Nonsense! There were more loose fragments of tinsel swirling about in this kaleidoscope than he could pull into focus at the moment and he was not going to lose track of a single element. The face of Francine Raissac had stayed with him. He remembered clearly her terror. Her warnings. He'd take her seriously and he'd listen to Pollock's parting words of advice and stay alert.

He performed his automatic checks for surveillance as he strolled along the rue du Faubourg St Honoré but with no sense of urgency. If anyone cared to follow him from the Embassy to his hotel, they were welcome to do so. He paused in front of the window display in one of the bookshops along the street, decided they probably didn't have what he was looking for and moved off. Finding what he wanted a few yards further on, he went in and spent a few minutes examining the stock before he made his choice.

* * *

The receptionist at the Hotel Ambassador greeted him and told him a telephone message had just arrived for him. Joe took the note. A brief one from Bonnefoye.

We have Wilberforce. Has agreed to meet Fourier at 11.30. Be there!

Joe telephoned to congratulate Bonnefoye on his speed of performance.

'Not difficult! He was at the third hotel on our list. Having breakfast. Confirms he was at the theatre that night and says he'll be pleased to be of help. I'll see you both at Staircase A?'

* * *

Joe, freshly bathed, shirted and suited, met Bonnefoye at the entrance to police headquarters and waited with him for Jennings' taxi to drop him off. The man stepping out was easily identified by his English overcoat, bowler hat and rolled umbrella. Bonnefoye suppressed a snort of laughter at the image of propriety the man presented as Joe stepped forward to enquire: 'Mr Wilberforce Jennings, I presume? How do you do, sir. Commander Sandilands of Scotland Yard liaising with the Police Judiciaire. May I introduce my colleague, Inspector Bonnefoye?'

Jennings relaxed on hearing Joe's suave voice and shook hands with each man.

'This is to do with the killing at the theatre, night before last, eh? What? Not sure I can be of much help. I know people always say they saw nothing but, in this case, it's absolutely true! I saw nothing of the killing, that is!'

Joe allowed him to chatter on nervously as they crossed the courtyard. These forbidding surroundings would give anyone the jitters — even a man fortified by a bowler and a brolly. At the door to Staircase A, he turned to Jennings, reassurance in his voice. 'Don't be alarmed, sir. Just a few questions to be put to you by the French Chief Inspector in charge of the case. He's obliged to cover all bases, you understand? Explore all avenues.'

Jennings nodded vigorously to indicate he understood this calming drivel.

'Many people are being interviewed — one of them may have seen something he was not aware that he had seen. Just answer the questions carefully. I will be on hand to translate.'

Chairs, Joe noted, had been provided in Fourier's office. The files and papers were aligned in rows. After introductions all round, he and Bonnefoye settled in a group with Jennings between them, facing Fourier and a sergeant who was taking notes at his elbow.

'I say! However did you know I was there? Clever of you to find me! I shall have to hope my wife is less vigilant than the French police, eh? What? I read about this sorry affair in the papers. Fellow Englishman knifed to death, they're saying. And that's the extent of my knowledge, I'm afraid. I've never met the dead fellow. I was in the stalls. Thought you might like to see my ticket stub.'

Fourier looked carefully at the number on the ticket. He took a pencil and a sheet of paper and in a few quick strokes sketched out a floor plan of the theatre. He placed it on the desk in front of Jennings. 'Can you confirm you were sitting where I have marked an X?'

'Yes. You've got it exactly!' said Jennings. 'I say — you know your way about, Chief Inspector! A regular yourself at the Folies, are you then?'

Joe didn't attempt a translation.

'I now add two boxes,' said Fourier, supplying them. 'Take my pencil and mark in the box where you understand the murder to have taken place.'

Jennings obliged.

'Well done! Quite correct! Box B.' Fourier's attempt at bonhomie was unconvincing. 'Now, tell us who and what you observed in that box.'

Jennings' account was disappointing. He was

quite obviously doing his best but his best was not pleasing Fourier. An unknown man (dark-haired), an unknown girl (fair-haired), had been noted before the lights went out and again when the lights came on again in the interval. Between and after those times — nothing of interest.

'Of course, had one only known, one would have . . . ' Jennings burbled. 'Tell you what, though! Why don't you ask the chap opposite? May I?' He took the pencil again and marked Box A. 'Now, if you can find *me*, I'm jolly certain you can find *him*. He had a perfect view of the deceased. And he knew him,' he announced.

'And I understand the witness in Box A was known to you also?' said Fourier with mild interest.

'I say! This is impressive! Yes, he is known to me. Only seen him once or twice since we were at school together — reunions and so on — but there's no mistaking that nose. Jardine. It was George Jardine. I'll bet my boots. Something important in India, I believe. Showing off as usual. In the Royal Box. But where else? Wouldn't find *him* rubbing shoulders with hoi polloi in the stalls.'

'And you think he was acquainted with the man opposite?'

'Oh, yes. Undoubtedly. They were *talking* to each other.'

Fourier stirred uneasily. 'Across the width of the theatre, sir? Talking?' His strong witness was showing signs of cracking. He looked to Joe to correct his interpretation but Joe shook his head.

''Communicating', I ought perhaps to have said. Exchanging messages. Just the sort of showy-off Boy Scout stuff Jardine would have indulged in. He always enjoyed an audience, you know. Incapable of fastening his shoelaces without turning round to acknowledge the plaudits of the crowd.'

Joe summarized this and added, 'Fourier, may I?'

Fourier spread his hands, amused to delegate.

'Would you mind, Jennings, demonstrating the form this communication took?'

'Certainly. As the lights were being lowered . . . ' Jennings got to his feet and went to stand, back to the wall, looking down at an imagined audience. His face froze in a parody of George's lordly style. 'He put on his white gloves . . . '

On went the gloves.

'And then he did this sort of tick-tack nonsense with his hands.'

The hands flashed rhythmically, fingers stabbed, thumbs were extended.

'You'd have thought he was leading the Black and White Minstrels in the show at the end of the pier. People were beginning to think he was the first act.'

'And did the man opposite take any notice? Did he reply?'

'Yes. Same sort of thing but a shorter response and he wasn't wearing gloves so it wasn't so obvious. I thought, at that moment, it was a game. Yes, I was sure it was a game. He was laughing, joining in the fun.'

'You *thought*?' asked Joe, picking up the tense.

'Yes. Changed my mind when I saw the *last* gesture though!'

'Describe it,' said Fourier.

'He did this,' said Jennings.

Face twisted into a threatening mask, he gave a flourish of the hand and trailed the forefinger slowly across his throat.

No one spoke. The sergeant stopped writing. Fourier turned to him and advised: 'Sergeant, why don't you put down — 'The suspect was observed at this point to make a life-threatening gesture announcing his intention of cutting the victim's throat.'?'

The sergeant noted it down.

Jennings knew enough French to take alarm at the twist Fourier had put on his words. 'Look here! That's a bit strong, don't you know! Sandilands, put him right! I wasn't implying that . . . Oh, Good Lord! He wasn't in my House but I didn't come here to drop old Jardine in the quagmire . . . '

'Did you not?' drawled Joe. 'Well, you've made a very good fist of it. But before we ask you to check and sign your statement, just tell us, will you — what was the reaction of the second man playing this game? Did he appear alarmed? Did he seem menaced by Jardine's gesture?'

'Well, no. Not at all. Most odd. He laughed. Damn near slapped his thigh, he thought it was so funny.'

* * *

When Jennings had been thanked and escorted from the premises by the sergeant, Fourier turned to Joe and Bonnefoye with a pitying smile. 'The case firms up, it seems,' he said. 'And unless you two are about to produce some late entrant like a jack-in-the-box to surprise me . . .' He left a pause long enough to annoy the younger men. 'No? Well, there is one more amusing little excursion I've laid on for you.'

He gestured to his sketch of the theatre layout. 'Forget the audience. What no one else seems to have observed is that there were a hundred or so other potential witnesses and all much closer to the scene of the murder at the moment of the murder. The cast! Lined up for the finale, their eyes would have been on their audience. They say that Miss Baker herself is always acutely aware of the reactions of the crowd before her and responds to their mood. Dark, of course, out there, I should imagine. Up to you to see how much you can make out. How close the boxes are to the stage. Which performer was standing underneath.

'I've arranged with the man in charge — Derval's his name, Paul Derval — for you to be given an hour to scrounge around before the matinée performance this afternoon. I guaranteed you wouldn't get in anyone's way. He'll send someone to open up for you if you present yourselves at the stage door. That's about it . . . Jardine behaving himself, is he?'

He started to collect up his papers. As they reached the door he said: 'Oh, I fixed a ten-minute interview for you with Mademoiselle

Baker. Thought you'd make a better impression on her than I would. She wants to help, apparently. Tender-hearted girl — keeps a menagerie of fluffy animals in her dressing room backstage, I'm told. She was upset to hear some admirer had bled to death while she was singing her heart out a few metres away. See what you can do.

'We may be getting closer to that headline,' he added with a chuckle they left.

18

'Some time to kill before our two o'clock tryst in the avenue Montaigne.' Joe emerged with relief into the sunshine. 'The theatre's not all that far from my hotel . . . Why don't I take you to lunch there first — Pollock assures me the cuisine is excellent. And I think we've earned it! But first — a short walk. What *is* it about this place — ' he stabbed a thumb backwards over his shoulder — 'that makes me want to burst out and run ten miles in the fresh air?'

'Fourier?' grunted Bonnefoye. 'Medieval architecture . . . medieval mind? Know what you mean, though. Which direction do you want to take? I'll gladly trot alongside.'

'Let's cross over into the Tuileries, cut through the gardens and make for the place Vendôme.'

'Why would we want to do that?'

'Off the place Vendôme, running north towards the Opéra, we'll find the rue de la Paix. Not a street I've frequented much. Wall to wall with *modistes*, I'm told.'

He took Francine's scrap of blue fabric from his inside pocket. 'Well, you never know. This is from the House of Cresson, according to Mademoiselle Raissac. It's a lead we ought to follow up. It may take us to the beauty who showed a clean pair of heels before the show ended. Think of it as Cinderella's slipper, shall we?'

'Not *we*, Sandilands. They would be instantly suspicious of two men arriving with a strange enquiry.' He looked at Joe then tweaked the sample from his fingers. 'I'll deal with this. You can loiter outside, window shopping. I suggest the jeweller's. That's safe enough. You're choosing a ring for your girlfriend.'

It took a considerable amount of confidence to put on a routine such as Bonnefoye was demonstrating, Joe thought, in this smartest, most exclusive of streets. There *were* men to be seen entering the salons but they followed, dragging their heels, in the slipstream of their smartly dressed wives. Their role was clear: parked in a little gilt chair, they were required to smile and admire everything they were shown until, finally catching a nod and a wink from the *vendeuse*, they would come to a decision and pull out their wallets. The solo flight Bonnefoye was contemplating was daring. Professional, well-disciplined and having the sole aim of charming large sums of money from rich and fashionable women, the elegant assistants Joe caught glimpses of through the windows were truly daunting. They moved about with the easy arrogance of priestesses tending some vital flame.

Bonnefoye looked smart enough — he wore his good clothes well — but he would be entering hostile territory. He watched the young Inspector's reflection in a shop window opposite the gold and black façade of Maison Cresson as he straightened his tie, tilted his straw boater to a less rakish angle and strolled inside, humming an air from *Così fan tutte*.

He was in there a very long time, Joe thought suspiciously. He saw Bonnefoye emerge finally, scribbling on a page of his little black book. He slipped it away into his breast pocket. Joe sighed. An address had been added to his list. But whose?

'Another success, Inspector?' he asked. 'How did you manage it?'

'Two successes!' Bonnefoye gave a parody of his best slanting Ronald Coleman smile to indicate method. 'But the one that concerns you, my friend, is the identification of the fabric. It wasn't easy. Sacrifices had to be made! There's a good café just around the corner. Why don't we walk on and have our second coffee of the day?'

They moved off out of the sight lines of the salon.

'A charming girl greeted me . . . Delphine . . . I told her I was desperate. I wished to buy something special for my mother — for her birthday. And the trouble with rich spoiled old ladies . . . I was quite certain Mademoiselle Delphine would understand . . . was that they had everything. I had noted (sensitive son that I am!) on a recent visit to the theatre that she had been very taken with a certain evening cape being worn by a blonde young lady. I produced the swatch at this point. A dear friend of mine — the Comtesse de Beaufort — had advised me that such a garment might be found at the Maison Cresson.'

'A moment, Bonnefoye . . . the Countess? You've lost me! Who's this? Does she exist?'

'Of course. And I know the lady to be a devoted patron of this establishment — Cresson labels right down to her silk knickers! I arrested her husband two months ago for beating a manservant nearly to death. The Countess was duly grateful for the brute's temporary removal from the family home. And the suggestion of intimacy with a valued customer impressed Delphine. She was very helpful. She identified your scrap — though claims the stuff they use to be of better quality. Twice the weight and a richer dye, apparently. She remembered the garment for a very particular reason. They had designed and sold no fewer than four as a job lot, a highly unusual procedure, and all in the same size and fabric. The capes had been commissioned by a certain customer with whom they do a good deal of business. To reproduce a copy for my mother, it would be only polite to seek permission, of course.'

'Understandable. The thought of *five* examples of a designer piece out and about in Paris would horrify your Delphine. Suppose the ladies all chose to wear it at the same occasion? The reputation of the House for exclusivity would be ruined! Have you noticed, Bonnefoye, that we men all try to look alike, toe the fashion line, cringe at the thought of looking different, but a woman would die rather than be seen in the same get-up as one of her friends?'

'Exactly! So why on earth would they want so many cloaks? Not kitting out a nunnery, do you suppose?'

Bonnefoye produced his book again and

flipped it open. 'Delphine was very happy to undertake the negotiations on my behalf. I'm certain she didn't take me for an haute couture pirate or anything of that nature but, all the same, the training prevailed. No address was forthcoming, I'm afraid.' He grimaced. 'And I even went to the length of ordering one of those things. There on the spot! I heard myself selecting twilight blue silk. Grosgrain. Lined with pigeon's-breast grey.'

'Shantung?'

'Of course. Have you any idea of the cost? A month's pay! But I thought I ought to underline the urgency. Birthday next Thursday, I said. It seemed to work!'

'That — or the appeal in your spaniel's eyes, liquid with filial affection?' said Joe.

'We have a saying — *A good son makes a good husband*. Perhaps that's what Delphine was thinking? But whatever it was, it did the trick. She swayed over to the telephone and asked for a number. I memorized it.'

They settled at a café table outside on the terrace and ordered coffee.

'The temptation,' said Joe, 'of course, is to nip straight inside and use their phone. See who answers . . . but . . . '

'We could do that. I have ways of tricking identities out of people who answer their telephones. Ordinary, innocent people, still slightly bemused by the new device on their hall tables. I wouldn't expect any success if we're dealing with a criminal organization. And if I mumbled, 'Sorry, wrong number,' or 'Phone company — just checking,' and cut the connection, it might alert them.'

'I don't want to be boring,' Joe began tentatively, 'but in London — '

'*And* here in Paris!' said Bonnefoye. 'We have the same facility. It's not so exciting as establishing a direct contact with a suspected villain but I'm about to go inside and ring up a department on the fourth floor at the Quai. They hold reverse listings of all the numbers in Paris.' He took out his book again. 'Won't be a moment.'

Joe was drinking his second cup of coffee before Bonnefoye emerged again. In silence he passed the notebook across the table to Joe.

'Ah! I think we might have been expecting this,' said Joe, smiling with satisfaction. 'Let me teach you another London expression, mate: *Gotcha!*'

* * *

Vincent Viviani strode smartly down the avenue Montaigne towards the Pont de l'Alma. He was glad that his schedule had led him back to this part of Paris. He'd make time in his day to go and have a look at his favourite bridge over the Seine. Not being a theatre-goer, there was little to bring him to this increasingly smart area. Like everyone else passing by, he gave a swift, unemphatic glance at the three-storey, art nouveau façade of the Théâtre des Champs-Élysées. Overblown, sweet-toothed, but perfect for its purpose, he supposed. Offering rich men the chance of parting with large sums of money for the privilege of gawping at acres of jiggling, gyrating female flesh — of all colours now, it seemed. He flicked an interested eye sideways, following the two men on the opposite side of the road. They ducked into the alley that led to the side door of the theatre. Stage-door Johnnies? Yes, they looked the part. At least the boater was a good attempt. Vincent wasn't sure the grey felt would open many doors.

He pressed on without a break in his stride down towards the bridge. The bridge itself wasn't much but he'd always been fascinated by the four stone figures that decorated it. Once, when he was a small boy, his father had brought him here and pointed them out. He'd thought that's what a soldier's grandson would like to see. He was right. Vincent had been enchanted by the four Second Empire soldiers. The Zouave was his favourite. He stood, left hand on hip, neatly bearded chin raised defiantly against the current, swagger in his baggy trousers, tightly cinched jacket and fez.

His father had been pleased with his reaction. '*Les Zouaves sont les premiers soldats du monde*,' he'd said. 'That was the opinion of General St Armaud after the Battle of Alma when we licked the Russians. And your grandfather was one of them. A *real* Zouave. Not one of the ruffians they recruit from the east of Paris these days — no, he came straight from the mountains of Morocco . . . Kabili tribe. Second regiment, the Jackals of Oran. No finer fighters in the world.'

Vincent had signed on as soon as they would take him. He'd managed to see action in North Africa before the war broke out in Europe. He'd been a seasoned hand-to-hand fighter like the rest of his men, wearing just such a flamboyant uniform. A lieutenant by then, he'd slashed, burned and bayoneted his way through the forests of the Marne at the beginning of the war, realizing that he and his regiment were finished. The red trousers, the twelve-foot-long woollen sash, the red fez all cried, 'Here I am! Shoot me!' And the Germans, lying holed up in every village, wasted no opportunity. He'd witnessed the arrival of the British gunners, coming up late to their aid. Not creeping or dashing along — marching as though on the parade ground, camouflaged in their khaki clothing, stern, calm, standing firm when the sky above them was exploding. Machines of war.

And, of course, his regiment had adapted. They'd been kitted out in *bleu d'horizon*, issued with more suitable weapons. He'd survived until Verdun. He'd been there at the storming of the fort of Douaumont. He'd been collected, one of a pile of bodies, and sorted out at the last minute by an orderly more dead than alive himself, into the hospital cart instead of the burial wagon. Months later, he'd come back to his old mother in Paris and she'd seen him through the worst of it. And he was flourishing. Not for Vincent a nightly billet under a bridge with the other drunken old lags. He had his pride and as soon as he had his strength back he'd got himself a job. It had taken a stroke of luck to get him going but he was in full-time employment. Employment that demanded all his energy and used all his skills. What more could a retired soldier ask? The pay was better than good, too, and his mother appreciated that. She had a fine new apartment. When he'd told her he was in the meat industry, she'd not been impressed but she'd accepted it. Something in Les Halles — a manager in the transport section — she told her friends. Out at all times of night, of course. She didn't know he was still soldiering.

He smiled and strolled the few metres down to the place de l'Alma where he greeted the old lady keeping her flower stall by the entrance to the Métro. He spent a few rare moments idling. Paris. He never took it for granted. After the grey years of mud and pain, the simplest things could please him. The walnut-wrinkled face and crouched figure of the flower seller, surrounded by her lilies and roses, beyond her the glinting river and the Eiffel Tower, so close you could put out a hand and scratch yourself on its rust-coloured struts, this was pleasing him.

His smile widened. He'd buy some flowers. And he knew exactly which ones to choose.

* * *

'Two inspectors and both speaking French? Monsieur Derval understood that we were about to receive a visit from a gentleman of Scotland Yard. I was sent along in case there were language problems. I do not represent the theatre, you understand, but I speak English.

Simenon. Georges Simenon. How do you do?'

Joe handed his card to the young man. 'Monsieur Simenon? You are French?' Joe asked.

'No. Belgian.' The man who greeted them at the stage door was reassuringly untheatrical, Joe thought. Of medium height and soberly dressed in tweeds with thick dark hair and a pale complexion, he looked like a lawyer or an accountant. Although not far into his twenties, Joe judged, he had already developed a frowning seriousness of expression. But the lines on his forehead were belied by a pair of merry brown eyes, peering, warm and interested, through heavy-framed spectacles. A strong, sweet smell of tobacco and a bulge in his right pocket told Joe he'd been passing some time at the stage door waiting. He seemed genuinely pleased to see them.

'Everyone else is doing what they usually do an hour before the matinée. You may go wherever you please in the building — just try to keep out of the way as far as you can. I'll come with you. You'll be needing a torch, I think. And a guide. I know where the light switches are. Front of house is empty — the orchestra drag themselves in at the very last minute. The cast are thumping about backstage. Clattering up and down stairs and being drilled by Monsieur Derval. Soon they'll be screaming and yelling, tearing each other's hair and stealing each other's lipstick! Oh, and you're expecting to see Josephine?' He paused for a second, and continued with a slight awkwardness. 'Can't promise anything as far as she's concerned, I'm afraid. Not the most reliable . . . In fact, she's usually late. She's not arrived yet and may well drift in, still eating her lunch, and go straight onstage. We'll just have to wait and see. I'll give you a call when she gets here.'

He seemed to tune into the two policemen's puzzlement. 'You must be wondering what I'm doing here, answering for the star? Wonder myself sometimes! I'm not an employee of Josephine's — more of a friend. I'm a journalist in fact. I met her last year when she arrived, fresh off the boat. I was a stage-door admirer, I'm afraid, turning up with a bunch of roses. She talked to me. I discovered she knew not a word of French.' He smiled. 'Her English isn't wonderful either! She was an instant success and, as you can imagine, began to receive sacks full of mail. Every day there were invitations from some of the grandest people you can imagine, offers of hospitality of one sort or another, gifts, proposals of marriage — thousands of *them*. And, of course, the poor girl was unable to answer a single one of them. Couldn't even manage a thank-you note for a diamond necklace or a De Dion-Bouton! I began to help her out. She'd tell me how she wanted to reply, I'd put it into suitable French — or English — and see that the notes were sent off.'

'You're her secretary?'

'It's not that formal. No. As I said — I'm a news reporter. And I'm a friend who writes for her. But — to business. I expect you'd like to inspect the scene of the crime first? The box? It hasn't been used since the killing. Nor has the other one. All entry barred. The police squad didn't spend a great deal of time up there . . .' His voice was slightly quizzical. 'Commissaire Fourier in attendance. The big gun! They hauled off the corpse and the weapon — and a suspect they claim to have caught red-handed — gave firm instructions to leave the site alone and that's the last we've seen of them. Wondered when you'd be back . . . There must be much still to discover . . . Have they made an arrest? Have they charged their Englishman with murder? Did they have any success with the fingerprinting, do you know?'

'*Which* branch of journalism are you employed in, monsieur?' asked Joe with the air of one who knew the answer.

'Crime,' he replied, smiling.

'Then you'll never be without material in Paris,' said Bonnefoye acidly.

'And we're working on the assumption that the suspect they carted off is an innocent man,' Joe felt bound to assert.

'I never thought otherwise,' Simenon said graciously.

* * *

Their guide switched on the house lights and the inspection began. Joe and Bonnefoye opened up the two boxes and tick-tacked rude messages to each other over the void, agreeing that Wilberforce Jennings' account was probably entirely accurate. The reporter went obligingly to occupy a position centre stage, confirming that he had a clear and close view of Joe in one and Bonnefoye in the other box, sight limited only by the available light. With nothing of note in Jardine's box, the three men gathered at the murder scene and looked about them. The grey upholstery with its sinister dark stain was witness to the exact spot on which Somerton had breathed his last.

Simenon waved a hand at the walls where patches of graphite from the fingerprinting brush stippled the paintwork. 'Dozens, you see! Not one of them bloodstained. I expect the ones they've taken belong to the world and his wife — and his mistress; everyone who's been in here since it was last cleaned. And the knifeman could have been wearing gloves. Not much of a tradition with us, I understand, Inspector — fingerprinting? Chances are, if they can pick up the murderer's prints on these surfaces, they'll have no records to compare them with. You'll have to catch him first and then match them up.'

Joe took the torch he was offered and trained it systematically along the walls, since it seemed to be expected of him. He wasn't hopeful that this murderer had left a trace of himself behind. He wasn't likely to have paused to decorate the walls with his calling cards, but he had to come and go through the door. Yes, the door, if anything, would be the most revealing, Joe thought and said as much.

'Unless he had the forethought to leave it ajar,' murmured Simenon. 'And shove it open with his foot. That's what I'd have done. He was right-handed, I assume? Is it known?'

Bonnefoye nodded. 'And Somerton's lady friend who nipped off early could have ensured it was left open when they entered — had to have a draught of air or some such excuse — so he could push it open with an elbow.'

'Indeed? Mmm . . . So he's in and out with no need to touch anything with or without bloodied hand or bloodied glove?'

'Wouldn't he have closed the door behind him in anticipation of his private moment? Instinctive, you'd think,' said Joe, 'covering your back?'

'A man with cool nerves would chance it. With the finale going on . . . star on stage . . . no one's going to be prowling about the corridors. And his back could have been covered by his blonde conjurer's assistant keeping cave outside, holding his cloak ready to slip over any bloodstains he might have on him.

'You know — I think the man probably *wasn't* wearing gloves . . . '

Joe was enjoying the man's musings. 'Yes. Go on. What makes you say that?' he asked.

'Not their style. It's a tricky manoeuvre slicing through flesh — muscle and gristle. They like to have complete control of the blade in their fingers. I've witnessed a demonstration.' He shuddered. 'They'll tell you a gloved hand can slip. And why bother when it's easy enough to wipe the blade afterwards? It had been wiped clean?'

'It had,' said Bonnefoye.

'There you are then. No gloves.'

'But tell me, monsieur: *they*? Who might *they* be? Do they have a name and number? An address, perhaps? Where they might be reached?'

'The professionals. *You* must be aware of them, Inspector. You clear up their nasty little messes often enough.'

'The gangs of the thirteenth arrondissement? The Sons of the Apaches, I've heard a romantic call them.' Bonnefoye grinned at Joe.

'No, no! Those buffoons are window-dressing! Practically a sideshow for the tourists. Did you know you can hire them by the hour to stage a knife-fight in the street, right there on the pavement in front of whichever café is opening that week? They even have stage names: Pépé le Moko, Alfrédo le Fort, Didi le Diable, La Bande à Bobo. Two rival gangs will fight it out with blood-curdling oaths and threats, egged on by their molls. And all to an accompaniment of delighted squeals from the clientele. Then, after a suitable interval,' he looked slyly at Bonnefoye, 'on they come — the *hirondelles*, the swallows flashing about in their shiny blue capes. The boys in blue sweep up on their bicycles and confront both gangs who, miraculously, always seem to turn around and join forces against the flics. Oh, it's a pageant! You could put it on at the Bobino! The bad boys always know exactly the moment to disappear down the dark alleys, leaving really very little blood behind them. Just a few spots for the *patron* to point out to his customers. These — as you might expect — are perfectly unscathed but have worked up quite a thirst in their excitement. No, this is not their work. And no, I can't give you any names. They have none.'

'Is what we're hearing your theory or your

evidence, monsieur?' asked Joe, intrigued.

'I've told you what I do for a living. To report on crime you have to be close to the criminals. As close as they will allow you to approach. I know, or think I know, a good many people who are known to you also — by reputation. I've shared a drink with them . . . talked to them . . . drawn them out. I have friends in some pretty low places! Brothels, opium dens, absinthe bars . . . Sometimes they shoot me a line for their own benefit. But even their lies and false information can give much away if you're not taken in by it . . . are prepared to analyse it. I'm aware of what they can do — of what they have done — but I have no name to offer you and would not offer if I knew it . . . The last man who let his tongue run away with him was found two nights ago in the canal with his mouth stitched up. They have a brutal way with those who would . . . *vendre la mèche* . . . ?'

'Sell the fuse?' said Joe, puzzled. 'Oh, I see . . . Give away the vital bit? Squeal. Inform.'

'The warning is reinforced periodically. Whether it's called for or not, I sometimes think,' he added with chill speculation.

'Is that all you have for us? A portentous warning empty of any substance?' Joe's voice was mildly challenging.

The reporter was spurred to make his point. 'There's a small group of villains — six at the most. Deadly. Discreet. For hire. When the Corsican gangs folded their tents and moved on after the war, a central core of bad boys, the survivors, stayed on. Licensed to kill, trained and encouraged to kill, they came out on the other side of it ruthless, skilled and, above all, older and wiser. They regrouped themselves. They're careful. And that's most unusual; gangsters have a touch of the theatrical about them as a rule . . . they like to have their names known, their exploits vaunted . . . there are even songs made up about some of the more flamboyant villains! But the men I have in mind are silent. Or else they're being run by someone capable of imposing discipline on them. And when they work, it's not in public, for a handful of francs in front of a Saturday night audience of voyeuristic merrymakers, it's for thousands, in the dark. In secrecy. In anonymity.'

'Well . . . Well, well!' said Joe. 'No name, perhaps, but every man has fingerprints. And he can't change those every six months. You roundly declare our chap was not wearing gloves? Let's see what we can do, shall we? Perhaps the officers who worked here on the night of the crime have, inadvertently, recorded his prints. Though, amongst this profusion of sticky dabs, they are not aware of what they have.'

Bonnefoye stared and sighed. 'So many! It's going to take a month to process this lot. If they haven't given up already. And — really — are they going to bother when they have so many of Sir George's on the victim's chair?'

'Ah! *Le pigeon! Le gogo!*' was Simenon's verdict on Sir George and Joe was encouraged to hear it.

'The 'patsy' you might say. Our supposition also.'

The beam of Joe's torch illuminated the last section of the wall, to the left of the door, passed on and then jerked back again. 'I wonder if we can reduce the area of search?'

He moved closer to a powdered print on the left door jamb. 'Here's a remarkably sticky print, wouldn't you say? Just look at the detail there!'

'Not blood?' said Bonnefoye.

'No, not blood. The greasiness is pomade! Hair grease. I had some of that muck on my fingers yesterday. It's the pathologist's theory that the killer seized Somerton by his hair with his left hand from behind to hold his head in the correct position and then slit his throat with his right hand. So, his right hand might well have been covered in blood and he was obviously at some pains not to touch anything with that but, possibly leaning out to check the corridor was free, he placed what he thought was his clean left hand here . . . ' Joe extended his hand without touching the wall into a natural position and found he had to move it up an inch. 'Tall man,' he commented. 'Just over six feet tall? Bonnefoye? Could you . . . ?'

'As soon as I can get back up to the lab! Focusing! That could save them a bit of time!'

* * *

'That policeman! Is he still in the building?'

The voice boomed out from the rear of the stage. Urgent. Powerful. Alarmed.

'We're up here, Monsieur Derval,' Simenon called back. 'Just finishing in the box. I have two inspectors with me — one Police Judiciaire, the other Scotland Yard.'

'The more the merrier. Bring the Grand Old Duke of York as well if you've got him. Quickly! To Josephine's room.'

The figure exited at speed, stage left, pursued, Joe would have sworn, by all three Furies.

Joe checked his watch.

Their escort turned an anxious face to them and he muttered something abstractedly, indicating that they should follow him. So evident was his concern, Joe speculated that the young man's relationship with the star was warmer than he had declared. It wouldn't have been surprising. Josephine was rumoured to enjoy a vigorous and fast-changing series of romantic involvements. But if the reporter had been a fixture in her frantic life for over a year, he must occupy a position of some trust and intimacy.

He led them at an ankle-breaking pace down staircases and along narrow corridors, burrowing always deeper into the vast unseen reaches of the theatre. They swept through gaggles of girls, practising steps and formations in any space they could find, skirted around others standing rigidly enduring the pinning up and repair of flimsy costumes. Someone threw a tap shoe along with a curse at them as they blundered by. Finally, they climbed a spiral staircase which brought them out on the level of the dressing rooms. The first three rooms were crowded with dozens of girls with sweaty towels round their necks, offering greasy faces to over-bright mirrors, dipping fingers into pots of Crowe's Cremine or peering closely to apply layers of Leichner make-up. They were screeching at each other in English, breaking off to shout louche invitations to the three men as they hurried by. All perfectly normal behaviour. Joe felt he could have been backstage at the London Palladium. Nothing untoward going on here.

At the end of the corridor, a group of three men stood guard in front of the closed door of the star's dressing room. They were agitated. They did not wait for introductions. One, the director, Derval, who'd boomed at them from the stage, put a hand on the door knob.

'Come in quietly! No fuss please! We haven't disturbed or touched anything. We'll stay outside until you call us. This is Alex, our stage manager. He found her.' He nodded to one of his companions. 'He went to check whether she'd arrived yet.'

Simenon frowned and chewed his lower lip but said nothing.

'You'd better go in with them, Georges,' Derval added, touching the man's shoulder gently.

* * *

She was lying in the middle of the room, on her front on the floor with the back of her glossy black head to the door. Her high-heeled shoes had fallen off. They were green satin, exactly matching the shining cocktail dress that had slid up, revealing brown thighs and strong calves. Joe at first wondered whether the room had been ransacked. Everything was in disorder. Clothes and stage costumes hung from every picture rail and spilled from open couturiers' boxes littering the floor, towels were draped on every chair back. There was a stench, overpowering and at first inexplicable. A potent cocktail of death and dung. Joe wrinkled his nose, trying to identify the elements. A farmyard? A zoo? And then he noticed the menagerie. In cages and boxes, small animal faces pushed forward, grunting, growling, mewing, sensing their presence, eager for attention. Dog, cat, two rabbits, a small goat, a leopard cub asleep on a cushion in a cardboard box, and — Good Lord! — a snake, thankfully securely boxed.

Well, that at least explained the trail of cereal of some sort that had spilled from the dead girl's hand all over the carpet. She'd dropped a bag of pet food and must have been preparing to feed her animals when she was attacked.

The reporter had rushed forward and sunk to his knees beside her before they thought of calling a warning, touching her sleek head with a caressing hand. 'She's dead,' he whispered. Then he recoiled and froze, eyes starting. He gasped and cursed and, taking the body by the shoulders, turned it over.

19

It was Joe's turn to draw in his breath in surprise. 'It's not her . . . No — that's not Miss Baker!'

He stared at the face and added, 'No scarlet thread. Thank God for that at least.' His gaze lingered uncertainly. 'But all the same, there's something odd here . . . something missing . . . '

'You're right, though. It's Francine,' said Bonnefoye. 'Francine Raissac.' He moved to the body with quiet authority. 'Would you both move aside?' Bonnefoye checked for signs of life and shook his head. 'Dead — and very recently. Within the last half-hour. After a second's inspection, I'd say she'd been strangled. No — wait a moment — neck broken. Better leave that to the pathologist. But what on earth was she doing here? By herself in the star's dressing room? All dolled up for a party but feeding the animals? It's unreal!'

The reporter, visibly shaking from the shock, had taken a pipe from his pocket and was attempting to hold a match steady enough to light it. 'No, you're wrong. Everyday scene. The girls were very thick,' he started to say, between puffs. 'Josephine liked her. They were always giggling together. She had the run of the place.'

'I understood from Francine herself that she often modelled new outfits for Josephine. They're the same size and I suspect Francine may have worked hard at acquiring the new fashionable Baker look. Not difficult with her dark skin and hair,' Joe said.

'She would choose clothes for Josephine to wear after the show. Josephine always goes on somewhere after she's performed. She's tireless, you know! Usually to a nightclub. To her own, first of all. Chez Joséphine, it's called. In the rue Fontaine. And then on somewhere else. Brick-top's more often than not. She's not *captivated* by fashion as Francine is . . . was — she takes her word for it that what she's picked out for her will be just right for whatever party she has in mind.' The words spilled out, a confusion of thoughts and tenses, a reaction to the relief he clearly felt. Relief that the dead girl at his feet was not Josephine but also guilt that, in these circumstances, he could be feeling relief at all. He collected himself. He stared at the body and frowned in pity. 'Francine always got it right. This green satin gown is probably the one she'd selected for whatever Josephine was planning for this evening.

'And she used to come in before work to see to the menagerie.' Simenon waved a hand with distaste in the direction of the animals. 'Josephine adores them but she isn't all that consistent in her care . . . no more than she is with people, I suppose. Francine couldn't bear to see them go without attention. She even cleaned up after them and took them for walks. The ones that *can* walk. I suspect Derval slipped her a little extra for her trouble. She never stopped working, that girl.'

They watched in fascination as Bonnefoye in total silence poked and prodded his way through a textbook examination of the corpse. Joe determined to extract as much information as he could from the man who was so close to both girls. For Joe, listening to witnesses' early reactions was more important than firing off the usual series of routine police questions. And he'd never met a witness so involved and so insightful, he thought, as this man. He would encourage him.

'Are you thinking that this may be — if indeed it is murder we're looking at — a case of mistaken identity? Finding Francine, looking as she does, in Josephine's clothes, going about what ought to be Josephine's chores, perhaps with her back to the door, one can understand that a mistake might have been made.'

'They're really meaning to kill Josephine, you mean? I had feared as much.' He took two deep puffs on his pipe and the atmosphere in the room thickened further. 'She has enemies, you know. Quite a lot of them are American. Successful, self-opinionated, liberated black girl that she is — that's too much for some of them to stomach. I was with her at a dinner party the night before last — we were celebrating the arrival of Lindbergh. Some oafish fellow countryman announced in ringing tones across the table that black girls where he came from would be in the kitchen cooking the food, not sitting at table eating it with civilized folks. I think sometimes it breaks her heart. Strong heart though.'

'And, I've heard — enemies in the theatre,' said Joe. 'Rival ladies wishing to be the paramount star in the Paris heaven. Ladies with influential lovers, prepared and able to indulge them.'

'She nearly died when that device she comes down from the roof in misfired. Death trap! There was a fuss and they sacked someone. But there never was a serious enquiry. Certainly no one called the police in.' He looked at Joe across the body, startled. 'It could have been arranged. Someone could have been paid to foul up the works.'

'The most spectacular exit ever on the French — or any other — stage, that would have been,' said Joe thoughtfully. And with a memory of Fourier's avid face, 'What headlines! *Black Venus plummets head-first into death pit*.'

'*Dea ex machina*. It was just a rehearsal, thank God. But it could have gone to performance, you know. I might have been in the audience, witnessing the death with my own eyes,' murmured Simenon with a shudder. 'What a waste of an opportunity! Because, I can tell you, it's not an article I could ever have written.'

Joe believed him and was glad to hear him say so. And yet Joe was, while struggling with his shock, touched by a feeling of resentment. He could find no comfort in the realization that this was not the star lying dead at his feet. There was no need to mourn Josephine. But this was Francine, the girl he had flirted with, sipped coffee with, and, by his unwitting clumsiness, annoyed the hell out of only yesterday. He'd liked and admired her. More than that. He flushed with guilt as he acknowledged he'd been planning a further meeting with Mademoiselle Raissac. In fantasy, he'd taken her to a performance at the Comédie Française — more her style than the cabaret, he thought — and then he'd walked with her along the Seine and dropped in at the Café Flore for a brandy before . . . well . . . whatever Paris suggested.

He looked again in sorrow at the chilling flesh and realized how much of her attraction had sprung from her movements, her light gestures, the slanting, upward challenge offered by her dark eyes. He remembered her head tilted like a quizzical robin and now permanently tilted, it seemed, at that angle by a broken neck. The last throaty, gurgling laughter he'd provoked by his clowning beneath her window in Montmartre replayed in his memory. Stylish and intelligent. He was saddened that such a girl had thought it necessary to copy the looks of anyone, even an entertainer like Josephine. The thought startled him into a gesture.

'Bonnefoye! There *is* something wrong here!' He bent and looked closely at the dead face. 'Her hair. Look, there — d'you see? — it's been cut. Raggedly. She had a kiss curl on her forehead, I'm certain, when I met her yesterday. You know — one of those cowlick things . . . stuck down on her forehead like Josephine.'

'*Une mèche rebelle*,' said Simenon. 'Yes, she had. There's a pair of scissors — over there on the floor.' He went to peer at them, carefully refraining from touching them. 'And there's a black hair trapped between the blades.' He looked back at Francine. 'She's cut it off. Perhaps that was yesterday's fashion?' Concerned, he went to the waste basket and turned over the contents. 'No hair.' He checked the crowded surface of the dressing table. 'No hair anywhere.'

With mounting dismay, Joe pointed to the girl's mouth. 'Her lipstick's badly smudged.' He touched her cheeks gently. 'And her face is puffy.'

'Time for the opening of the mouth ceremony?' said Bonnefoye quietly. 'What did you say, Joe? Release the *ka*? Let's do it, while we can — before rigor starts to set in!'

He delicately ran a finger between her lips and slid it under her top teeth. With his other hand he tugged gently on the lower jaw and the mouth sagged open. The fingers probed the inside of her mouth and drew out the contents.

With an exclamation of disgust, Joe spread his handkerchief on the floor by the corpse to receive the damp bundle.

Bonnefoye poked at it. 'A wad of currency and . . . ' He flipped the folded notes over revealing something wrapped tightly up in them. 'There it is — the curl of hair.'

He sat back on his heels, confused and defeated. 'Now what the hell are we supposed to make of that?'

'*Mèche*! That's what we're meant to understand!' Simenon's voice was urgent, trying to stifle triumph. 'It's a play on words! It means 'kiss curl, strand of hair' but it's also a candle wick . . . or a fuse. And if someone informs on you in criminal circles you'd say: *on vend la mèche*. They're selling out. Selling information. They got the girl they wanted, you know. It was Francine they intended to kill. No mistake!'

'And the choice of currency, I believe, was not random,' said Joe bitterly. 'Significant, would you say? That the notes are *English* ones? Have you noticed? Those elegant white sheets of paper are English treasury fivers. They're saying she sold out to *me*. To the English cop. They've crammed in ten of them. Fifty pounds! No expense spared on the death of a little Parisian *ouvreuse*? More money than she ever had in her life.'

He turned away to hide his sorrow and anger.

Simenon's eyes flashed from one policeman to the other. 'Ah. Little Francine whispered more than she ought to have done into a sympathetic English ear, did she? Alfred? He's the connection. He talked to *her* and she talked to *you*, Sandilands. Brother and sister both got their rewards then. They're suspicious of family relationships. One sees why. Word of this will be on the street by the end of the day. And people like me will be silenced for another year.' He turned to Joe and finished quietly: 'Whatever you charmed out of her, keep it to yourself, will you? I don't want to hear. Not sure it's even safe to stand next to you.'

Joe began to pull himself together and turned again to the body, though he noticed the younger men looked away, unable to meet his eye, alarmed by his expression. For a fleeting moment, the two sides of his face came together, disconcertingly in harmony, uniting to give out the same message. A message of fierce hatred.

Joe made the sign of the cross over the dead girl and knelt, tugging down and straightening the hem of the green satin dress. 'Even in death, she looks beautiful,' he murmured. 'She'd be pleased to be making her last appearance in something special. Not her black uniform. What is this little number do you suppose, Bonnefoye?'

'I know what this is. I checked the label. It's a Paul Poiret. Her favourite.'

* * *

The three men gathered at the door, pausing to adjust their expressions, regain control and prepare for the flood of questions waiting for them in the corridor.

On the point of leaving, Simenon took a parting glance around the room, then, one element of the chaos evidently catching his attention, he pointed and exclaimed.

'Look! Over there! That's how he got in!'

20

They followed his pointing finger to a lavish bouquet of two dozen large white lilies abandoned behind the door and beginning to wilt on the floor. The smell of death. Funerals and weeping. Joe had seen too many lilies.

Bonnefoye sighed. 'A special delivery! They must be three feet high! Walking along behind those, no one's going to notice your face or challenge you. 'Who are you and what's your business here?' Pretty obvious, I think. You'd feel silly asking!'

'And flowers arriving at the stage door — it's a daily occurrence. There's usually someone on duty to receive them, though, and bring them on here to her dressing room.'

'I'm thinking this must have been a particularly forceful delivery boy,' said Joe. 'Too much to hope there's a card with them, I suppose?'

Bonnefoye checked and came up with nothing more than a shrug.

'Well, gentlemen, are we ready to face the crowd?' asked Joe.

Information, explanation and requests for back-up followed in an intensive quarter of an hour. Derval hurried away to carry out Bonnefoye's instructions.

'I hope you don't mind but, in the circumstances, with the performance about to start, we've kept all this quiet,' said the stage manager, assuming authority. 'Josephine turned up five minutes ago, strolling down the corridor, munching on a ham sandwich, cool as you please. God! I nearly fainted! We guessed what had happened and when Derval could get his voice back he told her there'd been an accident in her room, a spillage . . . Had to get the cleaners in . . . When we could reassure her that her animals were all safe she agreed to borrow a costume, use the general dressing room and go on as normal. She doesn't make a fuss . . . used to bunking up . . . gets on well with the girls. Goodness only knows what I'm going to tell her when she comes off! She was very fond of Francine, you know. We all were.'

Joe launched into an angry outburst. 'Then you should take better care of your staff, monsieur! Where is your security in all this? A murderer walks in from the street and kills what he assumes to be the star? What next? One killing on the premises, I will call chance, two, a coincidence. But three? That's known as enemy action! If you call us back here for a further crime I shall send Commissaire Fourier to arrest *you*! Good day, monsieur.'

Joe and Bonnefoye each felt his arm taken in a firm grasp and they heard Simenon's voice in their ears growling: 'The bar's open! Come on, lads — we all need a brandy. This way!'

* * *

'It's not your fault. I'm talking to both of you! I haven't got the whole picture by any means, but

I see enough to say: I can see you're both knocked sideways by that girl's death — more than professional concern calls for perhaps? I don't know what more you could have done or shouldn't have done and why you should hold yourselves responsible, but it wasn't *your* hands around her throat. Hang on to that! All you can do now is find those hands.'

'And break every last bone in each one,' muttered Bonnefoye viciously. 'Slowly and one at a time. Then stamp on both of them.' Catching sight of Joe's wondering look, he added, 'Excuse me. My uncle was in the Foreign Legion.'

They had found a quiet corner behind a screen of potted palms and were sitting, heads together, sipping generous measures of cognac, half an hour before the doors opened to admit the crowds.

'It seems that, unwilling as we were to believe it, what we've got is a double — at least — murder, carried out, gangland-style, to punish informers and send out a warning,' said Joe. 'Alfred and Francine.'

'You said you knew about Alfred?' Bonnefoye asked the newsman.

'Her brother? Rumours only. Nothing for certain. Feel like telling me?'

Bonnefoye obliged.

' . . . So it would seem to me that these clever dicks not only punish but signal ahead the identity of their next victim,' Joe summarized heavily.

'See what you mean,' said Simenon. 'All that stitching done on Alfred was a very personal warning to his sister.'

'She perceived it as such. Yes.'

'And her own death is meant to carry with it a threat to the next name on their list?'

'Oh, good God! Those English banknotes, Joe!' said Bonnefoye. 'It was more than a cocky way of saying, 'Look, this was all your fault. She sold out to *you*, you English copper.''

'Yes. I'm afraid so. Though they got that wrong. The notes they provided from their own resources. She had nothing from me but a red rose, a cup of coffee . . . and a laugh.' With an effort, he pulled himself together and battled on: 'I think the next name on their list is Joseph Sandilands. As Simenon here has remarked, I'm not safe to stand close to and I take the comment seriously. I've no intention of being the death of anyone else in this hellish chain. I think we know the source of the infection. Let me go in and lance the boil.'

'What! You know who's responsible for all this? Then why are you sitting here on your bums . . . excuse me . . . ?'

Joe and Bonnefoye exchanged looks.

'Are you quite sure you want to listen to this?'

Simenon looked from one to the other doubtfully then his curiosity overcame his wariness and he nodded.

'Very well. A further theory that we dismissed out of hand, I'm afraid,' said Joe. 'Perhaps we should reconsider. Alfred was involved with the nameless crew you have mentioned to us. He became addicted to drugs and, we must assume, less reliable on account of that. Confused, lacking judgement . . . desperate. Perhaps the reason they wanted to get rid of him? These soldiers appear to maintain an absolute discipline. He remained close to his sister — dependent on her — and, as they rightly feared, had confided information to her. Not exactly key information — I suspect he was something of a fringe figure . . . messenger boy . . . back-up. But information we — ' he glanced at Bonnefoye — 'heave been able to make use of. An address,' he added vaguely. 'Look — we know nothing for certain. We merely have a fervid imagining that there may be an assassination service operating from these premises. One of rather special quality.'

'Do you know who's running it?' Caution overcame eagerness and Simenon hurried to add: 'Don't give me a name.'

'We couldn't anyway. No idea. There obviously is a mind devising and controlling all this nastiness and, whimsically, we've called him Set after the Egyptian God of Evil. But that's since proved to be a distraction.'

Joe told him of Dr Moulin's theory which had been shot down by Jack Pollock's evidence.

Simenon stirred excitedly and began to stuff his pipe again. 'You're saying the villain who committed the murder in the Louvre confessed to it and died by his own hand, thus breaking the continuity? He didn't take responsibility for any of the others?'

'Not yet known for certain. Pollock is a good authority but I'll check the records. Shouldn't be difficult.'

'Then, consequently, the series of deaths the

pathologist recalls must all be personal, unconnected acts of imaginative staging? Not impossible, of course. Most murders are impulsive but boring, spur of the moment stuff . . . the push downstairs, the carving knife through the heart over the Sunday roast . . . Not many would have the confidence or the patience to kill as you've described. Though I can imagine the satisfaction. There's this editor I've worked for who's just asking to be . . . Never mind! Tell me — when, in Moulin's chain of suspicious events, did this Egyptian one occur? Do you know? The *first* he was aware of? So the concept died with him? Hmm . . . But there *is* a thread, you know . . . stretching all the way from the Louvre, forward to poor Francine. This obsession with the mouth. Things, revelatory things, spilling out.'

'I shall keep my mouth shut,' said Joe lugubriously. 'At all times.'

'I'd say you'd got their message,' said Bonnefoye. 'And so have I. I'm going to put you on the next Silver Wing service back to London. Gagged and bound if necessary.'

* * *

'If you're looking for a feller, always try the bar first.' The voice was female, joking and warmly American.

Simenon had shot to his feet a second before the other two men were aware of her presence. He introduced the two policemen to Miss Baker and went off to fetch her a glass of mineral water.

Like and yet unlike Francine. Joe was startled to see she was wearing a silk Chinese dressing gown the replica of the one the French girl had been wearing in her room in Montmartre. Seeing the girls side by side no one would have confused them, but from a distance or an odd angle or from behind it would have been all too easy to take one for the other. Judging by her lightness of tone and her smiles, no one had hurried forward to tell Josephine the truth of what lay behind the closed door of her dressing room. Cynically, he calculated they would not reveal it until the end of her performance. The show would go on, regardless of Francine.

'Two fellers? Well, how about that! Joe and Philippe? Say — I'm sorry I'm late! Long night! Didn't get to bed till six. Louis played until four in the morning! Can you imagine! And no one walks out of a Louis Armstrong performance. Have you heard him play? Come! Tonight! Pick me up here and we'll make a night of it,' she said, batting eyelashes flirtily at Bonnefoye.

For a moment, Joe was so disconcerted he could not remember why on earth they were seeing her. The three men exchanged glances, silently and shamefacedly acknowledging that they'd get the best information out of Miss Baker if she remained for the moment in ignorance of her friend's death.

Josephine herself came to their rescue. 'That poor old gent!' she exclaimed. 'I hate to think the guy was up there dying . . . could have been just above my head . . . while we were wiggling our way through that last Irving Berlin number. Why would anyone want to *do* that? At a show?'

'We were wondering, Miss Baker,' said Joe, 'if you could recollect anything — anything at all — of the occupant of what I'll call the murder box.'

'Sure. I'll try. Can't say I'd remember any old night. But this was special. Lucky Lindy made it, did you know that? Someone rushed in with the news and I went on in between numbers and announced it. Crowd went wild! And so they should! What a feller! I remember looking up at both boxes. But you'll have to tell me which one the dead guy was in.'

Joe touched her right hand and said, 'From the stage, he would have been on this side.'

'Okay. Up there.' She looked up to her right, and extended her finger, fixing the imagined box. 'Got it. Not that it makes a heap of difference, ya know — I could have been seeing double! Two gents. Wearing tuxedos, the both of 'em, and each with a girl. All snuggled up hotsy-totsy. Nothing out of the ordinary. Clapping. Seemed to be having a good time . . . '

She sipped her water with a smile of thanks for Georges and thought hard. They waited in silence. 'Can't say I noticed anything odd about the fellers but the *girls* . . . '

'Yes?'

'Yeah . . . that *was* kinda strange . . . I was struttin' about, leading the applause. Watching *them* watching me. Everybody was getting very excited about the flight. Clapping and whistling and screeching like you'd never heard but they were talking to each other as well, smacking each other on the back, standing on their seats. Gathering together into one big shout of congratulations. But not those girls.'

'Girls?'

'Yeah, the two of them. You'd have sworn they were agreeing with each other. Exchanged a look and turned and left. Without a word. No goodbyes. No nothing. It was choreography. And I know choreography! The men were left on their lonesome for the finale.' She frowned, doing her best to call up her fleeting impressions.

A good witness, Joe thought.

'The one you say died . . . ' Out came the right hand again. 'I last had a glimpse of him halfway, I suppose, through the finale. I don't have a lot to do in that routine — just prance around in gold feathers — and I remember being something put out — he was looking at his watch! Turning it this way,' she held up an arm and demonstrated, 'towards the stage lights, you know, to get a look at it. And he stared across at the other box. I was beginning to think we were losing the audience. Feller looked as though he couldn't wait to take off.'

'Strange behaviour?' murmured Joe.

'Well, exactly! Lord! If a hundred naked girls — and me! — can't knock his eye out, whatever will?'

'A good question, Miss Baker. What better entertainment can he possibly have wanted?'

Bonnefoye looked curiously at Joe, who had lapsed into silence, and he seemed about to speak but he was interrupted by Josephine who, half-rising, was drawing the conversation to a close. 'Still, sorry to hear the old goat died.'

'Don't be,' said Bonnefoye, getting to his feet. 'The man was more of a cold-hearted snake and he got off lightly. Don't give him another thought.'

* * *

Simenon showed them to the side door and said goodbye. 'You will let me know how all this turns out?' he said hesitantly. 'I've been most intrigued . . . '

'And helpful,' said Bonnefoye. 'We've been interested to hear your insights, monsieur.' He hesitated for a moment. 'Look. You're a crime reporter. You must be keen to see how we live over there at the Quai? Take a peek inside? Have you ever been? Well, why don't you come over and see me there when this is all over? I'll fill you in. My turn to give *you* the tour!'

'Bit rash, weren't you?' Joe commented as they walked away back into the avenue de Montaigne. 'Fourier won't like that.'

'Sod Fourier! I can swing it! Anyway — with the ideas you've been stuffing into his head, a newsman might be just exactly what he wants to encourage . . . 'Now, my dear Simenon, just take this down, will you?' Chaps like that are very useful to us. They're a channel. They're not exactly informers but — well, you heard him — he talks to people who'll accept a glass from him and open their mouths but who wouldn't be seen within a hundred yards of a flic. They can pass stuff to the underworld we can't go out and shout through a megaphone. He seemed to be able to take a wide view of things. Man of the world.'

'And quite obviously something going on between him and the star, wouldn't you say?'

'Oh, yes, of course. Good luck to them! How did he say they met? Stage-door Johnny, didn't he say? Just turned up on the off-chance?'

'Yes. But not empty-handed,' said Joe thoughtfully. 'Said he brought her a bunch of roses. Roses . . . lilies . . . ' He looked about him. 'We're a long way from a florist's shop here. But there must surely be some enterprising merchant out there catering for star-struck young men on their way to the theatre?'

'Place de l'Alma,' said Bonnefoye, turning to the right and walking towards the river.

⋆ ⋆ ⋆

'Lilies? Two dozen? Yes, of course. Not every day I shift two dozen in one go! Lucky to get rid . . . they were just on the turn. I told him: 'Put them straight away in water up to their necks.' Must be nearly two hours ago. That's right — the bell on the Madeleine had already rung two. But not the half past . . .

'What did he look like? Oh, a handsome young chap!' The *fleuriste* turned a toothless smile on Joe and cackled. 'To my old gypsy eyes at least. Rather like you, monsieur. Your age. Young but not too young. Tall, well set up. Dark skin. Southern perhaps? North African even? Mixed probably. Sharp nose and chin. Well dressed. Nice hat. Lots of money.

'You'd need lots of money to buy all those lilies! His wallet when he took it out to pay for them was stuffed! Wished I'd asked double! He didn't really seem interested in the price. Some of them haggle, you know. This one didn't. Paid up, good as gold.

'Scar? Can't say I noticed one . . . I did notice the bristles though. He's growing a beard. It'll be a fine black one in a few weeks' time.

'Where? Oh, he walked back up the avenue towards the theatre.' The old woman grinned. 'Probably spotted some young dancer on the front row. He'll certainly impress her with those flowers anyway!'

Sensing they were about to close up the interview, she recalled their attention: 'Do you want to know what he was doing before he came to my stall?'

A further five francs changed hands.

'He was wandering about on the bridge. Looking at the statues,' she said. 'Now, gentlemen, I've got some lovely red roses fresh in from Nice this morning if you're interested . . . '

'Heard enough?' said Bonnefoye using English, in a voice suddenly chilled. 'She's scraping the barrel now.' And then: 'He's not exactly hiding himself, is he? He must have known we'd trace him here to this stall.'

'He's watching us at this moment,' said Joe, managing by a superhuman effort not to look around. 'Down one of those alleys, at one of those windows. Under the bridge even.'

Bonnefoye carefully held his gaze and Joe added: 'So, let's assume that, just for once, it's we who have the audience, shall we? And give him something to look at.'

He turned to the flower seller. 'Thank you, madame. I'll take two dozen of those red roses from Provence.'

The old woman stood and moved a few yards to watch them as they went down to the river. When she saw what they were about, she shook her head in exasperation. Idiots! Mad foreigners! Had they nothing better to waste their money on? They'd taken up their position halfway along, leaning over the parapet, and, taking a dozen blooms each, were throwing the roses, one at a time, downstream into the current.

She pulled her shawl tighter about her shoulders and crossed herself. She watched on as the swirls of blood red eddied and sank. How would those fools know? That what they were doing brought bad luck? Flowers in the water spelled death.

21

Bonnefoye had returned to the Quai des Orfèvres to pass on instructions for the fingerprint section and to check whether they'd made any progress with the Bertillon records of scarred villains. He'd been reluctant to let Joe turn up unaccompanied at the jazz club on the boulevard du Montparnasse, offering, as well as his own company, the presence of a team of undercover policemen in reserve.

Joe had reassured him. 'Don't be concerned . . . Just think of it as a visit between two old friends . . . Yes, I think I can get in. I'm prepared.' He patted his pocket. 'A bird has led me to the magical golden branch in the forest. I only have to brandish it and the gates to Avernus will swing open. As they did for Aeneas.'

Bonnefoye had rolled his eyes in exasperation. 'The gates can swing shut as well. With you inside. And I'm not too certain that Aeneas had a very jolly time. Full of wailing ghosts, Avernus, if I remember rightly. If you're not out by eight, I'm storming the place. I mean it! Now here's what I'm offering . . . '

* * *

Joe waited until six o'clock when the crowds hurrying in through the door made him less conspicuous. He went to the bar and ordered a cocktail. He asked for a Manhattan and threw away the cherry. A Manhattan seemed the right choice. The combination of French vermouth and American bourbon, spiked with a dash of bitters, was in perfect harmony with this atmosphere. Throaty, fast Parisian arpeggios studded a base of slow-drawing transatlantic tones and the band also seemed to be an element in the blend. Setting the scene, in fact, Joe thought, as he listened eagerly. Excellent, as Bonnefoye had reported.

A black clarinettist doubling on tenor saxophone was playing the audience as cleverly as his instruments this evening and there was a jazz pianist of almost equal skill. A banjo player and a guitarist added a punchy stringed rhythm. Not an accordion within a mile, Joe thought happily. Generously, the instrumentalists were allowing each other to shine, turn and turn about, beating out a supporting and inspired accompaniment while one of the others starred. To everyone's delight, the pianist suddenly grabbed the spotlight, soaring into flight with a section from George Gershwin's *Rhapsody in Blue* and Joe almost forgot why he was there.

Damn George! If it hadn't been for his officious nosiness, Joe could have been here, plying Heather Watkins with pink champagne, relaxing after a boring day at the Interpol conference, just a couple of tourists. She'd have been laughing at the new cap he'd bought and flattened on to his head, wearing it indoors like half the men in the room. Instead, he was crouching awkwardly, sitting slightly sideways on his bar stool to disguise the bulge of the Browning on his hip and hoping that no friendly American would fling an arm around him, encountering the handcuffs looped through his belt at the small of his back.

He glanced around at the crowd. Not many single men but enough to lend him cover. The one or two who appeared to be by themselves had probably chosen their solitary state, he reckoned. He saw two men line up at the bar, released from the company of their wives whom they had cheerfully waved off on to the dance floor in the arms of a couple of dark-haired, sinuous male dancers. What had Bonnefoye called them? Tangoing, tea-dance gigolos. Everyone seemed pleased with the arrangement, not least the husbands. On the whole, a typical Left Bank crowd, self-aware, pleasure-seeking, rather louche. But then, this wasn't Basingstoke.

He enjoyed the clarinettist's version of 'Sweet Georgia Brown' and decided that when he spiralled to a climax, it would be time to move on.

He ducked into the gentlemen's room and checked that, as Bonnefoye had said, it was no more than it appeared and waited for a moment by the door he held open a finger's breadth. No one followed him. A second later he was walking up the carpeted stairs towards the three doors he'd been promised at the top on the landing. And there they were. The middle one, he remembered, was the one behind which the doorkeeper lurked.

The building itself was a stout-hearted stone

and rather lovely example of Third Empire architecture seen from the exterior. But it had been drastically remodelled inside. The original heavy wooden features had been stripped away and replaced with lighter modern carpentry and fresh bright paint. Entirely in character with the new owner. Joe suspected.

He fished in his pocket for his ticket to the underworld, thinking it might not be wise to be observed digging about as for a concealed weapon at the moment when the door-keeper turned up. And the mirrors? Just in case, he offered his face to the fanlight, grinned disarmingly, and waited for Bonnefoye's promised monster.

A moment later the door opened and he was peremptorily asked his business by a very large man wearing the evening outfit of a maître d'hôtel. Bonnefoye, for once, had not exaggerated. The attempt to pass off this bull terrier as a manservant could have been comical had he not seemed so completely at ease in his role. He was not unwelcoming, he merely wanted to know, like any good butler, who had fetched up, uninvited, on the doorstep.

Joe held out the book he'd bought that morning.

'This is for madame. Tell her, would you, that Mr Charles Lutwidge Dodgson . . . ' He repeated the name. ' . . . is here and would like to speak to her.'

It's very difficult to avoid taking a book that someone is pressing on you with utter confidence. The man took it, looked at Joe uneasily, asked him to wait, and retreated, closing the door behind him.

A minute later, the door was opened again. He saw a slim blonde woman, giggling with delight and holding out her arms in greeting.

'Mr Dodgson, indeed!' She kissed him on each cheek. Twice.

'We can all make use of a pseudonym at times,' he said, smiling affably and returning her kisses. 'Good to see you again, Alice.'

The giant appeared behind her, a lowering presence. She turned to him and spoke in French. 'Flavius, my guest will hand you his revolver. House rules,' she confided. 'I see you still carry one on your right hip, Mr Dodgson.'

Joe traded steely gazes with Flavius as he handed over his Browning. The man's head was the size of a watermelon and covered, not in skin, but in hide. Cracked and seamed hide, stretched over a substructure of bone which had shifted slightly at some time in his forty years. Wiry grey-black hair sprouted thickly about his skull but had been discouraged from rampant growth by a scything haircut. It was parted into two sections along the side of his head by an old shrapnel wound. Or a bayonet cut. His hands resembled nothing so much as bunches of overripe bananas. Joe wondered what pistol had a large enough guard to accommodate his trigger finger.

'Thank you, that will be all, Flavius,' said Alice daintily. 'I'll call you if we need to replenish the champagne.'

'Or adjust the doilies,' said Joe.

'May I just call you, as ever — Joe?' she said, switching back to English when her guard dog had stalked off on surprisingly light feet. She held up the copy of *Alice's Adventures in Wonderland*, with a peacock's feather poking out from the pages as he remembered it on her shelf in Simla. The hat maker in the rue Mouffetard had been puzzled and amused by his request that morning and had refused payment for such a small piece of nonsense but it seemed to have worked. Alice was still laughing. 'Do you know, I never did get further than the page marker! I got quite bogged down in the middle of a mad tea party.'

'The reason most of us leave India,' Joe suggested.

'Yes indeed! But, as you know, it wasn't boredom that drove me away! I was having a happy time. It was Nemesis in the shape of a granite-jawed, flinty-eyed police commander who chose to delve too deeply into my business affairs.'

Joe decided to bite back a dozen objections to her light summary of a catalogue of murder, theft and fraud. 'Not sure I recognize *him*. Shall we just say something came up and you had to leave India in a hurry?'

'*You* came up, you toad! And here you are again, doing what toads do! Now the question is — shall I step on you and squash you or invite you inside and give you a kiss?'

'I think it's *frogs* that are the usual recipients of osculatory salutations,' he said cheerfully.

Alice groaned. 'Still arsing about, Sandilands? Can't say I've missed it! But come in anyway.'

He followed her trim figure along the corridor. Dark red cocktail dress, short and showing a good deal of her excellent legs. Her shining fair hair, which had been the colour of a golden guinea he remembered, was now paler, with the honey and lemon glow of a *vin de paille*. It was brushed back from her forehead and secured by a black velvet band studded with a large ruby over her left ear. Had her eyes always had that depth of brilliant blue? Of course, but in the strait-laced society of Simla, she had not dared to risk the fringe of mascara-darkened lashes. She still had the power to overawe him. He found himself looking shiftily to left or right of her or down at her feet as he had ever done and was angry with his reaction.

'Joe, will you come this way?' She turned and, stretching out her right hand, invited him to enter a salon. Distantly, sounds of the jazz band rose through the heavily carpeted floor and he realized they must be directly over the jazz café. She closed the door and they were alone together.

'Champagne? I was just about to have a glass of Ruinart. Will you join me?'

'Gladly.'

She went to a buffet bearing a tray of ice bucket and glasses and began to fill two of the flutes, chattering the while.

'Cigarette? I'm told these are good Virginian . . . No?' She screwed one into the end of an ebony holder and waited for him to pick up a table-lighter and hold the flame steady while she half-closed her eyes, pursed her scarlet mouth and drew in the smoke inexpertly. Joe read the message: English vicar's daughter, fallen amongst rogues and thieves and ruined beyond repair, yet gallantly hanging on to some shreds of propriety. He was meant to recall that, for someone of her background, smoking was a cardinal sin. He smiled. He remembered her puffing away like a trooper at an unfiltered Afghan cigarette in Simla.

'Five years?' she asked, her thoughts following his, back into the past. 'Can it really be five years since we said goodbye to each other on the steamer? You're doing well, I hear. And I hear it from George of all people. We met at the theatre the other day. Did you know he was in Paris?'

'Yes, I did. But tell me how *you* knew he was going to be here, Alice.'

'No secret! You know my ways! In India I was always aware of who exactly was coming and going. It's just as easy to keep track of people over here if you know the right man to ask. And the French are very systematic and thorough in their record keeping. A few francs pushed regularly in the right direction and I have all the information I need at my fingertips or rather in my shell-like ear . . . ' She glanced at a telephone standing on a table by the window. 'Bribes and blackmail in the right proportions, Joe. Never fails. Tell me now — how did you find George? Is he all right? I heard a certain piece of nastiness was perpetrated after I left the theatre. I'm guessing that's why you're here?'

Alice shuddered. 'I blame myself. If I hadn't shot off like that, he would never have gone over and got himself involved with all that nonsense. Look, Joe, I'd rather not break surface and I'm sure you can understand why but if he's desperately in need of help, then — oh, discretion can go to the winds — the man's a friend of mine. I do believe that. I always admired him. If I can say anything, sign anything to get him out of that dreadful prison, then I will. That *is* why you're here, Joe?'

'No, it's not. And don't concern yourself about George. No action required — I'm sure I can manage.'

'I'm assuming he is still over there on the island?' she asked less certainly. 'Or have you managed to get him out?'

'He's in police custody,' said Joe, looking her straight in the eye. Alice had, he remembered, an uncanny way of knowing when she was being told a lie. And she was likely to have developed such a skill leading the dubious life she'd led. He wouldn't have trusted himself to tell her anything but the truth. 'Still in the hands of the French police,' he said again. 'He's not enjoying the downy comfort of the Bristol which is where he ought to be but I'm pleased for him to be where he is. For the moment. I don't believe Paris to be an entirely safe place for him. I've persuaded Commissaire Fourier, in charge of the case, to go more easily on him — the Chief Inspector seems to think he ought still to have the use of medieval methods of extracting a confession as well as the medieval premises.'

'Poor, dear George! You must do what you can, Joe!'

'Of course. I visit every day. I'm happy to report the bruises are healing. He enquired after you when I saw him this morning. Wanted to know that you are well and happy.'

'Ah? You will reassure him then?'

'Can I do that? Tell me — what should I report of little Alice in Wonderland? Business good, is it?'

For a moment she was taken aback. 'My businesses always do well. You know that, Joe. Until some heavy-footed man comes along and stamps them into the mud.'

He decided to go for the frontal attack. 'So — how do you get on with the management of the Sphinx? Your competitors can't have been too enchanted when you came along and set up here in their rabbit patch. Have you come to some amicable agreement? Equable share of the lettuces? They have a Paris bank underpinning them financially, I understand. I wonder how you manage, Alice? A single, foreign woman?' He shook his head. 'No. Wouldn't work, would it?' And, abruptly: 'Who's your partner?'

He saw the moment when she made up her mind. Alice hadn't changed. She was behaving as she had done years ago. Why not? It had deceived him then. Wide-eyed, she was about to plunge into a confession to a sin she knew would revolt him, a sin in his eyes so reprehensible it would distract him from and blind him to the deeper evil she must keep hidden at all cost.

'Very well. I see you've worked it out. I run a brothel. The very best!' She made the announcement as though she'd just made a fortune on the stock exchange and wanted him to share in celebrating her good luck. 'Even you, old puritan that you are, Joe, could hardly object. My clients are the cream of society. The richest, at any rate . . . They demand and I supply the loveliest girls, dressed by Chanel, jewels by Cartier, conversation topics from the *New Yorker*.'

'I understand. Expensive whores. Is that what you're dealing in these days? But, of course, you learned a good deal from Edgar Troop, Brothel-Master Extraordinaire, branches in Delhi and Simla.'

'These girls aren't whores! They are *hetairai* — intelligent and attractive companions!' Pink with anger, she put out her cigarette, creasing her eyes against the sudden flare of sparks and smoke. Calculating whether she was wasting her time in self-justification. 'You are not in England, Commander. Are you aware of the expression *maison de tolérance*?'

'I have it on my information list, just above *magasin de fesses* and *abattoir*,' he said brutally. 'Knocking shop and slaughterhouse, to translate politely.'

'Tolerance!' she replied angrily. 'These establishments are exactly that — *tolerated* — not hounded out of existence by hypocrites like you. As long as the ladies succumb to their weekly health check — the doctor visits — we break no rules. So, if you've come to threaten me, I'm not impressed. If the Law can't close down those abattoirs in the rue de Lappe, they're hardly likely to turn their attention on *me*. Not with the list of habitués I have . . . *députés*, industrialists, royalty, diplomats . . . senior police officers,' she finished triumphantly. '*You* will be seen leaving. You may be sure of that! I may even send your superior a photograph to show how his pet investigator adds to his expenses.'

Her lip curled as she played with an amusing thought. 'Though, in the manly English way, he'd probably summon you to his office to compare notes.'

'Probably,' Joe agreed, the further to annoy her. 'Tell me — where do you recruit? I can't see you standing in line with the other pimps at the Gare du Nord?'

'My girls are top drawer! Your sister was probably at school with some of them . . . ' she added defiantly. 'Some of them I found in the music hall line-ups, some had just run away to Paris for excitement, some are escaping violent men in their lives . . . Not many openings for unsupported girls in these post-war days, you know. Men have flooded back and elbowed women out of the jobs they'd found in fields, factories and offices — '

'Spare me the social treatise, Alice!' Joe growled. 'You look ridiculous on that soap-box, champagne glass in hand, a hundred quid's worth of ruby over your left ear and twenty girls on their backs down the corridor, working for you.'

If she attacked him now, as he was hoping, he could have the handcuffs on her without a second thought. He'd find it easier than requesting politely that she extend her hands.

'Very well,' she said, ignoring his jibe, and

added angrily to annoy him: 'Starry-eyed romantic that you are, I know you'll not believe it when I tell you — some of my girls actually don't at all mind the way of life. They're paid well and cared for. *I* care about them and their welfare. They're fit and happy. See for yourself if you like. An hour or two on the house? No? Well, perhaps you can accept another glass of champagne?' She put out a hand.

He nodded, looking at her with stony face. 'Why don't you let me do that?' He went to the sideboard and refilled his glass, taking the opportunity of positioning himself between her and the door.

'And is *she* well and happy, the little miss who was encouraged to enter the wild animal cage with Somerton the evening before last? The bait you hobbled for the tiger? Did you warn her about the character of the man she was to entertain?'

Alice laughed. 'Watch out, Commander! Your soft centre's oozing out of that hard crust! Something you have in common with Sir George. Makes me very fond of the pair of you! My girl wasn't in the slightest danger. I was on hand.'

'Because you knew it was never intended that she should finish the evening with him. At a given signal the two of you donned your silken cloaks and disappeared into the Paris night. Or did one of you — both? — lurk behind to ensure the killer had easy access to the box?'

'How the hell?'

'A wardrobe of four midnight-coloured cloaks

— I'm guessing that your girls, or a small picked unit of them, are actively involved in the other branch of your operation here. A sort of alluring Flying Squad? An undercover ops unit? You were always a showman, Alice. You enjoy playing games. And reading novels. Inspired by *The Three Musketeers*, were you? Well — listen! — this is where it all gets terribly serious.'

He put down his glass on a low table and stood ready to knock her to the floor if she tried to get past him or move towards the bell. To his surprise, she retreated away from the door and went to stand, a hand on the mantelpiece, at the other end of the room. He followed her, careful to position himself ready to block her exit.

'I've got handcuffs in my pocket. Real, steel ones, not forgiving flesh and blood ones. They'll be round your wrists and I'll be pulling you with me down the stairs and out into the street before you can say knife. And I'll hand you straight over to the lads of the Brigade Criminelle who are waiting below. You can sample the accommodation at HQ for yourself. Not sure which of the murders you'll confess to but eventually you will confess. I don't imagine even your partner's influence spreads as far as the inner reaches of the Quai des Orfèvres. He wouldn't be trying hard to ride to your rescue at any rate, I'd guess. And you'll have lost again, Alice, to a man who's made use of you. He'll wait, knowing you won't give him away, because by doing so, you implicate yourself. He'll sit it out until the storm's blown over . . . until the guillotine at La Santé has silenced you permanently and then he'll start up again. Madames are ten a penny. He can probably raise one from the ranks with no bother at all.'

'I'm not sure what you expect me to say. How can I respond to these maunderings? Partner? Who is this partner you rave on about?'

'The head of the assassination bureau. The undertaker of delicate commissions. Murder with a flourish. That partner. Or should I say — boss? Two compatible services under one roof. The White Rabbit, the jazz club, and its escape hole up here into Wonderland — your part of the organization, I would expect — and then there's the other. The Red Queen, I suppose we could call it. Wasn't she the one who rushed around calling 'Off with his head'? Or didn't your perusal of the text take you that far? She was quite insane, you know, and incapable of discriminating. Innocent or guilty, it didn't matter to her. Heads rolling was all she cared about. And so it is with your partner in crime.'

His voice hardened. 'I've seen his handiwork. Somerton's head was damned near severed. A youth of sixteen had his living lips stitched together. His sister had her neck broken and her mouth stuffed with banknotes because someone thought she'd spoken to me. Three deaths in as many days! You're sheltering Evil, Alice!'

'By God! You haven't had time to put all this together! Who've you been talking to?' She looked wildly around the room.

'You'll be safer with me in my handcuffs, so

stop looking at the bell. Every street urchin, every tramp under the bridge will know by this evening what you've been up to. It'll make the morning editions. The authorities may turn a blind eye to whoring but they still disapprove of murder. From this moment, you're a liability. Perhaps if I left you running loose he'd devise in his twisted, sick mind a way of bumping you off in a spectacular and appropriate way. Let me think now! What could it be? Found strangled with a silk stocking in the bed of Commissaire Fourier? I like that! I'm sure I'd be amused by the headline. Kill two nasty birds with one stone. Alice, you're finished here. Yes, you're safer with me.'

She was looking at him in horror. Distanced. Shocked. But still calculating. 'Safer with you? You're mad!'

'Possibly. Leaves you with a narrow choice, Alice. You walk out of the front door with a mad puritan and negotiate your future career or stay behind with a mad sadist and die. Which is it to be?' He looked at his watch. 'A taxi arrived just a minute ago in front of the jazz club. I expect your sharp ears picked it up?'

She turned her head very slightly to the window. The thick cream and black curtains and closed shutters reduced the traffic noise on the boulevard to a low murmur.

'It's sitting there with the engine idling. We can be inside it and away into the night in thirty seconds.'

Alice had never been indecisive. The last decision he'd seen her take had been witnessed by him down the barrel of a gun. A gun trained on him.

'Top left drawer of the sideboard,' she said. 'There's a Luger in there. 9 mm. It's loaded. Eight rounds. Safety's on. You're going to have to use it.'

22

'Your guard dog's standing right outside, isn't he?'

'Yes. He's as tough as he looks and he understands English. That's why I lured you down to this end of the room. Laugh a little, Joe. If you go on snarling at me, he'll come crashing in.'

She gave a peal of laughter that sounded genuine enough but he couldn't bring himself to join in. 'You won't be allowed to leave here alive, you know. I don't think we ever expected you'd come here . . . just walk in. Flavius will have sent a message by now . . . To the boss. I'll be expected to entertain you — to keep you on the premises until he gets here. He'll want to think up something original for *you*. It's high time the police had a warning shot across their bows.'

Joe decided to ignore her bluster and concentrate on the present danger. 'Tell me about him quickly, your Flavius. Is he a one off or is he at the head of a pack?'

He looked again at his watch.

'He's from the south. Not bright but quick enough. Vicious. Ex-Foreign Legion. Knife or gun, he doesn't mind. He'll have one of each in his hands at the moment. He's right-handed. He'll use the knife if he can — we like to avoid noises up here — but if he has to, he'll shoot you with his pistol. It's fitted with a silencer. He's top house dog but there's a security staff of four more always on the premises. They are wolves. Two North African, two Parisian. Armed. They have discreet house guns for indoor work. Beretta 6.35s. Last year's model. At the first sign of trouble, two will go out through the back exit and circle round. Two will come straight down the main corridor to back up Flavius.'

'Where are they all at the moment?'

'Flavius is right there, as you guessed, at the door. The others?' She shrugged. 'Playing cards in their room. It's ten yards down the corridor to the left. Playing with the girls, given half a chance. They won't be expecting trouble at this early hour and the girls won't be busy. We like to keep the staff sweet.'

Joe went to the sideboard. 'More champagne, m'dear?' he asked in a louder, drunken voice. 'Jolly good drop of fizz you keep! What?' He clinked a glass against the bottle at the moment he pulled open the drawer. It opened silently. He took out the Luger.

'It's fully loaded. I did it myself,' she mouthed.

Joe checked it anyway.

She shuddered as he reached behind his back and took a pair of handcuffs from under his jacket. 'I borrowed these from a colleague,' he murmured. 'I think I can make them work. Do I need to put them on you?'

'No. I'll be more use with my hands free. And don't forget we have to get out through the club. They're not used to seeing women in cuffs. And they're not very fond of the police. They might object.'

He slipped them back through his belt.

'Come closer to the door but stay well to the side. I don't forget he's got my Browning. If he fires that into the room the bullet won't stop until it hits the towers of Notre Dame. Remind me — which way does the door open?'

'Inwards.'

'Listen! When I nod, you're to squeal. Not loudly. Enough to encourage him to come in to investigate. Okay?'

'Ready.'

Joe took a deep breath then nodded.

Alice squealed.

Joe waited one second then blasted the door with four rounds. The wood splintered as the bullets tore through the flimsy structure. A lozenge pattern of blackened holes marked out a target area two feet square which would reach from throat to abdomen on a six foot two inch man standing at the door.

If, indeed, he had been standing at the door.

Joe heard no scream or oath. Not even a grunt.

Crouching to the side, he listened. Not a sound. No time to wait. The wolves would be slamming down their cards, saying, 'What the hell was that?' or murmuring 'Excuse me, ma'am' and unsheathing their Berettas. Covering the door space with his gun, Joe reached out, turned the knob and flung the remains of the door open into the room.

Alice made a little wuffling sound in her throat.

Flavius was utterly silent. His huge body lay

collapsed, sandbagging the doorway, still pumping out blood from at least two wounds. No screams because the highest and first of the bullets had shot out his throat.

Alice was faster than Joe. She leapt straight at the obstacle, scrambling in high satin heels over the twitching body. Joe followed. As they reached the door to the stairs Alice fiddled with the bolt and double lock and a gathering roar rumbled down the corridor after them. As the door yielded, Alice took off down the stairs.

Joe turned and raised the Luger. He watched the door Alice had mentioned, waiting. The door creaked open and the snub-nosed barrel of a pistol started to slide out. Joe fired. The gun crashed to the ground. Someone howled in pain. Joe fired again blindly through the wood. Two bullets remaining. He waited a heartbeat and fired them off, warning shots down the length of the corridor, then wiped the gun and threw it back towards Flavius's body. He turned and leapt, three steps at a time, down the stairs. Alice had already disappeared.

When he reached the entrance to the jazz club he paused and listened. The music had stopped, women were shrieking, men shouting. He was in greater danger of being torn apart in a mêlée of angry jazz fans, he calculated, than by the wolves.

He turned and backed into the door, bumping it open. He held up both hands, clearly unarmed, and gestured with a hand towards the stairs, a soldier indicating an enemy position. He yelled, '*Au secours!* Help!' He looked over his shoulder, eyes wide in alarm, and shouted into the horrified silence: 'Hell! A feller goes to the john and World War Two breaks out over his head! What sort of joint *is* this?'

Two hearty Americans leapt to his rescue and dragged him backwards to safety into the café. All three of them were instantly caught up and struggling in the general surge towards the exit.

⋆ ⋆ ⋆

God! It was there! Joe hadn't heard and really didn't believe in Bonnefoye's promised taxi but there it was, as he'd described it, panting and choking at the kerbside. A petulant Alice was locked in the back. Bonnefoye was leaning nonchalantly against the driver's door. He greeted Joe as he dashed up and unlocked the rear door.

'Do you mind, Joe? Sitting in the back? Standard procedure when we're carrying a dangerous prisoner. The lady took me for the driver. Understandable, as I was sitting at the wheel. Jumped in and told me to drive to the Gare de Lyon. In quite a hurry. Peremptory, even. Promised me a reward if I arrived on bald tyres! Another woman fleeing your company? What on earth do you say to them, Joe?'

He climbed in behind the wheel and turned off the engine. 'Well now — what do you have to tell me, Joe?'

⋆ ⋆ ⋆

'Four others on the premises, you say?' Bonnefoye was calm, enjoying the moment. 'We found the rear exit and covered it. There's a *panier à salade* round there blocking the alley and ten of our best boys raring to have a go. A section of the Vice Squad are on their way as well. They'll go in and clear up. Um . . . heard the noise. Are we likely to put our feet in anything up there, Joe?'

'I'm afraid so. One rather large casualty, bleeding copiously. Not our man — the doorman. Name's Flavius. Not that he's answering to it. Problem with his throat.'

'It was self-defence!' Alice spoke up firmly. 'He was threatening me and the Commander had to shoot him.'

'Much as I dislike contradicting a lady,' said Bonnefoye pleasantly, 'I have to say I think you've got that wrong, madame. Your guard was shot by one of the other bits of scum you keep about the place with the house gun. I expect if we search carefully we'll find the . . . '

'Luger,' supplied Joe.

' . . . Luger, yes. Wiped clean? Yes, of course. And we'll establish that the fracas was no more than a fight over a girl. The usual. We'll just have to wait and see which one confesses to what, won't we? But I'm sure one of them will be only too pleased to assume responsibility. Do you want to stay and see the fun, Joe, or shall we take off for the Quai?'

'Hold on a moment,' said Joe, still getting his breath back.

Alice had shrunk away from him as he pushed

himself into the back seat alongside her.

He stared at her and burst out laughing. 'Two minutes ago this woman, you'd have sworn, was on her way to the Ritz, sporting the last word in cocktail frocks! And now look at her! Milady de Winter! Fully caped. Booted and spurred probably too if I could be bothered to check. And — ' he kicked a soft leather bag she'd pushed away behind her calves — 'packed and ready for the weekend, I see. Now where were you off to, I wonder?'

'Not planning on helping us with our enquiries,' said Bonnefoye with mock resentment. 'I was watching her. She tore into the café and spoke to the barman. He handed that stuff to her from under the bar.'

'My exit bag. I always have it to hand,' she explained sweetly.

'And what were you intending to do at the Gare de Lyon, Gateway to the South? From where so many adventures start?' Joe asked. 'Return to your old haunts on the Riviera?'

'Change taxis? Head north . . . or east . . . or west,' she said, tormenting him. 'You'll never know. Not sure I do myself. Joe, are you ever going to introduce me to your charming young colleague? He seems to have the advantage of me.'

'No. You don't need to know him. You just need to do as he says.'

He had counted on annoying her, but Joe was taken aback by the fury in the glare she directed at him.

A small black police car screamed to a halt a

few inches in front of them.

'Here he is,' said Bonnefoye. 'My associate in Vice. I'll just leave you for a moment while I fill him in then we can leave. We'll make for a nice quiet place and put a few questions to the lady. If she answers correctly and reasonably, it may be that she can go free — after signing a statement, of course. If we're concerned by what she has to say then she may have to proceed as far as Commissaire Fourier. Won't be a minute.'

'How long will he be?' Alice's voice was strained. He could hardly see her face. She had flung the hood over her head and was shrinking down into the upholstery. Her eyes were scanning the crowds milling about on the pavement. 'We must leave now, Joe! Call him back! He — *you* — have no idea . . . '

Joe was reminded of George's remark about Alice's strange behaviour. ' . . . eyes quartering the room like a hunter,' he'd said and then corrected himself: 'No — more like the prey. There was someone out there in the auditorium . . . '

And there was someone out there at this moment on the pavement, coming closer. He began to catch Alice's fear. He spoke softly to her. 'Alice, we are surrounded by at least a dozen assorted flics. You're quite safe. For the moment.'

She looked at him, incredulous. 'You think that will stop him?'

Uneasy, he muttered, 'Damn! I haven't got a gun. I really did remember to wipe the Luger and drop it a suitable distance from the body. And — oh God! — I didn't get my Browning back. No time, even if I'd thought of it.'

Alice bent and fished about in her bag. 'Here. Take this. It's only a .22 but it's a little more effective than pointing a wagging finger.'

He took it warily, resting it along his thigh between them, finger on the trigger.

'You make me nervous, Alice,' he said finally. 'As nervous as you made Sir George on Saturday night at the theatre? And for the same reason perhaps? I'm afraid for my life. *Should* I be afraid for my life? What are your instructions this time? The same as last? Kill the Englishman?'

She looked at him, eyes darkening with suspicion inside her silk hood. 'What on earth do you mean?'

'I mean that I *know*, Alice. I know that you'd gone to the theatre that night, not for the pleasure of seeing Sir George again, but to kill him.'

23

'To kill him. At the very least, to participate in his killing.'

She swallowed but remained silent, still staring through the windows.

'Sir Stanley Somerton was never the target, was he? His death has brought freedom, much relief and even unholy joy to a good number of people but it was never intended, was it? No one put cash in an envelope and asked for *him* to die? Am I getting this right, Alice?'

She nodded her head. 'As usual.'

'Do you want to know how I guessed?'

'No. Not particularly. I assume you to be omniscient.'

'Well, I'll tell you anyway. Because I shall enjoy the satisfaction of making you and your filthy organization aware that you've been tripped up by no more than a couple of bystanders, neither of them connected in any way to the murder that went wrong but both sharp-eyed, observing accurately and passing on their observations to those who could make sense of them.'

Alice appeared not to be listening. 'Where's your friend? God! Now where's he off to? Do we have to wait for him?'

'The star of the show, Miss Josephine Baker,' Joe pushed on, 'was kind enough to grant us an interview. She's a responsive girl who feeds off her audience, is aware of them and their moods.

She remembers that evening particularly because the routine was broken. Lindbergh flew in and she took it upon herself, being from St Louis, to invite the audience to celebrate with her. She was aware of you, Alice, and your young employee in Somerton's box. She was aware enough of the two men to tell me the boxes were a mirror image of each other. Two elderly gents, two blonde young women with them. She didn't even know which man had died. Left or right, they were much the same to her. It made no difference to the star but it was life or death for one of those men. And then it struck me. For me, the kaleidoscope suddenly shifted and settled into a different pattern when she said that.

'And, taken with the strange behaviour of Somerton, the behaviour reported both by Sir George and by a treacherous school friend of his who happened to be in the audience, it all began to pull together. They said the same thing. George, compassionate man that he is, attempted in the only way open to him to ensure — not the virtue — but the well-being of your little tart across the way. Before the show started and you showed up, he got to his feet and in soldier's hand language told Somerton to back off. 'Or else!' he added. Accompanying his threat by a very familiar gesture. This!'

Joe performed the slow dragging of the index finger across the throat.

'George was relieved to see his old enemy signal: 'Message received and understood.' He was puzzled, though not disturbed, by the man's further reaction. He fell about laughing. The witness in the stalls, Wilberforce Jennings, told us that Somerton 'damn near slapped his thigh, he thought it so funny . . . '

'And it was funny. In the circumstances. Very. Ironic might be a more accurate word as no one but Somerton would have been genuinely amused by the gesture. Because George was the one who was supposed to die and in exactly the way he'd mimed — by the slicing of a dagger across his throat. And the man who supplied the dagger, chose the killing place and the time, and paid for the assassination show was Somerton *himself*. George's prophetic gesture added to the gaiety! The cherry in the cocktail!'

Joe didn't care that she was barely listening to him. His outrage pushed him to try to make an impression, to make her admit an understanding. Regret and shame were out of the question, he supposed.

'The vile Somerton discovered that Jardine, the man who'd disgraced him and ruined his life — as *he* saw it — was to be in Paris at the same time as himself. He wanted the satisfaction of watching while his old enemy was filleted in front of his eyes. But a solitary viewing is not an entirely satisfactory experience for a man like Somerton. He wanted to share it. He arranged to be seen, flaunting female company of the choicest kind, knowing that this would annoy Sir George. And he intended that his companion should join him in witnessing a real-life bit of theatre.'

'You know that's not what happened, Joe.'

'No. And I'm wondering what went wrong — or should I say right? It seems to me that someone threw a sabot into the works and put all the cogs out of mesh. Are you going to tell me?'

'Me! It was me! You know that! *He* didn't tell me, for once, the name of the target as he usually does. Sometimes he allows me a veto when he's getting his schemes together. He trusts my judgement. But in this case, he must have been offered a great deal of money and he didn't care to hear my objections.' Alice paused and bit her lip, still working through her reasoning. Not quite happy with her thoughts, Joe guessed. 'He might have expected me to balk at killing off someone I knew from India. And he was right. I would never have agreed to harming George. He confided in Cassandre — that's the girl's name — and set up the whole theatre episode with her. The assassin had been told to kill the Englishman in Box A, the one sitting alone. The client himself would have one of our girls with him, a protective marker, so there was no chance he would get it wrong.

'Cassandre consulted me about the outfit she should wear that evening and I discussed it with her. I was concerned that I'd been sidelined in this — suspected Cassandre herself of making a try for my own position. No such thing — the girl was just as much in the dark as I was. I got the whole thing out of her. It wasn't difficult, she assumed I knew. I was horrified. I knew nothing of this Somerton but I did know I wasn't going to let Sir George die. I thought by arranging for the other man to be killed in his place, I could put it down to a ghastly mistake on the part of the knifeman. And there'd be no client left behind to complain that he hadn't had his show, after all! No consequences!

'At the appointed time — the killing was fixed for the moment when the applause for the finale rang out — I left and went down the stairs. I met our man coming up and berated him. 'Idiot! The bloke you want is over the other side! B, not A. Don't you listen? Or don't you know your alphabet? I'm with this chap, can't you see? The other, the dark one, is the one sitting by himself. Go quickly!'

'Cassandre had got away by then, leaving the door ajar, and the fiend got in and did the business. So long as he had someone to carve up, he wouldn't give a damn. If someone had made a mistake it wasn't his fault. He would put it down to a management mix-up. He isn't paid to think. But stupid Sir George! Why the hell did he have to go over and foul everything up?'

'Because he's got what you've never had, Alice — a kind heart and a conscience. But . . . here comes Bonnefoye at last. Just time to say — thank you!' He scrabbled around for her hand and lifted it, cold and trembling, to his lips. 'For those dim glimmerings of human kindness, I thank you.'

'Dim glimmerings? Fool! I saved his life! And now see where it's got me, my human kindness! Sharing a taxi with two rozzers and on the way to prison.'

* * *

'You took your time,' Alice accused Bonnefoye. 'Can we go now?'

'Fun's nearly over,' he reported, settling back in again and easing out into the traffic. 'Didn't entirely go to plan. A problem. Apart from the corpse — four armed security, you said? We've got three of them. Two dead, two injured, trying to shoot their way out. They loaded the lot into the police ambulance and headed off for the Quai. At the first halt, corner of the boulevard, one of the wounded leapt from his pallet, bashed the attendant on the head and jumped out into the traffic. He's covered in blood — his or someone else's. We should be able to pick him up with no trouble.'

Alice groaned. 'You're saying you've left one of the wolves on the loose? He'll go straight to . . . ' She teetered on the edge of a name.

Finally Joe had thought she was about to give him what he wanted but she caught herself in time. Losing patience, he said: 'To whom, Alice? Who *is* this bogeyman you're so frightened of? Who's out there? How many of them?'

'Not many. He likes to keep it small. Very small now, but there are always men available to swell the ranks. There's the one you've allowed to escape, the knifeman, and the boss. But they've got a network that runs all through Paris. And beyond. They'll track us down wherever we go . . . Where *are* we going?'

'Yes — where *are* we going?' Bonnefoye repeated. 'I'm just the driver, madame. Better check with the gentleman.'

'Follow that ambulance!' said Joe, suddenly

coming to a decision. 'I wonder if you knew . . . in times of danger, the Parisii tribe who settled here — before the Romans arrived and spoiled things for them — would make for the central island and pull up the drawbridge, so to speak. We'll do the same. Île de la Cité, please, driver.'

'Oh, Lord! Not Fourier, Joe! Not sure I'm quite prepared for that yet!'

'I'm certainly not! No, I have in mind a different location. In the law enforcement buildings, but not involving a trip up Staircase A. A quiet spot . . . none quieter. We're off to the morgue!'

* * *

Moulin was already gowned, gloved and masked, standing ready. He was accompanied by three young assistants, similarly clad, sorting through trays of instruments. At their approach, he removed his surgical mask and gave them a puzzled smile of welcome. 'I was just on my way out for the evening,' he grumbled. 'Under this,' he indicated his white starched gown, 'I'm dressed for the opera. We were alerted by telephone. Rush job on. Someone warned us to expect incoming dead.'

'Ah, yes,' said Bonnefoye. 'That was me. Sorry to foul up your evening, doctor. Gangland fracas in the boulevard du Montparnasse. They'll be a few more minutes yet. They were told to drop the wounded off at the hospital before coming on here. When you check your laundry list, you'll find you have three bodies, unless another succumbed en route. There's one commander and two soldiers. Gun shots, all three.'

'Ah. Anything to do with you?'

'It's all right, doctor. The commander, a person with the proportions of a small whale, died first with not a scrap of police-issue hardware in him. Luger bullets from the house gun. That's what started it all. The other two . . . were reckless enough to fire on the officers sent to arrest them.'

'I say, excuse me, but is this an entirely suitable conversation for a lady's ears?' They heard the slight reprimand in his voice as Moulin turned a concerned face to Alice. She had been standing listening, not, apparently, looking for a formal introduction. 'I'm sorry, mademoiselle? Madame?' He broke off with a bemused and reproving glance at Joe.

'Don't worry, Moulin. The lady's seen and heard and, indeed, perpetrated much worse. May I introduce you to a genuine example of *Latrodectus mactans*? We're here seeking sanctuary. Her life may be in danger — from the villains who are responsible for all this mayhem. I don't think they'll be looking for her in the morgue. Though that is where they'd *like* to see her. She has certain confidences of an intimate nature she's bursting to make, confidences including the identity of the gentleman we have been calling Set.'

'Indeed? *Set*? I wondered if he'd bob to the surface again!'

'The interview is to be an informal one, for

the moment. Moulin, I wondered if we might impose on you for an hour? May we borrow your room?'

After a flash of astonishment, the doctor did not hesitate. 'Certainly. You remember the way? Coffee's on the stove. Help yourselves. Oh, and before you go off, Bonnefoye, Sandilands — a word with you, please. Something's come up about Somerton . . . Ah! Here's our delivery!'

⋆ ⋆ ⋆

They settled Alice in the armchair furthest from the door and positioned themselves in front of her, Joe to her right, Bonnefoye perching on the footstool to her left. She smiled slightly, watching their manoeuvres. 'What a simply ghastly room!' she said, staring around her with a particular look of distaste for the tacked-up theatre posters. 'Don't you think? Looks like Quasimodo's idea of a snuggery. Dr Moulin's? How can he bear it?' She removed the antimacassar from her chair between delicate fingers and dropped it to the floor.

'He doesn't like it any more than you do but people will keep sending him corpses to be dealt with,' said Joe, angrily. 'This is his attempt at a retreat from your handiwork. Six bodies you've fed him over the last three days . . . how can *you* bear it? The alternative is Fourier's office. Shall we take you there? It's not far. No lace frou-frous there, no common thespian mementoes to curl your toes and shrivel your sensibilities. Spartan, you'd say. Entirely functional decor. But what you *wouldn't* like is the spot marked in the centre of the room where he will make you stand.'

Alice shrugged her shoulders, unimpressed.

'And stand . . . and stand . . . Have you any idea how much stress that puts on the body after a few hours? George is still suffering. So, be thankful you're sitting in an overstuffed armchair being served with coffee, talking to two understanding chaps making notes.'

'I'll have mine black with one lump of sugar, please, Inspector,' she said, capitulating. 'And you can put your thumbscrews away. I'm going to talk to you. Look on this as a practice run. You must advise me regarding the contents of my official statement. If, that is, you are still requiring me to make one when I've got to the end of what I have to say. You may be begging me to tear it all up by the time I reach that point. And hustling me aboard the next transatlantic liner with my head in a bag.'

Relishing their sudden wariness, she added: 'No, gentlemen — you won't be pleased.'

24

'The Zouave, I'll start with him,' she said, accepting a china mug of coffee.

'The knifeman as you call him, though he's more versatile than the name suggests. He was in the same regiment as the dear departed Flavius. Yes, I think you've detected that there's a military thread running through all this. I met him nearly five years ago when I arrived here from India. Alone and friendless and trying to establish myself in a hostile city . . . '

She caught Joe's eye and went on hurriedly: 'The man tried to rob me! There in the boulevard, in broad daylight. A scarecrow! A heap of rags and bones, he suddenly appeared in front of me with his hand held behind him, like this . . . '

She got to her feet and, with a frisson, Joe recognized the Apache gesture.

'He put his other hand out and demanded that I give him money. He wasn't thinking clearly or he'd just have snatched my whole bag and run. He seemed on the point of collapse . . . wobbling rather. I realized he was incapable of running anywhere. The man was at death's door. Desperate. I opened my bag as though to look for money and took out the gun I always keep by me. You still have it in your pocket, Commander. He wasn't worth a bullet, I thought. Certainly not worth the time it would take making statements, having my pistol confiscated and all that rigmarole, so I hesitated. And then he did something rather extraordinary. He brought his knife hand forward and showed me it was empty. Too poor even to possess a knife. And then he smiled, his chin went up and he saluted. I could hardly make out what he was saying at first but he repeated it. '*Vive la France!*'

'He thought he really was living his last moment. 'Don't be so silly,' I told him. 'When did you last eat?' I took him to a pancake stall. He wolfed down about six. I made him walk ahead of me to a park bench and sat him down at the opposite end. Perfectly safe — I had my gun in my pocket, covering him the whole time. He told me his story. Perfectly ghastly! He'd drifted back from the war where he'd been badly wounded and was searching for his mother in Paris. He hadn't seen her for eight years. He'd been reported missing, presumed dead, and she'd moved on. He was destitute. Dying of neglect. A common story. They sweep up a dozen like him from under the bridges every morning. But there was something about this one . . . the tilt of his chin, the glare in his eyes. It was like finding a rusty sword by the wayside. If I polished it up, sharpened it, I would have a weapon worth owning.'

'So you bought yourself a Zouave, Alice? For an outlay of six pancakes? Were you aware of the reputation of these men? I'd be more comfortable in the close proximity of a mad bull terrier with a stick of ginger up its backside!'

'I had a use for his skills. I know they are

fierce, implacable, terrifying fighters and none more effective with a knife. And there was someone in my world at that time that I needed to terrify. I gave him food, drink, money and a purpose in life. I asked him to undertake a small task for me in return. He was happy to repay my kindness. Loyalty is another of their virtues, you know. And he has never been asked to do something he has not been delighted to do. Clean work compared with what his wartime commanders expected of him. He re-established himself and in time introduced some old army acquaintances. They became the core of my organization.'

'*Your* organization?' asked Joe.

'Yes. Initially it was mine. I bought the premises in the boulevard du Montparnasse. Girls need protection, you know that. And I needed to show a tough face to the world to make it understood that my affairs were not to be interfered with. There was a power-shift going on at that time. Corsicans killing each other, North Africans moving in . . . an unsettled and dangerous time for one in my business.'

'Alice, couldn't you have set yourself up in a tea shop and bought a pair of poodles?' Joe burst out.

Alice and Bonnefoye both turned a pitying glance on him.

'A cup of tea brings in one franc,' said Bonnefoye. 'A girl, between a hundred and a thousand. A dirty business but a calculatedly short one, I'd guess. Five years . . . I'd say you were pretty well poised to make off with your ill-gotten gains?' he guessed.

'I am,' she said with a confident smile.

'So — tell us about the moment when *your* organization became *his*.'

'Ah! A sad story! And one you will have heard many times before. I became friendly with one of my clients. Over-friendly. I fancied myself in love with him. He reminded me very much of someone I had been fond of in my past and I allowed him to get too close to me. He also was recently arrived in the city, finding his feet, totally without female companionship. Someone introduced him to the establishment. We were a comfort and a support to each other.'

Joe was remembering just such a confession in a moonlit garden in Simla when she'd talked of a man she'd loved, and he wondered.

'I was rash. I confided in him. But why not? He gave me good advice and he brought me more clients — he's a well-connected man. I told him one day, for his amusement, of a fantasy shared with one of my girls . . . Thaïs, it was . . . A regular customer of hers had whispered in her ear. They do. And my girls are required as part of their job to pass on their confidences.'

'God! I'd like to get a look at your little black book, madame,' Bonnefoye chortled.

'Clients assume — perhaps you will know the reason for this, Inspector — that the head on the adjoining pillow may always be disregarded. The woman, by nature of her employment, must be empty-headed, deaf or have a short memory. None of that is true.

'Thaïs told me that her client, a regular visitor

and an agreeable young man, was suffering at the hands of his old uncle. Known for years to be his uncle's heir, he had been played with, tormented beyond reason by the old man on whom he was financially dependent. Finally the chap had informed his nephew that he was to be cut out of the will, that he (a keen theatre-goer) was leaving the entire fortune to the Garrick Club in London, to be distributed to indigent old actors. Our client spent some time outlining to Thaïs exactly what he wanted to see done to his uncle by way of retribution. His fantasy was amusing. He saw his uncle centre stage at the Garrick Theatre, spotlit of course, knife in his heart and an orifice unmentionable in mixed company stuffed with banknotes.'

'Oh, good Lord!' said Joe. 'November 1923?'

Alice smiled. 'I told my friend jokingly about this and to my surprise he didn't laugh. He was intrigued. He gave way to a fantasy of his own. 'What a cracking notion! Well, why not? Tell Thaïs to whisper in the boy's ear that all his dreams can come true! Overnight he will become a very rich and very grateful client, will he not? Let's put a proposal to him. We undertake to set the stage and provide the body for a fee to be agreed. How much?'

'Thinking he was playing a game, I suggested a sum.

''Ridiculous! Triple that. The overheads will be tremendous. People to pay off . . . Thaïs must be rewarded . . . and Vévé.''

'Vévé?'

'Vincent Viviani, my Zouave. In the end, my

friend went to London with him to smooth his path.'

'Obviously a successful outing. I remember the case. No one was ever arrested. Yes, a smooth beginning. You were inspired to continue?'

'Yes. Suddenly he was talking about what 'we' would do and I realized I'd lost control. There was nothing I could do about it — I've told you, he is well connected and powerful.'

'And you made a profit from these excursions into Hades?'

'Oh yes. But it was more than that. He enjoyed what he was doing. A game, you know.'

'You must have exercised a measure of control over him? In the selection of victims, Alice?'

For a moment she was puzzled, trying to guess his meaning.

'You appear, like the black widow spider, only to kill the males of the species. I have yet to hear — apart from the unfortunate Mademoiselle Raissac who merited punishment as an informer — of a female victim.'

Alice breathed out — with relief? 'Of course! You must have noticed our clients are men? They have aggressive fantasies about other men in their lives. Men blocking their advancement, men deserving an act of revenge on the battlefield or in the boudoir, questions of inheritance. Sometimes a vengeful fantasy will be triggered by a hurt done to a female in his circle: the father who requests that his impressionable daughter's young man, whom he has discovered to be a penniless male vamp, be thrown from the Eiffel Tower . . . '

'You don't jib at academics, Alice?' Joe asked, interested in her methods. 'I'm thinking of a case in 1923 — must have been towards the very start of your activities. A professor who ended up inspecting, rather more closely than he would have liked, the inside of a mummy case. In the Louvre? In front of a delighted audience of fellow academics? No?'

'No. Not one of ours. I'm sure if we'd been asked . . . . he couldn't have resisted.'

Joe was tiring of her games. 'Bonnefoye, Alice here confessed to me while we were alone in the back of the taxi that she went to the theatre that night to save the life of Sir George who was — as we suspected — the real target.' He filled in the details, which came as no surprise to the Frenchman.

'I'm sure Sir George will be most relieved to hear that he survived!' He grinned. 'And doubtless pleased to hear that Miss Alice did what she could to divert the knife from his throat on to a more deserving one. Can't wait to tell him! But, Joe, there is one detail in this nasty piece of entrapment that puzzles me. The tickets and the note that drew him in — I'd like to hear her account for that.'

'You'd shudder if you knew how much they cost, those tickets! But Somerton was determined to have his fun — you might almost say, desperate — and offered to pay well over the odds for a good performance.'

'And the note? The note that lured George to the theatre? How did you know about his relationship with his cousin at the Embassy? Did he speak of it in Simla?'

A trap.

She looked puzzled. 'Why no. I believe I must have left India before ever his cousin took up a post here . . . Not certain. He never mentioned a cousin at any rate.'

Then she looked at him and smiled. And Joe felt the furry feet of the spider easing their way up his spine. Selecting a soft place for her fangs.

'My boss, as you call him, wrote the note himself.'

'Taking a reasonable shot at the handwriting, it would appear?'

'Why would it not be an entirely reasonable shot? Not necessary to fake one's own handwriting, Commander!'

25

'Before I say another word, Commander . . . Inspector . . . I want your reassurance that I may walk free from here when I've told you what you want to know. I came here as a witness and will leave as a witness. I'll sign any statement you care to draw up but I must go free. I will give you an address at which I may be reached. If you require me to attend a magistrate's hearing or a trial I will, of course, do that. So long as the man I denounce is in custody.'

'And if we don't agree to that?'

'Then, one morning, you'll find me dead in my cell in the women's prison. His reach is a long one. And the killings will go on. Is that the proof you will be looking for?'

'Up to you, Bonnefoye. I don't trust her.'

He could see his young colleague had been fired by the chance of landing a male suspect. A foreigner, a well-to-do foreigner. Fourier would not have hesitated. Was it likely that the madame of a brothel, no matter how successful, could devise these murderous attacks? No, there must be a male intelligence and will underpinning everything. And who was to say he was wrong? Here was Alice on the verge of trading a devastating betrayal for her freedom.

'I agree to your terms,' Bonnefoye said after a long pause. 'And, madame, please do not think of deceiving me. I too have a very long reach.'

'John Pollock,' she said simply and held out her mug for more coffee.

Joe got to his feet, agitated, barely able to keep his hands off her. He wanted to shake her until she told the truth. A different truth. 'I don't believe a word of this. Nonsense! I've met the man. A cousin of Sir George's would never . . . ' He stopped himself from further reinforcing her jaundiced view of men. He was quite certain that she resented the easy camaraderie between them. Why should he trust John Pollock after a half-hour's interview and herself not at all after five years, was her flawed reasoning.

'Pardon me, madame,' said Bonnefoye, icily polite, 'but to clarify: you are accusing Sir George's cousin not only of masterminding a series of improbable murders in the French capital and now we must understand in London also — but of accepting a commission from a fellow countryman to kill his own cousin? You say he did not question the projected crime but went along with it, planned it, and had it not been for your intervention, would have executed it?'

Alice considered. 'Yes. That's just about it. Well done. Will you write that down or shall I?'

'I think we ought at this point to mention the word 'motive'. Why on earth would he do that?'

'Oh, come on! Can you be so unaware? What sort of detectives am I dealing with? Must I do all the work?'

'Be kind, Alice,' warned Joe.

'Very well. George doesn't talk much of it but he's actually filthy rich, you know. Stands to reason! The man had a finger in every pie in India and many of them are full of plums. That's what India was all about, you know. John Company . . . exploitation . . . Empire . . . it all boils down to cash. In accounts in Switzerland in many cases. George, with his knowledge of the way things would go — and he it was who pushed them where he wanted them to go on occasions — was well placed to make the most spectacular investments. He's retired and come home to enjoy the fruits of his labours. He has no heir. For many years his cousin has been — still is — named in his will as recipient of his wealth. But John has lately become concerned about his cousin's intentions . . . his state of mind . . . Unleashed from the stifling routine of India, he seems about to plunge into a world of gaiety. Who knows? Perhaps he might even be entrapped into marriage by some girl on the make? And produce an heir of his own within the year? It happens a dozen times a season in Paris! Pity I didn't think of it myself! Much safer to accept Somerton's timely commission. After all — the responsibility lies with the client, doesn't it?'

'Jack Pollock earns a perfectly decent salary. He may well be ennobled in the near future off his own bat. He doesn't need, like Frederick Somerton, to wait around to inherit a title.'

Again he was rewarded with the pitying, world-weary gaze. 'Do you have any idea how much it costs to underpin the life of a titled man? The estate? The household? The ceremony? The motor cars? The city house? The upkeep of a future Lady Pollock? He is like, yet not like

George. Don't be deceived. They are opposite sides of the same coin. Made from the same metal but the features are different. Jack is extravagant, fast-living. Ruthless, they are both ruthless, but, unlike George, his cousin has no conscience.'

'Set and Osiris,' Bonnefoye murmured. 'I knew that ugly creature would stick his bent nose in before long. Good God! That little scene at the Louvre must have given him the idea for all this carnage! Planted a seed!'

Alice looked from one to the other in puzzlement. They didn't bother to explain.

Half an hour later, a document had been drawn up to Alice's satisfaction and she signed it.

'My gun, Joe? May I?'

He took it from his pocket and handed it over hurriedly as though it would burn his fingers.

'Well, I think I'll be off now. Don't bother to get up. I'm sure I can find my way out. I'll mind my manners and pause to thank Moulin graciously for his hospitality and be on my way. I'll leave you to curse me when my back's turned.'

* * *

'Moulin keeps his brandy in a bottle behind *The Man in the Iron Mask*,' said Joe heavily. Bonnefoye poured out generous measures into the dregs of the coffee and they sipped it silently.

'Which of us is going to tell George?' asked Bonnefoye.

‘I will. You must be getting pretty fed up with all this palaver. Foreigners messing about in your life, murdering each other on French soil. Jolly bad form, what!’ he finished in an imitation of Wilberforce Jennings’ braying voice. ‘And I must find time to stroll into the Embassy and slap the cuffs on Pollock.’

‘And we’d better watch our backs on the streets. I haven’t forgotten there’s a pet Zouave slinking about.’

‘Well, well! Who’d have thought Fantômas, stalking the streets of Paris, would turn out to be a blue-eyed Englishman reciting the latest cricket scores!’

⋆ ⋆ ⋆

On their way through the morgue, Joe averted his eyes from the busy scene at three of the marble tables. He’d had enough of death for one day. But he was not to be allowed to ignore it entirely. Moulin called out to them as they appeared. He was holding something blood-stained up to the light in pincers and, carrying on with his work, said: ‘Somerton. Your last customer but one. The toxicology report came through. No, he wasn’t poisoned but they mentioned that he had a very high level of an opiate in his system. A pain-killer. I took a further look at the body. And there it was. A cancer. Well developed. I’d say he had no more than a month at the most to live. Pity the killer didn’t know that. He could have saved himself a tidy sum.’

Quietly Joe absorbed the news and, going to stand at Moulin's shoulder while he worked on, murmured: 'The killer did know. The killer, the instigator of the crime, was Somerton himself. He knew, then, he hadn't got long and was determined to treat himself to a variety of luxuries before he snuffed it. He wanted to see Sir George suffer and in the most dramatic way . . . ' He filled in the story as far as it was known to them.

'Mon Dieu! But — what a lucky escape! You must take your friend out to celebrate his good fortune.'

'He's not going to be much in the mood for celebrating when he learns the identity of the man we've been calling Set.'

'Great heavens! You managed to get it out of her? I heard no squeaks of outrage, no rattling of irons?'

'In the end she was all co-operation. Largely, I think, because the information she was giving us, she knew was most unwelcome to our ears. Set is, in fact, the alter ego of Sir George. The obverse of the medallion — his young cousin. Very sad and disturbing. And it's not over yet. We're just off into the night to find and arrest Set. Can't say I've ever tangled with the God of Evil. Any suggestions? Ah well . . . '

'Do I need to prepare a few more slabs?' said Moulin lugubriously. 'For goodness' sake, take care, Sandilands. What gun are you carrying? Are you armed?'

'Not so much as a toothpick,' said Joe.

'Here, take this,' said Moulin, selecting a

shining silver tool from his tray and rather embarrassed by his gesture. 'Put it away in your pocket. It's my best scalpel. Razor sharp. Don't touch the edge! Handle with extreme care.'

26

They stepped out into the grey and gold light of a spring evening. There was a faint glimmer in the sky to the west and, across the river, dying rays were caught up and given a last flicker of life by the open windows of high attic rooms, still hot from the day. But a mist was already beginning to curl up from the Seine and Joe shivered.

'Now I know you won't want to hear me say this,' Bonnefoye began cheerfully, 'because I'm quite aware you're all fired to go and stick your newly acquired weapon into the black heart of Set, but there are two people we must see first. Fourier and Sir George. Any preference?'

'As we're on the spot — Fourier. Let's start with him, shall we?'

'I'd prefer it. I have to report back on the fracas in the boulevard just now. He'll be waiting to see me. Seems to be taking more of an interest. He grudgingly gave me ten blokes to mount the raid, after all! Feel up to the stairs, then, do you?'

Police headquarters was busy. Fourier, they were told, was busy but he had asked to see them as soon as they arrived. The Chief Inspector appeared not to have left his desk or changed his clothes since Joe had last seen him on the morning after the murder. A closer look, however, revealed a different pattern of coffee stains on his shirt front.

Juggling papers and cards, the Chief Inspector demonstrated his busy-ness and asked them to take a seat. The enquiry, he informed them, was progressing. His sergeant dashed in with a sheet of foolscap. Fourier was instantly absorbed by what he read there and, taking out his pen, made a few alterations and additions to the text.

'The copy,' he announced. 'The copy, as we call it, for the press. I have it. Anything vital missing? Not having had your report yet, Bonnefoye, I'm working in the dark. What do you think?'

He began to read out the salient points. 'Now then . . . *Brigandage in Bohemia*. Here we go. Guaranteed to get them going, a reference to brigandage . . . *Officers working under the direction of Commissaire Casimir Fourier . . . dramatic shootout . . . three gangsters dead . . . no bystanders hurt . . . police squad remain on the alert and ensuring public safety in this erstwhile peaceable quartier* . . . Well? What are you thinking?'

'Can't argue with the facts, sir,' said Bonnefoye. 'It will do as a preliminary account.'

'Had you thought, Fourier, you might insert something on the lines of: *The peace of Mount Parnassus was shattered last night when* . . . '

'Good. Good.' He scratched in the insertion. 'Now. Next. Take a look at this line-up, will you? You requested it, I believe. Anything there you like the look of?'

He passed them a hand of six Bertillon identity cards. They shuffled ugly face after ugly face complete with cranial measurements and descriptions of distinguishing features. Three had accompanying fingerprint records stuck along the bottom of the card. All the men were aged between twenty and forty and all had a scar on the right jaw.

They spotted him at the same moment.

'That's him!' said Joe.

'Gotcha!' said Bonnefoye.

He handed one of the cards to Fourier. 'Everything we need to know about our knifeman. Vincent Viviani. You'll find, sir, he's known in his milieu as Vévé. Ex-Zouave. Scar as reported by Miss Watkins. He works for the outfit who run, or have been running until this evening, the premises in the boulevard du Montparnasse. And — icing on the cake! — some genius in the ID department bothered to take his prints when he was last a guest here, evidently. Sir, if you can get someone to check the fingerprints from the box at the theatre, you'll find a sticky one to the left of the exit. Fixed in pomade from the dead man's hair. We think it will correspond with the prints recorded here.'

Fourier exchanged a glance with Joe. It trembled on the edge of enthusiasm.

'Though, of course, we need to take the man into custody in order to make a comparison,' Bonnefoye said carefully.

'You're telling me you haven't got him yet? I would expect him to be standing in manacles outside the door by now,' grumbled Fourier.

'We've been busy tracking down, not this

underling, vicious killer though he be, but the mastermind who has set the whole organization in operation,' said Joe. 'Bonnefoye, will you tell him?'

Bonnefoye's account was succinct, sure and surgically precise. It just managed not to be sarcastic.

'And now I'm to understand that, though you have an identity for the killer, he's beyond our reach? Another bloody diplomat! Buggers! Corral the lot in their embassies and you'd reduce the crime in the city by half! I sometimes think they send their rogues and scallywags over to us to get rid of them. Now what the hell do we do? Can't touch him. He can sit in there as long as he likes, drinking tea. And when he's ready, he can jump in the back of an embassy car, pull a rug over his head and scuttle off back where he came from on the next plane.'

His eyes narrowed in cunning. 'You!' he said, addressing Joe. 'These are your countrymen. You can gain access. Go in there and get him out. As soon as he's out of protective custody, so to speak, he can be provoked into a rash act and you can shoot him. We'll back you up — swear it was self-defence. There'll be an almighty stink but they'll just have to accept it. And better if the whole thing is set up by one of their own. It's the only way. What do you think?'

'You're suggesting I enter the Embassy, slap his face with my glove, and call him out? 'The Bois de Boulogne at dawn, Pollock! Your choice of weapon,'' Joe drawled. 'Oh, very well. It's a plan, I suppose. Just leave it to me, old man.'

* * *

As they made their way over the courtyard to pick up a taxi Bonnefoye spoke, concerned. 'Sandilands, you're not — '

'Of course not!' said Joe. 'But, all the same, I'd rather Fourier left it to me. Not that he has much of a choice. You know how slow these negotiations with embassies can be. It was crudely put but Fourier was right. There'd be representations, accusations, rebuttals, counter-accusations . . . oh, a mountain of work for the eager young tail-waggers they employ over there. And it would all end exactly as he forecast. Pollock would disappear in the night and the French would retaliate by blackballing the English entrant in the Gold Cup race at Longchamp. Or even worse — withdrawing the loan of their string orchestra. We've got to sort this out ourselves. And we'll take advice from the best-placed source.'

'Sir George?' said Bonnefoye. 'Oh, my God! Right then. It's back to the Mouffe!'

* * *

Sir George and Amélie Bonnefoye were playing a game of piquet at the kitchen table and attending to what smelled like a lamb stew when the two men arrived.

After a shrewd look at their expressions, George put his cards down and said quietly: 'Would this be a good time to have a drink of wine or do you have to maintain a clear head for the rest of the evening?'

'Both,' said Joe. 'So — one glass would be most welcome, Madame Bonnefoye.'

She brought a bottle and four glasses and a dish of olives and settled down with them in the salon.

'Maman, if you don't mind . . . we have some disturbing things to reveal . . . ' Bonnefoye started to say.

'I don't mind. So, go on then — disturb us.'

'Sir,' Joe began, 'I have now met and interviewed your cousin at the Embassy. He is well and sends his warmest regards and hopes to see you when this is all over and you come out of hiding. Though whether such a reunion will ever take place now remains to be seen . . . '

Sir George listened calmly to the account, occasionally shooting a question to Joe or Bonnefoye, but without exclamation or hand-wringing or hair-tearing.

'So that's why she was there, at the theatre,' said Madame Bonnefoye. 'Your guardian angel! She was protecting you. Fearful for *your* life, not her own. Thank God she was there!' She patted his hand comfortingly.

Confidences, it seemed to Joe, had been exchanged over culinary activities at the kitchen table.

'But where is she now? You let her go like that, unescorted, friendless, into the night? She must be feeling very uneasy at large in the city with two men pursuing her. I'd have taken my chances with you and Jean-Philippe,' Amélie Bonnefoye said loyally.

Finally George spoke up. 'You're right, Amélie, so we must assume that she, in fact, is *not* in any danger. She's a calculating woman. Always comes out on top. I admire her for it. Wouldn't want to see a woman of her quality humiliated by the likes of this pair of hounds, in fact. And, to look at this positively — of whom exactly does she have to be afraid? I think she's been pulling the wool over your eyes, you fellows. Her Zouave? Saved his life, did you say? Well, there you are! Sounds like an eternal ally to me. He was probably waiting for her on the street corner. Seen this with the roughest, toughest fellows you can imagine in India — give their lives to protect the Memsahib.'

Bluster, Joe thought with a stab of pity. Even Amélie looked away, uneasy.

'And her other nightmare is, as she and you would have it — my cousin. My cousin! Little Jackie. No, he's a good fellow. Self-opinionated, over-active, too clever by half and something of a bounder in his early years but — by God! — the man's a gentleman!' He thought intensely for a moment and added: 'I think you'll probably recognize *me* in that description? And you're right. He's very like me, you know. Do you seriously believe *I* would go about taking orders for bespoke crimes?' He put on the unctuous tones of a Savile Row assistant: ''And does Sir have a style in mind? We can offer the assisted leap from the Eiffel Tower, the dagger in the ribs at the Garrick, and, on special offer this week, blood-letting in the Louvre? A snip at two and six!''

'I understand, sir, that you have met your cousin at long intervals . . . people change . . . similar men may have just one slight distinction which sends them spinning off in different directions. You've heard of the villain Fantômas? Bonnefoye tells me his twin brother was the police inspector Juve of the Brigade Criminelle. Two men incredibly alike in their cunning, perseverance and energy. But at some point in their history, their paths diverged and their similar qualities carried them off towards opposite ends. One good, the other evil.'

George considered this. 'Balderdash!' he concluded. 'Psychological piffle! Fiction! This is real life we're considering.'

'But real death also, George,' murmured Madame Bonnefoye.

'Amélie,' he said. 'My coat! Only one way to settle this. I'll go and find Jackie and ask him.' Catching her dismay, he hesitated and then added gently, 'But not, perhaps, before we've sampled the *navarin d'agneau printanier*. I've put a bottle of Gigondas to breathe. Hope that was all right?'

'Perfect! But, listen! It's a stew. It will reheat beautifully,' she said comfortably. 'Tomorrow, or later this evening. Just come home for it. All of you.'

27

'Sir George! At last! Welcome, sir. How good to see you out and about again . . . Gentlemen . . . '

Beneath Harry Quantock's bluff greeting Joe sensed a trickle of tension flowing.

'To see Pollock? Well, of course . . . and yes, he is in the building at the moment. Um . . . look — why don't you come along to his study and wait for him there? I'll have him paged. He's upstairs in the salon dancing attendance on the Ambassador's lady. Actually,' he confided, 'this could be rather a bad moment. They're just about to take off for the opera. His Excellency can't abide the opera so John usually undertakes escort duties. Are you quite certain this can't wait?' Oh, very well . . . '

They went to wait in the study, choosing to stare at the cricket photographs rather than catch each other's eye. George was looking confident, in his element. Bonnefoye was looking uncomfortable. Joe was just looking, taking in the neatness and utter normality of everything around him. All papers were filed in trays and left ready for the morning's work. The flowers in one corner of the desk had been replenished. On the mantelpiece, the photograph frame surrounding his mother's smiling Victorian features had been polished up. In the bin, a week-old copy of *The Times*, open at the crossword puzzle. Completed.

Pollock swept in a few minutes later, handsome in evening dress. He surprised Joe by heading at once for George, who had risen to his feet, and enveloping him in a hug. The two men muttered and exclaimed together for a while, holding each other at arm's length to verify that, yes, both were looking in the pink of good health and Paris was obviously agreeing with them.

He turned his attention to Joe and Bonnefoye, and George introduced the young Frenchman. Pleasantries were exchanged. Joe had the clear feeling that Pollock was trying hard not to look at his watch.

'I'm sorry to disrupt your evening, Pollock . . .' Joe began.

'So you should be!' he replied with an easy grin. 'I'm just off to hear René Maison singing in *Der Rosenkavalier*. A first for me — do you know it?'

'Yes, indeed. Charming entertainment. Full of disguises, deceit and skulduggery of one sort or another. The police dash in and solve all the problems in the end, I recall. I think you'll like it.'

George threw him a withering glance and took up the reins. 'We have a problem, Jackie. Or rather, these two Keystone Cops have a problem. Which you can solve. I want you to tell them you're not a degenerate and a multiple murderer.'

'I beg your pardon? I say, George, old man . . . what *is* going on? I really do have to rush off, you know. Look — can you all come back and play tomorrow?' He looked uneasily over his shoulder, hearing a party forming up in the foyer.

'I'm afraid it's no joke, Pollock,' said Joe. 'A certain accusation has been made . . . ' He abandoned the police phrasing. 'Alice Conyers has shopped you. She's told us everything. Her — your — organization has been shot to pieces, literally, while you've been sipping sherry and humming arias in Her Excellency's ear. It's over. The crew in the boulevard du Montparnasse are stretched out either in the morgue or on a hospital bed.'

Pollock tugged at his starched collar and sank on to a chair. 'Alice?' he murmured. 'Is she all right?'

'Right as rain. Not much looking forward to seeing *you* again. But she's gone off into the night — armed.'

'You know Alice, Jackie?' George was unbelieving.

'Yes. 'Fraid I do! Oh, my Lord, I knew all this would catch up with me! Never thought it would be *you*, old man, who brought the blade down on me, though. I say — is there any way of keeping this under our hats?' He looked anxiously at the door again. 'I wouldn't like His Excellency to find out his aide is a bit of a bounder.' He grinned sheepishly. 'I'd have to kiss goodbye to my evenings at the opera and the ballet and the gallery openings. And I enjoy all that sort of thing enormously. I'm sure he'd understand if I explained it all in my own words and in my own time . . . I mean — we're not Puritans here — we're men of the world, don't you know! The gossip would soon burn itself out . . . in fact, my image might even be burnished in some people's eyes . . . '

Bonnefoye could keep silent no longer. 'Bloody English! Is this the understatement you are so proud of, Sandilands? Six deaths in three days, your own life in danger, Sir George a candidate for the guillotine and the perpetrator confesses he's a bit of a bounder! Well — rap him over the knuckles and let's be off, shall we?'

He got to his feet in disgust.

Joe joined him, shoulder to shoulder.

'No joke, Pollock,' he said stiffly. 'Alice has told us how you took over her business and turned it sour. Used it as a base for a very hideous assassination bureau. I don't think you were involved in any way in the Louvre murder — except as a man casually caught up by circumstances — but I do believe that you learned from that episode . . . were inspired by it . . . recognized there a service that was not supplied by anyone else. You could name your fee. No client could complain about the outcome without condemning himself. Absolute security. You became Set.'

Pollock slumped in his seat, lost in thought. Finally he waved them back to their chairs. 'I think you'd better hear this,' he said, heavily.

'I fetched up here in . . . what was it, George? . . . 1923. I liked my employment. I'm good at what I do. Round peg in round hole. Ask anyone. Only two things I missed, really.' He looked shiftily at Joe. 'Yes, you've guessed — the cricket. But apart from that — female companionship. I had a mistress . . . or two . . . in Egypt, my last posting, and I was lonely here in Paris. Yes — lonely. They do things differently here.' He smiled. 'Oh, lots of commercial opportunities, street girls, chorus girls available. Not my style. I like women, Sandilands. I mean, I really like them. I like to talk with them, laugh, swap opinions, have a nice hug as well as the more obvious things.

'I met Alice at the theatre one night. She spilled her drink on my shoes in the bar. Scrambled about on the carpet with her handkerchief, trying to make all well. One of her tricks, I was to discover later. Who can resist the sight of a beautiful, penitent woman at his feet? She took my address, saying she wanted to write a note of apology. She was swept off at that moment by a large and protective gentleman. You can imagine my astonishment when, next day, a box arrived for me. Containing a wonderful pair of shoes. My size — she'd established that much while she was down there. And much more expensive than any I could have afforded. I was flattered, intrigued, drawn in . . . '

Bonnefoye stirred impatiently.

'Upshot was — I met her for tea. She told me about herself . . . quite openly . . . and the way she made a living. I was interested. I went along and approved. And then I realized what she really wanted me for.'

'Go on.'

'Contacts! I was to be her opening into the diplomatic world.' He paused, reflecting, and then smiled his boyish smile again. 'Not quite the teeming pool of skirt-chasers she had anticipated, varied lot that we are here! But I liked what she had to offer. I liked Alice! I became a regular customer. And, I had thought, until you burst in here with your hair-raising and ludicrous stories, a friend. I trusted her. I had thought we were very close. How could she? I don't understand . . . How could . . . ?'

To Joe's horror, he saw the blue eyes begin to fill with tears and looked tactfully away.

'My poor chap!' said Sir George. 'Many suffered similarly in India. Ask Joe! We all learn that the woman keeps no friends. She is totally self-interested. Unscrupulous.' He turned angrily on Joe and Bonnefoye. 'Now do you see what we've done? Jack is not one of your criminal insensitives, you know.'

'You're generous to say 'we', George. You should know, Pollock, that your cousin would hear not a word against you. He didn't believe Alice's story. And he was right. She used your relationship, the details of her close familiarity with you, to convince us that you were the guilty party behind these crimes.' He gave a sharp, bitter laugh. 'She traded a man's reputation and possibly his life for her freedom. And who knows where the hell she is now?'

'Out in the mists, armed, calling her Zouave to heel, planning her next murderous display?' said Bonnefoye. 'What clowns we are! She's made monkeys of the lot of us! She's the one behind it all, isn't she? There is . . . never has been a Set.'

'More of a Kali, perhaps,' muttered George. 'Indian Goddess of Death.'

* * *

'Look, you fellows, you've already ruined my evening. Bursting in here like Ratty and Moley with old Badger brandishing his stick, come to tell me the game's up . . . ' Jack Pollock grinned at George. 'Why not come back again tomorrow and ruin my day? I've heard only a fraction of what you have to tell me but really — you will understand, George — when Her Excellency calls, the aide comes running. That was her calling and here I am — running.' Pollock got to his feet. 'Fascinating story! No — truly fascinating! You could make an opera of it.'

He went over to the desk and plucked a red rose from the vase. 'Must get into the part, I suppose. Der Rosenkavalier — here he comes!' He nodded his head to the three of them, stuck the rose defiantly between his teeth and made for the door.

With a sickening vision of the red roses swirling away on the current down the Seine, Joe called after him impulsively: 'Pollock! If you have to go over a bridge, take care, won't you? Oh, I'm so sorry! How ridiculous! Do forgive me!'

Pollock, wondering, took the rose from his teeth and threaded it through his buttonhole. 'No bridges between here and the Opéra, Ratty. It's a straight dash down the river bank. See you all again tomorrow, then? Harry will show you out.'

'Bridges?' said Bonnefoye when the door

closed behind Pollock. 'What was that all about?'

'Oh, a phobia of mine. Some people fear snakes, some spiders, others heights . . . me — I can't abide crossing rivers. It was the rose that triggered that display of weakness.'

George wasn't listening. 'Look — Jackie's got the telephone,' he announced. 'Why don't you use it to ring up your mother, Jean-Philippe? She'll be concerned. Tell her we're all coming home safe and well.'

'But I never ring my mother — '

'Then I think you should start. Not easy being the mother of a policeman.'

Bonnefoye made no move to oblige and, with a snort of exasperation, George seized the receiver and took up the earpiece. He spoke in his Governor's voice, friendly but authoritative: 'Hello? This is Sir George Jardine here. I'm down below and I want you to connect me with this number. It's a city number. Got a pencil to hand, have you?'

After the usual arrangement of clicks and bangs they heard Madame Bonnefoye reply. 'Hold on a minute, will you, madame? I have your son on the line.' He beckoned to Bonnefoye and held out the earpiece.

'Yes, it is me, Maman. Oh — well! Yes, it went well. A waste of our time, I think. False alarm. Nothing sinister to report. Look, we're all going to climb into a taxi and come back for supper. We'll need to stop off for a minute or two at the Quai to brief Fourier . . . we don't want him inadvertently to go laying siege to the British

Embassy . . . and then come straight on home. Half an hour.'

As their taxi moved off, a second, which had been waiting across the road and a few yards down, started up and slid into the busy traffic stream behind them.

28

They had left George sitting in the back of the taxi in the courtyard while they trudged up the stairs to confess to Fourier that they'd been given misleading information. They emerged fifteen minutes later, silent, dismayed by the Chief Inspector's glee at their predicament.

Before they could cross the courtyard, they were alerted by the sound of running feet clattering down the stairs after them. Fourier's sergeant shouted their names and they waited for him to catch up with them. 'Inspector! Sir! Message just came through to the Commissaire. Emergency down by the Square du Vert Galant. Roistering. There's been roistering going on. They will do it! Young folk got drunk and someone's been pushed in the river. You're nearest, sir. Can you go down and sort it out?'

'No. I'm busy,' said Bonnefoye. 'Do I look like a life guard? We have a two-man detail down there from nine o'clock onwards for these eventualities. This is for uniform. They'll deal with it.'

'That's the point, sir,' said the sergeant, puzzled. 'Can't be found. They've buzzed off somewhere. What should I do then, sir? You'd better tell me . . . just so as it's clear.' He evidently didn't want to go back upstairs and report the Inspector's refusal of an order.

Bonnefoye groaned. 'I'll go and take a look.

But I warn you — looking's all I intend to do. I won't get my feet wet!'

Turning to Joe: 'Look — not sure I like this much, Joe. It's . . . irregular. I'd rather deal with it myself. I'm not so quixotic as you — you'd jump in to save a dog! You go on back with Sir George. I'll grab another taxi when I've found those two sluggards who ought to be here.'

'No — I've a better idea,' Joe replied. 'I'm coming with you. But we'll send George home as advance warning that we really are serious about supper. George!' he shouted, opening the back door. 'Slight change in arrangements. Something to check on down by the river. You carry on, will you? Jean-Philippe and I will be along in say — half an hour. Driver, take this gentleman to the address he will give you as soon as you're under way.'

He banged peremptorily on the taxi roof to deny George a chance to argue and watched as the taxi made its way out of the courtyard.

They began to run along the Quai des Orfèvres towards the bow-shaped point of the city island beyond the Pont Neuf. A romantic spot, green and inviting and dotted with willow trees, it was a magnet for the youth of the city with proposals and declarations to make but also for the many drunken tramps who seemed to wash in and out with the tide. A hundred yards. Bonnefoye gave warning of their approach by tooting insistently on the police whistle he kept in his pocket. No duty officer came hurrying up to join them with tumbling apologies.

'Why *us*?' Bonnefoye spluttered. 'A whole

bloody building full of cops behind us and who's rushing for a dip in this open sewer? We are. Must be nuts. Where are the beat men? I'll have their badges in the morning!'

They paused to get their breath back on the Pont Neuf. The loveliest bridge, Joe thought, and certainly the oldest, it spanned the Seine in two arms, divided almost exactly by the square. Centuries ago it had been a stage as well as a thoroughfare and market place, a paved space free of mud where comedy troupes could perform. The Italian Pantaloon, the clown Tabarin, uselessly flourishing his wooden sword, had drawn the crowds with burlesque acts of buffoonery. In an echo of the rather sinister jollity, each rounded arch was graced with a stone-carved gargoyle at its centre, grinning out over the river. Joe and Bonnefoye added their own stony profiles to the scene as they peered over the parapet into the gloom, searching the oily surface of the fast-flowing water, the only illumination the reflections of the gas lamps along the quays and a full moon dipping flirtatiously in and out of the veils of mist rising up from the river.

'Spring surge,' said Bonnefoye. 'Quite a current running. If anyone's fallen in there, they'll be halfway to Le Havre by now. Hopeless. Listen! What can you hear?'

'Nothing.'

'Exactly. No one here. Not even a *clochard*. At the first sign of trouble they're off. So there has been some trouble, I'm thinking. Sod it!'

A strangled scream rang out from below in the

park and to the right. Male? Female? Impossible to tell.

'Here we go,' groaned Bonnefoye. 'I'll go down and investigate. You stay up here and be spotter. Give me a shout the moment you see something.' He clattered off down the stone staircase to the lower level, still tooting hopefully.

Left alone on the bridge, Joe clung with tense fingers to the stonework of the parapet, steadying himself. It always hit him like an attack of vertigo. A combination of height and the insecurity of seeing a dark body of water sliding, snakelike and treacherous, beneath his feet. He closed his eyes for a moment to regain control and heard Bonnefoye's whistle cut off in mid-blast.

Joe looked anxiously to his left, aware of a slight movement along the bridge. A tall figure was approaching. He moved nearer, coming to a halt ten yards distant, under a lamp, deliberately showing himself. Dark-jawed, unsmiling, chin raised defiantly to the light, right hand in pocket. The Zouave. Waiting.

Angrily, Joe looked to his right to check his escape route and his second nightmare hit him with the force of a bolt of electricity. His body shook and he fought to catch his breath. A figure, also ten yards distant. Not so tall as the first but infinitely more terrifying. He could have been any gentleman returning from a show, shining silk top hat on his head, well-tailored evening dress, white waistcoat, diamond studs glittering in his cuffs. Urbane, reassuring, romantic even, until you noticed the black mask covering the upper half of his face. In a theatrical gesture, he raised his left hand, white-gloved, to cup his chin, looking speculatively at Joe. His right hand, ungloved, went up and slightly behind his back. Slowly enough to show the gleaming zarin it held.

Joe began to breathe fast, steadying his nerves. Two men. He didn't fancy his chances much. He thought, on the whole, he'd go for the toff first. The leader. Though by the time he'd closed with him, the Zouave would have sunk his knife into his back. Take the Zouave first and the Fantômas figure would be ripping his throat out from behind. He remembered Dr Moulin's hands in the morgue, clutching his hair, demonstrating the hold, and his skin crawled. That's how it would happen.

No gun, he'd have to fight with his fists and feet. Then he remembered the doctor's parting concern and his strange gift. He felt in his pocket, encountering the cold steel of the surgical instrument. Better than nothing and they wouldn't be expecting it. These creatures only attacked the defenceless and the unready, he told himself. 'It's razor-sharp,' the doctor had warned. But all Joe's instinct was pushing him to explore, to handle his weapon. To decide — slashing or stabbing? Which would be the more effective? His safety — his life — depended on the quality of the steel implement. By the time he closed with his assailant, it would be too late to find out. Worth a cut thumb to be certain. And the quick flare of pain would jolt his senses fully awake. Tentatively he ran a thumb along the cutting blade. He repeated the gesture, more urgently, pressing his thumb down hard, the whole length of the cutting edge. And moaned in distress.

There was no edge. It was blunt. Not a scalpel. It was as much use to him as a fish knife. He held it in his hand anyway because he had nothing else. It would still glitter in the gaslight. It might fool them into thinking he was armed. And then, with a rush, with a flash of insight that came hours too late, he realized.

He could deceive no one. He was himself the fool. No mistake had been made when he was handed the useless tool. It was a stage prop. He was standing here, gaslit from both sides, at the stone prow of the island, framed up for his audience below, a modern-day Mr Punch. The only thing lacking was the cap and bells on his head and the hurdy-gurdy musical accompaniment.

Strangely, he felt a compulsion to play the part handed to him. To let them know that, however belatedly, he had worked it out. He held up the instrument before his eyes in a parody of a scene from *Macbeth*. 'Is this a scalpel which I see before me?' he mused. 'Or could it be an earwax remover?'

He looked to the right again and saw the smile start in the masked eyes, the nod that acknowledged his moment of understanding. He looked to his left and the Zouave with panther stride began to close on him. He pushed the scalpel back into his trouser pocket, took a deep breath, put both hands on the parapet and vaulted over, leaping as far out into the void as he could manage, hoping he'd miss the built-up quayside and hit the water.

The cold of the spring surge waters knocked the breath from his body and he struggled to the surface gasping and choking. The stench of the river water was sickening. An open sewer, Bonnefoye had called it. He stared as a dead dog, bloated and disgusting, swept towards him and then bobbed away before it made contact. He struck out for the bank, glad enough to be carried by the current at an angle to the Pont Neuf, away from the two creatures on the bridge. He wasn't a strong swimmer and his jacket was heavy with the weight of water, dragging him down. He spent a few moments treading water while he struggled out of it. Noises behind him. A gunshot rang out. He ducked under the surface and allowed himself to drift a few more yards.

They could with ease plot his course downstream, he thought, with the treacherous moon now lighting up the river like a satin ribbon. One could remain on the bridge watching for him to break surface, the other could intercept him at any point along the quay, and be there, standing waiting, while he struggled on the greasy cobbles that revetted the quayside. He would have to slip and slide and claw his way up over the green scum only to find a fresh and armed adversary looking down on him. Might as well drift straight down the centre and head for — what had Bonnefoye said — Le Havre?

And then anger took over. He'd been fooled. Completely fooled. He raged. His aggression mounted. He kicked out for the bank again. They could at least only take him one at a time now. And he wasn't intending to go down easily. Whichever man had run down to confront him there on the quay was going to take his life at some cost. He didn't want his body to be pulled, leaking water and bodily fluids, from the Seine miles downstream. To fight and die up there in the open air had, in a few short minutes, become his only goal.

A dead rat floated by, brushing his face. Retching with horror, Joe trod water, waiting for it to pass, but then, on an impulse, he reached out and seized it and squashed the swollen body down inside the front of his shirt. A gassy eructation burst from the rat and Joe gagged and spluttered. Then he gritted his chattering teeth. 'Brother Rat!' he muttered, knowing he was on the verge of hysteria. 'More where that came from? Let's hope so!' He was as prepared as he could ever be for the confrontation. He just hoped that his enemy would feel impelled, as most villains did, to explain himself. To talk. To give Joe time to get his breath back and plan his retaliation.

If he encountered the Zouave he could rely on no such reaction. His only language was Death and he would deliver it in one unanswerable word.

Taking his time, steadying his breathing, he judged the moment and made for the part of the quay where a set of slippery steps had been made for the use of the river traffic. Panting, he pulled himself together, taking the useless scalpel in his right hand.

'Thought you'd make for this place. How are you enjoying the show, so far, Commander?' The remembered voice purred down at him from the top of the steps.

There was the Fantômas pose again. Eyes glittered through the holes in the mask.

Joe responded in short panting phrases, one for each step as he climbed. 'Not the best evening I've spent in the theatre. Never been fond of melodrama. Overacting sets my teeth on edge. Kinder not to look, really. I've decided to bale out at the interval.'

He'd got almost to the top. Near enough. This would do. Affecting a gulping cough, he put his left hand to his chest and seized the rat, grasping its slimy fur in his fingers. 'I was wondering, Moulin . . . ' he began and a moment later had hurled the squashy and stinking corpse into the masked face. The man took an instinctive step back, with an exclamation of disgust, hitting out at the creature with his left hand. In an instant Joe had closed with him, pushing him off balance, a frozen but iron-hard left fist closing over the knife hand and squeezing with the fury of a madman. The zarin clanged on to the cobbles and the man looked down and sideways to find it.

A moment of inattention which cost him the sight of his left eye. Joe brought up the blunt scalpel and drove the point through the nearest hole in the mask.

A yell and a curse broke from him but he struggled on, strong right hand breaking free from Joe's slippery clutch. He scrambled to pick up his knife. With the scalpel still sticking out of his eye socket, he rounded on Joe, screaming, beside himself with fury, knife once again clutched in his hand. With both his feeble defences used up, Joe crouched and circled, only his fists left and his cunning. He was intending to work his way around his enemy, wrong-foot him and push him into the river.

Just as he was beginning to think he stood a chance, another shot rang out. The nightmare figure was hurled backwards away from Joe by the force of the bullet tearing into his chest. A dark stain was already spreading over the white waistcoat before he collapsed on to the cobbles inches from the drop into the river.

Joe, shaking with cold and effort and shock, could only turn his head and mumble, 'Bonnefoye? Jean-Philippe, is that you?' into the darkness.

'Er, no. It's me, my boy,' said Sir George, emerging from the shadows, Luger in hand. 'Thought you were up to something sending me off like that. Nosy old bugger, as I keep reminding you. Not so easy to shake off. Had to investigate. Who's your friend?'

He moved over to the body, pistol at the ready, Joe noticed.

'Who *was* your friend. He's dead. Police not very popular in these parts, I see. I had to take strong action to disable the other bloke on the bridge who seemed to be taking too close an interest. Vévé, I'm assuming. He's dead too, I'm afraid. But, Joe, who was this fool?'

George bent and tugged the mask off the dead face, carefully pulling it away from the scalpel which still projected.

'No fool! Madman perhaps? Moulin. The doctor. The pathologist.'

'Pathologist? Is he so short of customers he has to . . . oh, sorry, Joe. It just seems very peculiar to me. So, he's the one who fancied himself as Set, is he? But why on earth is he got up like this? Was he on his way to a masked ball?'

'He didn't have time to explain. I'm just guessing this was his last commission. Someone paid to watch me die, George. But where on earth has Jean-Philippe got to? He was down in the square, whistling . . . Oh, my God! There were three of them!'

29

Joe doubled over and vomited up a litre of river water before he was ready to run on unsteady legs back along the bank, up on to the bridge and then down again to the level of the small park, calling out Jean-Philippe's name. In his exhaustion, he found that George was well able to keep stride with him. They paused by the statue of Henry IV. The dashing young monarch, Le Vert Galant, the Green Sprig himself, peered majestically down from his horse at the panting old man and the drowned rat as they battled to get their breath and take their bearings.

'There was a third man on the loose. One of the wolves. Got away during the raid. I heard Jean-Philippe whistling down here on this side. We'll split up and search.'

'No we won't,' said George firmly. 'You stay by me. I'm not losing sight of you again. No telling what you'll get up to. Fancy dress balls . . . midnight swimming parties . . . some fellows live for pleasure alone,' he muttered, checking his pistol. 'Six left. Should do it. And in the dark I don't want to put one of them into you by mistake. Eyes not what they were, you know.'

Back to back, they quartered the ground, working their way out towards the pointed tip of the park.

They found them under a willow tree.

Bonnefoye had had no time to draw his revolver, his hands were empty, thrown out one on either side of his body. The handle of a zarin gleamed in the half-light, sticking out of his back.

George groaned. 'Ambushed. Taken from behind.' He expressed his grief and rage, cursing in a torrent of Pushtu.

Joe was on his knees, feeling for any sign of life. 'George, do shut up! He's trying to speak! He's alive . . . just. It's all right, old man. We're here. Look, try to stay still. You've been stabbed . . . I expect you noticed . . . yes. What we'll do, if you can bear it, is leave the blade where it is — it's actually stopping the blood from flowing. We'll summon up a stretcher party and get you to the hospital . . . it's only a step or two away.'

He bent his ear to the chill mouth which was barely able to move, yet determined to convey something. 'What's that? Oh, yes, you got him. Or *someone* got him . . . The wolf. He's lying here right beside you.' Joe glanced down. 'Shot through the back of the head. Small calibre bullet, I'd say. .22? But well placed. Not you, I take it? No? Ah, there's a puzzle . . . Sorry, what did you say? . . . Yes. I'll send George in a taxi to tell her. I'll stay by you . . . What day? It's Monday, old fruit . . . We've just had what we call in England a long weekend.'

He was grateful for the soldierly presence of Sir George, still covering the pathways with his Luger. Gently, Joe removed Bonnefoye's police revolver from its holster and held it at the ready. But he knew the flourish was in vain. The wolf's killer had made off into the night and was a mile away by now.

* * *

The next three days gurgled their way down life's plug-hole, barely distinguishable from each other by Joe. A day of sickness and shivering, spent in Bonnefoye's room in the rue Mouffetard, being Amélie's replacement son while her own boy was in hospital, passed like a bad dream. He remembered the bowls of chicken soup, the cool hands on his forehead, George's gruff voice from the doorway: 'Just back from the hospital. Thought you'd like to hear — the lad's going to be all right. Blade went in at an angle — the thought is that the attacker was disturbed before he could place his blow more accurately. No vital organs damaged but he lost a lot of blood. He's on his feet already and clamouring to come home.'

The day after, which must have been a Wednesday, he spent in Fourier's office making statements, colluding in the fabrication of various pieces of subterfuge. Nodding in agreement as the Commissaire outlined the dashing attack of the Brigade Criminelle officer (trained and directed by Fourier himself) who had gone in against great odds to the rescue (from an attack by a gang of Apaches) of two theatregoers, one a visiting tourist, his companion a Parisian and a distinguished doctor. Sadly, the latter had succumbed to a bullet fired by one of the gang, the former was lucky to survive being hurled into the river by his assailants.

This lively scene was, as they spoke, being worked up by an artist into a cover for *Le Petit Journal*. Under Fourier's direction, of course, he reassured them. These creatures were attacking in the very heart of the city now! But thanks to the bravery of the aforementioned police officer, two had been shot dead and would trouble the peace of the city island no more. Patrols on the Square du Vert Galant had been doubled.

'Seems to be paying off, Fourier,' said Joe. 'Though I'd have preferred on the whole not to be summoned down to the river on a wild-goose chase on Monday night.'

'Ah, yes. Clever devils! Some bugger diverted the two *agents* on duty down there. And rang directly through to my office, someone knowing my number, leaving a message so official-sounding my sergeant passed it straight on. Moulin. He knows . . . knew the numbers, knew the tones that get attention. Probably expected to catch you while you were still up here sitting in front of me.'

He frowned and fiddled with his pen. 'I can make this sound convincing enough, Sandilands, for general consumption, I mean, on paper. But I can't make any sense of it — ' he gestured to his head — 'up here. What in hell did the stupid bugger think he was doing? Clever man. Reliable. Thorough. My best.'

'Well placed to cover up a whole crime wave of his own creation?' Joe suggested. 'You'll never know now.'

'And who's going to take his place? Good Lord! He's down there on the slab as we speak! I haven't been to see him yet . . . I don't suppose . . . ? No?'

'Who's going to perform the pathology on the pathologist?'

Fourier burst out laughing. '*Quis medicabitur ipsum medicum?*' he said, surprisingly. He rose to his feet to show Joe to the door.

'And I'll add a second thought on similar lines,' said Joe cheerfully. 'Who will police the policeman? I'll tell you — I will!'

In a moment his foot had come out to trip up the Commissaire and his hand simultaneously pushed him hard between the shoulder blades. Fourier's head banged against the corner of his desk as he went down and he swore in pain and confusion.

'Bad luck,' said Joe. 'You really ought to have that rug tacked down, Fourier. There was a loose end there somewhere, I think.'

⋆ ⋆ ⋆

'Poor old thing! You look jolly peaky still,' said Heather Watkins, pouring out a cup of tea for Joe at Fauchon's. 'But I can't understand why that woman would *do* such a thing . . . I mean . . . Well, I can just about see why she would undertake . . . um . . . the profession she undertook . . . ' Heather blushed and hunted about for the milk jug. 'But how could she have let herself be led into a life of crime by that appalling villain?'

'I think what she gave me and Bonnefoye was a true bill. Ninety per cent of it. The client who insinuated himself into her establishment probably had some strong hold over her . . . blackmail . . . contrived involvement in one of his early excursions . . . I think he took over her life like a cancer, eating it away. He was using her girls as agents in his schemes. Alice was left only nominally in charge and beginning to realize she was herself replaceable. Good liars tell the truth as far as they possibly can and slip in one big falsehood. She told us truthfully what happened — just gave us the wrong name. Picked an entirely innocent Englishman, knowing he would be able to talk his way out of it — and anyway, Jack Pollock was safe enough behind the walls of the Embassy. The worst thing that could have happened to him in the event of an enquiry was a rap on the knuckles from Her Excellency! And a suspension from opera escort duties. But I believe Alice was truly alarmed by the sadistic nature of the man she found herself tied to. By his complete ruthlessness. It defies explanation, Heather! A professional man, clever, sharp, kind to me when in role. And the other side of him, dark, greedy and murderous.'

'But why? I know men murder others for the satisfaction, even enjoyment it can bring them.' She shuddered. 'But his victims were not known to him in a personal way. Where was the satisfaction in that?'

'I think he was a bit mad. Working in that place — it would send any man off the rails. And I believe he sensed this was happening to him.

He made an effort to keep the stone walls, dripping with sorrow, at bay. It didn't work. The corpses kept piling up and he kept on slicing and carving and witnessing the very worst man can do to man.'

'He lost his sensitivity? Like a knife losing its edge?'

'I think so. He had been a sensitive man. He enjoyed the theatre and the opera — he had posters and programmes all over his room and, Heather, the strangest thing — I'd noticed a photograph on his desk. A pretty dark girl. Her face was vaguely familiar. I checked his room yesterday — I went to return a book he lent me . . . ' Joe's turn to shudder. 'I thought it might be his girlfriend. I asked one of the assistants if they knew who she was. They looked a bit shifty, I thought, but one of them spoke up. "Don't you know her, sir? That's Gaby Laforêt. The music hall star. Nuts about her, he was! Went to every show. Used to joke that one day when he'd made his fortune he'd . . . Well, we all need our fantasies, working in a dump like this, don't we?" '

'But why would he want *you* dead, Joe? How did *you* figure in his fantasies?'

'He overrated my insight, I think. Thought I was nearer to putting it all together than I actually was. After all — I'd confided in him, shown him my cards, in fact. One professional to another. And if you see your opponent is holding a Royal Flush, you assume he's going to play it. He never suspected that I hadn't recognized the significance of what I had. So — I had to be eliminated. And — possibly as his grande finale — he couldn't resist stepping on stage himself for a change. I think no one paid him for that display on the bridge. He treated himself to a private performance. He fancied himself as Louis XIV perhaps, that ardent supporter of the theatre, the Sun King, strolling on in the final scene.'

'Horrid notion! All the same, it's doubly depressing to think that a man got his thrills by carrying out another fellow's fantasies! I expect the money was the more important element, you know. But, there, you survived! And so did Jean-Philippe. That's all that matters. Is he back at work again?'

'Oh, no. He's been given a week's leave. But he's back at home, firing on all cylinders, driving his mother to distraction. Claims he's fully fit and she must stop fussing over him. She's given up on him and decided to go and spend a few days with her sister in Burgundy. George went back to the Bristol to put up his feet for a bit, get his heart rate down and then start on his packing.'

'Poor soul! Has he had enough of France then?'

'Not a bit of it! He's bought a first class ticket on Friday's Blue Train to Nice. The overnight express. Paris seems to have lost its charm but he's not quite in the mood for Surrey yet. I think his cousin has cause for concern there! George is showing every sign of going off the rails as soon as he can get up the right speed. He's booked himself in at the Negresco! Best food in the world, he tells me. And I'm dug in again at the Ambassador for the next day or two. Lively scene! I say, Heather, they've got a dinner dance and jazz band on tonight if you'd be interested?'

'Oh, Joe, I have to leave on Friday — that's tomorrow! — for the Riviera myself. First game of the tournament on Sunday morning. Must be fresh for that. So, if you can guarantee you won't step too heavily on my feet and break a toe or try to get me drunk — yes, I'd love to! And then you can wave me goodbye on Friday — I'm on the same train as Sir George. Joe, why don't you try to get a few days off and come down and watch me play? You look as though you could do with a bit of southern sun . . . '

* * *

The Gare de Lyon was bustling with smartly dressed travellers, porters hurrying along behind carts piled high with luggage. Trains whistled and panted and whooped. Joe and Bonnefoye struggled with Heather Watkins' hand luggage and packages, hunting for her compartment. Finally settled, she leaned out of the window to talk to them.

'Well, here we are . . . Oh, good grief! Joe! Jean-Philippe! Do you see who that is — down there, thirty yards off, just getting in. Crikey! Shall we pretend we haven't seen them?'

Joe looked along the train, puzzled. 'George! It's George! I said goodbye to him this afternoon at the hotel . . . I don't need to show my grinning face again.'

'The last thing he'd want to see at this moment, I think,' said Heather mysteriously. 'Look! He's with a woman.'

Bonnefoye saw her at the same moment. With one hand she picked up the hem of her dark blue evening cape and with the other grasped the hand of Sir George standing gallantly at her side. Laughing, she stepped nimbly up into the train, turned and pulled him up after her into her arms.

'They've gone into a sleeping compartment,' said Bonnefoye, astonished.

'That's what people do on the Blue Train,' said Heather, giggling. 'What fun! How smart! She's very pretty! And — I have to say — what a lucky lady!'

'That was no lady — that was my mother!' spluttered Bonnefoye. 'What the hell! Visiting my aunt Marie indeed! And she has the nerve to go off wearing my birthday present.'

'Glad to see it got there on time,' said Joe, smiling.

'It was *you*, wasn't it?' Bonnefoye rounded on Joe. 'Duplicitous fiend! It arrived with a card — *Amélie, with eternal gratitude from an English Gentleman*. She thought it was from George!'

'If he'd been aware, I'm sure it *would* have been,' said Joe. 'I didn't quite like to disillusion her. Delphine in the rue de la Paix was very understanding when I nipped in with my cheque book and a disarmingly salacious story. Let's hope they're as understanding at Scotland Yard when I present them with my expenses! So that's what you earn in a month, Jean-Philippe? You're really doing rather well, aren't you?'

Other titles published by
The House of Ulverscroft:

TUG OF WAR

Barbara Cleverly

Summer, 1926. Working for Interpol, Joe Sandilands is despatched to Reims representing British interests in an unusual case. French war-widow Aline Houdart runs a champagne estate on the Marne, and is determined that Joe should support her claim that a shell-shocked soldier in the local sanatorium, without speech or memory, is her husband. But a strange conflict has arisen — the patient has also been claimed by three other families . . . Aided by Inspector Bonnefoye, he investigates all the claimants. Amid a tangle of lies and manipulation Joe uncovers a murder committed during the war. And when he discovers who the soldier is, Joe and Bonnefoye face an even greater dilemma. They must work quickly, not only to solve a past crime, but to avert a fresh tragedy.

THE BEE'S KISS

Barbara Cleverly

When Dame Beatrice Jagow-Joliffe is bludgeoned to death in her suite at the Ritz, it looks like a burglary gone wrong and Scotland Yard detective Joe Sandilands is despatched to conduct an inquiry. Joe soon discovers this was no tweed-wearing dame — in couture gowns and a cloud of expensive perfume, her tastes included a younger lover as well as the company of an ex-chorus girl. As more murders follow, Joe begins to suspect that Beatrice was killed by someone very close to her. But suddenly he finds that the case is being closed, and his superiors demand that he surrenders the files . . .

5 6 7 8 9 10 11
26 27 28 29 30
46 47 48 49
66 67 68

101 102 104 105 106
116 117 … 120 121 122
131 132 … 135 136 137 138
146 147 148 … 150 151 152 153 154 155
161 162 163 … 166 167 168 169 170 171
176 177 178 … 181 182 183 184 185 186 187
191 192 193 194 … 196 197 198 199 200

201 202 203 204 205 … 207 208 209 210 211 212 213 214 215
216 217 218 219 220 … 222 223 224 225 226 227 228 229 230
231 232 233 234 235 … 237 238 239 240 241 242 243 244 245
246 247 248 249 250 … 253 254 255 256 257 258 259 260
261 262 263 264 265 266 … 268 269 270 271 272 273 274 275
276 277 278 279 280 281 … 283 284 285 286 287 288 289 290
291 292 293 294 295 296 … 298 299 300

301 302 303 304 305 306 307 … 309 310 311 312 313 314 315
316 317 318 319 320 321 322 … 324 325 326 327 328 329 330
331 332 333 334 335 336 337 338 … 340 341 342 343 344 345
346 347 348 349 350 351 352 353 … 355 356 357 358 359 360
361 362 363 364 365 366 367 368 … 370 371 372 373 374 375
376 377 378 379 380 381 382 383 384 385 386 387 388 389 390
391 392 393 394 395 396 397 398 399 400

401 402 403 404 405 406 407 408 409 … 411 412 413 414
416 417 418 419 420 421 422 423 424 425 426 427 428 429
431 432 433 434 435 436 437 438 439 440 441 442 443 444
446 447 448 449 450 451 452 453 454 455 456 457 458 459
461 462 463 464 465 466 467 468 469 470 471 472 473
476 477 478 479 480 481 482 483 484 485 486 487 488
491 492 493 494 495 496 497 498 499 500

501	502	503	504	505	50									
516	517	518	519	520	521									
531	532	533	534	535	536	5								
546	547	548	549	550	551	552								
561	562	563	564	565	566	567	56							
576	577	578	579	580	581	582	583							
591	592	593	594	595	596	597	598	59						
601	602	603	604	605	606	607	608	609	61					
616	617	618	619	620	621	622	623	624	625					
631	632	633	634	635	636	637	638	639	640	64				
646	647	648	649	650	651	652	653	654	655	656				
661	662	663	664	665	666	667	668	669	670	671	67			
676	677	678	679	680	681	682	683	684	685	686	687			
691	692	693	694	695	696	697	698	699	700					
701	702	703	704	705	706	707	708	709	710	711	712	713	714	
716	717	718	719	720	721	722	723	724	725	726	727	728	729	
731	732	733	734	735	736	737	738	739	740	741	742	743	744	745
746	747	748	749	750	751	752	753	754	755	756	757	758	759	760
761	762	763	764	765	766	767	768	769	770	771	772	773	774	775
776	777	778	779	780	781	782	783	784	785	786	787	788	789	790
791	792	793	794	795	796	797	798	799	800					
801	802	803	804	805	806	807	808	809	810	811	812	813	814	815
816	817	818	819	820	821	822	823	824	825	826	827	828	829	830
831	832	833	834	835	836	837	838	839	840	841	842	843	844	845
846	847	848	849	850	851	852	853	854	855	856	857	858	859	860
861	862	863	864	865	866	867	868	869	870	871	872	873	874	875
876	877	878	879	880	881	882	883	884	885	886	887	888	889	890
891	892	893	894	895	896	897	898	899	900					
901	902	903	904	905	906	907	908	909	910	911	912	913	914	915
916	917	918	919	920	921	922	923	924	925	926	927	928	929	930
931	932	933	934	935	936	937	938	939	940	941	942	943	944	945
946	947	948	949	950	951	952	953	954	955	956	957	958	959	960
961	962	963	964	965	966	967	968	969	970	971	972	973	974	975
976	977	978	979	980	981	982	983	984	985	986	987	988	989	990
991	992	993	994	995	996	997	998	999	1000					

M/c 3318